SAVAGE TEMPTRESS

When Adam Frane rescued Nita from Indian captivity, he swore he would civilize her. But each time he washed the paint off her face she calmly put it back on.

Adam's temper rose with each act of defiance. The next time she flaunted her contempt for him he roughly threw her into an icy creek . . . Her deerskin dress parted. Angrily, Adam jerked it back into place. Then, for the first time, he heard Nita laugh. Tauntingly, deliberately, she tore out the lacing and bared herself with a mocking smile.

THE CAPTIVE WITCH
By Dale Van Every

The Captive Witch

Dale Van Every

BANTAM BOOKS
Toronto • New York • London • Sydney

This low-priced Bantam Book
has been completely reset in a type face
designed for easy reading, and was printed
from new plates. It contains the complete
text of the original hard-cover edition.
NOT ONE WORD HAS BEEN OMITTED.

THE CAPTIVE WITCH

A Bantam Book / published by arrangement with
Julian Messner

PRINTING HISTORY

Messner edition published September 1951
2nd printing .... October 1951
3rd printing ..... January 1952
Doubleday Book Club Selection February 1952
2nd printing .... May 1952
3rd printing ..... August 1952
Peoples Book Club Selection for special offer by
Sears Readers Club 1952
Bantam edition published March 1953
2nd printing ..... March 1953
New Bantam edition published January 1962
2nd printing .... May 1968
3rd printing .... October 1973
4th printing ... September 1982

ISBN 0-553-22523-5

Published simultaneously in the United States and Canada

PRINTED IN THE UNITED STATES OF AMERICA

H   13 12 11 10 9 8 7 6 5 4

The Captive Witch

ONE

THE sun, low in the west, broke through the overcast to make everything look whiter and blacker, as if a kind of thin checkered cloth had suddenly been dropped across woods and town and river. The gray patches of melting snow, the lime-washed garden fences and the ice-rimmed riverbanks became a glistening white; the leafless trees, the muddied paths and trails and the holes in houses made by the English cannon became the more black. Anybody who moved in the hard, flat light stood out like a buffalo in a snowbank.

Honore Dorion with his oxcart was trundling a barrel of sap from his sugar bush to the big kettle steaming behind his house. From the Indian camp on the edge of town two Piankashaw squaws were paddling a leaking canoe across the Wabash toward a tall buck Indian waiting on the other bank with the carcass of a deer at his feet. Major Bowman was wading in the marsh south of the fort shooting ducks. Captain Williams and Lieutenant Rogers were splitting a bottle of brandy in the bow of the war galley moored in the stream. Men not on duty were wandering restlessly through the town, eying the French girls and looking for some way to spend their prize money. Before the gates of the stockade stood the blanketed pack of Miami chiefs still waiting to talk to the colonel. Even the two commanders were in sight. The captured English lieutenant governor, Lord Henry Hamilton, paced moodily within the fort he had surrendered, his scarlet uniform black in the shadow of the palisade. And George Rogers Clark, standing alone on a rifle platform, idly smoked his pipe in full view of the Indians below so that they might know that he was keeping them waiting another day— not because of any press of business but because he was in no hurry to listen to their protestations of friendship. The young colonel of Kentucky militia had just won the one great victory of the Revolution since Saratoga, and he had won it because men who knew him, glimpsing that tall figure always ahead, were willing to keep on following him into no matter what hazard he led them. Now to hold what he had won he had still no more substantial resource than to present that same commanding figure to the eyes of the enemy.

1

All this Adam Frane saw with his first glance from the edge of the woods. Then, deliberately, he looked to see if the shawl was hanging in Therese's window. It was there, all right, just as he had been nearly certain it would be.

There was still a good hour before dark. He had spent the day so far pretending to hunt, though he had shot nothing but a turkey that had gotten so fat eating acorns uncovered by the thawing snow that it could no longer fly. He was about to toss it aside when he looked again at how plump it was. It wasn't much of a present but he might as well take it to Therese. That Spanish woman who lived with her could certainly cook. He cleaned the bird and washed his hands in a pool of snow water.

As he beat his hands dry against his woolen capote the ripples in the pool smoothed out. His reflection stared back at him with watchful gray eyes. The lines around them, weathered by seasons of wind and sun, gave him an older look than his twenty-four years. He took an uneasy second glance at the reflection. In the sacklike capote which he had taken to wearing since reaching Vincennes his form had the bulgy outline of one of those damn Frenchmen. He shook back the hood, disclosing the thatch of close-cropped, tow-colored hair and the muscular neck thrusting up from shoulders made to seem even wider by the garment's bunched folds. He grinned. A week's carrying on with a Frenchwoman could hardly have already begun to give him the look of a Frenchman.

The sun dropped into a cloud bank and the woods grew darker. He ran his fingers along the line of his jaw. He had shaved upon getting up but there were already one or two rough spots. He dabbed his face with cold water from the pool and with his hunting knife scraped his chin smooth again. Not since his beard had started to sprout could he remember shaving twice in a week. Now he'd come to shaving twice a day. The week in Vincennes had brought him to that, at least. He squatted back on his heels and reflected, in the main with satisfaction, on how this had come about.

Wading shoulder deep across the flooded prairies with Clark's little army, he, like all the rest, had seethed with an ever-growing fury. The incredible weather had made the march impossible—by every human standard. Yet men used to doing only what the chose to do, even when Clark was leading them, had stubbornly floundered on, day after day. Vincennes had become more than an English fort in a French town somewhere ahead. It had become the one place in the world they must reach, even if they died getting there. With the capture had come a complete reversal in their every outlook, and there had been rewards to match all previous trials. Division of the English stores among soldiers who had not been paid since they had enlisted had made every man rich. His own share had amounted to more than five hundred Spanish dollars. And for him, to the sudden surrender of the town there had been added the equally sudden surrender of Therese. The first time he'd gotten into her house he'd broken in during the attack in order to fire from her bedroom window into the English fort. Every time after that there had been the shawl in that window and she had opened the trap door to let him in.

No matter how sharply you reviewed it you couldn't find much wrong with a week like this one had been. It had given him a part in a great military victory, had filled his pockets with money and had furnished him more pleasure by far than he'd ever before had with a woman. A man couldn't ask much more than that of any week. And he'd be a fool to catch himself still wondering how it would be if, instead, he were somewhere else, doing something else. It was dark now in the woods. It would be full night by the time he got to the river. He'd be worse than a fool to have anything on his mind except being down there the very next minute after that. He picked up the turkey and angled across until he could walk in the ruts left by Honore Dorion's oxcart.

Skirting the Indian camp he saw that the blanketed chiefs had given up for the day and returned. They were huddled about the council's fire, murmuring and wagging their heads like men who, having already suffered much, expected momentarily to suffer more. Warriors stood about in restless, uneasy groups, whispering and watching the chiefs. The women were keeping the horses hobbled within close reach and had their family belongings packed so that the whole outfit could make a break for the woods at any minute. A strangled dog, painted white, splashed with dots of vermilion and decorated with silver shillings and strips of wampum, was hanging to a pole beside the fire. A rack alongside the pole was covered with blankets and baskets and sacks of pemmican and every sort of Indian valuable. From time to time one of these objects was thrown into the fire. Ordinarily a white dog sacrifice with all these trimmings was offered only to head off some very great threat to the tribe such as drought or pestilence. Clark's temper was the pestilence that had these Miami shivering. Adam could enjoy their consternation. He had grown up hating Indians.

He got down to the riverbank but then had to veer away from it again to keep out of the light from the big fire back of Laurient Bazidon's trading store where most of the Holston

3

company was barbecuing an elk. They had bought a keg of brandy from Laurient and though it was only the start of the evening some of the boys were already beginning to roar. Alarmed French families in the nearer houses were peering from windows, drawn, in spite of their concern, by the chance to study this newest sample of American behavior. However, since it was from these inquisitve French eyes that Adam had the greatest need to hide, he circled more widely around the church.

The little board chapel had suffered more than any other building in town during the night of the assault when the English cannon had blazed wildly at the invisible attackers. Jim Beggs and Cory Poynter were somewhere among the tangle of fallen timbers and each had a bottle. In the darkness Adam could tell who they were and what they were doing only by the sound of their voices and the occasional gurgle.

"Yuh know what we bin a-doin' the whole week we bin here," Cory was saying. "Yuh know what we bin a-doin', don't yuh? We jes bin a-squattin'. We got us a big jump on 'em when we tuk this place—a big jump. So now what do we do? We jes squat. We'd orter be halfway to Detroit by now —thet's where we orter be."

Cory's aggrieved voice trailed off into indistinctness as Adam kept on. Every man in the regiment had more ideas than Clark himself about the next move in the campaign. Adam worked his way down in the shadow of Francis Vigo's warehouse back to the riverbank. Along here he had kept a special lookout for Bert Cogar. This was certainly no time to have Bert spot him sneaking past. Bert had already worked up enough curiosity about where he'd been spending so much of his time. But the warehouse door was closed and locked. Bert was away somewhere. Adam turned downstream, keeping close to the bank, below the whitewashed garden fences of Gabriel Picotte and François Adehemar, and crept among the pilings supporting the boat landing before the house of Jacque Papin, the keelboatman.

Jacque, Therese's husband, had left Vincennes three weeks ago with a cargo of buffalo hides for New Orleans. Nevertheless, there was still plenty of need to take care. The family of Michel Menard, Jacque's brother-in-law, shared with Therese the occupation of the house above, while the sister-in-law did a lot of snooping to keep track of what Therese was doing, though there was no way of telling whether she was trying to look after the interests of the absent husband, her brother, or was suspicious of her own husband.

Adam crawled back through the pilings until he was under the section of the house that projected out from the bank.

Here he paused to listen. The Menards, in their part of the house on the other side of the central storeroom, were quarreling as usual and one of their children was crying. From Therese's kitchen, on this side, came the muffled, cheerful chatter of Angelina, the Spanish woman, gossiping with some visitor. Directly overhead Therese paced up and down in her bedroom. Her sudden stops and quick turns were like those of an animal in a cage.

The sounds in the house overhead mingled with those more distant; the faint yells of the increasingly festive Holston company, the tap of a drum accompanying a change of guard at the fort, the murmur of conversation in the Bailly boathouse where Grandpère Bailly's five trapper grandsons were making preparations for their spring voyage to the Missouri. Adam squatted, listening, reminding himself that this was a moment worth savoring. The willful impatience of the footsteps overhead echoed his own impatience and there was the added excitement of the risk they both were running. They had to be on guard against more than her family. There was probably not a man in town who would not condemn his presence here, including those among the Americans who, had they the chance, would have been quick to take his place. Discovery could stir no end of trouble between the French inhabitants and the new American garrison.

He reached up and scratched on the trap door. Instantly the bearskin on the floor was pulled aside and the door lifted. He tossed the turkey through the opening, shoved his rifle after it and swung himself up. As always the place was dark except for the iron pot of glowing charcoal in the corner. The familiar warmth of the room enveloped him. He knelt to replace the trap door and spread out the bearskin over it. Rising, he leaned his rifle against the wall and began to grope for her in the darkness.

This had always been the signal for her to retreat. She liked each time to pretend that she was as much of two minds about him as she had actually been the first time. Sometimes her breathless flight took them all around the room, each taking care to knock over nothing and to make no sound that might be heard by Angelina in the kitchen or by the Menards in their quarters. Even when he caught her she would continue to hold him off for a while. She knew how the most was to be gotten out of everything at every bend in the trail.

But tonight it was different. She came right to him and wound her arms around him as if she had an idea he might be the one to run. She was breathing fast and shaking all over. She pressed against him as hard as she could and then she began to kiss him over and over again. Backing up a step he

5

struck his heel against the turkey on the floor. He pulled loose from her grip to pick up the bird and give it to her.

"Turkey I brought you," he whispered. But there was no use trying to tell her anything since she knew no more of his English than he did of her French. *"Weenecobbo,"* he started again in Chippeway, on the chance she might know the word.

She reached out to feel the turkey and when she had comprehended what it was she let out a gasp of surprise and then a sigh of satisfaction. She clasped the turkey against her and turned to look toward the kitchen as if already thinking about how to cook it. He reached over and began to undo the buttons at the throat of her dress. She neither struck his hand away nor lifted her own to guide his. She kept right on looking toward the kitchen.

"Oui," she whispered with sudden decision.

She had made up her mind about something and whatever it was she wasted no more time. She pushed the turkey back into his arms, grabbed him by the wrist and led him firmly toward the door which opened into the storeroom. When he saw that she was taking him away from the bedroom he balked. *"Oui—oui—oui,"* she kept whispering insistently. He reached for his rifle and allowed her to lead him on.

She guided him swiftly and silently the length of the dark storeroom, in and out among the barrels of pitch, the hanging coils of rope, and the racks of spars and oars. When they reached the main front door which led to the yard outside she unbarred it, and once the door was open she began to exclaim loudly with surprise and pleasure. She slammed the door noisily and then hurried him toward the door to her kitchen. On the other side of the storeroom the Menard door opened a crack and the sister-in-law peered out. Therese laughed carelessly as she threw her own kitchen door wide open so that the light fell full on the both of them.

Adam was catching on. The turkey had been important after all. She had some reason for making it known that he was in the house tonight and she had seized upon his bringing it as an excuse for letting him in. So he was prepared for the great to-do she made as she took the turkey from him and held it up for Angelina's inspection and cries of appreciation, which were as loud as if the bird were stuffed with silver brooches. But he was not prepared for the other visitor he'd heard Angelina talking to when he'd first listened under the house. It was Bert Cogar.

Bert looked as if he had been mighty pleased with his situation up to the minute Adam came in. This was one kitchen in Vincennes no American had so far found his way into. He'd been feeling right at home, his feet stretched under the table, nodding and grinning at Angelina while he picked his teeth with his thumbnail, his broad, usually slightly worried face creased with an expression of complete satisfaction. But his mouth fell open when he looked around to see Adam in the doorway with Therese.

"What brought you here?" Adam demanded.

Bert shoved back from the table with the offhand innocence a reasonably honest man can still put on when appearances are against him. "All I know," he said, "is I was comin' past just before dark and the fat one there"—he nodded toward Angelina—"she stuck her head out the door and asked me in."

Adam took a quick look at Angelina. "She know English?"

"She knows Spanish." Bert glanced at his empty plate. "And she sure knows how to cook."

He didn't ask what Adam was doing here. But he kept looking Therese up and down and then back at Adam. Adam sat down on a bench.

"You can see for yourself," he said. "I brought 'em a fat turkey."

He wasn't making much of a try at fooling Bert. Bert knew how many nights he'd spent away from the warehouse this past week. The longer Bert looked at Therese the more his eyes bulged. He was licking his lips as if Adam's luck had been in part his own.

Adam, too, took a look at Therese. She was standing in the shadow over by the fireplace but it was still the best light he'd seen her in since that first night. She had glossy black hair and big black eyes; her skin was so white that it made her mouth that much redder, while the way she was formed was enough to take a man's breath away. Bert had a right to sit there blinking. She was far and away the best looking French girl in Vincennes. And you could throw in Kaskaskia, Cahokia, Prairie du Rocher, Ste. Geneviève and St. Louis, for that matter.

The women's voices had dropped to low, intense whispers and they had forgotten the turkey. But their excitement was real now. Therese was insisting on something. Angelina was objecting violently. Therese kept right on insisting. Angelina drew her shawl over her face and began to cry. Therese shook her angrily. Angelina surrendered. She turned her tear-streaked face to Bert and began to speak to him in Spanish. Bert had known Spanish since the winter he'd worked for that Spanish trader. He was the sort who had the patience to try to figure out how foreigners talked. Adam began to see why Bert had been called in. There was something Therese wanted him to know. Now she could tell it to Angelina in French,

7

Angelina could tell it to Bert in Spanish and Bert could tell him in English.

"They've heard I'm a good friend of yourn," said Bert. "She," he indicated Therese, "wants to know how far you can trust me."

Adam had known Bert off and on for nearly four years. He counted him about as good a friend as he'd ever had. But there certainly wasn't anything he wanted Bert to tell Therese for him. "Tell her about half as far as I could throw you," he said.

Bert began to explain to Angelina. According to his tone and gestures he was swearing that Bert Cogar and Adam Frane had been all but rocked in the same cradle and that in any event they were closer than brothers.

Therese and Angelina whispered together, from time to time turning to eye Bert with continuing doubt. But finally Angelina squared around to Bert and began to tell him something.

"No!" Bert exclaimed.

Angelina kept on with her story. Bert began to grin. Angelina ended on a squawk of dismay.

"You'd best hunt you a deep hole or a real tall tree," Bert told Adam. "Her husband's due back—maybe tomorrow."

"Talk sense," said Adam. "By now he's halfway to New Orleans."

"Nope," said Bert. With each word he was finding more relish in his news. "At Kaskaskia he heard about Clark's marchin'. He got to worryin' about his place here—so he turned around and started polin' back. One of his wife's cousins come ahead by land from Kaskaskia. That's how come she knows."

Back in the shadows Therese was looking as if the world were coming to an end.

"Tell her this," said Adam. "Tell her she's got nothing to be afraid of. Tell her if he so much as hollers at her real loud I'll cut his ears off."

Bert still thought all this was funny. "From what I've heard," he cautioned, "this husband of her'n is six four and about as mean as these Frenchies ever git."

"Tell her what I said," said Adam.

His message started a new argument between Therese and Angelina. The Spanish woman burst into tears again. When at last she wiped her eyes and turned to Bert he did not seem to find what she was saying so funny. And when he looked at Adam it was with something like awe.

8

"She ain't afraid of her husband," Bert said. "He allus does whatever she wants. She just don't like him so much as she does you. She wants you should take her away."

"My God!" said Adam. "Where to?"

This inquiry, traveling through Bert and Angelina, brought a prompt reply from Therese.

"She says anywheres," said Bert. "So long's it's far. She's heard you're from Virginia. She says why not take her back there with you."

"Well," said Adam, "that's far, all right."

Therese was staring hard at him, watching feverishly for the first hint of how he was going to feel about this. Her face came closer to the candle as she leaned forward, gripping the table. He could see how tight the skin was drawn across her cheekbones and around her mouth and at the corners of her eyes. She must be somewhat older than he had supposed. Young or old, he'd never liked her half as well as this minute. She knew what she wanted and wasn't afraid to go for it. But he knew what he wanted, too. He hadn't wanted the week to end as soon as this but it was ended now. He stood up.

"Tell her she'll hear from me before daylight," he instructed Bert.

Before daylight he'd see to it that Clark had sent him off to join one of the ranger parties watching the Detroit portages. Bert stuttered over the importance of his message. The two women embraced. Angelina was weeping again. Adam reached for the door.

"Hey—wait," Bert protested. "Don't rush off before they've fixed you somethin' to eat. Might be the last good grub you'll have for quite a spell."

But when he saw that Adam was really going he bolted after him. "The fat one," he continued to protest when he had caught up with him on the road outside, "she's got a pot of venison stew on the fire that's tastier'n any venison you ever laid lip over."

"You sidle up to her just right," said Adam, "and she might cook you that turkey, too."

"Take more'n a turkey," said Bert. "Shes got a mustache —and she sweats." He peered up at Adam, trying to see his face in the darkness. "You sure enough goin' through with it?"

"Through with what?"

"Makin' off with Therese?"

"Why not?"

Bert wagged his head, torn between envy and concern.

"Might myself," he boasted, "was a piece so smooth as that to rub up against me. A man could stand bein' chased no matter how far if he had that in camp every night."

He kept breaking into a trot in his anxiety to get Adam back to their quarters where they would have a better chance to talk. He dropped the key twice before getting the door to the Vigo warehouse unlocked. Adam watched him fumble, speculating on the good it would do Bert if some woman did take him in hand. Bert was short and wide and a little bow-legged, but he was no fool; he had an honest freckled face, and he made friends quick. Women were ready enough to like him, too. But though he didn't scare easy in other ways there was something about women, unless they were old or fat or ugly, that took all the spunk out of him.

There were still live coals on the hearth in the little bunk-room that occupied one corner of the warehouse. Bert threw on some sticks, got a blaze started, put a tin of water over the fire and got the jug of rum, the sack of maple sugar and the crock of butter out of the cupboard.

"One thing was said I didn't tell you," he said. "The fat one said somethin' about Therese leavin' a rich husband that owns a keelboat but that with your prize money you'd be fixed so's you could take good care of her, too. You done any figurin' on the money this stands to cost you?"

Adam sat down on the rawhide bed. Now that the excitement and novelty that had marked the week had come to so sudden an end the usual and all-too-familiar restlessness was gnawing at him again. Teasing Bert wasn't much help. "What's the good of money except for what you can get for it? What do you expect you're going to get for yours?"

"I don't expect—I know," said Bert. "Four five real good pack horses—that's what I'm gonna git for mine. I'm goin' back to the valley of Virginia where you can find better horses for less money. With more folks comin' to Kentucky all the time and with the Indians keepin' right on stealin' what horses they got—a man's gonna be able to do right well with his own pack string to hire out."

"Suppose you've picked just what day you're lighting out for Virginia?"

"That I have," said Bert, unruffled. "The first day I can git me shed of the army. For a while today I had an idee that might be right now. That's somethin' that come up while you was off in the woods that I ain't had a chance to tell you yet. Clark's made up his mind to send Hamilton and Jehu Hay and that French polecat, Maisonville, together with fifteen or twenty common prisoners, back to Virginia. He wants to git 'em outta the way so's he won't have to fret about their maybe bein' recaptured—and I reckon he wants to prove to people back east what a haul he's made. Anyway, soon's I heard about it I put in to git sent along as one of the guards. But Clark said no. He's pickin' out men to go who's been sickly or has got family troubles back home or who he'd just as soon spare." Bert bent down, dropped a lump of maple sugar in each mug, added rum, boiling water and a blob of butter and began stirring the steaming mixtures with a stick.

Adam was staring at the wall as if he could see through the logs all the way to the Virginia toward which the guards and prisoners of the escort party would be journeying. He could see every foot of their course—down the Wabash, up the Ohio, across Kentucky, over the Wilderness Road. It would take them months. But from the moment they set out they'd be on their way to Virginia. Each morning they'd be starting on, each night they'd be nearer their journey's end.

"When they getting off?"

"First thing come daylight."

Sudden excitement gripped Adam. The opportunity was so perfect that it already seemed something he must have planned. The impulse to take advantage of it was overpowering. He wasn't really thinking. He wasn't making up his mind. Even an ignorant Indian, in deciding upon his moves while hunting or fighting, was governed by signs he saw in the shapes of clouds or the flights of birds. At least he was governed by something. There was a Spanish dollar in the bottom of Adam's game pouch. He drew it out between thumb and forefinger. Head's he'd go—tails he'd forget it. It was tails. He dropped it back in and drew it out a second time. Tails again. Before he could try a third time Bert handed over one of the mugs and settled himself comfortably.

"One thing I don't git the hang of," began Bert, warming his hands on his mug, "is what made her want me there tonight."

"So's she could tell me what she had to say."

"You mean she don't know no English a-tall?"

Adam nodded and took another drink. Bert squirmed and laughed uneasily. "So you got that well acquainted that quick without having to say aye, yes, or no."

"She knew the Chippeway word for turkey," said Adam. Bert's eyes opened wide.

"I never thought about it that way before," he admitted, "but I can see how it might work." Bert might never have come real near any woman but there was nothing he liked to talk about as much as the way he imagined she was apt to behave once he did. He began to glow in the new light that was breaking over him. "I can see how much trouble you

11

save. When you start to fuss around a gal of your own kind you have to keep on talkin'. And no matter how she feels she's got to keep on sayin' no—cause she'd be ashamed to come right out and say yes out loud. And oncet she's said no she's obliged to act like she meant it. But when you git with one of these gals that don't know your lingo and there ain't nothin' you have to say—or *can* say even if you got no better sense—then you can just keep on movin' in and there ain't no easy place for her to take a stand before things git along so far it's already too late. Beats me how come I never figgered that out before."

Bert kept on nodding reminiscently, as if this general principle exactly fitted some of his own experiences. He picked up Adam's empty mug and began mixing a new draught. "Your folks's eyes will sure bug out when you show up in Virginia with Therese."

"I don't have folks in Virginia."

"No? It's a fact I never heard you mention 'em. What happened to 'em?"

"Indians. When I was eight."

Bert handed over the refilled mug. "That was bad," he said. "Don't know that I ever said what happened to mine, either. They was took off by smallpox. When I was fourteen. All 'cept paw—and he might better have been. He married a Yankee woman that was too mean for any man to have to stand." Bert sat down and resumed nursing his drink. He shook his head once or twice over the twin tragedies. But the loss of whole families to Indians or pestilence was no uncommon event. He came back to the present. "If you got nobody there what's the reason you're taking Therese to Virginia?"

"No reason," said Adam.

Bert lifted his mug, not to drink but to press his face against the warm pewter. "No matter where you go," he said, treating himself to all the pleasure he could in contemplating his friend's prospects, "she'll be the best looker folks there has ever seen."

Adam pulled out the coin again. It was still tails. "No," he said suddenly. "Not if I was to go one place in Virginia."

Bert rose to this like a trout when a bug hits the water. "You ain't never told me you ever knowed a gal like that."

"I'm not telling you now."

"But accordin' to what you just said, that—whoever she was back there—she was a handsomer piece even that this Therese."

"No question about it."

Bert started to take a careful sip of his drink but in his irritation swallowed a gulp that almost choked him. "But

12

you've told me twenty times you ain't been back to Virginia since you was sixteen."

"That's right."

Bert stared at him. "You're just talkin'."

"Too much," agreed Adam.

By now Bert was completely disgusted but his curiosity got the better of him. "What happened—her people run you off?"

"No."

"She wouldn't have you?"

"I never found out."

"That," pronounced Bert, "I wouldn't believe if I read it in Holy Writ."

Adam took another drink. Already he'd talked too much. But he couldn't stop now. Some of this he had to tell, if only in the hope that telling a story so simple would help him get a grip on himself.

"I never so much as spoke to her," he said. "I was apprenticed that year to an old man named Stull who had a store at the upper crossing of the Mechum River in Albemarle County. He worked hell out of me by day and then made me sit up most of the night getting in the licks I needed on my reading and writing. When I'd improved enough so's I could keep his accounts he started in hammering on me to study to be a lawyer. This girl used to ride past the store. She'd turned sixteen that spring, same as I had, but I was still all arms and legs and big feet, while she'd all of a sudden started to look grown up. Since her father lived up the road one way and her oldest brother down the other, she came past almost every day. I got so I knew the gait of her horse and whenever I heard it I'd find some excuse to take me out front so I could get a closer look at her. After a while she got so sometimes she'd nod and smile."

It was remarkable how clearly he could remember the rosy blaze of the rhododendrons massed along the riverbank, the feel of the sunwarmed dust between his bare toes, the smell of blossoms from the wild crab apple tree at the corner of the store, the approaching thud of her horse's feet in the sandy road—and his secret, guilty excitement as he waited for the first glimpse of her when she rode into view. Never since had he seemed able to see or hear or smell or feel anything quite so keenly as he had that spring.

"Then what?" prompted Bert, by now more polite than interested.

"Come summer she went somewhere down in Henrico County to visit with relatives. When I heard she was back I couldn't wait for her to ride past next. That night I sneaked over to her father's place and climbed a tree so's I could see in a window and maybe catch sight of her. The way it turned out the window right next to the tree was to her room. She must have been tired from her trip because she was already undressing and going to bed. I was so shamed to be peeking that I near to fell out of the tree but I couldn't bring myself to stop looking."

Bert's interest perked up. "What happened then?"

"Nothing. Except that right now I can picture the way she looked that night just as well as if she was standing over there by the fire."

Bert looked quickly toward the spot by the fire and then back at Adam. "Couldn't you git the window open?"

"It was already open. But soon's she blew out the candle I slid down the tree and ran like all her old man's dogs were after me."

Bert grunted his dissatisfaction with the story. "Well—no good cryin' about it now. That was eight years ago. If she was the looker you say, there ain't no manner of doubt she's married by now and got her a raft of young'uns."

"I can't say about the young'uns. But I know she's married. She got married that same week to a gunsmith she'd met down at Richmond. Everybody was dancing at the wedding the night I left." He set down his empty mug with a sudden angry movement. "I ran away just like a scared rabbit."

"The night she was gittin' herself married," said Bert, "that was kinda late to count yourself runnin' away."

Adam reached for the jug and then drew back. The way liquor was hitting him tonight he'd better stop drinking. And stop talking, too.

Bert again tried to dismiss the far past. "You ain't told me yet how come you got next to Therese so quick."

"That," said Adam, "was just an accident."

Bert waited patiently. Adam said no more.

"Well," said Bert angrily, "what you aimin' to do now? Just set here and wait for another accident to happen?" Bert rose to his feet with the air of a man compelled to take full charge of a situation. "You'll need a canoe and some grub. And you'd best git to lookin' for 'em. You'll need to be out of sight by daylight." He relented a little. "All you got to do is speak up if they's some way I can help."

Adam didn't bother about looking at the coin again. He knew now he'd told Bert his story for the pleasure there had been in at last allowing himself to talk about it, not to keep himself from doing something foolish. All the time his mind had been made up.

"Yes—there is," he said. "McCarthy's in command of the guard tonight, isn't he?"

"That's right."

"He's a friend of yours. Go find him and talk to him like you have to ask his advice. Tell him you're upset because you're afraid I'm thinking about running off with a French-woman."

"But that's crazy. McCarthy'll not waste a minute runnin' to tell the colonel."

"Sure he won't. I'm not going to run out on Clark without giving him a chance to stop it. I owe him that much."

"He'll throw you in the guardhouse. That's the way he'll stop it."

"You know that when I get ready to go nothing can stop me. Now go do as I say."

Bert went out, shaking his head and muttering. Adam stretched out on the bed. For the first time in eight years he was at peace.

It seemed to him that he had hardly more than dropped off before Bert was shaking him awake again. Clark hadn't waited to send for him. Clark was standing just behind Bert. Adam threw off the blanket and stood up.

"Got a candle?" said Clark, very grim. "I want light enough to see him by."

Bert found the stub of a candle and lighted it at the fire. Clark took it from him and held it up to Adam's face. Clark was very nearly as tall as Adam and able to look him straight in the eye. His unbuttoned greatcoat fell apart in front to show his nightshirt tucked into his breeches. His tousled red hair stuck out all around the edges of his three-cornered hat. He'd piled straight out of bed to come here. But his blazing black eyes were awake enough. Their gaze struck into Adam with the sharpness of a knife.

"What makes you so goddamned sure I can't take Detroit?"

Adam blinked. But when Clark asked you a question you answered without stopping to ask what he meant by it.

"I'm not. I'm close to sure you can."

"You are?"

"Yes. Unless you give the English so much time they get themselves pulled together again."

"That's what you think?"

"Yes."

"Everybody around here's picked up a way of telling me not what they think but what they think I want to hear. Is that what you're doing?"

Adam was beginning to get the drift now. "No. And if you

15

jumped out of bed to find out if some kind of new fool talk might have started going around among the boys I can settle that for you, too. I've heard talk enough but none you wouldn't be glad to hear. I don't know of a man in your whole outfit that's not ready to start for Detroit tomorrow if you say the word. Or ask Bert there. He gets around more than I do."

"I don't give a damn about Bert. I want to know what you think."

"I've told you."

Clark lowered the candle and turned to put it down. He started to stick it in the open mouth of the jug, but after first shaking the jug and discovering there was something in it, he dripped grease on the table top and set the candle in that. Bert jumped to shove the tin of water back against the coals.

"Never mind the water," said Clark.

He sat down at the table, splashed rum from the jug into a mug, rinsed it around thoughtfully for a moment, then swung back to glower at Adam again.

"Then will you tell me what in hell's got into you to make you feel like running out on me?"

"Nothing that has anything to do with you or Detroit."

"I ain't got a single solitary man that's not got something to do with me and Detroit."

"Kentucky's full of men that could afford to spell some of us for a while."

This was a reminder that brought the thundercloud back into Clark's face. "Crawling with 'em," he agreed. "All of 'em running around staking out land claims while you and a few more like you wade around in the swamps out here trying to keep the Indians off their necks." A sudden ring of pride replaced the anger in his voice. "There's a parcel of them that could take their turn all right but not so many that's man enough to take your place. I don't have to tell you that. You know it as well as I do. You were one of the first. You joined up before Corn Island and you've stuck straight through everything since. You've been more good to me than some that's officers. Want I should make you one?"

"No."

Clark drew a slow, deep breath, looked at the ceiling, at the floor and then at the mug on the table at his elbow, while his lips moved as if he were counting ten. He picked up the mug and took a drink.

"Sit down."

Adam sat down on the edge of the bed.

"Well, there must be some way to get to the bottom of this," said Clark. "You must have something stuck in your

16

craw. Maybe—since all you men carry on like you're generals —maybe I should tell you why I stopped here after taking this place. I knew that if we kept right on going—while the English and Indians were still wondering what hit 'em—that we'd stand a good chance to take Detroit, too. And nobody likes chances better'n I do. But with something so important as taking Detroit—important to the whole western country and maybe the war—it's not right to take any chance you don't have to. It's a fact that while we wait the English are probably getting themselves set so that they can stand off the few men we have here. But we've got something to wait for, too. Ben Logan and John Bowman will be here within the month with five hundred more men from Kentucky. With that much extra help there'll be no chance to it. We'll be sure of Detroit."

"I don't doubt that for a minute," agreed Adam.

Clark leaned over and tapped Adam's belt, weighted with the flat leather pouches packed with silver dollars. "You didn't do so bad here. You can guess how much better you'll do at Detroit."

"Yes, I can guess."

"And doesn't that make any difference to you, either?"

"No."

Clark got up, walked over to the fire, stared into it, kicked a couple of unburned ends in among the coals, came back, sat down and took another drink. "All right," he said. "Who is she?"

Adam shook his head. "You just might figure some way to stop me."

"Married woman, eh?"

Adam shrugged.

"And there's no might to it. I have to figure some way to stop you." Clark threw back his greatcoat and folded his lean, wiry arms. He grinned, for a second looking as young as his twenty-seven years. "Best way, of course, would be to larrup hell out of you myself."

Adam surveyed Clark's long, slender figure while he rubbed his jaw thoughtfully. "I don't think you could," he said. "But I wouldn't put it past you to try."

"Another way would be to lock you up and keep you locked up."

"Just to give the boys an idea of how sweet you are on the French?"

"The boys mightn't like that too well," conceded Clark. "But just the same I do have to think about the French. There're four of them here for every one of us. They've already changed sides three times in the last two months.

They don't like us so much as they dislike us just a little less than they do the English. And nothing can sour them on us quicker than starting to fool with their women. On top of that you've managed to pick out one where you can make the most trouble possible. That Jacque Papin's got more gumption than most of these Frenchies—together with a keel-boat crew of thirty and a townful of relatives. Once he gets back and finds his wife gone the fur can fly."

Adam turned to scowl at Bert, then got up and started for him. Clark smiled.

"You've no call to pick on Bert. He didn't name your wench. But it wasn't hard to guess who she was. You weren't born a fool. I can think of but one woman in town up to making you one." Clark was still smiling. "So you've made up your mind you have to have her, eh?"

"Some things once you start you got to finish."

Adam sat down and waited. Clark got to his feet. He had stopped smiling.

"Stand up."

Adam arose.

"I'm still your commanding officer. Have you also made up your mind to refuse a direct order from me?"

"Not a military order."

"Then I'm giving you one. I'm sending a party of prisoners back to Virginia. They're leaving first thing in the morning. I'm assigning you to the guard detachment. This is a direct military order. Can you see a way around it?"

Adam slowly shook his head. "No," he said. "I can't."

Clark smiled again. "And I'll give you another order to go with it—a written discharge—good once you get to Virginia."

"What's that for?"

"I want you back. And I've an idea you're likely to show up sooner if you feel free to come or not as you please."

Clark began drawing his coat around him.

"Before you go," said Adam, "I'd like to shake hands."

"I wasn't going without it," said Clark. "Or without saying that I owe more to you—and to Bert, here—and a few dozen more like you—than any of you'll ever owe me."

Bert came back from seeing Clark out, walked up to Adam and pulled him around. "You bastard," he said. "All the time you was countin' on his packin' you off to Virginia." He dropped on the bench and groaned. "You beat me. You're harder to catch up to than a mouse in a mattress." His indignation boiled over. "And me—me that's got a sensible reason to git to Virginia—me, I'm stuck here in this swamp. I'm gonna git drunk." He reached for the jug and then paused to glare at Adam. "You better weasel over there and break the news to Therese about how short her end of the stick is goin' to be."

"No," said Adam. "Anything I could tell her would only make her think worse of herself. Not that it's going to kill her to stay with a husband who wants her. In the morning you get word to the Spanish woman that Clark sent me to Virginia with the prisoners."

Bert forgot about the jug and stretched out on the bench. He groaned again. Then he raised on one elbow with another accusing glare. "I s'pose was you to run into this Virginia gal again—you'd count on havin' the same luck with her you been havin' with Therese." Adam did not reply. This brought Bert bolt upright. "So that's it. I ain't never put much beyond you but this takes tongue, hump and all the marrowbones. This long after—and this far away—you work yourself up to gittin' ideas about a woman you never seen but on a horse or through a window and that's been married eight years to another man."

Adam poured himself another drink and then set it down without tasting it. "You always figure everything the hard way," he said. "What's wrong with a man's getting sick of this war—like everybody is—and, when he finds his pockets all of a sudden full of money, wanting to go somewhere he can spend it. What's wrong with that for an answer?"

"Nothin'. Only if that was it he'd head for New Orleans. That's the place you can git the most fun for money."

"But Virginia is where I was born. Why shouldn't I want to see it again?"

"No reason. Only this gal's in Virginia. And you're aimin' to make a beeline for her." Once he'd make a point in an argument Bert stuck to it like a good dog did a tree that had a coon up it.

"Maybe your sights are set a little low," said Adam. "Might be I just want to see how she'll look to me now that I've grown up some."

Bert spat scornfully into the fire. "If that's all there was to it—you could wait 'til the war's over."

"A man could get himself shot in this war."

"Never heard you fret much before about gittin' shot."

Adam walked over to the fireplace and began thoughtfully kicking the unburned ends of sticks into the fire. Bert was watching him with the pained expression of a man whose best friend has all of a sudden begun to show signs of being slightly touched. Adam cleared his throat. Maybe if he put it in fancier words Bert would be better satisfied. Bert was a great hand for the general principle behind a thing.

"There's something I have to find out first. It's like going back over a trail to look for sign you missed the first time. You have to do it."

Bert shook his head. "You ain't aimin' to go back over no old trail. You're aimin' to break yourself a new one."

TWO

ADAM left the deer path and trotted around the shoulder of the ridge toward Logan's Station. This was familiar country. The year the station was founded he'd hunted for Ben Logan. Four years ago it hadn't been much of a job to keep the place supplied with meat. In those days buffalo came to wallow in the big spring within sight of the stockade. You had to stop to think to keep it straight in your mind that there wasn't a settlement in Kentucky more than four years old. Today he hadn't seen fresh buffalo sign for the last five miles. Game was getting scarce that close to every settlement. And people had more than ever to depend on it because the Indians kept killing any cattle they tried to pasture.

The amount of Indian trouble in Kentucky had been a surprise to him and to all the men of the escort who had spent the last year with Clark in the Illinois gabbling about the easy time people in Kentucky were having. They had no more than landed at Louisville than they had begun to realize the shoe was on the other foot. There had been no big attacks but all winter small parties of Indians had prowled among the Kentucky settlements, making it nearly impossible to hunt or to turn stock out to graze. People had had to spend the time cooped up behind their palisades, cut off even from news from any distance. At Louisville, for example, the whole winter had passed without their learning of Hamilton's recapture of Vincennes. They had finally heard of the disaster only the day before the word had come that Clark had taken it again, along with the English governor.

Adam came out on the cliff above Logan's Station. The place hadn't changed much. It was still the same solid log stockade planted on the little knoll, its houses, built against the inner walls, facing each other across the stock pens in the center, the roofs sloping inward to make it easier to get water to the blazes started by Indian fire arrows. Logan had had to fight to hold the place, almost from the day he had built it, but probably he hadn't changed much either. More than likely this little valley was still the one stretch of land on earth he was bound to have.

To the north two horsemen rode out of the woods into the blackened valley bottom where the cane had been burned to deny Indians cover in the neighborhood of the station. Captain Williams, in command of the escort, had had to keep outriders on the trail ahead and behind, and scouts, such as Adam today, farther out on the flanks, ever since they'd left Louisville, just as if Kentucky were enemy country. To the chance that some roving war party might make a stab at rescuing the prisoners was added the greater likelihood that the enraged settlers might try to get at them. Everybody accepted the story that the English governor at Detroit paid more for Kentucky scalps than for Kentucky prisoners, and there was no question it was English policy to encourage and supply the Indian attacks on the settlements. The fact that Hamilton was now a prisoner of war made him no less an enemy. Men who had lost homes and families had none too much regard for military niceties.

Adam slid down the ravine that cut the face of the cliff and started across the flat for the station. People were running out to stare, muttering, at the little column of soldiers and prisoners plodding out into the open. Since Williams had been unable so far to requisition horses among the hard-pressed settlers of Kentucky, his party's foot pace had allowed news of its nature to run ahead. Though the captives were not yet within hearing, some of the Logan's station women were already beginning to scream threats and insults. Ben Logan, standing in the gateway, saw Adam coming in from the side and strode out to meet him. His thick curling beard had become well sprinkled with gray since Adam had last seen him, but his powerful figure was as erect as ever and his eyes, which had looked upon more danger than most men's, were still as serene.

"We been countin' on you turnin' up again one day," he announced with amiable calm. "But we sure didn't count on you turnin' up with the Hairbuyer in your pocket. How'd you leave your redheaded boss?"

"Fit to buy your hair when he finds out you're not joining him. What happened to your arm?"

Logan glanced down at the arm tied to his belt. "Buckshot," he said. "I was out lookin' for Ann's only fresh cow and let a Wyandot see me first. Same damn arm they busted for me last summer. Come on in and see Ann before the crowd gets back."

Most of the station's people were streaming out along the

21

trail to get a quicker look at the prisoners. Logan linked his good arm with one of Adam's and walked with him through the gate. After the fresh air of the wooded hills from which Adam had come, the smells of the station—of manure and ashes and privies and soft soap and bedding and pigsties and drying hides and brine barrels and wet dogs and cooking grease—were sharp in his nostrils. Logan had always insisted on his people's keeping the place cleaned up better than was the case with most stations. He had even dug a ditch to the nearest spring—so that there was water enough for washing as well as cooking—running right through the stockade. But since a station was a place where stock was kept herded in small pens, and families lived seven and eight in a room, it was bound to smell like a station.

"How'd you know?" asked Logan. "Bowman been talkin'?"

"Not to me. We saw him at Harrodsburg. He slapped us on the back a lot but he didn't tell us anything."

"Then what give you the idea we don't aim to join Clark?"

"Bowman would have had plenty to say—and so would you—if that was what you still had in mind."

"Clark thinks nothin's important except takin' Detroit." Logan released Adam's arm, then stopped, and turned to face him, waiting for his protest. Adam shrugged. Clark and Logan and Bowman and Todd and Calloway and Boone and Harrod were colonels. They had charge of the war in the West. If they couldn't get their minds made up about what they could agree on, nothing was to be gained by everybody else in Kentucky trying to put in his say. But Logan seemed uneasy, for once, and anxious to justify his position. "He can't get it into his head that there's somethin' more important than takin' Detroit."

"What is?"

"Keepin' Kentucky. We go on lettin' the Indians devil us like they been doin' folks is all goin' to pull out."

"I reckon the way Clark looks at it—best way to keep the Indians off your backs is to take Detroit. That's where they get their powder and shot and most of their meanest ideas."

"Mebbe. But even was we to help Clark go for Detroit the good wouldn't last long. The English would only take it right back. It's set off from us here by a sight of mighty rough country—while they can get to it from Canada by boat."

Logan's point was so shrewd that Adam started to argue after all. "But you just said yourself that you're going to get pushed out of Kentucky if you don't do something. What are you and Bowman going to do to stop it?"

"I'll tell you. Though we ain't started to sing out about it

22

yet. You're right. We have changed our minds about joinin' up with Clark. We're aimin' to do somethin' that'll be more real quick use to Kentucky than pawin' after Detroit. Once folks get their corn planted so's they won't have so many excuses about answerin' to muster call Bowman and me are raisin' all the men we can and goin' for the Shawnee towns on Mad River. That's where most of the parties that's been pesterin' us is comin' from. We'll burn out their main nest and stomp on as many rats as we can catch. That'll keep 'em off our backs for a while."

Before Adam's eyes flashed a picture of Clark's face when he heard that he was to get no support this season from his own Kentucky and that he had lost his chance to seize Detroit, key to an empire, because his fellow Kentuckians had turned instead to the burning of a couple of Indian villages. The fact that Benjamin Logan, of all the Kentucky leaders the one he liked and trusted most, was the principal author of his disappointment would not soften the blow. Adam was stirred by an impulse to return to Clark. But as quickly he dismissed the idea. It was now too late for any of Clark's plans this season. The independent design of the Kentucky settlers had already committed him to spending the summer hanging on to Vincennes and Kaskaskia. For that he had men enough. Adam saw that Logan was waiting for his verdict, the first opinion from one of Clark's men he had had a chance to hear.

"Clark will make out somehow," said Adam. "He's used to going it alone."

"Adam Frane," came an excited cry from somewhere behind Logan. "Come here this minute."

Ann Logan stood, beckoning, on the doorstep of the Logan house. Logan seized Adam's arm again and hurried him toward the doorway, immediately more concerned with placating his pretty young wife than by Clark's opinion of him. "I was just on my way to tell you Adam was back," he called out to her.

"So I could see," said Ann. "After you'd palavered there in the gate for an hour or two—with me the last thing on the minds of either of you." She looked at Adam with equal severity. "Come into the kitchen where I can kiss you without the sight giving folks wrong ideas."

She pulled him away from Logan and through the doorway. Logan followed.

"What kind of ideas are you aimin' to give me?" he said.

"Nobody's ever able to give you any that's different from the ones you already have." Ann put her hands on Adam's

23

shoulders, pulled him down to her, kissed him on each cheek and stepped back to look him over again with critical affection. "I can see it's been a waste of time worrying about how you've been getting along. You've put on thirty pounds and you look as pleased with yourself as a weasel coming out of a hen coop."

"Or on his way in," said Logan.

"How many times do you generally have to kiss a man before he begins to look pleased?" said Adam.

"And as brash as ever," Ann said. "Seems like just once I might take to a man that minds his manners."

From the gateway where the escort was coming in with the prisoners the yells, whistles and catcalls from the accompanying crowd took on a new and more menacing note.

"Sounds like there's a parcel of folks out there better mind their manners," said Logan, starting for the door.

"I've got plenty of side meat and hominy for any that needs it," Ann called after him, indicating a great iron pot swung on a crane alongside the fire. "But send somebody in to carry out the kettle. I don't want a single one of the scrubby pack traipsing through my kitchen."

"Fine way to talk about the English lieutenant governor." Logan turned in the doorway to grin at Ann and wink at Adam. "Fact is—she's scared to look at prisoners. Last week we brought in a stinkin' Shawnee we'd run down with dogs over around Burdett's Knob and after she'd took one look at him she couldn't sleep all that night." He went out.

"He's right," admitted Ann. "I can't stomach anything that's live fixed so it can't move the way it wants to."

The commotion outside had risen to a roar, accompanied by the sound of blows and one or two yells of pain.

"Might be I could help," said Adam. "I know most everybody out there—our people as well as Ben's."

"Ben can handle it," said Ann. "Notice?" The uproar began to die down. Her eyes became bright. "The Good Book says pride is a sin. But how can a woman help being proud when she knows she's got the best man there is?"

There came a sleepy wail from the cradle in the corner. The sudden silence had roused the child as the noise had not. Ann ran to the cradle and lifted the two-year-old boy until he could stand against the headboard. "Hush, Billy." The child instantly quieted. This was one command frontier babies were taught to obey. "This is William," she said to Adam. And then to William: "See. That's Adam. You don't remember but he rode all the way from Harrodsburg through a blizzard to fetch your father in time to see you born. And now you watch while I get him something to eat before he rides off somewhere again."

"Looks as much like his father as David did at his age," said Adam. "Where is David?"

"Somewhere out in the crowd," said Ann complacently. "Probably been yelling louder than anybody. He's near as tough as Ben already. Day before yesterday he was bound to shoot Ben's rifle. It kicked him flat on the ground. Ben thought that had cured him for one day but when he offered to let him try it again Davy was just as ready as the first time. Sit down." She placed before Adam a platter of salt pork and hominy, flanked by bowls of pea soup and clabber. "Corn pone will be hot in a minute. We ran out of coffee about the middle of last summer."

"Don't know how I can get along without coffee."

Adam was hungrily lifting the first spoonful of thick, buttery pea soup when he saw something that took most of his appetite away. Bert was standing in the doorway, staring with a wide grin of appreciation, first at the steaming dishes set before Adam and then at Ann.

"Hello, Adam."

"Case you can't guess," Adam said to Ann, "he's one of Clark's men—named Bert Cogar." He stared coldly at Bert. "And you're in Mrs. Logan's kitchen."

"Pleased to know you, ma'am," said Bert, snatching off his cap and sidling in.

"A special friend of yours?" Ann asked Adam.

"Off and on he tries to act like it. But I've got no idea what brings him here unless he run off from the regiment."

"He's wrong, ma'am," said Bert. "I didn't run off—I come here to see that he don't."

"I suppose Clark gave you written orders," jeered Adam. Bert nodded. "Day after you left."

Ann put another bowl on the table. "Well—if you're a friend of Adam's you're welcome here. Help yourself. William's ready for his dinner, too." She scooped the baby from the cradle and started for the next room, her fingers busy with the buttons of her dress. She turned in the doorway. "If you see Ben before I do tell him I'll sit down at the table with Governor Hamilton—if Ben thinks it's his place to ask the man to have supper in this house."

Bert felt around on the table top for his spoon, his admiring attention still on the doorway through which Ann had disappeared. He turned to Adam, wagging his head in new wonderment. "They's some you can always count on findin' their way into a kitchen. And some that you can generally

25

locate by lookin' for the fetchiest piece of calico around. But what beats me is the way you can always git next to both at once."

"Best hold your tongue," threatened Adam. "She's Ben Logan's wife."

Bert helped himself liberally to the salt pork and hominy and began wolfing it down. "Can't see no harm in lookin' at her," he said with his mouth full, "and that's sure easy to do."

Adam's stare was still cold and suspicious. "Well?" he demanded.

"I'll tell you just how it all happened." said Bert. "The next mornin' Therese she went to Clark to find out what he'd done with you. She had some story cooked up about how you owed her for somethin' and she wanted you brought back to pay for it. Maybe I ought to say first that that night in the warehouse Clark he figgered you just wanted to see Virginia again like most of the rest of us did. It was his guess that you was usin' your business with Therese to put a little fire to him so's he'd have to send you back. But after he'd talked to Therese right in the same room with him, and looked at her for a while up real close, he got to worryin' may be he'd been wrong. It didn't seem to him a man was liable to get her out of his mind maybe for quite a spell. Anyway he sent for me."

"Wait a minute. You were the one that got her to go to Clark."

"I wasn't sure how it would work out," admitted Bert. "But it worked out fine. Clark told me to catch up with you as fast as I could. He wanted me along not to help watch the prisoners but to watch you. He knowed I knowed you well enough to keep track of you better'n anybody else could. He didn't want you crawlin' out of your blankets some night and headin' back for Vincennes."

"If that's your story—what took you so long to catch up?"

"You might need plenty of watchin'," said Bert. "But I knowed you didn't need watchin' to keep you from goin' back there. So when I left Louisville I come around by Lee's Town."

"What was that for?"

"I was lookin' for Joe Tusser. You remember old Joe. He brought that canoeload of jerked buffalo to Corn Island last summer. I recollected hearin' Joe say once he'd come from the Mechum River end of Albemarle County—and I figgered it might be from somewheres near where you come from."

"So—you took all that trouble to try to get your nose to a trail I left eight years ago?"

26

Bert waited, undisturbed by Adam's resentment, while he chewed and swallowed another chunk of salt pork. "Ain't had side meat so good as this since I left Augusta County. All I was aimin' at was bein' some help to you. Don't seem to me like there's much sense in your goin' at this blinder'n you have to. How do you know what might have happened among folks back there since you been away? That's the way it hit me. So I oiled Joe up a little with a pint of corn juice and purty soon he begun to remember good. He told me he used to work for a man named Nenifee that run a sawmill ten miles south of Stull's store. He couldn't recollect ever hearin' anythin' about you but he said he heard old Stull died of a flux year before last—that was the year Joe left to come out here."

Adam's anger softened for a moment. "I'd counted on looking up Alec Stull when I got back there," he said slowly. "I owe him more than I had much idea of when I left."

Out of respect Bert ate for a while in silence. But he couldn't hold back long. "And Joe remembered a family by the name of Wyeth that owned quite a piece of land along the Mechum River." He looked up from his eating to watch for the effect of what he was saying. "That name mean anythin' to you?"

Adam gave no sign that it did. "Keep going," he said. "I was mighty sorry to hear about old man Stull—maybe you dragged up bad news about somebody else I used to know."

"Ever know Paul—a big, redheaded galoot—one of the four Wyeth brothers?" Adam resumed eating without paying any attention to the question. Bert went on: "Joe said he'd heard this Paul was comin' out here this year to look at some land along the Licking the Wyeths once bought some kind of title to."

"When you hit on something that's so much out of the ordinary as a man coming to Kentucky to look for land," said Adam, "then you've picked up something worth sitting up all night talking about."

Bert chuckled. The more Adam tried to cover up the more he was enjoying himself. "If you can't remember a Paul Wyeth then maybe here's a Wyeth you can remember. Anyway, Joe did. He remembered about a Wyeth gal named Cynthia that married a gunsmith from Richmond. He remembered that because it was a big weddin' and folks for miles around was asked to it. And he remembered it was just eight years ago because it happened the same year Dan Boone was took by Indians the first time."

Bert paused on this note of triumph. Adam went on eating. "If you're waiting for me to tell you any more," he said, "you might as well stop flapping your ears. Your best bet is to go back to pumping Joe Tusser."

"You'll be glad I pumped old Joe like I did," said Bert, finally nettled by Adam's continued calm. "You'll change your tune when you hear the main news I got for you. This Richmond coot—Rowan was his name—that she married up with—he was killed at the Battle of Princeton back in '76." He leaned across the table and shook Adam's arm. "Can't you git it through your head? Your gal's a widow."

Adam pulled free and stood up. "I've known that since last summer. I saw a piece about it in a Richmond newspaper Vigo brought back with him that trip he took to New Orleans."

It didn't seem to upset Bert much to find out all his snooping had turned up nothing new. Instead, he began to look as pleased as if he'd finally caught the flea that had been biting him the hardest.

"Now I'm beginnin' to git the hang of it," he declared. "So you've knowed for a year she was a widow, eh? But all that time you didn't so much as twitch a nostril. You just went on foolin' along same's you had before. You was practicin' hard —but you wasn't ready. I remember that German bound girl at Harrodsburg and how every time you was in the neighborhood she'd light out to look for the cows a good hour ahead of milkin' time. She wasn't bad either—but she didn't prove enough for you. Then there was the Spaniard's daughter— runnin' to put on her best dress every time she seen you comin'. And that redheaded Carolina honey on the flatboat at Corn Island. Your luck was good—and gittin' better—but you didn't figger it was good enough yet. It took Therese to turn the trick. Then it got real good. There was one that had been used to every man that come around makin' a try for her. But for you she was no trouble a-tall. She was even ready to leave a rich husband and take to the bushes with you. That's when you made up your mind. You knowed you didn't have to practice no more. You was ready."

"You can get your mouth open so wide," said Adam, "you're lucky I don't stuff your elbow into it."

He walked to the door. He didn't like anything about Bert's tone or the sound of his laugh. Bert talked as if a man's ideas were as simple as those of a rooster in a hen yard. But there was no use shutting his eyes to the truth. When he'd first read that item in the Richmond paper it had started him to thinking about the woman Cynthia had probably become, in the place of the sixteen-year-old girl he had known, but it had not started him to thinking about seeing her again. Bert was right about that. That had come later, after his luck with Therese. But a man had a right to learn about women as he went along, just as he did about the balance of a rifle or the sign left by a Mingo war party. He'd be a fool if he didn't.

He stood in the doorway looking around for Logan and turning over in his mind what Bert had told him. There was another thing there was no good trying to fool himself about. There was one piece of Bert's news that made a great deal of difference to him. Up to now he had taken it for granted that when he got back he could drop in on Alec Stull, stay with him awhile, as would be perfectly natural for him to do after all these years, and make Stull's store, where he once had worked, and could again for a time, if he felt like it, a kind of center while he got his bearings. Now he had to hit upon some other excuse to take him into a neighborhood where he had no apparent reason to go. He could hardly ride up to the Wyeth house blowing a horn and announcing that he had come to take a fresh look at Cynthia.

The answer, prompted by another item in Bert's news, came to him almost at once, and kept recurring to him, each time with a stir of amused satisfaction, while he helped Bert carry out the kettle of hog and hominy to feed the soldiers and prisoners, while he visited with some of his old acquaintances around the station, while he spent half an hour telling David about the capture of Vincennes and while he sat at the table that night in the Logan kitchen with Logan and Ann, with Captain Williams and Lieutenant Rogers of the escort and with the captives Maisonville and Hamilton.

Logan had insisted on Adam's joining them. "Christ in a split stick," he declared. "If Ann and me can stand for lettin' that pair of injun lovers into our house we don't have to pay for it by shuttin' out somebody we want." Williams and Rogers, being militia officers, saw nothing odd in a common soldier eating with his military superiors, while Hamilton by now was astonished by nothing American. Logan had ruled out Major Jehu Hay, second in rank only to Hamilton among the prisoners, because Hay was a Pennsylvanian who had gone over to the English to become a deputy Indian agent. "I can put up with Hamilton," Logan said. "He was born on the other side. But that Tory turntail—he's lucky we was to let him eat with the dogs." Maisonville he had included after he had chanced to overhear Adam tell David how Jim Beggs and Cory Poynter had pulled the French partisan leader out of bed the night of the surprise attack and had used him as a breastwork in the ditch fifteen yards from the fort where they had crawled to shoot through the gun ports at the English gunners. The episode had left Maisonville excessively nervous. "I like to watch that tic around the Frenchie's left eye," said Logan.

Hamilton honored the occasion by wearing a handsome blue broadcloth coat produced from the modest baggage he had been allowed to bring with him. The stunning defeat he had suffered at Vincennes and the many personal humiliations to which he had been subjected while traveling through Kentucky had made him a grim and unhappy man. After bowing gravely to Ann upon entering, he maintained an icy composure.

"Mind you, Ben Logan," Ann had ruled. "You'll all behave like white folks. No matter how you feel about the Englishman you'll not go to badgering him at my table."

The meal began in a strained silence. It wasn't easy for men on this frontier this year to find much to talk about that had no connection with the war or with Indians or with the prospects of staying alive. The silence continued and became increasingly awkward.

"This is most excellent chicken, madam," said Hamilton himself, finally.

"Thank you, Colonel Hamilton," said Ann. "Usually I like to make my stew a mite richer than this is but we've been a little short of butter."

Logan felt of his broken arm. "Been a job lately to find the right kind of pasture for cows," he said.

She shot a warning glance at her husband and hastily changed the subject. "The laugh was surely on me when I was out in the pen catching these chickens," she said with forced brightness. "There was an old hen making a terrible to-do because she thought she'd lost one of her chicks. She couldn't seem to find it though the chick kept cheeping like it was in real misery. I'd started to help her look when I saw the catbird on the palisade. It was making sounds like a scared chick just to devil that old hen."

She looked to Logan to keep the ball rolling now that she had it started.

"A catbird's liable to make most any kind of a noise there is," said Logan gravely.

"I knew one once that could make a sound just like pulling the stopper out of a jug," contributed Adam. "Used to bother my grandfather because he'd always start doing it when the old man came out in the yard."

"There was a young Indian guide hunting with me last summer," said Hamilton, "who could imitate the bleating of a fawn so successfully that it brought the doe running."

"Indians is most as cute as catbirds at makin' tricky noises," said Williams, with the sudden, unexpected volubility of a man customarily taciturn. "I ain't never forgot the first one I ever come up with. I was maybe twelve and out lookin' for our old mare. I could hear the mare's bell and followed the jingle-jangle farther and farther into the woods. The bell kept startin' and stoppin' just like the mare was feedin' along—pickin' at one thing and another. But when I finally got right up to it there was a Mingo a-shakin' it."

Logan glanced reflectively at the top of Williams' head. "You still got most of your hair."

"Captives was worth more than scalps them days," said Williams. "Took most everythin' my folks had but they bought me back."

Lieutenant Rogers, seated beside Williams, gave him a ferocious dig with his elbow. Williams' neck turned red and he stared miserably at his plate, afraid to look at Ann. Her eyes flashed angrily in the direction of her husband whose remark had led Williams astray but she turned swiftly and smilingly to Hamilton. "That's a real handsome coat, Colonel Hamilton," she said, leaning nearer to look admiringly at the blue broadcloth. "I remember an uncle of mine had one of the very same material. His came from London, too."

"This didn't come from London, madam," said Hamilton. "I bought it at a trading store in Vincennes just before we came away. After the capitulation my extra uniforms, along with those of the other officers were—ah—shall we say—sequestered—as if they were a part of the post's military stores."

Logan choked and then met Ann's sharp look with one of bland innocence. She forced another bright smile. "Ben, start the chicken around again. Now—please—don't anybody hold back. There's plenty more in the pot."

Adam had been watching David. The boy had left his bed in the loft and had crawled to the head of the ladder where his solemn gaze was fixed on the person of the captive English governor. Presently Logan noticed him, too, and nudged Adam.

"Best pick us trees to get behind," he whispered. "Davy's gettin' ready to let fly."

"Maw," rang out the clear childish voice from directly over Ann's head. "Why do you always call him Colonel? Ain't Hairbuyer his real name?"

Hamilton slowly laid down his knife and spoon while as slowly his florid face whitened.

"David," said Ann sternly, though she was looking not at him but at Logan as if even this were in some way his doing, "get back to bed this minute." She turned to face Hamilton. Her tone was rueful but curiously unapologetic. "I hope you will not take it too much amiss. He is only four years old."

"Madam," said Hamilton, "these past days I have become inured to insults from all ages."

Silence returned to the table, this time not broken even by Ann. Hamilton looked defiantly around at the other men. Maisonville, who knew too little English to attend what was being said, continued to stare straight before him, while from time to time he lifted his hand to quiet the twitching muscle in his face. Williams was industriously mopping gravy from his plate with a piece of bread. Rogers with equal industry was wiping his mouth with his handkerchief. Adam's attention was fixed on the blue broadcloth coat. Only Logan met Hamilton's gaze. He extended the wooden serving platter.

"Have some more chicken?" he asked cheerfully.

"No, thank you," said Hamilton. There were little beads of sweat on his upper lip. "I know what all you Kentuckians think. You've taught even your babies to believe it. This business that you charge me with—let's bring it out in the open. Colonel Logan, if you were invading Canada and the Indian nations offered you their support would you accept it?"

"You're damned right I would."

"I'm relieved," said Hamilton, "to meet one honest man this side of the Ohio."

Ann gasped as if she had been struck. She sprang up, her blazing eyes turned first on Hamilton and then on her husband. Her face was dead white except for two spots of color just under her cheekbones. "Honest—so you two can call that honest," she cried. "Ben Logan—I'd sooner see you hanged—as you very likely would be if they caught you—as any man should be who dared to turn murdering savages loose on people's homes and children."

Hamilton rose eagerly. He was almost beaming as he confronted Ann. "I must thank you, madam, for your plain speaking. I welcome the opportunity to give an equally plain answer. Would you, then, hang every soldier? Do you forget that the first duty of the soldier—the single purpose of war, in fact—is to inflict suffering on the enemy? Or can you doubt that in war, as with a surgeon's knife, it is sometimes more merciful to cut quickly and deeply?"

"All my life I have heard how soldiers talk," said Ann, more quietly but still breathing hard. "But nobody can be so wrong as a good soldier."

"Right or wrong—war is war—it never changes—its one aim is to injure."

Logan had been kicking Adam's leg under the table. As he watched Ann his eyes shone. "Well," he said, getting to his feet, "looks like we've baked that cake good and brown.

32

Colonel Hamilton, I don't need to tell you we're kind of crowded here in this station. Where'd you sooner sleep—here by the fire alongside of Adam—or in the mill loft where we've spread straw on the floor for you men?"

"The mill," said Hamilton. "I've already imposed enough on your hospitality." He bowed to Ann. "For which—and I beg you will believe me—I am deeply grateful."

Williams and Rogers went out with their prisoners. Logan grinned at Ann and winked at Adam. "It's a blessing you're staying the night with us. If it wasn't for company Ann would be at me with a broomstick."

"Takes more than a broomstick to straighten out a man," pronounced Ann. She placed her hands on the table and leaned forward thoughtfully as if addressing the array of dirty dishes. "A man can talk bigger'n a woman—just as he can swing an ax harder or lift a heavier load—but there's times for all his talk he can't see through to the end of what's right and what's wrong any better'n Davy can when he packs a toad full of buckshot to see if it can still jump." The ghost of a dimple appeared in her cheek. "Still—he has to be a man—else what good is he to you?"

She began to scrape and stack the dishes. Logan and Adam sat down by the fire and got out their pipes.

"I don't like to change the subject," said Adam.

"Go right ahead," said Logan. "Ann will be wakin' me up nights for the next month to tell me the rest of what she thinks."

"More'n likely," said Ann. "About the only time I *can* think is when you and the children are asleep. And right now I'd as soon hear what Adam has to say. He had something on his mind all through supper."

Adam gave her a startled look but she continued picking up dishes. "I heard today about some Virginia people I used to know who are looking for land in Kentucky," he said.

Both Logan and Ann were instantly as interested as he had known they would be.

"What kind of people?" asked Logan.

"Fairly well-to-do family—four grown sons—when I knew them they were farming maybe three hundred acres—they had about sixty head of beef stock—good horses—eight or nine slaves." He could tell without looking how this was hitting Logan. So substantial a family group would make a welcome addition to any Kentucky settlement.

"Where do they figger on locatin'?"

"One of the sons is coming out this summer to look along the Licking."

"Plenty of good land there," said Logan. "But too near the

33

Ohio. Mighty easy for the Indians to get at you on the Licking. All they have to do when they come across the river is to trot down that main buffalo trace and they're right in your dooryard." Adam waited. Logan scratched his beard uneasily. "They'd ought to look at some of the country around here before they make up their minds. There's a bottom just over the hill along Quail Creek that's better land than any I ever seen on the Licking. They'd be a sight better off here."

Adam nodded. "I think maybe they would."

"You goin' to be seein' them when you get back there?"

"I might."

"Then you can tell them how much better off they'd be here."

"I don't know them that well," said Adam. "You have to know people real well to try to advise them about land—either that or not know them at all."

Logan grunted regretfully. "Well, you know best. But they do sound like the kind of people it'd be an advantage to have locate here."

"You could write them a letter telling them about your place here and the kind of land they could expect. I can certainly see that they get the letter."

"That's a good idea," said Logan. "Ann—see if there's any of that paper left." But Ann was no longer in the room. "Ann," he called. She came back. She had paper, pen and inkhorn in her hands. Logan eyed her suspiciously. "How'd you know we wanted to write a letter?"

Ann merely smiled. She pushed aside the dishes and sat down at the table. "You tell me what you want to say—and I'll set it down and"—she glanced at Adam and now there was no question about the dimple in her cheek—"and Adam will deliver it."

"Better address it to Joel Wyeth," said Adam, still businesslike. "He's the oldest of the brothers."

He didn't have to worry about what Ann might be guessing. It was when he got to the Wyeth house that he had to watch himself. And, at least, with this letter in his pocket, now he wouldn't have to ride up to the door blowing a horn.

THREE

LEAVING Logan's the party left Kentucky, for from that day on, and for many days, they were in the Wilderness. People had known that region of brush-covered slopes, cane-choked gorges and forested mountains by that name as long as they had had a name for Kentucky. They called the way across it the Wilderness Road because it was the only way to get back and forth between the settlements of southwestern Virginia and the new ones in Kentucky. The road was no more than a narrow track through the brush, an accidental linking up of old game trails, along which men and horses pushed single file, and no better a thoroughfare now than when Boone and the Skaggs brothers, or the Indians before them, had first known it. For two hundred miles it climbed rocky ridges where storms howled, dropped into soggy bottoms where the cane grew thirty feet high and as thick as a man's waist, coming out again and again on the banks of foaming rivers to be crossed only by swimming or on laboriously constructed rafts. Anybody who knew the Wilderness or had heard about it regarded it with a special dread. It was a region where the worst could always be expected, where a misstep could mean a fall from a cliff, where a horse's stumble could mean a broken leg, where any thicket could mean there was an Indian in it.

However, this was no party of defenseless movers. Adam, each day studying the trail an hour ahead, from time to time found Indian sign but no sign of Indians in sufficient number to tangle with a company of Clark's hard-bitten veterans. He liked the hard and lonely going. It gave him more chance to think. When headed for dangerous country you needed to think about what you might be getting into, and he was headed for country more dangerous than the Wilderness. He couldn't send spies ahead into Albemarle County to bring him back notice of what to expect. Since hearing about old man Stull he'd also known he couldn't hang back after he arrived while he studied the situation. Once he got near he had to keep going. And the letter took him only to the door. What then? There was the one possibility, of course, which he didn't like to think about. Eight years was a long time. By now she could be fat or sickly or the mother of four. But if this were so all he had to

35

do was back away as fast as he could. He would feel a fool, yet not so big a fool as if he had never found out. But suppose not. Then he would be in the really dangerous country.

For three days the peace and calm so unnatural to the Wilderness continued. The faces of soldiers and captives alike grew brighter. The Americans could feel that they were getting on toward their onetime homes in Virginia, while the English, if denied that solace, at least that they were leaving the scene of their disaster behind.

The usual luck of the Wilderness Road caught up with them, however, at the Hazel Patch, where the northern fork came in. Colonel Richard Calloway had come down from Boonesborough and was waiting to take command of the detachment for the remainder of the journey. As the wearied column straggled in off the trail to the camp site his first command was a bellowing: "Fall in."

The puzzled, disgusted men pushed and elbowed into a semblance of company front.

"What ails yuh? Ain't yuh ever stood in line before?" The colonel surveyed them with a cold and disparaging eye. "Maybe you've forgot you're soldiers, but, Goddammit, from now on yuh'll start rememberin'."

All evening the outranked Williams moved from fire to fire, trying to soothe his irritated men. "What's the difference?" he said. "He's got folks up Boonesborough way to name him delegate to the Virginia Assembly. I spose he figgers he can git him more notice from the bigwigs back there if he shows up in Richmond with a parcel of English prisoners in tow. But nobody's goin' to forgit that it was Clark that catched 'em."

Nevertheless, from the moment the headstrong old soldier took over he saw to it that it made quite a difference. He liked to remember that he was a county lieutenant and that his military experience went all the way back to a captaincy in the French and Indian War. He valued his own judgment so much above any other man's that a year ago, in the course of a difference of opinion over defense plans, he had not hesitated to assemble a formal court-martial in order to prefer the fantastic charge that his old friend and neighbor, Daniel Boone, had suddenly turned into a friend of the Indians. Equally now he refused to listen to the suggestions of Williams or the complaints of the men. He continued to insist on the most rigid military formality. And though they were so deep in the Wilderness that any English prisoner was certain to starve if he tried to escape, and, in fact, was so frightened of the dark forest that he could not have been

driven away, the stubborn colonel required a full comple-
ment of pickets at every camping place. Soldiers of the escort
who had slogged along the trail all day were forced to stand
guard all night. The earlier good will evaporated. Men per-
formed their duties grudgingly, quarreled over rations and
snarled at one another under the slightest provocation.

Calloway brought with him bad weather as well as bad
temper. The mild winter turned into a stormy and frigid
spring. Sleet blinded them on the heights, frost crusted
their wet blankets at night and they came out from each river
crossing with their clothing sheathed with ice. Many men
sickened, slowing their progress, and this in turn caused their
already short rations to run out.

All welcomed the sight, when at last they came out through
Moccasin Gap into the open country along the Holston, of
substantial houses and barns, fenced fields and well-kept orchards. Here were settlements already so old that fruit trees
had begun to bear. Yet even here their troubles did not
lessen; they only changed again. Though so much farther
from the war the inhabitants here were more hostile to the
prisoners than had been the people of Kentucky. The Holston
settlers were eager to lavish acclaim and hospitality upon the
heroes of Clark's army but were bitterly reluctant to offer the
English prisoners so much as corn bread and water. At every
station there were near riots as the men of the escort sought
irritably to protect their charges.

Adam alone, among the travelers, had paid little heed to
their many trials—Calloway, weather, hunger or brawls. He'd
been occupied with his own concerns. His thinking ahead kept
hanging fire at about the stage of reaching the Wyeth door.
He could foresee the welcoming interest the letter would win
for him. But he could also picture himself arriving in his
bedraggled and weatherworn buckskins, apparently just another good-for-nothing young backwoodsman of the kind who
drifted back and forth over the mountains every spring, to be
received and treated kindly, perhaps, on account of the letter,
but to be bedded and fed out back somewhere with the
help. And from what he remembered of the Valley Road
ahead, he wasn't likely to find a store this side of Albemarle
County where he could buy new clothes that might pass, even
in a pinch. He could go on to Richmond first, of course, but he
was too impatient for that. Anyway, a brand new outfit wasn't
what he wanted, either. He'd better stick to his old buckskins than to run the risk of giving the Wyeths the idea he'd
decked himself out for their benefit. More and more his mind
kept turning to two garments he had seen when their owners

dressed up at Logan's and which he knew were still safely preserved in the party's baggage—Major Jehu Hay's doeskin breeches and Colonel Hamilton's blue broadcloth coat.

Of course they might not want to sell, no matter how much he offered. He didn't want to pay too much more than they were worth, either. He decided he needed Bert's counsel. Bert had worked for a trader. He always had ideas about the right price for things.

Bert caught on right away. And he took an immediate interest. "You'd best let me do your dickerin' for you," he said. "You'll pay too much. Or if they don't want to sell you'll git mad and come out nowhere."

He'd approached Bert while they were still back in the mountains during the worst of the sleetstorms. That same night when he got back to camp Bert had the doeskin breeches. They were almost new but not too new. Adam was very satisfied with them. He folded them carefully, wrapped them in oiled deerskin to keep off the wet, then put them in his pack.

"How much?"

"Nothin'."

Adam started taking them out of his pack. "You don't steal," he said, "even from a critter like Jehu."

Bert laughed. "I only meant no money. Jehu, he's been freezin' these last few nights so's he couldn't sleep. I traded him your bearskin robe for the pants."

Adam was still satisfied. The bearskin was heavy to carry and he'd always been used to rolling up in a single blanket in any kind of weather. He'd have thrown the robe away long since if the Logans hadn't given it to him.

The night they camped at Flat Lick Bert waited until they were alone together and then, making sure they were not being noticed, handed him the watch. It had a heavy silver case, a loud tick, and an enamel crest on the back—a very handsome piece.

"Ain't she a dandy!" said Bert.

"What you doing with Calloway's watch?"

" 'Tain't Calloway's watch no more," said Bert. "It's yourn now."

"Mine? What do I want with a watch?"

"Maybe you don't know it—but it's exactly what you want. Carryin' a watch sets a man up. Clothes that ain't out at the elbows is like keepin' your nose wiped. People expect it. But it says somethin' when you carry a watch. It says you're a real jump out ahead—and you don't have to keep lookin' back to see how far ahead. Ever see how old Calloway was always takin' out that watch to look at it? When you take out a watch folks take notice."

"How much?"

"Fifty dollars. And worth twice that. Solid silver. And look at that crown on the back. And every hour she rings a bell so you can tell what time it is even in the dark."

Adam continued to stare at Bert. "What I still want to know is how you got it from Calloway. That red-necked old buzzard wouldn't even speak to a common low-life soldier like you—let alone sell you his watch."

"That part was easy. I gave Cap Williams the money and he bought it off Calloway for me." Bert was aggrieved by Adam's lack of enthusiasm. "Long's you don't want it—give it back to me. Up to Richmond I can git seventy-five for it."

Adam looked at the watch again. He liked the feel of it in his hand. He had never before owned anything that was at once valuable and useless.

"No," he said. "I'll keep it. But get this into your head. Don't come up with any more ideas about what you think I ought to have. From now on all I want is that blue coat."

Bert sulked for a while but by the next day his interest seemed as lively as before. Still, more than a week passed without Bert's making any effort to approach Hamilton. "I got to wait for just the right time," Bert explained. "He's been through just as much brush as the rest of us. He won't want to show up in Richmond in a uniform the shape his is in. So far he wouldn't sell his only spare coat to his grandmother, was she naked."

The night they reached Sapling Grove in the Holston Bert tossed the coat in Adam's lap.

"How'd you do it?"

"By waitin' for the right time."

"When was that?"

"When he got mad enough."

"What made him that mad?"

"Seein' his own men go hungry while the rest of us has all we could eat. Calloway he's been doin' what he could to git people to loosen up a little, but every time Hamilton hollers about nobody feedin' his men all Calloway can tell him is nobody's furnished him funds to buy rations for prisoners. So Hamilton he wanted to buy grub for them hisself but folks along here they never seen a draft on a London bank before. That's when he got mad enough to sell me the coat for some of your Spanish dollars that folks would take."

"How many of my Spanish dollars?"

"Seventy-five. That's more'n the coat's worth but I knowed how much you wanted it."

Adam put the coat away in his pack. From now on he had nothing to worry about except how slowly the column marched. And though their route now led along an actual wagon road they were making no better time than back in the mountains. April passed and with early May the weather turned warm and then hot. The prisoners, disgruntled, hungry and footsore, sullenly refused to be hurried. Bert was taking advantage of the slow pace. Whenever off duty he made a point of visiting farms along the road to look at horses.

"I ain't aimin' to buy just yet," he told Adam. "I just want to see what kind of stuff they got for sale and what kind of prices they're askin'. 'Tain't easy to figger prices with this Virginia money worth less every day than it was yesterday."

"You happen to see a fair-to-middling colt for maybe twenty-five or thirty dollars," said Adam. "Pick him up for me. Before long now I'm going to spring my discharge on old Calloway and pull out. I'll need some sort of a horse."

At Fort Chiswell Bert came back to camp riding as beautiful a young mare as Adam had ever seen. She was a wine-colored bay with a starlike blaze and four white stockings and she moved as lightly as if she were on springs.

"I see you've found you a steady old bell mare to lead your pack string," said Adam.

"Nope," said Bert. "She's too fancy for me. I brought her in to show you. What d'ye think of her?"

"She's not bad."

"She's only the best mare I ever seen," said Bert.

"How much?"

"Git on her and try her," said Bert. "You never set a horse that moves as sweet and smooth as she does."

"How much?"

"She's just turned four and she ain't got a blemish on her the size of a gnat's whisker. And look at them quarters. She's really built."

"How much?"

"Two hundred and fifty dollars—saddle and bridle thrown in."

"Paper money?"

"Real money."

"Take her back."

"Just as you say," said Bert. "I only thought that where you was goin' you might want to ride up on somethin' that looked fitten." He dismounted and handed Adam the reins. "Hold her a minute. Before I take her back I want Calloway to see her. He's been lookin' for a horse."

The mare took a step nearer Adam and sniffed inquisitively at his buckskin sleeve. She had been gently raised. She did not shy when he lifted a hand to stroke her satiny neck. She was

40

wide in the chest and wide between the eyes and her nostrils were big enough to take in plenty of air when she needed to. Everything about her was right. She stretched nearer, her ears cocked forward, and nuzzled his shoulder.

"She got a name?" asked Adam.

"People that raised her named her Oriole. If she was mine I'd call her Queenie."

"I like Oriole better than Queenie," said Adam.

The next morning as he was saddling her Williams walked over. "She sure is a real honey," he said, eying the mare admiringly. "Like a chance to try her out? Ride ahead to Ingles' Ferry and tell 'em there we'll be gettin' in toward night. Bill Ingles he always likes to take good care of people comin' through and he'll be mad if we don't let him know how many of us there is in time so's he can git ready."

Trying out Oriole was a pleasure. Her every gait was smooth. She liked to go. She had no bad habits. And when he let her out she flew like a bird. The swift movement, after weeks of trudging along on foot, decided him. Traveling alone and this well mounted he could get to Albemarle in four days, five at the most. Staying with the detachment he'd be a month getting that far down the James. Now that they were well into Virginia the escort had no further actual need of him. Tomorrow he would make the break and go on ahead.

He found a big change in Ingles' Ferry since he'd come through here going the other way. The original Ingles log cabin had become a big frame house and had blossomed out with orchard, barns, garden—even a strip of lawn in front of the porch. Across the road there was a tavern and a general store and down by the ferry there were log stables for the freighters who were beginning to drive their overloaded wagons up and down the Valley Road as if it were the highway between Williamsburg and Richmond. William Ingles was one early settler who had managed to grow up with the country. The man who told Adam where to find him said the various Ingles establishments were doing upward of a thousand dollars' worth of business a month. But no matter how well Ingles was doing he had paid for being the first to build here twenty years ago when this country was no safer than Kentucky was now. His wife had never been the same since she got back after the Shawnee carried her off, while two of his children had died in captivity and another had been recovered, crippled, only after years of search. He remembered Adam at once, from the time Adam had stopped there to work out the price of a rifle, and he was intensely interested in what Adam had come to tell. Having done his share of Indian fighting his main interest, unlike most, was

41

not in the English prisoners but in the men who'd captured them.

"So Clark clamped down on the place so fast he catched Hamilton asleep in bed," he marveled. "Can't hardly blame the Englishman for not counting on anybody wading up to their necks through forty mile of ice water to get at him. We ain't had so much good news lately but what a piece like this is right welcome. One thing I don't quite follow. You say you didn't have so much as a grasshopper gun while they had twelve cannon and eighty soldiers back of a stockade. What made them give in so quick?"

This was Adam's first chance to talk to anybody who hadn't already heard about Vincennes and it was a pleasure. "Our showing up out of nowhere in the middle of the night to start with," he said. "And when it got light and Clark called on them to surrender he talked as big as if he had the French army and navy in each hand. He gave Hamilton just thirty minutes to make up his mind. Then while he was waiting something happened that might have helped a little. A pack of Vincennes Indians got back from Kentucky with scalps and prisoners. Instead of the big welcome they were counting on they walked right into our arms. Clark had them knocked in the head over in front of the main gate of the fort. After that Hamilton stopped arguing about terms."

"That George Clark—he is a caution," said Ingles. "I remember the last time he was through here—he was on his way to pound on the assembly at Richmond to send help to Kentucky. He had only one man with him—and he knew the people out there didn't even have gunpowder—but to listen to him you'd think he already had the English beat. Come on in and shove your feet under Ma's table."

Mrs. Ingles' haunted eyes did not brighten as her husband enthusiastically recounted the news. But when his three pretty daughters ran in to learn who was coming they became as excited as their father about plans for a sufficient welcome.

"We'll barbecue that white ox," said Ingles. "One of you run tell Pompey to get him butchered and hung up right away. And Sally you go find Zip and Sammy. Have them ride up and down the river letting everybody know what's up. They'll all want to be here."

The girls were already bubbling over with more and improved ideas. "We'll sweep out the threshing floor in the feed barn—there'll be more room there to dance. . . . Jeb Pleck's visiting out at Draper's Meadows—we'll get him—he's the swingiest fiddler I ever heard—remember him at Rachel Sweet's wedding. . . . We'll send for Rufus Settle to do the calling—nobody can call like he can. . . . We'll set up board tables under the arbor—and hang lanterns along the trellis . . . and. . . ."

"And I'll get that barrel of '71 whisky up out of the cellar," put in Ingles. "And a pint of cider for them that don't like whisky." He turned to Adam. "Tell Colonel Calloway he can keep his prisoners in the wagon stables down by the ferry. We'll count on him and his officers—and Hamilton—I reckon we better have him, too—to supper in the house with us—and we'll want everybody in your outfit here to help eat the ox and drink the whisky—and dance with the gals if they're a mind to. We want to show every man Jack of you the way we feel about you."

"Pull up a chair," said Mrs. Ingles to Adam with sudden loud insistence.

While the others had been talking she had been moving to and from the pantry. On the table before Adam was a platter piled with thick slices of baked ham and buttered wheat bread and a bowl heaped with wild raspberries. Mrs. Ingles poured a pitcher of clotted cream over the berries.

"Folks get hungry when they travel. You need a snack to hold you to supper time."

"Since Ma got so hungry out in the woods that time she ran off from the Shawnee," said Ingles, as casually as if she were not in the room, "she surely does like to see people eat."

Ingles and the girls scattered, intent on the various preparations. Mrs. Ingles watched, without expression, each bite Adam took until he had finished and then seemed to forget his presence.

He mounted and rode back south along the road to a meadow with a stream running through it which he had noted earlier. He unsaddled Oriole, rubbed her down and turned her out to graze. He then took a leisurely swim in the stream and dozed in the sun until the column appeared. It might be a while, he reflected, his anticipation slightly grim, before he again had so peaceful an afternoon.

"That's mighty white of Bill Ingles," said Calloway, when Adam told him of the waiting reception. "Ride back and say we will be right pleased to eat with him."

The men at the head of the column passed the word back and a ripple of weary, profane cheers traveled with the news. The military frown returned to Calloway's brow.

"You and Lieutenant Rogers can work it out between you," he said to Williams, "which platoon goes to the shindig and which stays at the stables to watch the prisoners."

As Adam cantered back into the outskirts of the village he heard the distant ringing of a hammer on an anvil. It was a

43

welcome sound, for Oriole was barefoot and if she were shod she could stand up better to the hard riding that was to begin tomorrow. Leaving word at the Ingles house that the column was near he rode on toward the sound of the hammering.

Around a bend in the road beyond the tavern there had once been a stockade. A blockhouse and a section of the back wall of the palisade still stood. The rest of the site was now occupied by a small, new brick house and an L-shaped row of log out-buildings. Under a shed before the center one of these there was a forge at which two gigantic young Negroes were working.

Adam rode into the yard and dismounted. The Negroes poked into the bed of glowing coals with tongs, lifted a large iron grating, the size of a lime kiln grate, placed it on the anvil and resumed their hammering. Both were naked to the waist and the sweat poured down in glistening streams over their tremendously muscled bodies. They handled the ponderous iron grating as if it were no heavier than a sheet of basketwork. Between the ringing strokes of their hammers they occasionally addressed each other in some outlandish tongue. Neither so much as glanced at him and he was beginning to get annoyed. Finally their hammering ceased and with the same ridiculous ease as before they swung the grating back onto the fire. One of the young giants began to work the bellows and the other stepped over to Adam. Now that he stood erect his size was still more impressive. He towered over Adam by a good three or four inches and he looked straight into his eyes without any of the uneasiness usual in a Negro when he addressed a strange white man.

"Yes, sir?" he inquired.

"Thought you might shoe my mare," said Adam.

"Yes, sir. We would be proud to. First thing in the morning." His speech was spaced and schoolbookish, as if in everything he said he was repeating something by rote.

"I'll be gone first thing in the morning," said Adam.

The Negro looked past Adam at Oriole. Then he shook his head regretfully. "We promised that grating to a man who's waiting over at the tavern to take it with him tonight and it will take my brother and me until dark to finish it." His regret seemed genuine. "If you would not mind asking my father." He indicated the door of an adjoining shop. "He does not do much shoeing any more but he might help you out."

"Thank you," said Adam. For a second he had lost the feeling that he was talking to a nearly naked, sweating black slave. Leading Oriole, Adam walked over to the open door. The father of the young giants was bent over a rifle barrel

44

fixed in a vise on a gunsmith's bench. A string running through the barrel was kept taut by a bent hickory wand, and he was sighting along this to get an accurate line on the bore. All Adam could see of him was his tremendously broad back across which the white cotton shirt was stretched like a tent.

"Any chance of getting you to shoe my mare?" said Adam.

The gunsmith turned and straightened, removing his steel-rimmed spectacles to look at Adam. He was if anything taller and wider in chest and shoulder than his sons. The dignity of simple strength that was in them in him mounted to the full consciousness of power. Every line of his age-seamed face said that he was aware that he had found a place in life and that it was not a lowly place. More than that, in his deep-set eyes there remained a gleam of his ancestral savagery. His bearing was that of some old king. Even the fringe of white hair around his bald black pate stood up like a crown.

He came over to the door and looked past Adam at the mare. He looked again at Adam.

"When I have finished straightening the barrel," he said. He indicated a bench against the wall outside the door. "Make yourself comfortable while you wait."

"My name's Adam Frane," said Adam.

"They call me Saul."

"Just wanted to say I'm much obliged, Saul."

Adam unsaddled and unbridled Oriole, tied her to the hitching post beside the horseshoer's rack and sat down on the bench. By the time he had smoked a second pipe the head of the column appeared around the bend in the road, marching at a brisker clip than for many days past. The prisoners must have guessed that even for them there might be a portion of barbecued beef. Adam walked out to the edge of the road. Calloway was not in his usual position out front. Adam called Bert out of line.

"Where's Calloway?"

"He stopped off back at the Ingles place. Didn't hardly expect to see you here. Both times you rode off ahead today I had an idea you'd git to feelin' your oats and keep right on goin'."

"No point sneaking off when all I have to do is tell Calloway first," said Adam. "But I am pulling out in the morning. How long you going to stick?"

"A spell. Long's I'm lookin' for horses along the road I might's well git my way paid while I'm lookin'."

Adam walked back to find Saul examining Oriole's feet.

"I would like to see her gaits," said Saul.

Adam mounted bareback and put the mare through her

45

paces up and down the yard. Saul nodded and went to work. Whether or not he was the best gunsmith in Virginia he certainly came near to being the best horseshoer. Adam told him so, paid him, saddled, then led Oriole out to the edge of the road. Never having had shoes on before she was puzzled and kept shaking her feet like a cat walking in paper bags.

The warm spring evening was growing dark. People were streaming past on their way to the Ingles party. Families from miles around were riding in, the men calling out ribald greetings to friends, their wives and daughters giggling and chattering. A great moon was climbing over the ridge. From up the road came the experimental squeak of a fiddle and then the player suddenly swept into the lilting swing of "Green Sleeves." It was the same dance tune Adam remembered dying away behind him the night of Cynthia's wedding. Again it seemed to taunt him.

So fine a moonlit night could better be spent on the road than dawdling here. He swung into the saddle, humored the mare for a moment while she danced around on her new iron feet, then straightened her out. There was no use fooling around any longer. He'd find Calloway now and be on his way.

The Ingles yard was filled with people eating and drinking, though some of the younger folks were already dancing in the barn. The officers and the Ingles family were still in the house. Impatient as he was, there wasn't much excuse for breaking in on the Ingles supper table.

He pushed through the throng around the whisky barrel and took himself a good, solid drink. The burning tingle had hardly started to cool in his throat when a group of people came out the Ingles back door to saunter, laughing and talking, toward the barn. In the shadows he caught a glimpse of Williams and the oldest Ingles girl but he did not see Calloway. Williams paused at the barbeque pit to light a cigar. Adam went over to him.

"Calloway still in the house?"

"Hello, Adam," said Williams. He had eaten and drunk well. "Enjoyin' yourself?"

"I'm doing all right."

"That's fine. Then what makes you want to see Calloway? A man can't enjoy lookin' at him."

"I want to tell him I'm through."

Williams laughed. "Hell—you don't need to see him for that—unless you want to kiss him good-by. He's knowed about your discharge—and Bert's, too—since the day he took over." He clapped Adam on the shoulder. "All you got to do is shake hands with me and git goin'." He gripped Adam's hand. "See you back with the regiment come next spring. And be sure to bring Bert with you." He clapped Adam on the back again and went on.

Adam had had it settled in his mind since leaving Vincennes that in Virginia he was to get out of the army. Yet now when the separation came it caught him unawares. It was an odd sensation, pleasurable enough but nevertheless a little disturbing, to realize thus suddenly that he was completely released from military restraint. With Clark, discipline had not been accompanied by too much of that but certainly a man had not been able to come and go as he pleased. Now he could. His first impulse was to get back to Oriole and to start riding. It was in this first moment of his new freedom, just as he was turning to go, that he saw her.

Cynthia, coming from the direction of the Ingles house, stepped into the pool of light from one of the lanterns hanging overhead in the arbor and stood, not ten feet from him, glancing around the yard as if looking for someone. Then she saw him and for a second she seemed startled. He was startled, too, for during that second it seemed almost as if it were he that she had been looking for. But then she looked past him, left the circle of light and moved on toward the barn.

He stood still, at first not even looking after her. He was not surprised suddenly to come upon her here, a hundred and fifty miles from Albemarle County. He was too busy thinking about how she had looked. She had looked exactly as he had remembered her. She had not even seemed any older except for the feeling she gave you that the way she was now was the way she actually was—and not the brief flowering of a young girl. The red glints in the sleek brown hair which was always so silkily neat, the flecks of gold in the brown eyes that were tilted upward slightly at the outer corners, the white softness of her skin which had so nearly the apparent texture of a camellia petal, the whole oval of her face shaped so as to keep you forever looking back to the promise of her mouth—all were just as he had remembered.

When he looked around to see where she had gone she was standing at the edge of the light from the barn doorway, talking to Ingles. Some sort of scuffle began over by the whisky barrel. Ingles left her and started for it. Adam crossed and caught him by the arm.

"That girl over there you were just talking to—"

"Know her?" broke in Ingles, oddly interested.

"She looks a little like somebody I once knew," said Adam.

47

"Funny," said Ingles. "She had the same idea. But she couldn't place you. I told her your name—but that didn't mean anything to her."

"How's she happen to be here?"

"Oh, she's a great friend of my gals. If you'll just wait until I knock a couple of heads together I'll take you over to talk to her."

But Adam didn't wait. He didn't want anybody to take him to her. She had noticed his talking to Ingles and she knew he was coming. She was taking a step forward to meet him and beginning to smile politely. There crossed his mind the thought of the letter and the watch and the doeskin pants and the broadcloth coat, tucked away in his saddlebags out front. It was too late now for any of his preparations. The moment had come and, as so often in battle, it was upon him without warning. He kept on walking toward her.

FOUR

SHE was looking intently up into his face, giving him a good chance to look at her, too.

"I don't often study to be so simple," she said. "I did say something to Mr. Ingles about wondering if once I might not have seen you somewhere—but I didn't realize he'd go straight to you with it."

She must long since have learned that with any man she could afford to be as mildly interested and as faintly amused and as completely calm as she was now. Her voice was soft, low keyed, yet rather deep for a woman's, giving to each word an odd note of importance.

"Suppose I have seen you before," he said, "should I remember—or not?"

"But do you?"

"Maybe we should just take us a fresh start. That other time—if there was one—couldn't have amounted to much."

"I somehow doubt a fresh start may amount to much more."

"Then I'd better remember when this other time was."

She had been on guard from the instant he had started to speak. She'd been startled, not so much by what he had said as by the way he had said it. Since he was one of Clark's men she'd been ready to accept him as a military hero but she'd hardly expected from him a manner that seemed to place him on an equal footing with her. That was the trouble with meeting a stranger on the road from Kentucky. You couldn't guess, right on sight, whether he was just another backwoods nobody or a Logan, a Bowman or a Clark. He'd be carrying the same rifle and game sack and wearing the same travel-stained buckskins, whichever he was. He was really better off by far than if he'd appeared before her in his new clothes.

They were being jostled by people moving back and forth through the barn doorway between the dance inside and the whisky barrel out in the yard. He took her arm and steered her toward a bench under the big oak at the end of the arbor. The warmth of her skin struck through the thin stuff of her sleeve into his finger tips.

"The fall before last," he was saying, "were you on a stepladder picking apples—just across a stone fence from the road—wearing a dress almost the same blue as the one you have on—and did the stepladder start to tip?"

"It's your story. Did it?"

"It did. But come to think of it that girl's hair was yellow. Then—let me see—it was the summer before—at that ford over the Holston below Wolf Hills—did your horse step in a deep hole and throw you into the water—and did you hang your clothes to dry on that big fallen sycamore just around the bend?"

They had come to a stop beside the bench. She made no move to sit down.

"And then what happened? Don't tell me you can't remember that."

"I can now. And it wasn't the Holston. I was getting that mixed up with something that happened once crossing the Clinch. But sit down. We've got to figure this out."

She shook her head.

"You've already tried so hard. Do you really think it's going to be worth it?"

"I certainly do. Right off I had the same feeling you did. I know I've seen you somewhere."

"Well, you're not making much headway. First you have to pretend one thing—then you have to pretend you can't remember what it was."

"I still know I've seen you—somewhere—sometime. It isn't as if you looked like anybody else. I'm bound to remember any minute."

"Maybe it'll come to you later. But I think we might as well give up for now." She was starting to go.

"Give me one more try. Maybe it's already come to me.

Do you happen to have a very small mole—just below your waist—around just a little to the back—on the right side—a little above your hip?"

She sat down then—with a gasp.

"Who are you?" she demanded.

He sat down beside her. "My name is Adam Frane," he said. "I—"

"How could you have known," she broke in, "about that —that—about what you just said?"

He smiled consolingly. "Of course, it could be I've still got you mixed up with somebody else. Lots of women have little moles—one place or another."

"Answer me," she insisted.

"Maybe the time has come to have us a drink," said Adam. He got up. "Now don't go away."

"Don't worry," said Cynthia.

He came back with two wooden cups of whisky.

"Want me to get you some water?"

She shook her head and tossed off the drink as a man might.

"Now," she said.

He sat down beside her again, politely took her empty cup and placed it on the ground, and then, leaning back against the oak and watching her reflectively, appeared to give her problem the deepest thought.

"Reminds me some of when Clark first got to Vincennes," he said. "He didn't have the men or the guns to take the fort. So he had to start making Hamilton think what he wanted him to think."

"I can't imagine what you're trying to make me think—if that's what you mean. And I sat beside Colonel Hamilton at supper tonight. It's hard to make that man think at all."

"Hamilton's not so bad. He's had a lot to put up with."

"He's a coldhearted monster. And tonight I was glad to give him something more to put up with. He asked me what was wrong with Mrs. Ingles. So I told him. I told him there was nothing wrong with her except that she couldn't stop thinking. That she'd had a baby the third day after his Indians—they weren't his Indians then but they were the same miserable lot he'd been using in this war—the third day after they'd burned her house and carried her off. And that when the chance came to get away from them she couldn't carry the baby . . . and had to make up her mind to leave it behind if she was ever to get back to her husband."

Adam looked at her with new interest. "Is that what you'd have done?"

"Certainly—that is, if I'd have had as good a man as
50

she did waiting for me. Though—just like Mary Ingles—I'd probably never have been able to stop thinking about that baby. But for heaven's sake, how did we get on this subject?"

"I was telling you about Clark and Hamilton."

"Instead of answering me."

"You mean—about the mole?"

"Yes."

"That's what I was trying to do. I was starting to say I was in the same fix Clark was. I have to make as big a show as I can to cover up what little I got."

"That's no answer."

He wagged his head regretfully. "You know—maybe you're making more of this than there's any real call for. Stop to think of all the common, everyday answers there could be."

"For example."

"Well—like I said at first—it could have been just a blind guess. Or I could have heard one of the Ingles girls mention it. Or—your old mammy—you must have one—or your mother —or somebody in the family—just could have said something about it to somebody I knew who just happened to mention it to me."

"Then what was the use of bringing it up at all?"

"I had to say something. If I hadn't you'd have been polite—and I'd have stood on one foot—for maybe two or three minutes—and that would have been all there'd have been to it. Now we're having a fine long talk and beginning to get acquainted."

"All right. Let's say you're Clark and I'm Hamilton. What fort are you trying to take?"

"I'm not trying—yet. So far I'm just reconnoitering."

"You do make me sure of one thing. We certainly could never have so much as spoken to each other before tonight— because I could never have forgotten a man able to say so many completely infuriating things."

She got to her feet. He rose beside her, fighting off an impulse to grab hold of her to keep her from leaving him. Then suddenly she began to laugh. He watched her warily.

"How can you stand there looking so solemn?" she gasped. "Don't you see anything funny?"

"Depends on who you're laughing at."

"Myself, of course. It just came over me. You're such a novel kind of rogue. What a flutter you must have left among the dovecotes—what a dither among the innocents! It was that crossing my mind which made me laugh. Because here am I—long since married—and widowed—and fast becoming an old woman—and yet look at the start you've even

51

been able to give me. Who are you? Where did you come from?"

"My name is Adam Frane, I—"

"*Please* don't start that again."

It was just then that over her shoulder he saw the pale, blond young man. He was tall and thin, remarkably handsome in spite of his hollow eyes and sunken cheeks, and dressed with elegance in broad-skirted maroon coat, yellow waistcoat and silk smallclothes. He was slapping his leg with a riding crop and prowling with nervous impatience through the crowd, evidently searching for someone. Then he caught sight of Cynthia and came straight for the oak.

"Man acts like he's looking for you," said Adam.

Cynthia turned. "Oh, it's Blake," she exclaimed. "And he is looking for me."

She ran to the newcomer and into his outstretched arms. The man did not seem even curious about Cynthia's recent companion. Keeping an arm around her he drew her with him into a slow stroll along the arbor—away from Adam. He was beginning quickly to tell her something that Adam could not hear. But he could hear her reply. It was a delighted exclamation: "Really, Blake!" Then she said: "Wait a minute while I run get my cloak."

She was turning toward the house. It was plain that his luck, which in the last half hour he had been crowding so recklessly, had taken a sudden turn for the worse. He strode over to join them.

"Just thought I'd better remind you I'm still here," he announced.

Cynthia turned back. "So you are," she said. "How could I have forgotten? Blake, this is Adam Frane, one of Colonel Clark's men. Mr. Frane—my brother, Blake." It had slipped his mind that she had a brother named Blake. Her whole family had always been unreal to him. She added, to Blake: "No doubt it was with Clark that he learned to be so—impulsive."

"Can't blame you, Mr. Frane," said Blake, unexpectedly affable. "You damn near have to bully her a little. If you don't she'll run right over you."

"Big disappointment—your taking her away," said Adam. "You see—we're both sure we've met somewhere before—and we were just beginning to work out again when it was—and what happened—and so on."

"Mr. Frane's imagination is really most unusual," said Cynthia hastily. "Come to think of it, Blake—if Joel just got in he's already had a long day. Suppose I ride out first thing in the morning."

"Fair enough," agreed Blake. In the glance he shot at Adam there was a spark of new interest. He kissed Cynthia and nodded to Adam. "Best of luck to you." There was a twinkle in his eye as he said it. He set off across the yard with the same air of nervous impatience as when he had come in.

"I've no doubt," said Cynthia, "that you feel you have taken at least—what would a soldier call it?—some sort of an outpost."

"No," said Adam. "Only a hilltop from where I can see a little better."

One thing he could see. She was fond of her brothers. He remembered how often in the old days she had ridden past the store to visit Joel. But tonight she was still here with him, her finger tips on his sleeve, walking demurely along beside him toward the oak.

"Blake bought a place last year out at Draper's Meadows," she was explaining. "He came in to get me because Joel, my older brother, has just arrived from Albemarle County."

The letter was addressed to Joel, but Adam decided to say nothing about it for the moment. He might have greater need for it later than he seemed to now. The fiddle in the barn struck up with new spirit.

"I've never heard that tune before," said Cynthia. "What can it be?"

"An old French dance," said Adam. "Though I forget the name."

"You do seem to remember and forget the most amazing things."

"Would you like to have me show you how they dance it at a place I remember in New Orleans?"

"Why not?" she agreed.

Instead of leading her toward the dance floor in the barn, however, he promptly took her in his arms.

"More room here than in the crowd in there," he said. "And we need room—it's that kind of a dance."

She took a quick look up into his face but she did not hold back. He swung her around on the heard-packed earth between the oak and the arbor. The music was a flamboyantly fast polka and the French danced to it with much jumping up and down and many dizzily whirling spins. But he was content at first to take it at half time. It was enough to have so natural an excuse to have his arm around her.

"But you dance very well," she said. "You are full of surprises."

He began to swing her around very fast, holding her hard against him, and kept on whirling until she was breathless. When finally he slowed to the former half time he continued to hold her as closely. The cessation of rapid movement made their clinging together suddenly intimate. Under her billowy skirts her thighs were against his. His breath rose and fell against the softness of her breasts. Her supple body seemed at once to yield and to resist. Her face was as near his as if she were about to whisper something to him. She was.

"In New Orleans—where they danced like this—what kind of a place did you say it was?"

"The governor's palace," he said.

The ecstatic fiddle came to the end of the piece and then happily started once more at the beginning. The laughter and chatter from the lighted barn seemed to fall away into the distance, to leave them entirely alone here in their shadow under the oak. They danced ever more slowly. It was no longer a dance. It was an embrace. Their continued silence made their case the more clear. The chance moment had become deliberate, and indulgent. They were acquiescing in sensation, willfully prolonging it.

The music ceased. He did not release her and even now she did not draw away. She only leaned back enough to look up at him. One bar of moonlight fell across her face. When he bent down her lips parted. He could feel the sudden rigidity of her finger tips digging into his shoulders. Her mouth was hot and sweet.

His only thought was to kiss her again. But near by a woman giggled. Some other couple had sought the seclusion of these shadows. The lighted and noisy yard was only just beyond the tree. Adam began edging farther away, guiding Cynthia with his arm still around her. He was instantly aware of her readiness to go with him. The significance of what they were doing rushed upon him.

They passed the shadow of a cattle pen. Ahead in the moonlight a stile rose quickly. They climbed over it, still without a word, their silence becoming even more eloquent than when they had pretended to dance. Beyond the stile there was a path leading down toward the murmur of a brook and into the shadow of a great sycamore.

When they reached this shadow he paused and drew her against him again. But she looked over her shoulder at the lights and commotion behind and shook her head. This time it was she who drew him on.

The path crossed the brook on steppingstones and then crossed back once more. They came upon a fern-covered bank made to seem the darker by a pool of moonlight in the glade beyond. Again he stopped but she wanted to go yet farther.

The brook splashed pleasantly over its hidden rocks. The path led into deeper shadows where he could not see at all. She took one of his hands in both of hers, and holding it reassuringly against her she led him on. They came to a huge weeping willow under the outspread branches of which they had to stoop.

Too late he realized that the tree trunk his outstretched free hand had brushed against was a post of the old stockade. The path had led to a narrow opening in the palisade and already they were through it. The embers in the forge glowed in harsh red contrast to the white moonlight flooding the yard. The figures of the three dark giants rose, looming, from the bench where they had been resting, and seemed to tower even above their daytime stature. A gaunt, erect, very black, very old Negro woman moved out from the house.

"You're home early, Miss Cynthia," she said. "I was just about to send Saul up to wait for you."

"Thank you, Hebe," said Cynthia. She turned to Adam. Her eyes were as wide as the most innocent maiden's. "And thank you, Mr. Frane, for seeing me safely home."

Adam pretended not to see her extended hand.

"So this is where you live," he said.

"Since last fall," she said. "It's a good location with so much new travel along the Great Road. We do gunmaking and blacksmithing and all sorts of ironwork."

"I know. I had my mare shod here today. A mighty good job it was, too."

"I'm sure of it," said Cynthia, smiling at the giants. "They're as good as they are big. My husband left them to me. Thank you again for a most interesting evening. Good-by, Mr. Frane."

Instead of taking her hand he took her arm and walked with her to the house, cheerily whistling several bars of the French dance tune. "What time tomorrow?" he asked, when they had reached the steps.

"Time for what?"

"For me to see you."

"But you know that I'm leaving for my brother's first thing in the morning. So I'm afraid this will have to be good-by, Mr. Frane. As I keep saying, this has been a most unusual evening. First you said something about which I shall probably always wonder. Now you have something you can always wonder about, too."

She went in and closed the door.

‖ FIVE ‖

THE whine of the fiddle rose only occasionally above the clamor of stamping and clapping in the barn. There was another clamor centered around the whisky barrel and a third in the taproom of the tavern across the road, to which sanctuary many men had drifted to talk, drink and fight out of reach of their womenfolk. Adam put Oriole in a stall in the stable back of the tavern, watered and fed her, then spread his blanket on the ground. He was in no mood for sleep but there was the moon to be watched. By the time it set the sun would be coming up on the new day. Each hour the moon seemed to move more slowly.

As soon as it was light enough to see at all he routed out Silas, the old freedman who kept the general store for Ingles. Silas didn't care much for being awakened so early but as the bargaining went on he took more interest. Adam bought a white shirt and neckcloth, a felt hat, stockings and riding boots. Although the sight of Adam's silver caused Silas to divide his prices by ten, the transaction still left the money belt considerably lighter.

Adam washed and shaved at the water trough in the tavern yard and then withdrew into the stable to change into the new outfit. Everything fitted well enough. The coat and breeches were wrinkled from being rolled up in the saddlebags but the fresh shirt and the new hat and boots were a help. The general effect was of a man who owned good clothes but along with them no great concern for how he might look at the end of a long journey. This was just the effect he wanted.

He led Oriole out and was starting to saddle up when Bert came running in. Bert pulled up, puffing and staring.

"Gawdamighty, I'd never of known you."

"My good man, what makes you think you ever did?"

Bert grunted and got around to what he'd come to say. "I just wanted to tell you that you can count on me pickin' me up some horses and gittin' back here for sure by the end of the week."

Adam grabbed him before he could get away and eyed him suspiciously. "Back here, eh? Why back here?"

"Beats me," declared Bert. "Beats me flatter'n a corncake why I ever fret so much about how you git along. But somebody's got to—because that luck of yourn is sure goin' to play out sometime. Sure I mean back here. Where else do you aim to be?"

"I didn't see you snooping anywhere around last night," persisted Adam. "Of course, I didn't look under every bush."

"I wasn't in no bushes," said Bert. "I didn't follow you when you and her went down in the bushes. All I seen was before that—and to save you hollerin' louder'n there's any call for I'll tell you just what I did see. I was late gittin' to the Ingles' cause first I went to a place across the river where somebody said somebody had some horses for sale. The horses was no good but I did happen to hear about your gal livin' right here. I started in lookin' for you 'cause I didn't want to see you prancin' off all the way up to Albemarle County only to find yourself lookin' foolish when you got there. By the time I did see you you'd already come acrost her. She was walkin' beside you along the arbor and hangin' on like she was feared you might git away. It took no more'n one look for me to see there was nothin' I could tell you. So I went down to the barbecue pit to see if there might be a rib of that beef left. From down there I couldn't help but notice you and her in the dark under the oak—on account of the lights in the barn on the far side of you." He edged away a step and added quickly: "But I didn't see nothin' after you and her climbed over the stile."

"You only watched us while we were under the oak?"

"Yes. Only I wasn't what you could call watchin'. Like I said—you couldn't help but see on account—"

"Yes, you said that before," said Adam. "Much of a crowd down there at the barbecue pit watching along with you?"

"No. Nobody but me—and Pompey, the nigger who was tendin' the fire. Except for Bill Ingles. He walked over to see if I'd found enough to eat. And the oldest Ingles gal. She stopped a while on her way to the house to git some resin for the fiddler. And a fat woman they called Aunt Regina who turned out to be some kin to the Draper cousin that's married to your gal's youngest brother. But nobody else."

"Nobody that wasn't right in the family, so to speak."

Adam's tone caused Bert to back away again. "I got to git me back to the ferry before the last boatload gits across— else I'll have to pay my own way. But like I said—I'll be back for sure in a week. There ain't no manner of doubt that by then you're goin' to need somebody to look after you."

Adam finished saddling and bought a cold chicken and a bottle of ale in the tavern kitchen. He paid his stable bill so he could leave in a hurry when the time came. But he was in no hurry yet. Cynthia would hardly have set out for Draper's Meadows until the ferry had been cleared of the last of the military. She'd not have chosen to cross with a boatload of soldiers and prisoners. Not with the chance of encountering him among them. Not after the way she'd slammed that door last night.

Before he'd heard Bert's story he'd counted on getting out to Draper's Meadows ahead of her this morning, delivering the letter to Joel and getting himself comfortably ensconced in her brother's household before she showed up out there. But the account of what so many people had witnessed last night cast a new light over his whole situation. All up and down the New River Valley there'd be talk today about how the young widow Rowan had carried on at the dance with the stranger from Kentucky. The story would have reached Blake's house by now. Far better therefore, whether she liked it or not, to ride out with her this morning and appear at her brother's house in her company.

He left Oriole in the stable, cut across the field below the bend in the road and slipped into the cedar copse crowning the little knoll across the road from the forge. From here he could see down into the yard between the smithy and the brick house, and what he saw caused him to settle back contentedly and begin leisurely to eat the chicken and drink the ale. Cynthia, wearing a leaf-brown riding habit, very new, by the look of it, that went exactly right with the color of her hair and eyes, was walking nervously about in front of her door, from time to time pausing to sip coffee from a cup on a tray held by Hebe. The old Negro woman was watching her with mingled concern and disapproval. Saul, equally concerned but more sympathetic, was holding the bridle of a fine gray stallion, whose restiveness indicated he'd been kept saddled and ready for a long time. Deep hoofprints showed that much earlier she had set out at a gallop toward the ferry and then had returned to the yard at a slow walk. Most revealing of all—one of Saul's sons was down toward the river where he could watch the ferry, now taking over the last boatload of soldiers and prisoners, and the other was across the road from the forge where he could see anyone coming around the bend from the tavern.

Adam watched Cynthia and speculated comfortably on the apparent meaning of all this. She'd come back to wait. She'd taken care not to be caught waiting. And she wasn't waiting patiently. She was out of sorts with herself and with everything about the morning.

He tossed the clean-picked chicken aside, drank the last swallow of ale and tossed the bottle after the chicken. The ferry was returning. The watcher from the river was running back to report the fact. Adam trotted across the field,

58

mounted and then rode out of the tavern yard. He'd timed it well enough so that as he rounded the bend Cynthia on her gray stallion was bolting out of her yard and down the road toward the ferry.

He had to let the mare all the way out to catch up before she'd got down to the landing. She heard the hoofbeats behind her but after one incurious glance over her shoulder she didn't look around again. Therefore it wasn't until he was riding right alongside her that she realized who he was. The surprise caught her off guard. For a second there was no mistaking the sudden light in her face, a look of mixed relief and delight. Then, before she could get her face set in the frown with which she must have intended to greet him, the nearness of the mare started the stallion to acting up.

Adam pulled Oriole to a stand and watched appreciatively. Cynthia knew how to handle a horse but she was a full minute getting the stallion settled down again.

"Shame to scare you," he said.

Controlling the rearing horse had further heightened her color. "You didn't."

He looked at her flushed face. "Just mad, eh?"

"Yes. I don't like being followed."

"I was following you, for a fact," he admitted. "At least, after I happened to see you on the road ahead."

"What made you think of it then?"

Adam had started the mare to walking on. The stallion, rolling his eyes and tossing his head, was keeping pace. "I remembered your saying you were going out to your brother Blake's today and it seemed like a good chance to have you show me the way."

"Why in the world should you want to go out there?"

"Just to be sociable. I liked your brother Blake when I met him last night. And long's your other brother Joel is here—seemed like a good idea to meet him, too."

She bit her lips a couple of times, then apparently decided there were safer topics to pursue. "How did you get away from your company—desert?"

"I didn't have to. I'm not in the army any more. I'm the most footloose man you ever saw."

They'd reached the landing and the ferryman was eying them with the greatest interest. Cynthia remained coldly silent during the crossing. Adam wasn't eager to talk. Neither said any more until they'd turned off the highway onto the road leading to Draper's Meadows. Cynthia pulled up.

"You're really serious about going out there?"

"Why not?"

"About some things my brothers have practically no sense

of humor. Any more than I have where they're concerned. And no matter how they take it—if you insist on coming out there I can't promise you I'll make anything easier for you. I'm giving you fair warning."

"Couldn't give a fairer one," agreed Adam.

She glanced at the road ahead.

"Want to race?" asked Adam. "Horses are fresh and the road's plenty wide."

She took onè quick look at the mare. "No. I don't want to race."

Adam folded his hands on the pommel and grinned sociably. "Certainly is a fine morning."

"You just can't be so simple as you're trying to seem. Surely you can see that to a woman there can be a certain difference between flirting with a passing soldier at a roadside dance—and then the next morning finding him following her around all dressed up like—like an earnest suitor."

Adam loosened his neckcloth. "The only clothes I had with me except for those old buckskins. But I wouldn't doubt you have to keep on the lookout for suitors back of every bush. And I wouldn't doubt, either, that when you feel like it you can make 'em wish they'd stayed there. But let's let it go for now. What you must be wanting right now is to get out to see your brothers. If we just ride along peaceably side by each then you won't have to worry about who's following who."

Cynthia shrugged, picked up the stallion and set off at a gallop. The mare drew alongside and kept pace. Cynthia continued to look straight ahead, paying no more attention to him. The road climbed the shoulder of a hill jutting down toward the river. She pulled into a walk.

"We're almost there," she said. "Have you planned what what you're going to say to my brothers?"

"Think I'd better beg them not to set the dogs on me?"

"Why do you laugh when you say that?"

"Take a while to explain. But it might help some if I didn't have so much to wonder about."

"That's one mistake I'll certainly never make again. Just what are you wondering?"

"Do you like being a widow?"

They had turned into a side road that led away from the river toward a clump of elms in a pleasant meadow.

"Just to save time—I'll tell you. No. I don't. I was married long enough—and I've been a widow long enough—to know I like better living with a man in the house."

"Got your eye on one?"

"No."

"Looking hard?"

"Not hard. I'm in no hurry. I have a good business. I'm free—independent—can come and go as I please—doing very nicely. I don't have to hurry."

"But you've got it all worked out—just the man you're looking for."

"Some things about him, at least."

"Skyrockets when you kiss him?"

"You can't forget last night."

"No, ma'am. I can't. Can you?"

"No. It was hardly something that's happened to me so often that I can manage to stop thinking about it right off."

"And you're thinking you don't want it to happen again?"

"No. But I'm thinking that there's something else I want more."

"What else?"

"I'm afraid there's really not much use trying to clear that up for you. You're a man that's bound to wonder. You might as well go right on wondering."

They had rounded the clump of elms and were drawing up before a porticoed, field stone house, one wing of which was still under construction. This, obviously, was brother Blake's. The Wyeths must have been doing well. Even the youngest of the sons had more of a place than old Man Wyeth's had been eight years ago. Adam surveyed the premises as if more interested in what he could see than in what Cynthia had just said.

"More new houses in this country," he observed.

"Prisoners from Burgoyne's army," she explained, matching his composure. "This last year people have hired Hessians to build stone houses and barns all up and down the valley."

A black stable hand ran around the corner of the house to take the horses. Adam dismounted and reached up to help her down. She started to lean forward and then drew back, staring down at him.

"That boy at Stull's!" she exclaimed.

He nodded. "I had an idea you knew all the time."

"Stupid as it sounds—I didn't. It just came to me this minute."

She dismounted and handed the reins to the groom.

"Where's Mr. Joel?"

"Somewheres out back wif Mr. Blake, Miss Cynthy."

She stepped up on the porch and turned to look down at Adam again.

"Looking down at you makes the difference. That's the way I always saw you then—out in front of the store as I rode past. Even now, when you have to look up—you don't look so

61

—so knowing about places in New Orleans—or so foot-loose—or so ready to race anybody any time. It's really such a relief finally to have placed you."

"What bush does this put me behind?"

"About the same one, I should think. With maybe one little difference. I'm beginning to remember there was something about that boy at Stull's I rather liked." She looked at him doubtfully, but as if disposed to give him the benefit of the doubt. "And I do have to admit that I can't dislike you even now quite as much as I should. Let's call a truce—for the moment, at least. I have so much to talk over with my brothers today. If you'll excuse us all now—I'll ask you to call on me here tomorrow. Won't that do?"

"You wouldn't be wanting the time to get more fences up, would you?"

Her eyes flashed. "Good-by, Mr. Frane."

"I'll be very happy to come again tomorrow, thank you. But I'm afraid I still ought to see them today."

She regarded him wonderingly. "You couldn't have some absurd idea—some intentions of some sort you feel you should announce to them—could you?"

"The shoe's on the other foot. I've an idea they've got intentions to announce to me—and without wanting to wait another day, either. You may not know it but half the valley seems to have been watching us under the oak last night."

"Good-by, Mr. Frane."

She went in and closed the door, just as she had the night before. This time he was more content with the maneuver. He'd been afraid she wouldn't go in before she had noticed the two men coming from the direction of the cattle pens in back. It was going to be much simpler accounting for himself to brothers Blake and Joel without her standing alongside.

He could see that one of the two was Blake and he took it for granted the other was Joel, though Joel was nothing like Blake. He was a foot shorter, squarely built, dark instead of fair and with an air of reserve that bordered on the austere. A slight limp and the empty left sleeve thrust into his coat pocket accentuated his military bearing. Though probably no more than forty his black hair was streaked with white. As he drew nearer Adam saw that the glance of the gray eyes under the heavy dark brows was as sharply penetrating as any he had ever met. They were eyes capable of taking in Adam, his apparel, his demeanor and his mare, all in one swift, decisive survey.

"Ah, Mr. Frane, we were just talking about you," said Blake, while still several strides away. "I was telling Joel—pardon—Mr. Frane—Major Joel Wyeth—I was just telling

Joel that if you'd run into Paul on the trail—Paul's another brother—you'd have said something about it when we met last night."

"I would," said Adam, drawing a long breath.

Joel took command of the interrogation. "There's only one trail between here and Kentucky, isn't there?"

"That's right."

"And when you just came over it you didn't see or hear anything of a redheaded man wearing new yellow buckskins with enough fringe on them to braid tie ropes for a drove of cattle—big man—tall as Blake here and twice as heavy—riding a black gelding—old backwoodsman named Eli Skaggs with him?"

"No."

"The chucklehead's got himself lost first thing."

"Not likely with old Eli Skaggs along. When'd he start?"

"Left Albemarle last week in March."

"When'd he come through here?" Adam asked Blake.

"Nobody knows," said Blake. "First I heard about his going was when Joel told me an hour ago. Whenever he came through here he took care to keep out of sight."

"I told him to stay away from you," said Joel. "I didn't want to risk your taking it into your head to go with him."

"What part of Kentucky was he headed for?" asked Adam.

"Licking River."

"That accounts for our not meeting him. He'd have turned north at the Hazel Patch. And two men traveling fast could have got that far and turned off before we got there."

"Sounds reasonable," agreed Joel, "though if there was any trouble to get into Paul would find it." He looked at Adam reflectively. "Know the Licking River country?"

"Hey," said Blake. "If we're going to start asking Mr. Frane about Kentucky—and I think we should if he'll stand for it—let's get in out of the sun and get out a bottle and get ourselves settled down where we can pick on him in comfort. What'd you do with Cynthia?"

"She went in the house," said Adam. "I rode out with her to deliver a letter from Colonel Benjamin Logan to Major Wyeth."

"You don't say!" Blake seized Adam by the arm. "Better and better." He took the letter, passed it to Joel and hung onto Adam's arm.

"I could have given it to you to bring out to Major Wyeth when I saw you last night," said Adam, "but I didn't think of it."

"We can probably thank Cynthia for that." Blake's eyes were twinkling again. "But glad you didn't. Come on in. By

63

dinnertime we'll know more about Kentucky than Paul's likely to find out all summer."

A slim, very young girl in a sprigged muslin dress stood in the open doorway. Her hair and eyebrows and eyelashes were straw colored and her eyes such a pale blue that they seemed almost without color, except when she looked at Blake when they glowed like sapphires. She turned out to be Blake's wife, Amy. By the time Adam had been presented and everybody had gotten through the doorway it was she instead of Blake who had hold of his arm. In the hallway she held him back to whisper to him.

"Cynthia came sailing through and right on out the back door. She was so busy thinking she didn't even see me. You surely must have made an impression on her last night."

"Last night?"

"Now, don't pretend you can't guess what I'm talking about. We didn't go to the dance because we were half expecting Joel but everybody else in Draper's Meadows did." She drew back to look up at Adam. "Anyway, I do hope so," she decided. "It's time she had some luck with a man."

"Does she need luck?"

"Every woman does."

"Where's Cynthia?" Joel was demanding.

"Out back looking for you and Blake," said Amy. "I'll fetch her."

Adam looked around swiftly. You could tell a good deal about people by noticing the inside of their houses, just as you could by the condition of their fields or the way they kept their stock. The portion of the house to the right of the central hall was still unfinished but the dining room to the left, into which they were moving, was a sunny, big-windowed room with maple flooring and wainscoting. The mahogany table and sideboard, the walnut chairs, the brass candlesticks, all were well worn and highly polished as if they were pieces that had been in the family for a long time. Adam had spent most of his life among people who considered a new pine bench an elegant piece of furniture. But here it wasn't the things themselves so much as the way—even in this unfinished house—they seemed to fit in with the people who lived here. He was more than ever glad that he had ridden up to this house on a mare as good as Oriole and was entering it wearing the Hamilton coat.

But everything he saw bewildered him the more. According to what Amy had told him everybody here already knew about last night. And still Cynthia's high-stepping brothers had made him welcome. It couldn't be that they didn't care what she did or that she made a practice of kissing strangers.

64

As a matter of fact, Amy had acted as if Cynthia's showing favor to any man had been something very much out of the ordinary. Then he began to comprehend. Her brothers had sense. They were glad to have him here because that gave them so good a chance to size him up. They might be interested in Kentucky, also, as was most everybody in Virginia and Carolina, but this only gave them a better excuse to question him.

Blake took the letter from Joel, tore it open with his two hands and handed it back to him. Joel sat down and started to read it.

"Sit you down, Mr. Frane," said Blake. "What's your first name? We'll be getting around to it by the third drink—might as well start now."

"Adam."

"Sit down, Adam." He raised his voice. "Titus—juleps."

Titus, a spare, stooped old Negro with a weazened face the exact color of the mahogany table, pushed through the door from the kitchen with five tall glasses on a tray. He had not only foreseen the demand but by some mysterious intuition had calculated the precise number. Adam took one of the frosty glasses. He wondered how they kept ice late in the spring. He could hear Amy calling: "Cynthia—Joel and Blake are in here." Three of Blake's hounds had come in with Titus. Two of them stretched out lazily on the floor but the third moved over to sniff at Adam's new riding boots.

Joel looked up from the letter. "I've heard a lot about Colonel Logan. He must be a good man."

"He is," said Adam.

"He speaks very highly of you."

Adam knew there had been no reference to him when Logan had dictated the letter that night. Ann must have slipped that in on her own hook. He could hear the voices of the women in the hall. Then Cynthia came running in and kept on straight to Joel, dropping on her knees and throwing her arms around him before he could get up out of his chair.

"You're a big help to a man trying to read an important letter," Joel complained.

"You silly old bear—it's been ages since I've seen you."

"I suppose that's why you rushed out to greet me last night?"

"If I had I'd only have found you sound asleep—and grumpier than you are now."

She rose, planted a final kiss on the top of his head, took a glass from Titus' tray and glanced from it to the other glasses and to Adam's—and then at the friendly hound which now stood beside Adam's chair with his muzzle resting on Adam's knee. "Well," she said. "I see you've even gotten around the dogs."

"Cynthia," demanded Amy, "why didn't you tell me that Mr. Frane had come all the way out here to tell us about Kentucky and about Paul and to bring Joel a letter from Colonel Logan?"

"You'd never guess. Because he didn't tell me. Mr. Frane is full of secrets—including some of the strangest ones. I'd like to know, too." She took a sip of her drink and glanced over at Adam. "Why didn't you tell me?"

"You didn't ask me."

Cynthia turned appealingly to the others. "That's only one small example. You'd never believe the ways he's taken advantage of me."

"We've heard a little about some of the ways," said Blake.

"Always ready to listen to any gossip." She turned back to Adam. "My brothers are possessed of the quaint conviction that I instantly become mad about every personable man I meet."

"While actually," said Amy, "there's not another woman in Virginia half so hard to please. She invariably compares every new man with her brothers and since nobody can come up to that standard she's always recovering from disappointments. I do have to agree about the standard—but I keep telling her she will just have to make up her mind to do the best she can."

"Let the man alone a minute," Joel commanded Cynthia. "Sit down and listen. You're just as interested in this as anybody. This is a good letter and Colonel Logan was kind to take the trouble but"—he tossed the letter on the table—"as long as Adam is here I'd rather hear what he can tell us."

"Adam?" whispered Cynthia with lifted eyebrows, sitting in the chair next to his. "Already?"

"Colonel Logan's more than kind to tell us about the land around his station," said Joel. "But we've already got twenty thousand acres somewhere along the Licking—though none of us has ever seen it. We bought the rights to it from the old Vandalia Company six years ago. I know such a title didn't amount to much then and probably a good deal less now."

"There's only one title in Kentucky that amounts to anything at all," said Adam. "That's to as much land as you move in on yourself and improve and hang onto yourself."

"That's what took Paul whooping out there this spring."

"Did you know about that?" Cynthia demanded of Blake. He shook his head. She looked resentfully at Joel. "Did you tell him to sneak through here in the night?"

"You couldn't have stopped him any more than I could,"

said Joel. He turned back to Adam. "My brother was bound to see for himself if this land was worth trying to hang onto."

"Take a good many families to hang onto that much," said Adam. "And the big trouble with hiring families to go out there is that they always decide after they've sweat and stood off the Indians for a while to hang onto it for themselves."

"You hear so much about Kentucky land. How good is it—actually?"

"Some of it's as good as the best you'll ever find anywhere."

"Then it might be worth our making quite an effort to hang onto all we can of ours."

"And all Paul wants is an excuse," said Cynthia. "If you don't watch out he'll be wanting to live out there. And look at the way we're scattered already—you and Paul still in Albemarle—Blake and me here—"

"I think myself," said Joel, "we'd be better off closer together—once we hit on the right place."

Amy sprang up. "Joel," she cried. She turned to look accusingly at Blake. "And you, too, Blake. You just can't be thinking even for one crazy minute of letting Paul move to Kentucky. Why, from all you hear everybody out there has to fight all the time—just to stay alive. And this family's had enough war. Look at Blake—he hasn't gained a pound since that fever he had at Valley Forge. And you, Joel, look at the way the war has left you. And even Paul—big and strong as he looks—he's still spitting blood every morning since that time he was left for dead at Saratoga. Think of Deck—and Henry—"

Her voice broke. Blake reached up and pulled her down onto his lap where she hid her face against his shoulder.

"Deck was my other brother," Cynthia murmured to Adam. "He was killed at Brandywine. And Henry was my husband."

"It's a fact," said Joel, "that the Wyeth family's done its part in this war." He walked to a window, looked out, then came back to sit down. "But Kentucky's not the only place there's a war going on. As long's the English own the sea it can spread anywhere. Any time they choose they can land in the Carolinas or here in Virginia. The time could come—I don't say it will—when Albemarle County—or even the valley here—might be no freer from war than Kentucky."

Blake was stroking Amy's hair. He looked over at Adam. "Clark's taking Vincennes and catching Hamilton—isn't that going to make a big difference in things out there?"

"Only for a while," said Adam. "There'll be Indians coming at Kentucky as long as the English hold Detroit. And one trouble with the Licking country—when they come across the Ohio they generally come through there first."

Amy lifted her head to look hopefully at Joel and then let it drop again when she saw he continued merely to look thoughtful.

"This Wilderness Road there's so much talk about," he said. "What's it like?"

"Just a track through the brush."

"Hard going, eh?"

"Well, when you leave the Holston, you climb Clinch Mountain, ford Clinch River, climb Powell Mountain, ford Powell River, crawl through Cumberland Gap, ford the Cumberland River—and from there on to Hazel Patch the going gets really hard."

"How far are you by that time?"

"About a hundred and fifty miles from the last settlement on the Holston."

"Nobody's ever settled along the way?"

"Nobody after you leave the blockhouse this side of Moccasin Gap until you're in sight of Logan's or Boonesborough."

"It's at Hazel Patch you said the trail forks?"

"Yes. One way you go through Logan's—that's another sixty miles—and on through Harrodsburg to Louisville. The other way you get to Boonesborough—about seventy miles—and, say, thirty miles farther is the Licking."

"Why has no one ever settled in between?"

"Indians. Country's too rough—gives them too many places to hide and makes them too hard to chase. And their Great War Trail—the main route the northern and southern Indians use to get back and forth—runs right through it so there's some of them always hanging around."

Amy had squirmed around on Blake's lap so that as she listened she could watch his face. Suddenly she jumped up.

"We've talked so much and been shut up here so long," she said. "Let's get out and get a breath of fresh air before dinner."

"What we're talking about is important," remonstrated Joel. "And we've got lots more to say."

Amy was tugging at Blake's hand to make him get up. "Adam might be interest in seeing your cattle. And anyway we have to get out of Titus' way so he can set the table."

Cynthia came to her support. "Come on. We've got all the rest of the day to talk about Kentucky."

Joel and Blake looked at the women, exchanged rueful glances, and reluctantly yielded. The five of them walked out to the cattle pens in the rear. Most of the herd was in a distant meadow but there were some cows and young calves in a holding field. Blake pointed out a bull that he'd brought over from England the last year before the war, but no special importance was attached by anybody to the inspection of the cat-

68

tle. Already Amy was linking her arms with those of Blake and Joel and steering them back toward the house.

"Cynthia," she said over her shoulder, "before you come in—why don't you show Adam the spring?"

"I'm sure he's just dying to see it," said Cynthia. "Come on, Adam."

"Half hour," warned Blake. "We'll hold dinner no longer."

Cynthia placed her hand on Adam's arm and walked beside him along a path toward a cluster of rhododendron at the base of a slope. Adam could see Amy still looking back over her shoulder, watching them nervously.

"I can't complain," he said. "She's a big help. But what's she shooting at?"

"She couldn't stand all that talk about Kentucky."

"Well, what's she want you to make it worth my while to do about it? Tell them that Kentucky's the sinkhole of creation?"

"She doesn't know them as well as I do. Chances are that would only make Joel and Blake the more interested."

"Maybe you're not so set against Kentucky as she is."

"I'm more. We're a family that belongs together. But there's still plenty of time to head off Paul's Kentucky ideas. Joel's the one who will decide. And he's not nearly as excitable as Paul or Blake. He'll stop to think—and to listen to me —and to his wife, Julia. Amy's getting scared too soon. Nothing can happen until Paul gets back and then we'll have all next winter to work on Joel."

"Are you always able to work things out the way you want them?"

"I only wish I were."

"Why'd you ever leave Albemarle if you were so anxious to keep your family together?"

"There wasn't enough land for all four of us."

"So now you plan to get Joe and Paul to sell out there and settle here alongside Blake. Then you can sit in your ironworks next door and you'll have everything fixed just the say you want it."

She smiled. "Nearly everything."

"Everything, then, but the man you were talking about."

"That'll come—sooner or later."

"What makes you think he hasn't already?"

They had come to the spring, a bubbling pool among moss-covered rocks. The dark green of the rhododendron seemed to have closed in around them. The air was sweet with the perfume of the great rose-colored blossoms. It was a spot in which only lovers should linger. A passing breeze caused the clusters of flowers in which Cynthia was framed to dance and shimmer and to send out new waves of scent. An exploring ray of sunlight wandered from her hair across her cheek and down into the hollow of her throat.

Probably he'd been a fool to speak out so soon. But it was too late to back away now. "Well?" he demanded.

She was looking up at him in wonder, as if as much surprised at herself as at him. "How can I be sure—yet?"

"Why not?"

"I can be more nearly sure," she admitted, still marveling, "than I've ever been before."

He put his hands back of her shoulders and drew her against him. She slipped unresistingly into his embrace but she did not respond as she had last night and her mouth remained passive under his kisses. She could still be thinking of what they had already said and what they must be about to say. For a moment her impassivity increased his desire, for she seemed quite willing to indulge him. His arms tightened about her. Then her apparent failure to share his emotion angered him. He started to shove her away. But he held her by the shoulders as soon as she was far enough away for him to look into her face. His anger left him. She was so wonderful to look at.

He tried to laugh. "Your brothers like me. Amy, too. Even the dog does. Why can't you?"

"I can. Or rather—I can't help it. Only—everything seems to be happening so fast I can't catch my breath."

"You'll have time to catch it," he said soberly. "I've never been much of a hand myself at making plans—but I've surely got to get at making some now."

She caught his meaning instantly and laid her hands on his, which were still on her shoulders. "No, Adam, that's one thing, at least, we don't have to worry about." This was dangerous ground and it was her turn to try to laugh. "Naturally, I'd not marry—just to get a man to run my business—but it does need a manager."

He stepped back, his hands dropping to his sides. His voice was harsher than he had intended. "And once you get him you'll have everything staked out just where you want it—all the way up and down the New River Valley."

"A woman doesn't often get anything the way she really wants it," she countered.

Lying awake last night looking up at the moon he'd tried to foresee the worst that could happen. But he hadn't guessed anything as bad as this. It was an issue too serious to be met head on. Better to circle around it, pretend they were still merely fencing.

70

"Sounds like you need an overseer more than you do a man," he jeered.

She was as anxious as he to treat the subject lightly. "Ought I to yearn instead for a cabin in Kentucky?"

But trying to pretend they still were only fencing was no good. Every word either said was crackling like a rifleshot. The cheerful clang of the dinner bell came from the direction of the house. Both welcomed the interruption and with one movement they turned to go. She placed her hand on his arm as they walked along and kept looking up at him questioningly but he stared straight ahead.

He had to have her. He was sure of that now. He'd been sure since the first minute he'd caught sight of her in the arbor. And he could have her. She'd made that clear enough. But he'd not be marrying her. She'd be marrying him. All he'd have to do was settle down in the brick house, spend maybe an hour a day bossing her blacks, another hour or two taking his place as one of the lesser members of the family—and the rest of the time giving her the idea she had a man around. It would be an easy life and a very pleasant one. But not at all the one he'd had in mind. They went in the back door and on into the dining room.

"Next week," he said to Joel, "I'm starting back over the mountains with a pack train. If you really want to see your Kentucky land I could take you there and get you back in two months."

Amy gasped. Blake looked past Adam at Cynthia with a low, surprised whistle.

"A very generous offer," said Joel. "So good a one, in fact, that I don't see how Blake and I can afford to refuse it." He glanced at Blake, who promptly nodded, and back at Adam. "But, though we welcome your help, I do have to ask one question—a very friendly one, I may say. What advantage do you stand to gain?"

"The chance you may decide to move to Kentucky," said Adam. "I am a Kentuckian and as a Kentuckian every increase in our number out there is an advantage."

He looked at Cynthia then. She was blazing.

"Do you take me for one of your Indian squaws to be managed by swinging a big enough club?"

Amy was crying softly. Cynthia put a comforting arm around her.

"I do declare," she assured Amy, "if I had a gun in my hand I'd shoot him this minute—right through the head."

"Or in the leg," said Blake, "to keep him from getting away."

71

SIX

"NOBODY'S luck can stay so good," said Bert. "Nobody's. Not even yourn."

"What's so good about it?" demanded Adam.

"How could it git any better?" Bert wagged his head, marveling anew. "That ironworkin' business of her'n—with them big smart niggers to run it—there ain't no kind of business could make you more and make it faster anywhere you settle west of Tidewater. And them brothers of her'n—they been bit by the Kentucky bug. Once people git that itch they never git over it. Sure as taxes they're all goin' to move to Kentucky. They're dry back of the ears—and they got their eyes open—but you know that country out there and they don't. Out there they'll need you. They'll need you and she'll need you. You got the whole kit and caboodle right in your pocket. Luck, my friend—you're havin' luck shoved into you every way there is."

At any rate, there was no question about the luck that accompanied their passage through the wilderness. The most forbidding heights were wreathed in the mild haze of summer. Their days on the trail and their nights in camp were neither hot, nor cold nor wet. The rivers had fallen since the spring floods and all were easy to cross. They were traveling light, with Bert's four pack horses loaded only with a few axes, shovels, saws, surveying instruments and sparse camp equipment, and able in the pleasant weather to move so fast as to reduce almost to nothing the risk that Indians, striking their trail, could follow them to make trouble. Here, too, the luck held. Joel saw his first buffalo, followed it on foot into a canebrake and killed it with a pistol. Blake's dogs flushed an enormous she-bear out of a raspberry patch and he succeeded in bringing the beast down with a single shot from nearly a hundred yards away. The brothers were equally delighted with the weather, the scenery, the swift progress and their marksmanship.

"Greatest country I ever saw," declared Blake.

"I've seen rougher going," said Joel, "right in sight of Williamsburg after a three-day rain."

They reached the Hazel Patch and turned north. Each day they traveled longer hours and more miles, as Joel and Blake's eagerness to see their land mounted. The evening of the ninth day after losing sight of the last habitation in eastern Virginia they came out on a ridge from which they could see, sprawled out on the bank of the Kentucky River below, the big stockade of Boonesborough. They rode through fields where the corn was twelve feet high and up to the gates of the station through which people were running out to meet them. In this, their first encounter with people who lived in Kentucky, the talk was all of favorable news. Bowman and Logan had invaded the Shawnee country, destroyed crops, carried off some hundreds of horses and burned the Shawnee town, Chillicothe, and since that exploit there had been much less Indian trouble in Kentucky. To Joel and Blake there was another piece of news that was even better. To the north of Boonesborough, Riddle's Station on the Licking was being strengthened and nearby a new station, Martin's, was building.

"With two stations between our country and the Ohio," Joel said, "sounds like we'll only be wide open to Indians coming from the direction of that war trail of theirs to the east."

"Those two stations could be a help, all right," agreed Adam.

They spent the night at Boonesborough, listening politely to the many eager descriptions of the excellent land yet to be had in the neighborhood, and set out in the morning more impatient than ever. From here on there was no longer even the rudest trail to follow. The scattered settlements of Kentucky all lay to the north and west of Boonesborough. They were turning to the northeast. They rode over the rolling hills up out of the valley of the Kentucky River, camping that night on the headwaters of a stream flowing northward into the south fork of the Licking.

Rising at dawn, Joel and Blake too excited by now to pause for breakfast, they started on. The luck still held. In the first hour Blake's dogs, whining with eagerness over a sudden familiar scent, led them straight to the half-faced camp of Paul and Eli Skaggs. Old Eli was dressing a deer. After one quick look, he waved casually, as if visitors from Virginia riding into camp were an occurrence to be expected any fine morning, and went on with his skinning. Paul was bathing in the stream. He reared up, his red hair and beard and great white body gleaming in the sun, stared and then began to bellow in wild delight.

"Get down," he cried. "Get down off your horses."

He capered about them like one demented, enfolded Joel and Blake in a dripping embrace and then continued to leap and gesture.

"Come," he demanded. "Just come with me."

73

Without stopping to dress or even to dry himself, he ran along the stream bank, beckoning to them to follow. He led the way around a bend and plunged into a thick patch of blackberry vines, paying no heed to the briars raking his naked skin.

"Come on," he kept crying. "Just keep coming."

Great clusters of ripe blackberries nodded in his wake. Covey after covey of quail boomed out from under foot. A long file of turkeys, gobbling angrily, ran through the undergrowth before him. He broke out into the open at the top of a slope beyond and turned to confront them.

"Now," he said in triumph, "just take a look."

The stream made a horseshoe bend below, tumbling meanwhile over two limestone ledges, then meandered away to the north through miles of a widening, marvelously green and lovely valley. On the encircling hills the forest here and there gave way to inviting expanses of grassland across which the wind's passing was marked by gentle waves in the carpet of rye and clover. In the valley bottom parklike meadows dotted by great elms and locusts were bordered by belts of towering cane. The stream, winding through the wild paradise, was a gleaming ribbon of blue and green and silver.

"You're looking at land that's just as rich as it looks," proclaimed Paul, waving his arms. "Notice the outcroppings of limestone, the size of the trees, the color of the grass, the height of the cane. That's the way you tell good land out here. Just look at everything—everything in sight."

"I'm looking at upward of eighty buffalo in sight," said Blake. "No—nearer a hundred."

"That farthest herd," said Joel, "that's elk. And there's some fair-sized trout in the stream. The one that bear's just fished out of the pool below the second falls must be all of three pounds. The creek got a name?"

Paul had bent to pick up several small sticks which he began to break hastily. "Nobody's ever seen it except a few hunters. According to Eli most of them call it Trace Creek on account of the buffalo trace that crosses just beyond that grove of walnut. There's a big salt spring there." He straightened up. "Near as I can make out, our piece of land takes in just about as much of the valley as you can see from here." He faced Joel and Blake, holding out one hand from which the ends of the sticks protruded. "Draw."

"What for?" asked Joel.

"For first choice among us on a place to build. If I win I plan to build there in the bend."

Joel looked and shook his head. "No place there for any

74

one of us to build. That's going to be the townsite. Spot for a sawmill at one falls and a flour mill at the other."

Paul let out another bellow of delight. "Hear that, Blake? Hear that? One look and old hard-shell Joel himself is converted. Already he's talking about mills and towns. Looks like you're all going to be in this as deep as I am."

"Beginning to," agreed Blake, grinning.

Bert dug his elbow into Adam's ribs. Joel's keen eyes seldom missed much.

"I suppose you two are used to the way greenhorns take on when they get their first good look at this country out here," he said.

"It's a mighty pretty valley, for a fact," said Adam.

Joel's attention returned to the view. "Go get yourself dressed and saddle your horse," he directed Paul. "Let's start right now taking us a closer look."

For the next month the three brothers explored their domain, ran survey lines, blazed trees and raised cairns of stones to mark their boundaries. The other three hunted for the pot and kept on watch for Indians.

At night in camp there was much talk—of horses and hunting and dogs and guns and cards and battles, of what Joel once had witnessed on a visit to London, on the right way to cure hams, of Adam's theory that the Missouri, not the Mississippi, was the main river, of the youthful experiences of the Wyeth sons on trading voyages to the West Indies with an uncle, of the proper weight of shot for canvasbacks, of the prices Bert had paid for his horses, of the precise amount of saffron to put in a terrapin stew, of Eli's conviction that the beaver was endowed with more than human intelligence, of everybody's opinions concerning the origin of Indian mounds, of the time Paul on a bet had rolled a hogshead of tobacco from Charlottesville to Palmyra, of the effect of weather on the way a trout rises to a fly, and, with much argument and many references to examples, of the comparative amorousness of white, red, and black women.

But there was no talk of the land in the green valley of Trace Creek, of the Wyeth opinions of it or plans regarding it. After each day absorbed in the exploration and examination they had come so far to make, at night they smilingly but firmly avoided the whole subject. The decisions which were in the making were to be theirs alone. When any question as important as this was to be dealt with the Wyeths closed ranks. The family was bound together by ties which excluded outsiders from their councils.

Weeks passed. Again and again Adam caught distant

glimpses of the three brothers, pausing to deliberate in the course of their daily surveying and soil testing and boundary marking. He could see them pointing to tracts of meadow or woodland, gesticulating in vigorous differences of opinion, nodding their heads in approaching agreement, coming to conclusions which Joel entered in his notebook. But never once did they summon him to ask the kind of questions or advice they formerly had so often sought of him.

Anxiety began to gnaw at Adam. His had been a sad miscalculation if they had already decided they had no further need of him. He thought continually of his parting from Cynthia. After her first rage had passed she had seemed to realize that she could not hold him entirely responsible for her brothers' obsession with their Kentucky land. At any rate, when the time had come to say good-by, she had offered her cheek to his kiss. Then she had smiled, her fingers tightening for a moment on his arm.

"Though maybe," had been her whispered half promise, "when you bring them safely back—"

But bringing them safely back was not going to be enough if thereafter he was thanked for his pains and left with no further part in their plans. Then, too, his liking for all three Wyeth brothers was growing the better he came to know them. He could barely remember his own kinfolk. He began to think of what it would be like to find himself belonging among these warmhearted Wyeths, beneath whose surface heedlessness there was so much loyalty to each other. Yet to be accepted as one of them was not an aim that he could pursue as he had set out to pursue Cynthia. There was nothing that he could do except to watch and wait and pretend composure.

Then, at last, there came a day when his suspense was relieved. He was coming back to camp, toward evening, with a brace of turkeys when he saw Joel, Blake and Paul gathered by the lower falls. For the first time since their arrival here they were sitting down during daylight.

"Adam," yelled Paul. "Come down here."

Adam joined them. The time had come. They had made up their minds about something and were ready to talk to him. It was odd to remember how recently he would not have felt concerned with anything anybody could be about to say to him. Now his outward calm was no more real than that of the young Indian brave waiting outside the council lodge to learn whether or no he will be initiated into the warriors' secret society.

"Sit down," said Joel. "You've had time to look around some yourself. What do you think of this section?"

"About as good as there is."

"That's what we think. So we've made up our minds to try to take up all of it we're entitled to. But we've been giving a lot of thought to the right way to go at it. We don't want to go off half cocked. And we certainly don't want to rush out here with our families until we're sure we've got everything set as it should be. First we want to build what we need, get enough land under cultivation so nobody'll go hungry and then bring in enough people to stand off the Indians."

"That's the way to go at it, all right," said Adam.

"But it's also too big an order for us to handle alone," resumed Joel. "So this is the way we've decided to go about it: We're going to keep the land on the east side of the creek for ourselves. Then we're going to form a company and sell it the ten thousand acres on this side. There'll be ten shares in the company and with each share will go an acre here at the townsite, ten acres alongside and a thousand acres of general farm land. Each share will cost a thousand dollars and the money will go for building the stockade and the mills and a store and whatever is necessary to give a new settlement the right sort of start. We'll buy four of these shares ourselves and sell the other six. This other six we don't want to sell just to anybody who happens to have a thousand dollars. We want only men who've got something genuinely useful to offer. And, naturally, we keep thinking about men we know well enough to know how far we can count on them. For example—there's Jim Menifee back in Albemarle who's run a sawmill all his life. A sawmill's about the first thing a settlement needs because once you get one set up you can get ahead so much faster with your building. Then by the time the first corn's up we'll need a flour mill. Probably a storekeeper. A doctor if we can get one. Maybe even a preacher. You've been out in this country quite a while and had a chance to watch new settlements getting started. See anything wrong with this plan?"

"No," said Adam.

"Good. Because the first share after our own we'd like to offer to you. Want it?"

Adam clung to his outward calm. The most he had expected was talk of employment, of their obvious need of him as guide, hunter, Indian fighter and general advisor. Instead they were really taking him in. They couldn't know he had just sixty dollars to his name. They were making him an offer in all good faith. They were looking forward to his becoming one of them. It was the next thing to the negotiation of a betrothal contract. Somewhere, and quick, he had to find a thousand dollars.

"I'd be a fool if I didn't," he replied.

"Good," said Joel again, this time with a sudden added warmth. "And by the way I can see Blake and Paul squirming I can see that they want me to add that we feel the advantage is mainly ours."

All three shook hands with him. There was no question that this was a great deal more than just a business deal.

"How soon will you need the money?"

"We don't figure to start building until next spring. That'll give you time to make any arrangements you have to. And another thing—there's no way these days to count on what money's going to be worth. So we'll reckon a dollar at the rate of twenty-five cents a bushel for corn."

Four thousand bushels of corn. All you could raise in a year on fifty acres of good cleared land. And no time to raise it if he had the land. People had gotten into the habit of talking easily about dollars because they'd become so used to the idea that dollars were only pieces of paper. But four thousand bushels of corn was more than a thousand horseloads.

Adam combed the woods to the north, in which it was Bert's day to watch the game trails Indians might use, until he'd run Bert down at the lower salt spring. Bert saw no great problem.

"I can git you five hundred silver for your mare, the watch and that blue coat," he said.

"How about the other five hundred?"

"Borrow that from your brother-in-laws. They want you so bad they'll let you have it."

"No," said Adam. "If I go into this I'm not going to back in."

"If you go in," scoffed Bert. "You're hooked as tight as they are."

"Anyway you look at it," said Adam soberly, "it's a good deal for me."

"It surely is," agreed Bert. "It's one you can't afford to let git away from you. So where you goin' to git the money?"

They both thought for a while. "What's saltpeter worth a pound?" asked Adam.

"Not bad," exclaimed Bert. "Not bad a-tall. Knew you'd come up with some sort of an idea but didn't count on you gittin' such a sensible one. Saltpeter's worth twenty, thirty, forty cents a pound—all depends on how short gunpower is that month out here. If it's real short you can git about what you want to ask for it. So you know where you can find some."

Adam nodded. "Cave down on Green River where I wintered first year I was out here. There's saltpeter a foot thick all over the bottom of it. Of course I'll need kettles to render it in. How much will they cost me?"

"Six to eight times what they're worth—anywhere in Kentucky. Near as bad on the Holston. Closest place they got any at any sort of price a man can afford is Pittsburgh. They make 'em there."

Adam thought for a while longer.

"Get the Wyeths packed back to Virginia," he said. "With Paul and Eli you'll have a stronger party than when we came out. Old Eli's sharp enough but you keep your eyes open, too. I promised to get them back safe."

"Don't fret about that," said Bert. "After the trouble I took findin' them horses of mine I don't aim to let no Mingo or Cherokee creep up on 'em."

"And take care of my mare for me."

"Now wait," grumbled Bert. "While I'm doin' all your work for you—what you goin' to be doin'?"

"I'm going to be on my way to Pittsburgh. I can make it faster on foot through that rough country along the Tug and the Kanawha. Then I can bring the kettles down the Ohio by canoe. In two months meet me at Louisville with your pack horses."

"I'll be there," said Bert, appearing to see nothing unusual in a man's setting out to travel alone over three hundred miles of trackless mountains and down six hundred miles of Indian-infested river.

SEVEN

"Two months to the day," was Bert's greeting at Louisville. "You sure must of pounded on it."

"I was in a hurry," said Adam.

"Reckon you still are," sympathized Bert, "so let's git goin'."

Bert inspected the kettles and reluctantly approved the price Adam had paid. They packed and set out at once, though it was already midafternoon.

"Near three hours of daylight left," said Bert. "Might's well use it."

Only five days later, having kept moving south each day every minute of daylight, the little pack train was winding through the rugged hills about the headwaters of the Green River. Adam was to spend the winter in a land more lonely than any through which he had traveled on his way to and from Pittsburgh. From Logan's on the Wilderness Road behind, no white man lived anywhere in this country to the south nearer than Natchez on the Mississippi, five hundred miles away.

"It's been eight years since I was through here," said Adam. "Maybe I can't find the place."

There was not much chance of that. A boy's first winter in the wilderness was not something he was likely ever to forget. Riding ahead of the pack train he circled to the west of the bald-topped hill—the kind Kentuckians called a knob—kept on through the stretch of open beech woods, climbed the next ridge, descended into the next cane-filled valley and here picked up the broad, beaten buffalo trace which provided the one way by which pack horses could have been worked through the cane at all. Though they could not see them they could tell by the grunting and rustling that there were hundreds of buffalo feeding in the cane on either side. Later, when the trace crossed a small stream, Adam turned down the stream bed so that for the next two miles the pack train splashed along in the water, leaving even less sign of its passing than on the trampled trace behind.

As they kept on, the little valley narrowed and the stream veered nearer the ridge on the south. Then, as they rounded a bend, the forest of cane on this side opened to disclose a strip of meadow running down to a long, flat rock shelving off at its lower edge into a pool in which a squadron of trout darted to and fro. Along the north bank the wall of cane reared up impenetrably. Above the meadow the ridge rose in an almost sheer cliff. The only approach was to wade along the stream as they had. After one glance Bert grunted his approval.

"For a boy and a greenhorn you didn't pick such a bad spot to winter in," he said.

But when they had dismounted Adam had more to show him about the virtues of the spot. Behind the drooping branches of a huge oak at the foot of the cliff there was the opening of a cave. Adam twisted a dried serviceberry bush into a torch and led the way. Just within the entrance there was a low-roofed, sand-floored chamber not much larger than a good-sized cabin. To one side were the ashes of the last fire Adam had built here and to the other crumbling fragments of the cedar bed upon which he had slept.

"Been nobody here since," said Bert. "How'd you ever find it?"

"On my way out that fall I ran into an old trapper named Jeb Sproat—back at Flat Lick on the Cumberland," said Adam. "He wanted somebody to talk to and so did I. Anyway, we started traveling together and one day we wound up here. The next morning while I was frying some trout he went out to take a shot at an elk he noticed up the mountain a ways. When he didn't come back I went out to look for him but he didn't answer no matter how much I yelled—and then it started to snow so I couldn't track him. I never saw him again—only what was left of him when the snow went off —where he'd fallen down a crack between two rocks."

"Must of been kind of a long winter for a boy by hisself out in the woods for the first time," remarked Bert. He looked around. "I don't see no saltpeter."

Adam moved to the back of the cave. Here there was a cleft in the rock wall which, a few feet beyond, took an abrupt turning. Bert followed and peered past him. The glare from the torch dispelled some of the nearer darkness in an enormous cavern, many times as large as the chamber at the entrance. As far as the light extended the floor of the cavern was white.

"I do now," said Bert.

Somewhere back in the darkness could be heard the gurgle and splash of running water.

"That's an underground stream," said Adam, "that runs off to the southeast. If you follow it far enough you come out on the other side of the mountain. So if Indians ever do get to nosing around your front door you can always go out the back. And notice this, too." He held up the torch. The flame was bending away from the outer entrance. "That's the way with these big caves. All winter the wind blows in like this. There's no chance for smoke from your fire to drift outside where it might attract attention. And all summer the wind blows out again. That's why the Indians call this cave country along the Green River the Land Where the Earth Breathes."

Much as he would have liked to stay, at least long enough to help Adam get settled in this most interesting place, Bert had to leave as soon as his horses were unloaded. At Logan's he had been engaged to take a party of discouraged movers back to Virginia.

"I had to git me back to Virginia before spring anyway, to pick up that sawmill gear for Joel," he explained for the tenth time. "So didn't seem like there was much reason I shouldn't git paid both ways."

"No reason at all," agreed Adam.

"When you want me back here to pack out your saltpeter?"

"Early in the spring as you can make it."

"Ought to be able to make it right early. Joel's goin' to want that sawmill at Trace Creek early in the spring as we can git over the mountains."

"That'll depend on how long the winter hangs on. So I'll start expecting you when it warms up enough for the hawthorn to start to bud."

"That's when you'll see me," said Bert.

Adam was almost glad to see him go. Working alone seemed better to fit the purpose of his winter labors. He threw himself into this work with immediate, fierce energy and with as much zest as if he were building the house in which Cynthia and he were to live. His hopes and expectations had become so definite that in his mind it seemed almost as if this were actually what he was doing.

His first need was timber for building and wood for fuel. He waded three miles up the stream to do his cutting. Cherokee hunters often circled through this Green River country. Even if no Cherokee ear picked up the actual ring of his ax, sooner or later some Cherokee eye might light on the litter of chips and lopped branches, and he didn't want attention attracted to a spot any nearer than this to his meadow and cave. The logs and poles and firewood he rafted down the stream. With the poles he built a pen for Oriole between the cottonwood and the maple at the lower edge of the meadow, a hundred feet from the mouth of the cave, and in it a shed to shelter her against the cold of the approaching winter. With the logs he built a wall across the mouth of the cave and fitted it with a door that could be barred, making the dwelling into a refuge stronger than any cabin and one that could be defended for a while, at least, even by one man. The wood he stacked in the main cavern. Keeping four big kettles boiling would eat up fuel, and once he had started rendering saltpeter he didn't want to stop to get more.

He had been none too forehanded with his preparations, for the morning he was ferrying his last raft of wood down the stream it turned very cold and began to snow. He thought little of it at first since occasional snow was not uncommon in late November. However, by midafternoon there was a blizzard of a ferocity such as trappers told about on the plains beyond the Mississippi but the like of which he had never heard the oldest hunters mention experiencing in this mild country south of the Ohio. And each hour it grew colder. The last of his wood was encased in ice before he had got it dragged in and added to his store in the cavern. He tied his extra blanket over Oriole, fed and watered her, saw that she was snug in the shed, against which the snow already was drifting, and, staggered by the tremendous gusts, floundered back to his own door. He had been working each day to the limit of his strength and, once sheltered and warm within, was glad of the excuse to eat early and then to start catching up on his rest.

He slept soundly from late afternoon through the night, stirring only occasionally to notice that the gale was still booming against the door. It was the intense cold creeping across the stone floor and under his blanket that finally awakened him at daybreak. The wind had ceased. His first thought was of Oriole and he was bending hastily to thrust some sticks of wood against the coals buried under the ashes of his fire, before going out to see to her, when he heard the gunshot. It sounded so close that he caught up his rifle and sprang to the loophole. Before he could get the block shoved aside so that he could see out, there was a louder report even nearer.

With his first glance he saw that the white blanket of snow was unbroken by tracks anywhere this side of the edge of the cane and, to his astonishment, that the cold had been so severe that the running stream had frozen over. There were several more shots in the distance. He began to realize that there must be some other accounting for the reports, since there could hardly be so many people, white or red, wandering about, this far from Kentucky settlements or Indian towns, aimlessly firing off guns. When he saw the big maple down by the horse pen he understood. The trunk was split wide open. The cold was so intense it had frozen the sap in the heartwood. Everywhere through the forest trees were splitting with these reports, which were like gunshots.

He swung open the door. The frigid, still air burned when it struck his face. Stepping into the open he could feel the cold strike through his buckskin shirt as if he had stepped in over his head into a pool of ice water. Under the metallic gray sky the whitenesss of the outer world was the whiteness of death. The lifeless silence was broken only by the squeaking of the snow under his moccasins and the occasional distant crack of another tree. He plunged through the drift between his door and the horse pen.

Oriole appeared in the doorway of the shed and whinnied her usual morning welcome. Clouds of vapor shot from her nostrils as she breathed and there was a lacework of tiny icicles about her muzzle, but under the protection of blanket and shed she seemed to have suffered little from the cold. He threw an armful of young cane in to her. One of the many virtues of cane was that the lesser leaves remained green at all seasons so that it made good winter fodder. To provide water for the mare and for his own use he had to chop through the ice of the stream. In only one night six inches of it had formed. On his way back to the cave he noted one advantage in the unprecedented cold. The quarter of venison hanging from a limb of the oak was as hard as a stone. As long as this weather lasted the meat would keep. He could hack off what he needed each day and would not need to drop his work to hunt more. And, he decided with a sudden gust of impatience, it was high time he got at his real work.

After breakfasting hastily he went into the main cavern, set up his kettles and started his fires. Of purifying saltpeter he knew only what he had been told. But it was not a complicated process. It consisted chiefly of gathering the impregnated earth from the floor of a limestone cave, washing the common salt from it with water, boiling down the residue with wood ashes and then permitting the solution to cool until the crystals of pure saltpeter formed. His first trials were unsuccessful but when he began to allow more time, both for washing and boiling, to his great satisfaction the first needlelike tufts of saltpeter crystals appeared.

It proved slower work than he had anticipated but by the third day he was able to estimate that, come spring, he would certainly have accumulated as much saltpeter as Bert's horses could carry. The long waits while the solution boiled were what took the time. He gave up sleeping through the night and took his rest in short snatches, rousing as often as was necessary to keep the fires going and the boiling uninterrupted.

In the cavern he was shut off from the weather outside. Here in the heart of the mountain there was no way of telling whether the season was winter or summer. Each time he emerged he expected to find a change. But there was none. Occasionally the wind had risen and there was a new fall of snow driving before it. However, these northwest gales were never succeeded by the flow of warmer air from the south that usually followed the worst winter storm. Each time, in the resulting calm, the bitter, intense cold descended once more. He could imagine the shock and dismay such an unheard-of cold spell was causing in the crowded settlements of Kentucky.

On the fifth day he discovered that the stream had frozen solid. The water of the stream in the cavern was too bitter to drink. Thereafter, to get water for himself and Oriole he had to take the trouble to melt snow. The following day he ate the last of his venison and realized the next morning he had to take time off for hunting. But with the morning came a real disaster that swept all thought of hunting from his mind.

Oriole did not appear in the shed doorway. When he got to her he found her inside lying on the ground. She was breathing in intermittent, struggling gasps; there was a bloody foam on her lips and her whole body was rigid and cold, except for her throat which was swollen and feverish. Prying open her mouth he saw the cuts on her tongue and the shreds of cottonwood bark between her teeth and guessed what had happened. With the perversity of a horse she had ignored her feeding of cane and had stretched through the bars of the pen to gnaw bark from the cottonwood. Usually cottonwood bark was good for horses and they would keep through an entire, ordinary winter with no other food. But when frozen hard it became dangerous. The sharp-edged shreds lacerated the throat and stomach until horses had been known to die from eating it.

He remembered that salt was reputed to be a specific for such a disorder. Desperately he forced salt into her mouth and down her throat, but the immediate result was to choke her and to stop her labored breathing almost entirely. He built a fire in the shed and kept her covered with one warmed blanket while he warmed the other at the fire. He soaked his one cotton shirt in hot water and applied the compress to her throat. Alternately he rubbed the swelling with pieces of ice.

Night came. And another day. She showed no improvement. But the hoarse, convulsive breathing never quite stopped. He grasped at one faint hope. A horse that was going to die generally died. When they hung on like this they had a chance. He boiled cane leaves into a mash. When a handful was shoved far enough back into her throat she swallowed weakly. With a section of a hollow reed he managed to get warm water into her rectum and to bring about a bowel movement.

After a second day and night without sleep he was nearly as weak as the mare. But he was saved from further starving by a turkey which, flapping forlornly to roost in the maple, was frozen on its perch during the night and literally fell at his feet. He propped the hastily cleaned carcass against a stone by the fire to roast but, keeping little account of time because of his concern with his nursing duties, he let his hunger drive him to eat a large portion of it before it was done. Already tense from anxiety and exhaustion, his gorging on the half-cooked, half-frozen meat gave him a colic. For many hours he was as sick as the mare. He was left with so little strength that it was only by the most painful exertion that he managed to get the remains of the turkey into the kettle and keep the fire going. When at last he began to sip the hot broth he saw something that did more to restore him than the soup. Oriole was able to lift her head and look at him.

The next day she stopped trying to fight off the mash and the day after he got her on her feet. The third day, though trembling and shaky, she could walk, so he moved her to the cave where it would be easier to attend her and to keep her warm. The effort tired her so much that she barely made the door, but after he had bedded her down again and she had ceased to pant she was more willing to eat than she had been before. Confident at last that she would pull through, Adam slept until he was rested.

Awakening, he was delighted to see her standing, her ears pricked cheerfully and inquisitively forward, and watching him with interest. There was no longer much question of her getting well. He sprang up, refreshed, and eager to get back to his long-neglected work, only to be struck a moment later by another crushing blow. The sound of running water in the cavern had ceased while he slept. Incredulous, he ran to look. The underground stream had dwindled to a trickle. He ran back to the door to discover that the cold outside was more intense than ever. What had happened was obvious. At some point nearer its source the cavern stream ran aboveground and there it had frozen solid as had all others. Until the weather changed there would be no water with which to make saltpeter.

For a time he stubbornly refused to bow to this preposterous disaster. Realizing he could not possibly carry enough snow to be of any use, he chopped ice in the meadow stream and carried the chunks in to be melted. But he was forced to admit after some days of angry persistence that the amount of water required for the washing was so great that this effort was senseless. He could only wait while each successive day his idleness became more nerve wracking.

Storms came and went but the great cold merely continued. The need to hunt for food provided no occupation for his time since almost within sight of the cave there were the frozen carcasses of four deer and three buffalo. Several times he circled more widely, curious, yet half reluctant, to observe more of the effects of the terrible weather. Everywhere trees were split and everywhere the snow-covered landscape was dotted by the gravelike white mounds where game animals had given up the struggle to exist. Much of the cane, even, had been killed. The country would be a long time recovering, if it ever did, from the effects of this winter of '79.

Depressed by all he saw outside, Adam spent days dozing by the fire. The winter, upon which he had counted so much, was passing; the spring, of which he had expected so much, when it finally did come, would find him with nothing accomplished. He dreamed constantly but in his dreams he was as frustrated as in his waking hours. These dreams were the most vivid and disturbing when he was neither quite awake nor quite asleep, so that his most nightmarish fancies carried over to color his real anxieties. He could hardly so much as nod without beginning to see running water, boiling kettles, the meadow green and sunlit, Bert's pack horses loaded with saltpeter—and yet without ever entirely losing the awareness that these were but dreams. Again and again Cynthia appeared in them, at first always near, smiling, often with her arms outstretched and her lips parted as if awaiting his kisses. But, invariably, when he reached for her she seemed to retreat just beyond his grasp, to drift toward him again when his arms dropped only once more to elude him, until the violence of his desire brought him fully awake, the sudden surge of longing undiminished, to realize unhappily how far away she actually was and how little he had so far been able to do to bring her closer. He was equally haunted by his desperate yearning for the winter to break and by his dread of the very idea of spring. For in the spring Joel and Blake and Paul would return to Trace Creek and he could not be there to keep his appointment with them—unless he appeared before them empty handed and defeated. His sole comfort was that the mare continued to improve.

He had not kept a careful account of the days but he knew the great cold had persisted well into a third month. At best there had been none too much time for all that he had planned to do. Already three months of it had been taken away from him. His rebellious impatience was like a fever. He could scarcely force himself to eat.

When at last the end came it came with as little warning as had the beginning. In the middle of the night he heard a faint splash of water in the cavern. It was a sound he had heard so often in his dreams that for a moment he could not believe he was actually hearing it now. He sat up, listened, made sure that he was awake—and still heard it. Lighting a pine knot at the fire he ran into the cavern.

The stream that had been dry so long was a trickle again and water by the cupful was gathering in the hollows of its bed. He rushed outside. The air was warm. The snow was soft under his feet. Trees were dripping. He yelled until he was hoarse.

Stumbling back to the cavern he rekindled his fires. Before the end of the day there was water enough to start one kettle and by the next morning he had all of them going. Deeper in the cavern the impregnated earth had formed a thick layer on the floor. It seemed whiter and might, he hoped, prove richer. He was able to notice no great increase in the deposit of crystals left eventually at the bottom of each kettle but thereafter he made the longer carry. It gave him more to do while waiting on the boiling. Now that he was working again he was driven by a fiercer impatience than had tormented him during the enforced idleness of the winter.

Spring, coming at last, had come with a rush, as if Nature was remorseful. In a week the snow was gone. The days remained bright and warm and the nights frostless. Waterfowl swarmed in from the south. Grass sprouted in the meadow on which Oriole, completely recovered, grazed happily in the sun between bouts of pawing and rolling. Every plant and tree and creature of the wild, not killed by the cold, stirred and leaped with new life.

The hawthorn buds appeared, swelled and burst into bloom. But Bert did not come. At first Adam thought little of his failure to appear at exactly the time agreed upon. Such a winter must have thrown off all travel schedules and even one who planned every move as carefully as Bert could have found some delay unavoidable. Also, at first, the delay was a relief. So far Adam was ready with less than half his cargo. When Bert did come he would only have to wait and he was sure to complain of the hire he was losing on later engagements for his pack train.

However, when a second and then a third week passed, still with no sign of Bert, Adam began to worry. Unless something serious had happened to him he would never be this late. The more Adam thought about it the more he was impressed by one possibility. While going to and from Virginia Bert had been with a fair-sized party. He'd have been running his geatest risk while traveling alone from Logan's to the cave.

Adam waited two more days, then saddled Oriole and set out to examine the track to Logan's. No foot had been set on it since Bert had taken it north the autumn before. Neither was there the slightest sign that Indians had been anywhere in the region since the snow had gone off. After such a winter Indians were almost certainly too occupied with hunting, to keep their families from starving, to be out looking for mischief this early in the spring. Adam's alarm subsided somewhat.

Halfway to Logan's an irritating possibility occurred to him. Instead of coming by way of Logan's Bert might have left the Wilderness Road at the Hazel Patch and from there struck straight westward through the hills for the headwaters of Green River. If Bert did take such a notion he would come down a creek bottom the other side of the high ridge that reared up to the east. The more Adam thought of this chance that Bert might be on the way to the cave, or even waiting there now, while he was wasting days hunting word of him at Logan's and Boonesborough, the more annoyed he became. He decided before going any farther to cut across to that other bottom and make sure.

The rocky ridge was more easily climbed on foot. He tied Oriole in a cedar thicket and set out. Three hours later he dropped down the other side to discover Bert had not passed along the old Indian trail which followed the creek bottom westward. After three more sweating hours he swung down off the ridge to the cedar thicket beside the track to Logan's. He had lost six hours at a time when every hour was precious. And here he discovered that he had lost far more.

Oriole was gone. To his rage it was apparent that she had been taken by Indians. A few circles, examining the ground about the cedar thicket, and he had worked out what had occurred as clearly as if he had witnessed it. There had been two of them, both Cherokee. The heavier one's left moccasin had a freshly patched heel and the other one must once have suffered some kind of a leg injury for his right foot toed out a little. They had been traveling south, fast, probably from their vagabond northern town in the Shawnee country, and had come upon the mare's hiding place by the purest chance. They must have come straight through Kentucky on their way, instead of taking the Great War Trail to the east, more than likely in the hope of stealing a couple of Kentucky horses. They had failed in that, for they were still on foot, and must have been well pleased to come, here deep in the woods, upon so fine a horse, all tied up and waiting for them.

The two Cherokee, Patched-Heel riding and Toe-Out running behind, hanging to the mare's tail, had hastily started on, keeping to the south, headed, without doubt, for the main Cherokee towns on the Tennessee. Adam's only impulse was to pursue. There were many practical reasons for his going to any length to recover his mare but they barely crossed his mind. His rage was reason enough. To permit a couple of stray Indians to take anything from him was not to be endured.

The Cherokee drew away from him all that first afternoon. They kept changing places in the saddle so that the one on foot was always fresh while Adam was already winded from running back and forth over the ridge. When night came he lost more distance. To follow their trail in the darkness he had to feel for the hoofprints with moccasined toe and sometimes with finger tips while they, for several hours, kept right on as fast as the nature of the country permitted.

The next morning, however, they slept well past daylight. He gained on them again at the crossing of the Cumberland. Oriole had no liking for water and they had a time making her swim the river. In the afternoon they were again slowed up a little. They stopped changing places in the saddle. Thereafter Patched-Heel did all the riding and Toe-Out all the running. He no longer hung to the mare's tail but kept a careful distance. Adam surmised with satisfaction that Patched-Heel had been kicked.

The next morning the ashes of their camp fire were still warm. Before the day was out, he began grimly to hope, he might come up with them. But toward midafternoon, just after crossing a considerable stream running northwest toward the Cumberland, they had encountered a third Indian, and after a conference with him they had turned abruptly east up a side creek, instead of keeping on south toward the Tennessee.

They had walked slowly, following an old deer trail, keeping abreast where the going permitted, the first two munching some dried venison that the third had given them. One of them had dropped a piece, which Adam picked up and chewed with relish. Several times they had stopped to face each other. Adam could almost see them jabbering and gesticulating. There was, no doubt, no end of tribal gossip to be exchanged with the two from the north. He kept a mile or two behind them. Before dark they would camp. Night would bring him his chance. He was not so much disturbed that now he had three instead of two to deal with. More than likely with three in camp they would be less watchful.

But later in the afternoon there were signs of a further change in the situation that did disturb him. The blue jays became more than usually noisy and excitable. Over a distant hilltop two eagles hovered low, as they did when attracted by something dead. Then in the deer trail he came upon deep furrows where a buck, running headlong, had all but plunged in among the three ahead before wheeling away.

90

He had been running toward them when he sighted them. Adam knew he was getting into a district that had recently been hunted.

The creek bottom widened with a glimpse of grassland ahead. He climbed a tree and saw with angry disgust exactly what he had expected to see. The creek circled around one edge of a meadow in the middle of which was a Cherokee hunting camp occupied by at least a dozen families. Since the moment he had set out on the chase he had had a general idea of what there'd be for him to do when he caught up. At the first night pause after he had come up with them he would creep in, kill the two, preferably before they awoke, take his mare, and be off. Even if they gained one of their towns before being overtaken there would remain a fair opportunity to do something. Horses had to be taken out to graze by day, necessarily to pastures at some little distance beyond the cornfields and orchards around a town, and the herdboys could be outwitted or otherwise dealt with. But this hunting camp was another proposition. There was good grass right in the middle of the camp. The hunters were too numerous to creep in upon by night and there was no occasion to take the horses anywhere to graze by day.

But there was no use hanging here in a tree worrying about it. Something might turn up and he had to make his try whether anything turned up or not. And whatever stab he made in the coming darkness he needed to study at closer range the way the camp was laid out while he could still see. He slid down the tree and waded up the creek under the edge of the overhanging shrubbery on the bank. He kept on until he was able to crawl into a fringe of brush from which the camp in the meadow was in full view and not much more than a long rifleshot away.

Smoke from the meat drying racks and the cooking fires before the circle of brush huts rose in the still evening air. Most of the hunters seemed already to have come in. The squaws were doing more laughing and yelling to each other than skinning and butchering and the whole camp was buzzing with excitement. The arrival of the two from the north had created a great stir and Oriole, in particular, was the center of attention. Patched-Heel and Toe-Out were strutting and nodding, making offhand gestures, pretending that the mare was no great matter, yet, without doubt, talking very big. They were getting wound up to tell the full story of the great things they had done while they'd been away, of which the mare was only one slight indication. The stay-at-homes would listen for a while, then each one would get around,

Indian fashion, to telling about everything he'd ever done since he'd shot his first squirrel. The parcel of them would sit up the whole night, eating, bragging, singing and counting coups. Adam watched, his discontent bitter in his mouth. Trying to get at Oriole tonight was going to be about as simple as stealing the Cherokee Ark. The change of luck which Bert had so often forecast, once it had come, was keeping at him with a vengeance.

The sensible course was to wait. Tomorrow night, after tonight's excitement, the camp might be sleepier and more approachable. Or the camp might break up and the hunters scatter for better hunting. Or Patched-Heel and Toe-Out might decide to go on alone to show their prize and tell their story to the bigger audience of their town. The only trouble with all this was—he couldn't afford to be sensible. He had no time to wait. He had to get back to find out what happened to Bert and to get at everything else he had to do. He couldn't wait a day—hardly an hour. Whatever try he was going to make he had to make tonight. If he got the mare—well and good. He'd take her and go. If he didn't—and yet got away himself—he'd still have to go.

A dry stick cracked just beyond the bushes on the other side of the creek behind him. No wild animal big enough to break a stick that size would be wandering this near the camp by daylight. Adam held his breath the better to listen. There was a rustle of dry leaves as of a moccasined foot.

He drew his feet in, turned over on his side, freed his right arm, drew his tomahawk and held it poised in his hand for a quick throw. He was fairly well hidden in a clump of scrub aspen and might remain unseen. But if whoever was approaching did chance to spy him he must be certain his tomahawk reached its mark ahead of any outcry that might be heard in camp. He waited, tense.

Across the stream and up some twenty paces a laurel branch trembled. Then it was drawn aside and a young Indian girl stepped into view on the bank. She was slender, light boned, graceful even under the straight, unbelted folds of the fringed and beaded dress that hung from her shoulders to her knees. Her wrists were thin and her hands small. She moved with the tentative lightness and delicacy of a fawn. Her hair was wet and the red paint on her forehead and cheek bones was fresh. She must have just finished making her toilet at some nearby pool. A frog hopped from under her feet into the water. She paused to watch, smiling, as it swam away, and then she began moving along the bank toward a spot opposite Adam's hiding place, glancing about her idly as if enjoying the evening.

Adam's fingers tightened on the handle of the tomahawk but he felt a little sick. He was not sure he could bring himself to make the throw, even if she discovered him and opened her mouth to scream, even though it might come to a choice between her life and his. She looked so young, so innocent of any intention to threaten him, so defenseless. Her movement along the bank brought her out of the shadow. Under the paint her face was not coppery. He had seen French and Spanish girls who had tanned to as dark an olive. She turned toward him, not to look along the ground where he was but over the aspen in the direction of the camp. He saw then that her eyes were blue, in startling contrast to her jet black hair and the paint on her brow and cheeks. Very possibly she was the half-breed daughter of some white trader, left behind to grow up among his erstwhile Indian customers.

She was immediately across from him now, not a dozen feet away. The sweet grass scent on her hair and garments drifted to him. The hem of her dress caught on a thorn and she turned to disentangle it. Her thigh, revealed momentarily as the dress was pulled above the top of her leggings, was as white as any white woman's. She might very well be white, Adam decided. And if white she was almost certainly a captive.

She moved on. He was safe from discovery now. But if she was a captive she might be persuaded to help him. She might be only too glad to do anything to discomfort her captors. All she'd have to do was to get up in the night and lead the mare out to where he was waiting. Whatever the risk of accosting her it was a far lesser risk than any other that faced him.

He sprang across the creek and ran up behind her, keeping bent down to make sure he could not be seen from camp over the top of the fringe of brush. She turned and saw him, her eyes widening incredulously, but she didn't scream. He grinned, made reassuring gestures and kept on toward her. She still didn't scream. She whirled and started to run. He lunged, caught her by the arm and pulled her around to face him.

"S-s-s-h," he warned, putting a finger to his lips.

She began to struggle desperately to break loose. He slipped the strap of his rifle over his shoulder, grabbed her other arm and shook her to bring her to her senses.

"Stop it," he said. "I'm here to help you."

The sound of his voice speaking English words brought her head up and she stared into his face. She must have it worked out by now that he was a white man and a friend. But when her lips parted it was not to address him but to give the Indian alarm call. He clapped his hand over her mouth and straightened up enough to look toward the Indian camp. The gabbling Indians around the fires had taken no notice but two squaws carrying baskets of water from a spring in the meadow had heard enough to set them to running toward camp. Adam gave the girl another shake.

"You little fool," he said. "I'm not going to hurt you. Can't you see I'm a white man?"

She sank her teeth into the hand he was holding over her mouth. He snatched his hand away and struck her on the jaw with the heel of it. In his exasperation he hit harder than he had intended and the blow knocked her senseless.

The squaws had given the alarm and the men were snatching up their weapons. There was no hope now of his getting Oriole. The best he could do now was to make sure that they did not get him. He dropped the girl to the ground and turned to run. But on second thought he swung back and grabbed her up again. If he left her here they would quickly find her, and whether or not she promptly revived they would soon figure everything out and be on his trail. It was better to keep them looking for her, to force them to spend all the time possible in circling and trying to work out what had happened. He threw her limp form over his shoulder, jumped into the water and started running down the creek.

The shadows gathered and it began to grow dark. Behind him he could hear the signal whistles and animal calls of the searching Indians. Though they must before now have discovered where he had lain in the aspens and where he had jumped over the creek they were still not sure what had become of the girl. It would be full dark in another ten minutes. They wouldn't catch him tonight, at any rate.

Almost alongside was the deer trail by which he had come and on which he could get along so much faster. But there he would leave tracks which the first thing in the morning would reveal the direction he had taken. It was in the daylight hours of tomorrow that the real pinch would come. After what he'd been through the last three days and nights he'd never have the strength to outrun them if they picked up his trail any time before noon tomorrow. His one chance to get away was to keep them guessing about which way he had gone. He kept to the stream, stumbling over rocks and sunken logs in the darkness and finally falling headlong.

The plunge into cold water brought the girl to. Instantly

94

she began to struggle again to break away from him. For a while she fought silently and with all the intent, vicious energy of a wildcat. When with his superior strength he had twisted her into a position where she could no longer move she started another yell. He clapped his hand over her mouth, this time taking care to avoid her teeth.

"Now listen," he whispered. "You might as well make up your mind to it. You're staying with me and you're staying quiet. Once I get a little farther away I'll turn you loose and you can go back to your goddam Indians. Until then all you got to do is behave yourself and no hurt's going to come to you."

She gave no sign she'd heard a word he said. The moment his grasp relaxed ever so slightly she began straining to break away from him again. She was an intolerable burden to his flight, but he didn't dare let her go. She'd have the Cherokee after him in a quarter of an hour. And he couldn't very well just knock her in the head.

He took the halter rope he'd intended for Oriole and began methodically to tie her up, forcing one length of the leather thong between her teeth and knotting it in position so as to keep her gagged. He thrust her trussed form into the middle of a willow thicket and bent the tip of one of the outer branches. Tomorrow the Cherokee would comb both banks of the creek and before the day was over some sharp eye would spot the bent twig. It would be too late, then, for what she could tell to help them much.

He started on down the creek. A wolf howled on a distant hilltop. He guessed it was one of the Cherokee until the call was answered from another slope to the west. It was natural for wolves to gather in a country that had recently been hunted. Wounded deer were easily pulled down. No prey got wolves so excited as something that was injured or still warm or trapped. Blood spattered on leaves along deer trails or where carcasses had been packed toward camp drove them into a frenzy of looking everywhere for whatever there was to find. A third wolf howled. Adam continued another dozen steps, stopped, slowly turned, plodded back to the willow thicket, dragged out the helpless figure, disgustedly threw it over his shoulder and started downstream again.

He kept on until he reached the wider stream and still kept on, wading shoulder deep at times, until he came upon a little island ringed with heaps of driftwood. He staggered to dry ground beyond the driftwood, dumped his burden and dropped to his hands and knees.

Fumbling in the darkness he made certain the thongs at his prisoner's ankles and wrists were tight. They were and, dry-

95

ing, would tighten further. She'd have a none-too-comfortable night. He was glad of that. She was lucky to be getting out of this with no worse than a big scare and a night's discomfort. Her idiocy had cost him his one last chance. It was due to her that he'd had to take so bad a licking, that his beautiful mare was still with the Cherokee, where from now on she'd have to stay, while he was left with nothing to show for all his pains and effort but maybe one chance in three of getting away with his scalp still on. He jerked savagely on the halter rope as he tied the loose end of it to his own wrist. He'd ought to get up and kick her around for a while until she'd worked up a real good scare. But he was too tired. He sagged forward to the ground, pillowing his face in the cool sand, and fell asleep.

EIGHT

AT dawn Adam opened his eyes long enough to take note of his island situation. Impenetrable belts of twenty-foot cane lined the banks on either side. No glimpse could be gained of the island from anywhere beyond the cane. He could be discovered only by pursuers coming down the stream. He felt fairly safe from that. The hunters had no boats and unlike the northern Indians the Cherokee had no talent for impromptu canoe building. He twitched the leather thong to make sure his captive was still fastened to him, turned over and went back to sleep.

Later, when the sun, climbing above the eastern mountains, fell on his face he turned over again. He was stiff and sore and not much less tired than when he had reached the island but he was too restless to sleep longer, though there was little for him to do for the next few hours but to sit and wait. He had already decided on his next moves. The Cherokee search would be pressed hard today and tomorrow, at least, making travel overland a continuing risk. Instead of running that risk he'd build a raft and drift down the stream tonight under cover of darkness. Reaching the Cumberland he'd build a canoe and tomorrow night paddle up the Cumberland to the big bend nearest the headwaters of the Green. Having left no trail behind him, the next day it would be reasonably safe to start across country for the cave and then, if Bert still had not arrived, to keep on to Logan's.

He sat up and looked at his captive. She had withdrawn as

far from him as the thong tied to his wrist would permit, and lay on her side, facing him, her body bent like a bow, her bound hands and feet outthrust toward him. She had managed to work the gag out of her mouth but the other knots had been too much for her. Her eyes were closed, her face impassive and she was breathing quietly as if asleep. It was more likely that she was listening with the greatest anxiety to his first stretches and yawns.

It angered him that she should be so stupid. If she was trembling inside with dread of what he next might do it served her right. She had set out to look like an Indian and to act like one and it was her own fault if she now had to worry about being treated like one. She probably knew that to the average white man on this frontier an Indian was no better than an animal and that the only difference he saw in an Indian woman was that she was a kind of animal that under some circumstances could afford him pleasure. And here she was, bound and helpless and completely at the disposal of a white man who had already set upon her and carried her off without any apparent purpose except ill will. She must think she had something to worry about, all right. She'd have had some slight reason to worry, at that, up to a few months ago. He'd not have taken her by force. But he might very well have whiled away the greater part of a day, during which he had so little else to do, to finding out if anything short of force would bring her around.

He noticed again the slenderness of her arms. They were smooth and rounded, like a child's. Her black lashes were so long that he could not be entirely certain she was not watching him under them, but her eyebrows had been plucked, in keeping with the Indian custom of removing all superfluous hair. This lack of marking to set off the brow and the general regularity of her thin, delicately molded features gave her face an appearance of unformed personality that was also like a child's. Even the profusion of outspread dark hair upon which her head was pillowed, and the bars and dots of ceremonial paint on her face, instead of seeming the badges of womanhood, gave her more the look of a little girl making believe she was a woman. She must be even younger than he had guessed at first, possibly no more than fourteen or fifteen.

Her defenselessness and childlikeness stirred a twinge of pity in him. For all the trouble she had caused him she was white, as white as he was, and no matter how ignorant and schooled to savagery it was a shame to turn her back to live among savages. His own aversion to everything Indian made this seem a special iniquity. It was probably his duty as a

97

white man to take her instead to live among white people. He was going to Logan's. Ann would know how to take her in hand. Ben Logan might be able to locate her kinfolk, if any had survived. But Adam dismissed this notion as soon as it had occurred to him. Taking her with him any farther than he had to would be an impossible drag on him. He already had his fill of duties, including a number to himself.

Her wrists were swollen and raw under the tight knots. He knelt beside her and began loosening them. Her eyes opened. There was no flicker in their calm gaze to indicate what she might be thinking. She merely watched him. He looked at the dried blood on her wrists.

"Your own doing," he told her.

He sat back, coiling the halter rope. She began wriggling her fingers and then her toes to get the stiffness out of them. Then, without the slightest warning, she sprang upon the pile of driftwood and dove into the water. Relieved as he would have been to see the last of her, this was much too early in the day to let her get back to tell the Cherokee where he was. He jumped over the driftwood and plunged into the water after her.

To his great annoyance it turned out that she was the better swimmer. Her head, the dark hair streaming on the water in its wake, coursed up river like an otter. With each stroke he could see he was falling farther behind. The wall of cane prevented his landing to run along the bank. Had his feet not struck a submerged sand bar she would have gotten away. Staggering upright, he threshed through the knee-deep water along the bar until he had drawn abreast of her, where she was swimming in the deeper channel, made a furious lunge and caught her by one ankle. When he had dragged her to the bar she refused to stand up and when he pulled her up she fought him in every way she could, clawing, kicking, biting, until he had to slap her hard a couple of times. She subsided then but he still had to carry her back to the island. He dumped her on the ground and regarded her angrily.

"Try just one more trick," he threatened, "and I'll whale you good and proper."

She seemed not to have heard him. She squeezed some of the water out of her hair and then, shaking it back to dry in the sun, sat impassively, her hands folded in her lap, looking off up the river. The paint on her face had smeared and run. Her stoic Indian composure, her stubborn refusal to give any sign that she realized he was talking to her or even looking at her, the red paint splotched across her expressionless, childish face, all reminded him of her preference for Indians and added to his resentment.

"Wash your face," he directed. "Then maybe you won't look so much like a stinking Cherokee."

He might as well have been addressing one of the logs of driftwood. River water had seeped under this driftwood to form a small pool beside where she was sitting. He seized her by the back of the neck, bent her over the pool and began washing her face. She made no new attempt to pit her strength against his and did not resist, even when he had to use sand, along with the water, to get her face scrubbed clean.

"There," he said, sitting back, "you look a little more like a white girl."

She calmly picked up a handful of mud and daubed it across her face. He was sorry he had started so foolish a game but he was committed to winning it now. He bent her over and washed her face again. Promptly she reached for the mud again and as promptly he reached for the back of her neck. Without looking at him she slowly dropped the handful of mud, rinsed her hand, sat back, again folded her hands in her lap and resumed her gazing up the river. He resumed coiling the halter rope. Apparently he had won another round though not one which gave him much satisfaction.

He continued to eye her. Now that it was clean her face had a certain fineness and nicety of feature. The eyes, the nose, the mouth, each in itself was agreeable enough. It was the absence of any feeling in the face as a whole that was objectionable. That shut-in, senseless Indian look didn't go with a white face.

"Hungry?" he asked. "You must be. You must have that much sense."

She paid no attention. He still might have been addressing one of the logs of driftwood.

"Well, I am," he said. "I'm going to have me a slather of fried fish. You can suit yourself."

He rose, cut a slim willow sapling, came back, sat down and began trimming it to fashion a shaft to which he would tie his knife to form a fish spear. She had not once glanced around to follow any of his movements. Her studied refusal to take the slightest notice of him made him determined to draw some response from her.

"I told you I'd turn you loose," he said. "I still will—when the time comes."

Hardly any subject could be more interesting to her. But she continued to sit with averted face, giving no sign that his words had had the slightest meaning for her. It could be, of course, that she had been a captive since earliest childhood and had no understanding of English. But even a trapped animal would have responded in some fashion to the sound of his voice.

"You're not simple-minded, are you?" he said. "You certainly act like it."

She did not so much as flicker an eyelash at the insult. There was the other chance that there was something wrong with her hearing. Repeated blows on the head, such as captives received while running the gantlet, sometimes had that effect.

"Look out," he cried sharply.

She didn't move. He suddenly whipped his knife into the log back of her shoulder. She was looking away so she could not have seen the movement of his arm as he made the throw. But the thud caused her to turn like a flash. He laughed.

"Anyway, you're not deaf."

He started to get up to recover the knife. The girl snatched the still-quivering blade from the log and sprang at him. He was both off balance and off guard and it was only by the narrowest of margins that he parried the blow which was driving straight at his throat. He twisted the knife out of her grasp and held her off.

She met his accusing stare without hesitation and without remorse. There was expression in her face now. It was easy to read everything she was thinking and feeling. She was glad she had tried to kill him, sorry she had failed, eager to try again if she got a chance.

"Told you I'd whale you," he said.

With the willow shaft he had just cut he began to beat her soundly, as a child is punished by the severe but just schoolmaster. She did not cringe, or cry out or make any attempt to avoid the blows. She stood still and after each deliberate stroke she smiled up at him scornfully.

He threw down the stick in disgust. It was like breaking a colt of tail switching. Beating never did the trick. The best thing to do was to get rid of the colt. He'd be rid of her before the day was out. It was a relief to recall that breaking and training her was not, after all, his responsibility.

He picked up the halter rope, tied one end to her ankle and the other to a young sycamore, splashed water on the knots so that while wet they'd be too slippery to untie and in drying would tighten beyond any possibility of her loosening them, made sure there were no sharp stones around with which she might cut the rawhide and then went about his fish spearing.

He came back with a twenty-pound catfish, carved half a

dozen slices from it, split a piece of dry pine driftwood into slivers, kindled a very small, very hot smokeless fire and broiled the slices on sticks. The first one he offered to her. She paid no attention. He put it down on a piece of bark within her reach. She continued to ignore it though he noticed her nostrils dilating slightly as she caught the smell. He was irritably tempted to force her to eat it but thought better of this project. Instead he sat back and ate fish until his hunger at last was satisfied.

After a glance at the sun to fix the time of day in his mind, he stretched out in the shade of the sycamore and slept three more hours. Awaking, much refreshed, he saw that the girl was chewing at the rawhide thong with great determination and persistence. He grinned. Let her chew. It was tough old elkskin and long before she'd got it bitten in two he'd be turning her loose anyway. He pretended not to notice what she was doing and began casting about for chunks of driftwood of the right size, shape and dryness to build his raft and for grapevine with which to bind it together. She was no longer staring up the river. She was covertly watching his every move.

The fatal flaw in his calculations only then thrust upon him. He had to start building his raft now in order to be prepared to embark with the first moment of darkness. He wasn't sure about the distance to the Cumberland and he'd have to take advantage of every hour of the night. But there she was watching him and she must already have seen enough to guess what he was doing. When she told the Cherokee about his raft they would know the general direction he had taken as well as if they had come upon his trail and, running along the ridges, might well get to the Cumberland before he did. He'd have to keep her with him another twenty-four hours.

She watched all his preparations for the journey with sharp and malicious attention. But by now he had had enough experience with her possibilities to be constantly on guard. He took care that his rifle, tomahawk or knife was never laid down within her reach and that he did not become too preoccupied with his raft building to keep an eye on her. However, she merely sat and watched and waited. When, at nightfall, he was ready to go, and signified that she was to go with him, she showed no new anger or resentment.

He tied to his belt the end of the rawhide that had formerly been attached to the sycamore. She did not hang back. But when the raft was launched and they were starting to float away down the river she stood up suddenly, grasped an overhanging branch and swung her weight from the raft to the tree. The rawhide, tightening against his belt and catching him leaning far over against the pole with which he was guiding the raft, jerked him into the water. The raft bobbed off downstream.

It was at this point that he came nearer to choking her than he had at any time yet. He dragged her ashore and attached the rawhide to a branch high enough so that the ankle to which it was fastened was held off the ground. Leaving her in this awkward position, he swam after the raft.

When, after great exertion, he brought the raft back, he found her lying quite comfortably on her back, waving the free as well as the tethered leg idly in the air. And when again aboard the raft she curled up like a cat and fell peacefully asleep. For him it was a night of unceasing labor—freeing the raft from obstructions, dragging it over sand bars, poling it away from mud banks. But she slept on through it all and thus, when they laid by at dawn, was rested and wakeful when he would sleep.

He had not reached the Cumberland, as he had hoped, but with the first streaks of dawn he poled into the reed-fringed estuary of a side creek where until nightfall he would be sheltered from observation either from the open river or the surrounding hills. He staked the raft against the bank, offered her some of the remaining cold fish, which she ignored, ate all of it himself, took up most of the slack in the rawhide so that she could make no move without his knowing it, disposed his weapons under him so that she could not snatch at them and then prepared to sleep. She remained outwardly as impassive as usual but there was a roving gleam in her eye.

Shielding his face with one arm he watched her through half-closed eyes. She was looking with sober yet alert interest at everything about her. She looked at the alternate bars of light and shadow on the water rippling past the raft, at a school of perch nosing along the shore among the roots of the reeds, at a pair of scarlet tanagers, incredibly brilliant in the sun, hovering momentarily just over her head before flashing away again, and, from time to time, at him, with malicious speculation. Then, suddenly, her attention became fixed on something beyond him. He turned, as if sleepily, and looked also.

Some fifty feet away a belated coon had come down to the water's edge to wash his prey, a captured mouse. Adam edged the tomahawk out from under him with a double purpose. Meat for supper would offer a change from fish, and there was no harm in the girl's witnessing a sample of his marksmanship. The throw was from an awkward position but it was true. The coon keeled backward, kicking, and the surprised mouse paddled thankfully away. Adam twitched the rawhide and gestured to the girl to retrieve his kill. To his astonishment she obeyed. Packing in game was such natural woman's work among the Indians that she probably hadn't stopped to think. He loosened the rawhide from his belt and watched her wading along the bank. The creek was too shallow to swim and if she made a break into the woods that long leash trailing behind her would soon trip her. He half hoped, when she picked up the tomahawk, she would try to throw it at him. He'd have enjoyed proving to her how easily he could catch it. But she waded back with the coon, let go of the weapon when he reached for it, and climbed upon the raft.

He refastened the leash to his belt and settled down again. He had all but dropped off before he noticed with what she was now occupying herself. Dipping her fingers in the gash in the coon's throat and using the water beside the raft as a mirror, she was with great elaboration once more painting her face—this time with warm blood. Wearily Adam rose, took the carcass away from her, bent her over the side and washed her face.

During the process of dousing her, none too gently, head downward into the water, the lacing at the throat of her fawnskin dress parted. When he hauled her upright again the unlaced dress fell apart, exposing one of her breasts. It was small but fully formed and firmly rounded and unmistakably not that of a child's. With guilty haste he jerked the dress back into position.

For the first time he heard her laugh. It was a taunting laugh, chilling in its amused malevolence. Deliberately unlacing the front of her dress she uncovered both breasts.

He realized that from her benighted point of view there was nothing wanton in the gesture. She had been raised among Indians and among Indians nakedness was commonplace. Exposure of her person was no trial to her. It was his guilty start when he had pulled up her dress that had given him away. She had immediately seized upon this as a wonderful new way to offend him, to flaunt her contempt for his authority.

He shrugged and turned away, hoping she'd lose interest in the device when she saw that it held none for him. Instead she began to draw the dress off over her head. Under this single, simple garment it became clear at once she was wearing no other.

"You're not a goddam squaw," yelled Adam. "And while I'm around you'll not act like one."

He grabbed the dress and yanked it down. There ensued an absurd contest. Everything about it was so contrary to all rhyme or reason that it was like a nightmare. He was struggling desperately to keep a woman's clothes on and she just as intently to take them off. Her taunting laughter continued while his swearing became more and more violent.

The thin fawnskin, already torn by travel and softened by water, began to part in widening gaps. Escaping his grasp for a second she was able to rip the dress altogether from her and to cast it into the creek where it floated away.

He was never able afterward to recall whether in that moment she had seemed to him child or woman, as she stood confronting him with her arms flung upward, her eyes glittering like a wild creature's, her laugh gay with malicious triumph. He was so blinded by rage that he could hardly have told whether she was black or white. He whipped off his own buckskin hunting shirt and, overcoming her frenzied resistance, forced her into it. The leather was too strong for her to tear, and to make sure she did not get it off again he kept her pinned down while he lashed several strands of the fringe around the bottom to the tops of her leggings and tied knots in the ends of the sleeves, which were so much longer than her arms, so that she could not get her hands out where she could use them.

He stood back and regarded his handiwork with the first trace of satisfaction he'd been able to feel since she'd first stepped into his view. The effect was almost worth the misery it had cost him. She was as safely out of mischief as if she'd been sewed up in a bag. He should have thought of something like this sooner.

She got up slowly and looked down at herself, plucking helplessly with her imprisoned hands at the heavy folds of leather bunched at neck and knees. When he laughed the venom in the look she gave him was more deadly than when she had come at him with the knife. For a moment she seemed of a mind to attack him, even though she could manage no more than to flail away at him with the stumps of her arms, but by a great effort she regained control, turned her back on him and moved away from him to the extreme edge of the raft. Here she sat down, her knees drawn up under her chin, and hunched herself together inside the shirt, which hung about her like a collapsed tent, as if trying to make herself so small she might avoid any contact with it.

Soothed by the advantage he had at last contrived to gain, Adam stretched out and slept until past noon. He awoke, full of new energy and new ideas. Though he hadn't reached the Cumberland he'd save time by making a canoe this afternoon so that he could start traveling faster tonight. He looked around at the girl. She hadn't moved. He tied the end of the rawhide to a log of the raft and went ashore.

Finding a red elm of the right size he cut a ten-foot strip of bark from it in a single piece. Bending the elm bark into shape he sewed the two ends with withes of linden bark, fitted the hull with struts of cedar and calked the seams with pitch softened on a flat stone beside the fire at which the coon was roasting. Well before nightfall it was finished. It was shaky and not handsome but it was a canoe.

He ate a good portion of the roast coon and wrapped the rest in sycamore leaves for later need. While eating he noticed a young ash well up toward the top of the slope above him. He intended to whittle a paddle from a piece of walnut driftwood he'd spotted on the shore near the raft. But ash made a better paddle and he'd completed the canoe early enough to give him time for the extra labor it would cost him. He trotted up toward the ash.

Reaching it, he dropped to the ground as suddenly as if he'd just seen a Cherokee. It was almost as bad. Along the crest of the ridge, just beyond the ash, ran a well-traveled Indian trail. This must be the new Cherokee trail he'd heard vague talk about. The last year or two they'd taken sometimes to circling west of the Kentucky settlements when journeying to and from the northern Indian towns, instead of always taking the Great War Trail through the eastern mountains. This path must cross the Cumberland about where the stream he was following hit the main river.

He crawled forward to examine the surface. No one had passed over it today or yesterday. But one thing was certain. Before giving up their search the Cherokee hunters would be bound to work the country along this trail as far as the Cumberland. It was a wonder they hadn't already done that. Another thing was almost certain. When he turned the girl loose this evening she'd strike the trail first thing. She probably knew about it and even if she didn't she'd follow it back and meet the searchers in time for them to get north to the Cumberland fast enough to cut him off. The brief satisfaction he'd taken in the shirt and the canoe evaporated. He couldn't let her go yet. He'd have to keep her with him another night— at least until he was around the corner and well up the Cumberland.

He spent half an hour carefully removing every trace of his approach to the trail. There was no use trying to cover up the sign where he'd built the canoe and the fire. If, when they came along, they prowled that far down the slope there'd be no help for it. But unless they came during the remaining hour of daylight they'd not find out he'd taken to a canoe until tomorrow morning and by then he'd have enough of a start on them.

He carried the canoe out and set it in the water alongside the raft. It would be one relief to be able to travel so much faster tonight. The girl hadn't moved. She didn't even look around at the canoe. He untied the sleeves of the shirt so that she could get her hands out and gave her a piece of the roast coon.

"Eat it," he commanded.

She wouldn't touch it. She'd presently starve if she stayed that stubborn. Again he had an angry impulse to force her to eat at least one mouthful. But he didn't have time to fool with her now. He began swiftly shaping a paddle from the piece of walnut while listening for sounds in the direction of the trail. But the peaceful wilderness silence continued while the shadows gathered.

Just at dusk there came one distant signal whistle from somewhere to the east. The girl gave no sign of having heard it. He loosened the end of the rawhide attached to the raft, jerked on it and gestured for her to get into the canoe. She didn't move. He picked her up, plunked her down in the bow, got in himself and pushed off.

The canoe turned out to heel to the left a trifle but he corrected this by shifting his weight. At the mouth of the creek he paused a moment to listen. The slopes behind remained quiet. It was full dark now. He shot out into the main stream. It was an immediate pleasure to feel the smooth swift glide after the sluggish gyrations of the raft last night. There was danger that in going so fast he might in the darkness run into some snag that would rip the whole bottom out. But that was a chance he had to take. He needed to be a long way up the Cumberland before morning.

The girl hadn't made a move since he'd dumped her in the bow. Now, when she did make one, it was a big one. Hoisting her legs suddenly into the air she swung them over the side. The lurching shift in her weight capsized the canoe instantly. By desperate grabs Adam managed to hang onto paddle and rifle as well as the drifting canoe. The girl dove off downstream with the current but was brought up short by the rawhide tied to his belt.

The water was no more than shoulder deep. Adam pushed the canoe ahead of him to a gravel bar and emptied the water out of it. When he pulled in his captive against the current she flopped and struggled like a fish on a hook, and by the time he had landed her he was happy to see that she was choking and gasping and half drowned. This time he stowed her away amidships where she was within his reach.

Afloat again, he leaned forward and gave her a solid whack with the paddle.

"Just one more wrong move," he threatened, "and I'll give you a clout that'll keep you quiet the rest of the night."

He gave her another whack to make sure that even if she didn't understand his words she understood his intentions. Apparently she did. For no one of the deep, long breaths she was taking ended in the defiant yell he half expected.

Leaning back to dip his paddle again he saw that the current was slackening. Around the next bend the expanse of starlit water ahead suddenly widened. They had reached the Cumberland. He'd pulled ashore this morning when he was almost in sight of it. He was getting on, after all, almost as fast as he had hoped. He kept in the shadow of the shore, made the turn, then started up the main river. In turning this corner he was passing the point of greatest danger. Any second might bring the sudden yell, the sudden hiss of arrows or crackle of shots. But nothing happened. He had heard no later signal whistles. On neither bank here at the junction of trail and river was there the gleam of a camp-fire, nor was there in the air the smell of smoke. He deepened and lengthened his stroke. It would be harder going from now on, against the sweep of the river, but at last he was headed for his own country.

He could see the faint gleam of the girl's eyes as she looked up at the stars, the slight cock of her head as she listened to the changed sound of the water beating against the side of the canoe. She was able to tell that he'd turned into the Cumberland and that now instead of traveling northwest he was headed northeast toward Kentucky. To her this was enemy country.

Her foot moved, barely perceptibly. She waited several moments. The toe felt for the side of the canoe. Her whole leg edged sidewise, began to inch upward. Since the rawhide still connected them she could not hope to escape. She only wanted to make more trouble, at whatever cost, out of pure cussedness.

Hardly breaking the rhythm of his stroking he lifted the paddle and brought it down hard across her shin bone. She made no outcry. Her leg dropped limply into the bottom of the canoe. The blow had made an astonishingly sharp crack. Adam took a dozen more strokes while he speculated, uneasily, on the chance he'd broken her leg. He shipped the paddle and bent forward to find out.

There was a dent in her shin which he could feel right through the legging. The flesh on either side was beginning to puff out. But after some vigorous twisting and prodding he decided the bone hadn't been broken. She didn't let out a whimper. He took hold of her and turned her over to lie face down.

"Now you stay that way," he told her.

She didn't stir the rest of the night, though, as usual, he had the feeling that this was merely saving her strength. He kept up a steady pace, not driving too hard. With the coming of daylight he was starting across country and might still have to make a run for it.

The first streak of gray in the east found him still short of the big bend, on a stretch of the Cumberland where the river meandered in long, lazy north-and-south curves so that he was paddling four or five miles to make one. He landed at the northern extremity of the next curve and pulled the canoe up after him.

The girl lay stretched out face down in the bottom of the canoe. She was shivering a little in the morning cold but giving no sign his landing made any difference to her. Huddled in the oversize shirt she looked small and lost and forlorn, in this early gray light, like a wet, stray kitten.

"Get up," he said.

To the last she was ornery. She didn't move. He bent down and turned her over. She looked up at him quite placidly. There was almost the hint of a smile on her lips. The little fool hadn't caught on that here was where he was turning her loose.

"Have it your way," he said.

He tipped the canoe, dumping her out on the ground. She lay where she had fallen. He cut three or four long slits in the bottom of the canoe, put a good-sized stone in bow and stern and shoved it out into the river. It drifted down a ways and sank from sight. She watched with no apparent interest. There was no reason now that whatever she felt should make the slightest difference to him, but this last example of her perversity annoyed him just the same.

"Get up," he insisted.

She didn't move. He took her by the shoulders and jerked her to her feet. When he let go her legs went limp and she slumped to the ground again. He grinned. After all, the joke was on her.

"You sure picked a smart time to play possum," he said. He picked up his rifle. "Hate to leave you that shirt—but suppose I have to."

He backed away a couple of steps and by very emphatic

gestures indicated that he was going his way and that she could go wherever she pleased. She didn't believe him. He walked off a few more steps and repeated his gestures. She still didn't believe him. She thought he was only trying to trick her into getting up. He remembered the remains of the cold roast coon in his game pouch. He walked back, tossed a shoulder to the ground beside her and started off again. This time he kept going until he was out of her sight.

He dropped to the ground then and crawled back to watch her, curious to see how she was going to act when she became convinced he was gone. She'd raised her head but only to listen. She still suspected he was playing some trick on her. Getting up on one elbow she looked toward the river and then in the direction he had gone, as if considering whether or not she could make it to deep water before he could catch her. The roast coon caught her attention. She snatched it up and began to gnaw at it hungrily. She ought to be hungry—she hadn't eaten for three days. After three or four mouthfuls the greasy meat made her sick. Adam chuckled. This alone was worth coming back to see.

She threw the meat aside, worked her feet under her and stood up unsteadily. Then she got herself together and set off along the boulder-strewn riverbank, wobbling and stumbling and limping decidedly on the leg he'd hit with the paddle. It was full daylight now. With the baggy, over-size shirt flopping around her she cut a sad and grotesque little figure against the broad sweep of the river.

The chuckle died in his throat. He was heartily sorry he'd lingered to watch. There was more to this than just turning her loose. She had no way to hunt, no way to make a fire. At this time of year the woods offered little to eat in the way of berries or nuts. She'd probably get a lot hungrier than she was now. And she had a long way to go—if she ever got there. Being an Indian of a sort she'd probably make it. But he'd have to go on wondering whether or not she ever did. And while he wondered he'd have to go on remembering that he'd not only sent a white woman back to live among the Indians but had left her to shift for herself in the middle of the wilderness—after he'd starved her for three days—and lamed her besides. He strode out into the open.

"Come back here," he called.

She didn't look around at the sound of his voice. She moved over to a patch of grass and deliberately lay down. Now that business could start again. More angry with himself than with her he walked over to her.

"Get up," he commanded.

She just looked at him. He may have weakened but she hadn't. He gave her a crack across the thighs with the handle of his tomahawk. By the cold glitter in her eyes he saw that it would make no difference to her which end of the tomahawk he hit her with.

"If I've made up my mind you're going with me," he said, "by God you're going with me."

He sat down with his back to her, drew her legs around his waist, tied the ankles together in front of him, caught her arms, drew them over his shoulders, pulled the long shirt sleeves tight, crossed them and tied the ends to his belt. She was fixed to his back now, like a pack. His arms were free while her hands were encased in the leather sleeves so that she couldn't scratch, or poke at his eyes or snatch at his weapons. He got to his feet, tugged her weight into the best carrying position, bent, picked up his rifle and set out.

He was so mad the first hour or two that he didn't notice the burden, but she got heavier as the day wore on. There wasn't much she could do but what she did was the worst she could have contrived. She just slumped down inside the shirt so that she became an inert, dead weight on his back. And surely, he reflected angrily, no man even packed a more unwanted, unwelcome, unprofitable dead weight a whole day through any woods, any time, anywhere.

He doubted the Cherokee search for his trail would range north of the Cumberland. Nevertheless until past noon he took the trouble at every opportunity to take to stony ground or to creek beds and did whatever else he could to make his sign harder to follow. After that he was confident he was safe, except from some such accidental encounter as had cost him Oriole. He swore every time he thought of the mare. A wonderful botch he'd made of recovering her. Instead of riding her back, he was coming back, himself a pack horse.

Through the late afternoon he shot an occasional squirrel. By the time he got in he'd need plenty to eat if he wasn't too tired to swallow. Paddling all night against the current and then packing a hundred pounds all day over hills was more at one stretch than any man should be made to endure. He'd not have had the strength to keep going the last hour if he hadn't been so anxious to discover if Bert had come. He was barely able to keep his footing as he plodded, finally, down his own stream.

The meadow came in sight. He saw at a glance Bert's horses were not there. He staggered on until he reached the door and got it open. No one had been here since he'd left.

Oppressed by this final disappointment he dropped to his knees, untied the girl's ankles, freed the sleeves from his belt and dumped her off over his head into the doorway. Turning his back on her he began disgustedly examining his feet. His moccasins had not lasted through the late afternoon and his feet were raw and blistered.

A rustle in the cave caused him to look around. The girl had gotten up. She was still weak but her eyes were curiously bright and interested and she was looking around at the cave with quick, intent glances. She came to the doorway and looked out at the untrampled meadow, the stream and the wall of cane beyond it, noting all these signs of his dwelling's isolation.

Then for the first time she addressed him—not in words but with vivid, questioning gestures. He lived here? He lived here alone? No one else lived near? There was no town? He nodded, watching her. She looked again at the lonely wilderness without, then back at the no-less-lonely cave and drew a long breath of unmistakable relief. He was mystified until he remembered that she counted herself an Indian. An Indian, when captured, expected his enemies to make a show of him and stubbornly set himself to make it as poor a show as possible. She was relieved to find this cave her destination. Her special dread had been of the public indignities she had anticipated upon her arrival in a white settlement.

"Don't grin too soon," he said darkly. "Like it or not, tomorrow I'm taking you on to a town where you'll have to start behaving like a decent white woman."

He got up and hobbled into the cave. She retreated before him and sat down on the floor with her back against the wall, watching his every move. He scooped a handful of bear's grease out of a bladderful he had laid away, rubbed it into his feet and got out a fresh pair of moccasins. There seemed barely enough strength left in him to draw on the moccasins and he wanted nothing except to throw himself down on his delightful-smelling cedar bough bed and sleep until he was slept out. But he knew he'd be in better shape tomorrow if he took something to eat first.

Moving stiffly and painfully, but with slow determination, he started a fire, got a bucket of water from the stream, set the brass kettle over the fire, went out again to skin and clean the squirrels, brought them back, dropped them in the pot and threw in a little salt.

"This is all work you could just as well be doing," he reminded his captive, "if you only had the sense."

She listened, now, when he spoke to her, as if she at

111

least wanted to understand. Her eyes followed everything he did, shifting only when he looked directly at her or when she studied, momentarily, some object among his belongings that caught her attention, such as the ax or the brass kettle. Her gaze lingered longest on a deerskin hanging on the wall. He'd dressed it with care last winter with some thought of making a spare shirt. Noticing her thoughtful look it occurred to him that wasn't such a bad idea. He took down the skin, found his awl and ball of waxed thread, took out his knife and dropped the lot in her lap.

"My shirt fits me better than it does you," he said. "Make yourself one of your own—that is, if you know how."

She caught on instantly and she seemed to know how well enough. She was particularly pleased by the chance to return his shirt to him. She would have stripped it off that very minute if he hadn't hastily prevented her. She promptly fell to work on the substitute.

He sat down on the other side of the fire, dozing and nodding uncomfortably until the smell of the squirrel stew told him it was ready to eat. Ladling out a cup of the liquid he gave it to her with instructions to sip it slowly unless she wanted to be sick again. His graphic pantomine referring to her early morning disaster on the riverbank brought a brief flash of fire into her eyes, but she relaxed and began to sip with a resignation that soon turned to increasing interest. He had no such need of babying his hunger and wolfed down three of the squirrels without stopping.

The food revived him somewhat, bringing him a little way out of the stupor of exhaustion. But this allowed him to start thinking and everything he had to think about was more painful than his fatigue. He could hear the stream in the cavern. His fires down there had been cold for nearly a week and would stay cold for another week, if not longer, while he rushed off to Logan's to try to find out about Bert. Having been forced to waste the winter he was now being forced to waste the spring. And after all his other bad luck there was this girl on his hands. That was the last straw. That was really too much.

He fished out another squirrel and began to eat it. He wasn't as hungry as at first. Anyway, he'd always liked squirrel roasted better than boiled. He'd only stewed these so that the girl could have the soup. At every turn she was a nuisance.

Now that his belly was full he was getting good and sleepy. But before he could go to bed he had to get up and fasten the door and gather up his weapons and even take that knife and awl away from her. That would likely bring a loud squawk out of her. She was busy with them, cutting and sewing the deerskin.

Suddenly there flashed across his sleepy mind a wonderfully cunning scheme. Why fasten the door? Suppose she did escape? He'd be rid of her. The thing to do was to appear to doze off here by the fire. She'd be sure to take advantage of that. He looked over at her. She was busy with awl and thread and deerskin but watching him, all the same, under her lashes. The moment she saw him drop off she'd make for the door. All he'd have to do about it was to try not to laugh too soon.

He picked up the squirrel, nibbled at it and then let the hands holding it drop into his lap. He let his head nod forward a couple of times, started, blinked, nodded again and then tried a small snore. He could tell how closely she was watching him. This was going to work out just like he'd known it would. Only one thing went wrong. In pretending to sleep he fell sound asleep—and slept on like a dead man.

NINE

THE familiar dream of Cynthia was with him again, though this time it was not quite the same and the difference was an improvement. She was far away, but journeying toward him—a tremendous journey over mountains and through forests—her purpose to join him clear and steadfast. Then, suddenly, she was very near and he was going toward her. She was standing on a hilltop and, as at the spring among the rhododendron, her eyes were golden in the sunlight and her mouth bright against her white skin. A brazen gust of wind was ruffling her smooth, sleek hair and pressing the folds of the blue dress against her. Behind her stretched the green slopes and meadows of the valley of Trace Creek. The pleasant splash of water pouring over the limestone ledges, however, was no longer the sound of Trace Creek but of his own stream in the cavern. He was heaping wood on his fires and he was on fire, too, with the feeling that he was accomplishing all and more than he had set out to do. Cynthia was still near. She was not actually helping him but she was at his elbow, watching him and smiling at him as he worked. Through this pleasant pattern there ran another thread of lesser but quite definite satisfaction, the reason for which he could not place.

He awoke with a start. The splash of the stream in the cavern continued as in the dream. He was sprawled beside the fire pit, very cramped and sore from yesterday's exertions and from lying so long on the hard-packed earth. There was a ridge across his ribs where he'd rested, as he slept, upon the end of a stick of firewood, that felt as if he'd been belted with a pickax handle. The sense of Cynthia's presence slipped away from him. But the other, lesser, thread of satisfaction persisted. Almost at once he was able to account for it. The door was wide open and the morning sun was in the doorway. The captive girl was gone. He'd slept the whole night and by now she was many miles away.

He got hastily to his knees and began to look, with instant sheepish concern, to see what she'd taken with her. After sleeping his head off the way he had it was no more than he deserved if she'd stripped him clean of everything he owned. He'd probably been lucky that she hadn't cut his throat besides. His first look was for his rifle and to his enormous relief he saw it leaning against the wall where he had left it. As long as she hadn't taken that, whatever else she'd taken was worth it. But as he continued to look around he saw knife, awl, ax, powder horn, tomahawk, flint and steel, all still in sight. The moment he fell asleep she must have jumped and run like a scared cat. But his shirt, he realized suddenly, was draped about his shoulders. Before doing any jumping and running she must have paused to get it off and to drop it over him as he slept. That didn't go too well with the scared cat picture. The deerskin, too, was gone, except for a neat ball of leftover trimmings, suggesting she'd waited until she'd got the garment finished. Continuing to look around he finally spotted one thing that was missing. His thin-bladed skinning knife was no longer stuck in the wall beside the door. He could hardly begrudge her a knife. Anyway, she was gone.

He sank back on his haunches. Already the single thread of satisfaction was beginning to fray. It was a blessing that she was off his hands but there were no other blessings for him to count. There was nothing else with which he could be satisfied. His mare was still gone. Bert was God knew where. His fires were still out and would have to stay out. First off he had to go to Logan's to see what he could learn. After all the time he had lost he had to lose more. He got stiffly to his feet. From head to toe his skin was caked with dust and dried sweat, his week's bristle of beard was crusted with mud and cold squirrel grease, he smelled like a wigwam in midwinter. Probably if he took himself down to the stream and cleaned up a little he'd feel more like facing what he had to do. He stalked gloomily to the doorway and as he reached it even the one thin thread of satisfaction snapped.

The girl was coming across the meadow toward the cave, carrying a bundle of dry sticks for the fire and a string of a dozen trout. The deerskin had become a sleeveless dress, neatly sheathing her slender figure from neck to knees. She must have bathed while she'd fished, for her hair, now in two long tight braids, was damp and her skin fresh and glowing. She did not look up at him as she glided past, calm, expressionless, apparently unaware of his existence. She went on into the cave, replaced the knife she'd used to clean the fish, dropped her load of wood, laid the trout on one of the flat stones beside the fire pit and stirred coals from the ashes into a blaze. Her movements were brisk, deft, businesslike.

"What in God's name changed your mind?" he demanded. "If you've got a mind."

She looked at him when he spoke, watching his lips until he had finished and then watching his hands, waiting for him to make some gesture to indicate his meaning. In her attitude there was no sudden new anxiety to please him, merely a readiness to consider his views if he could make them clear. When he continued only to glower at her she returned her attention to the fire and the trout.

He strode down past the horse pen to the next pool below the one at the foot of the meadow and began stripping off his leather pants, leggings and moccasins, puzzling angrily over what, conceivably, could have prompted her to stay. He'd have to take her with him to Logan's—there was no getting away from that. Traveling alone he could have made it in a day by driving himself hard. Now it would cost him an extra day. He plunged into the stream. There was no solace even in the cleansing tingle of the cold water beating against him. Refreshed, he merely thought that much more clearly and the more clearly he considered his situation the more unsatisfactory it became. He squatted at the water's edge to dry in the sun while he shaved. After all, the girl was only one small item among many. And when he got right down to it he didn't even know what to fret about the most. He hadn't the faintest idea how much things had changed while he'd been holed up here by himself. Anything could have happened since last fall.

There was the war, for one thing. All Kentucky could have been taken, for all he knew. Or the terrible winter could have made more difference than any number of Indian attacks. A country that could get so cold that trees

115

split and rivers iced solid and animals froze in their tracks was no land of promise. The Wyeths, or anybody else still in Virginia, could have given up any further thought of moving to Kentucky. Even the people already in Kentucky could have decided such a winter piled on top of all their other miseries was too much. In the summer of '77 there had been a lot of talk about giving up the settlements until the war was over. Now, after two more years of trouble, they could have done it. He might find nobody at Logan's when he did get there.

The bushes parted behind him and the girl stepped swiftly and noiselessly to his side. He leaped up angrily, grabbing for his pants. But she was paying little enough attention to his nakedness. She had her finger to her lips and she was looking over her shoulder upstream. His rifle was in her hands and she was shoving it at him. He took it and listened, too.

There was the faint splashing and muffled tread of a number of horses coming down the stream bed. It was hard for him to keep his mind on the possible nature of the approaching threat because he was so confused by the girl's running to warn and to arm him. Then he heard the ring of an iron-shod hoof against a rock. That meant white men's horses. It could still be Indians with horses they'd stolen. But it could also be Bert. He whistled the call of a quail, breaking it in the middle of the second phrase: "Bob white—bob." Immediately there came a cheery response, the call broken on the first note: "White—bob white." It was Bert, all right.

Adam transferred the rifle to the hand that was clutching his pants against him and gave the girl a pat on the shoulder. "It's a friend of mine," he said. "But thanks for fetching the rifle. That was the right spirit, I do have to admit."

The girl showed no response to this overture. Her face had taken on the closed-up Indian look the instant the two quail calls had told her that whoever was coming was someone Adam knew and expected. She started back to the cave. Adam jerked on his clothes and ran to the shelving rock at the foot of the meadow.

Bert came into sight, riding his lead horse, his three other pack horses stringing along behind. Right away Adam could see the horses were fat. They'd had a good long rest since coming over the mountains. Whatever he'd been doing Bert hadn't boiled over trying to get here on time. He tried to hang onto his anger. Bert's being late had lost him Oriole and gotten him tangled up with the girl. Some of his worst troubles had been brought on by Bert's failing to get here when he was supposed to. But his anger started to get away

116

from him as soon as he got a nearer glimpse of Bert's beaming grin. He had to be glad that Bert was still alive. He sat down on the rock and tried to hide how glad he really was. The very sight of Bert was a reminder that the world was taking a turn back to normal, back to a state in which things happened the way they were supposed to happen.

Bert dismounted and turned his horses loose to graze in the meadow. Some of Adam's doubts began flocking back. When you took a good look at him, Bert didn't look so normal, at that. Instead of buckskins he wore an old broadcloth waistcoat and a blue linsey shirt and woolen pants and cowhide boots and a wide-brimmed felt hat. His hair had 'grown long and was tied at the back of his neck with a twist of black ribbon. Even his face was different. He grinned a lot, just as he always had, but there wasn't that worried look back of his grin. He looked as comfortable with himself as if he'd just picked up a good horse for a quarter of what it was worth. After kneeling on the bank to take himself a drink of water he came over and settled down on the rock beside Adam.

"Reckon you'd about give me up," he said.

Adam grunted, eying Bert grimly. He didn't look guilty about being so late. He didn't even look uneasy. Adam was getting mad again. Bert took off his hat and turned his face up to the sun.

"Fine mornin'," he said, as offhandedly as if this were just any morning. "Seems like this spring a man can't git him too much sun."

He replaced his hat, got out his tobacco pouch and offered it to Adam. Adam shook his head. Bert began filling his pipe. Adam noticed the waistcoat, though threadbare and made for a man quite a bit thinner than Bert, was very clean. It still had every button and was neatly patched where it was most worn. Bert himself was as sleek and well fed as his horses. Wherever he had stopped to rest them Bert had found pretty good care, too. Adam waited for his excuses.

"Knew you'd fret some," said Bert, with another good-humored grin. "But I got myself what you could might call tied up." He laughed as if there were something unusually funny about the way this had come about.

"I might call it worse than that," said Adam. "I suppose you got yourself tied up so tight it took you a full month to get yourself untied." He glanced across at the well-conditioned horses. "Or maybe the winter was so bad it stove up your horses so's you couldn't get them over the mountains."

"Sure was a bad winter, wasn't it?" said Bert. "But not bad enough to keep nobody, afoot or horseback, from comin' over the mountains. Soon's the winter was over folks stopped carryin' on about it and started sayin' there'd never be another one like it. You never seen nothin' to beat the way people are a-comin' to Kentucky. More this spring than all the years before this put together. Wilderness Road's been a-crawlin' with 'em from one end to t'other. And day I left I heard three hundred boats got to Louisville just since the ice went out of the river."

"And it was packing 'em all in," said Adam, "that got you a month behind time."

"No—that wasn't what made me late." Bert laughed again but the fingers with which he was fussing with flint and steel and tow to get his pipe lit were all thumbs and he wouldn't look up to meet Adam's stare. "But they been a-comin' just the same. New settlements jumpin' up everywhere. There's even a new one they call Nashboro down on the Cumberland. And right in your own back yard Sam Glover's uncle's buildin' a station on the Green not twenty miles west of where we're a-settin'. Keeps on, land out here's goin' to be worth more'n what it is in Virginia."

"Anyway, makes you quite a story," said Adam.

"You ain't heard more'n the start of it yet," said Bert. "Lot been goin' on while you been stuck back here in the bushes. Can't hardly blame you for bein' a little slow to git it through your head. What got everybody so stirred up all of a sudden was the way the war's goin'. That's been mighty good. First, Clark knockin' down Kaskaskia and Vincennes and sendin' Hamilton all the way to Richmond so's folks all along the road could see the English governor that was beat. Then Bowman and Logan burnin' the Shawnee towns. Next, Washington he give General Sullivan near half the regular army and Sullivan he beat Brant and Butler and burned out the whole Seneca country most to Niagara. At the same time Brodhead took out from Pittsburgh and cleaned out the Mingo towns on the Allegheny. Between them they chased the Iroquois all the way to Canada. Before that Spain declared war on England and the Spaniards they've took Natchez and Mobile. We just about got this war won. On top of all that the Virginia Assembly sent land commissioners to Kentucky to prove up on land title and that made folks begin to figger that if they wanted Kentucky land they better crack along out here and git it before it was all gone."

"That all sounds fine," said Adam. "Now what's the bad news you're keeping back."

"I ain't keepin' none back," said Bert. But he still hadn't got his pipe lit. "We got the sawmill set up and been a-sawin' planks for near a month and a half. Stockade's finished. Most

118

of the houses more'n half up. Joel and Blake and Paul—they're goin' to be a couple of months late but that's only because they're bringin' their families out this year 'stead of waitin' 'til next."

Adam drew a slow, long breath. "So you weren't really hung up on anything. You just didn't see any hurry. Well, that's a good thing—since it'll be a month before we can get started back."

"A month?" Bert jumped up as if he'd been stung. "A month? Me—I got to get started right now."

Adam shook his head. "Be another month before I'll have a full load."

"What you been doin' all this time?" Bert demanded.

"A good piece of it I spent waiting for it to thaw so's I'd have water. Some more I spent chasing the Cherokee that took my mare while I was out looking for you."

Even then Bert didn't seem taken aback by the fact that it was mainly his fault the mare had been lost. "Tell you what I'll do," he said. "I'll leave the horses with you. Then you can pack out whenever you're a mind to. But me, I got to git me back."

"What for?"

Bert took off his hat and mopped his brow. "I sure do hate to hear that about your mare," he said. "The kind of people that are beginnin' to come to Kentucky this year I could likely of got you five hundred dollars for her. But there's one thing that might make up for it. Last fall when Colonel Rogers was comin' up the Ohio with five boatloads of army supplies from New Orleans he got picked off by Simon Girty and Matthew Elliott. Won't be much gunpowder in Kentucky this summer except for what folks make for themselves. My guess is you'll find saltpeter worth more'n it's ever been before."

"Why do you have to get back in such a hell-fired hurry?" persisted Adam.

"'Cause I said I would," said Bert, suddenly defiant. "That's why. 'Cause if I don't, Alice she'll—" He broke off, startled to realize he had spoken the name aloud.

"Alice?"

"If it'll save you badgerin' me longer," said Bert, "I'll tell you how it was. She's Jim Menifee's daughter. She come along with him when I packed his sawmill gear over the mountains." Bert was really sweating now. "Just this side of Flat Lick we was snowbound for the best part of a month and her and me we kind of got acquainted. Anyway, this spring when I got ready to come to git you she got to worryin' about somethin' happenin' to me. Jim—he felt the same way."

119

"I have to admit," said Adam, "that's a better excuse than I thought you'd have. Can hardly blame a man for feeling like staying home the first month he's married."

"Married? Who said anything about that? I ain't said I was—yet."

"You don't have to take it so hard. You're not the first man that's been collared by a girl's father."

"It wasn't that way a-tall," protested Bert. "It wasn't his idea—it was her'n. I mean it was mine—mostly."

"How do you like it?"

Bert sat down on the rock again, with a sigh of relief. "I like it fine," he confessed. "Another thing that's good about it. Alice she's knowed your gal since they both was little. You and me bein' friends like we are—that's goin' to make everything work out just right." He suddenly grabbed at his waistcoat and began to fumble at an inside pocket. "Talkin' about your gal just put me in mind of something I'd most forgot. She wrote you a letter."

"Well," said Adam, "can't you even remember where you put it?" He caught the folded square of paper, heavy with sealing wax, as Bert tossed it to him. "When'd it come?"

" 'Bout a month ago—last time we heard from Joel. It was brung by Joel's overseer Jesse Baker, when he come out this spring, along with his three sons and their families and a dozen Wyeth niggers to git the corn planted."

The paper was wrinkled and smudged from the long journey in various pockets and wallets and game pouches but there was the name—Adam Frane, Esquire—in writing that was clear and round and definite. Adam could see her strong, slender fingers tracing the characters, her head bent, her eyes intent on what she was writing. She must have written it while his cavern stream was still frozen, during the worst of his despondency. He broke the seal and read:

DEAR ADAM:

Joel, Paul and Blake are back, safe and well, for which I am most grateful. Their enthusiasm for Kentucky is boundless and to this, I fear, I must become reconciled. I do hope that you, too, will keep yourself safe and well until we meet again.

CYNTHIA

She'd come to the point as directly as had her brothers when they'd proposed he take a share in their land company. Taking the trouble to send to him at this great distance her admission that she was no longer opposed to the Kentucky venture was the same as admitting nothing longer stood between them. If Bert hadn't been sitting there, owl eyed, trying to catch his every flicker of expression, he'd have jumped up, whooped and fired his rifle in the air. He started reading Cynthia's letter again.

Bert gave a sudden start that caused Adam to look up. The captive girl was coming out of the cave, carrying a bark tray heaped with broiled trout. With modest, downcast eyes and maintaining her most stonelike calm she came up to them, bent and placed the tray of fish on the rock between them. She straightened, without glancing at either, and waited as if for some sign from her lord and master. She was the very model of Indian female subservience. Bert stared at her, open-mouthed.

"Gawdamighty," he stammered.

She gave him a look so cold, so hostile that he clapped his hand over his mouth.

" 'Scuse me, ma'am," he muttered hastily.

"You don't have to worry," said Adam. "She doesn't know a word of English."

He gestured for her to go back to the cave. She retreated obediently. Bert couldn't take his eyes off her. He watched until she had disappeared through the doorway.

"Gawdamighty," he repeated. He stared at Adam, blinking. "You take all there is—and then twicet that much more. Way out here in the woods—forty-eight and a half miles from nowhere—and still you find yourself a place in a kitchen just like you was in the middle of the settlements—with a gal to feed you and look after you—and not just anything in skirts but as smooth and sweet a young piece as a man could pick between Bluegrass and Tidewater."

"She was a Cherokee captive," said Adam. "I ran across her when I was trying to get my mare back. She's white but she's been with them so long she's wild—almost the same as an Indian."

"She might be a little wild but she don't look so Indian to me," said Bert.

"I was going to take her to Logan's today," said Adam. "But long's you're going right back you can take her."

Bert's broad grin couldn't have gone any faster if an arrow had nicked the end of his nose. "Me?" he cried. "Me—a man that's just married—come out of the woods with a young wild girl in tow? The story'd be all over Kentucky in a month. Alice is real easy to git along with but she wouldn't be after that. Oh—no. Not me." He picked up a trout and began eating it nervously.

121

"How about me?" said Adam. "Expect me to go on living with her in a cave? That'd make quite a story, too."

"You're not married—yet," said Bert. "And anyway you're already living with her here in a cave. You're already stuck with the story. Long's you've got to spend another month here you might as well make the best of it and git what good out of her you can."

"I've never touched her," said Adam. He glared at Bert until Bert stopping grinning.

"Sure—I believe you," said Bert. "Just like everybody in Kentucky will believe you once you catch 'em and make 'em stand still and listen while you tell 'em."

"It's the truth," said Adam bitterly. "You don't know her. She's not actually as grown up as she looks. She's hardly a woman at all. She's mean like only a young boy can be mean. She's really wild."

"You tryin' to tell me you can't handle her?" scoffed Bert.

"No," said Adam. "I'm trying to tell you she's"—he hesitated and then came out with the word—"innocent."

When Bert saw that Adam was in earnest he started grinning again. "Innocent, you say? She growed up among Indians and you say she's innocent?"

"I said it and I meant it," said Adam. "That's one of the things you can't fool me about."

Bert wagged his head sorrowfully. "Winterin' alone surely must of softened you up." He leaned toward Adam, speaking with the sober concern of a father enlightening a troubled son. "There's one thing a man has to remember, my boy. Soon's you git around enough you begin to learn it. That's that—underneath—when you git to know 'em—women ain't no different from men. They wants what they want just as much as a man does—sometimes a little bit more." He nodded toward the cave. "She's probably been laughin' at you for bein' so backward. Unless she's made up her mind there's something wrong with you." When he saw he was making no impression on Adam he stood up and wiped his fingers on his pants. "Just give me five minutes and I'll prove to you how innocent she is."

He started for the cave doorway. Adam watched him, marveling. A month snowbound and another month of marriage had certainly made a new man of him.

Bert disappeared through the doorway. It didn't take him five minutes to prove the issue. In something less than five seconds he bolted out again. The girl appeared briefly in the doorway, the knife flashing in her hand.

Bert slowed to a walk as he neared the rock. He wet his

122

lips. "She sure is wild, all right." He picked up his rifle and game sack. "Well, I got to git me started back."

"Tell them at Trace Creek I'll be there in a month."

Bert nodded. "But I won't tell nobody nothin' about your wild girl." He looked at Adam solemnly. "You want my advice?"

"What's your advice?"

"If I was you—I'd give her back to the Indians—quick."

Adam watched Bert splash up the creek and out of sight. The girl came out, looked vindictively to make sure Bert had gone, picked up the bark tray, rinsed it in the stream and returned to the cave.

One thing was certain, Adam decided. Bert was right about the amount of talk that would follow his appearance at Logan's with the captive girl. If she was able to talk or was homely or older or even had better manners it wouldn't be so bad. It was her being so young and ignorant and savage that would make it such a good story. There was no telling how Cynthia would take it when she heard about it. She might try to understand. She was levelheaded and a widow and far less foolish than most women. Still she certainly wouldn't like it.

Bert was right about another thing. He was already stuck with whatever name they'd give him for it—whether he took the girl to Logan's tomorrow or a month from tomorrow. He'd better settle down and get his work done first. Then when he took her out to leave her with Ann he could keep right on going to Trace Creek ahead of any story. Besides, there was always the chance that during the month she might decide to run away or that something might happen to get him rid of her.

Two young buffalo cows, browsing among the patches of feathery new green which had sprouted around the gaunt brown stalks of the winter-killed old cane, pushed, with a sharp crackling of the great dry stems, almost to the bank of the stream. Adam picked up his rifle. Meat that he needed for the next month's supply was walking right up to him.

The first cow dropped with the crack of the rifle. While he reloaded, the other sniffed curiously at her fallen companion and then swung suddenly to trot away. He shot hurriedly, hitting her a little too far back of the shoulder, and then, disgustedly, had to trail her a couple of miles before she finally fell.

He came back to get one of the pack horses to find that the girl had the first cow skinned and was well along with the butchering. She was working as hard and knowingly as

123

any squaw but she didn't look up or give any sign that she expected or wanted his approval. She seemed rather to regard this as a task which was natural for her to undertake. Nevertheless, he did heartily approve of her industry and before going after the second carcass he cut saplings to make a drying rack.

When he returned with the meat-laden pack horse she had the drying rack set up and a fire already going under it. However, instead of erecting it outside the door in the meadow she had it stretched down the middle of the cave, leaving them hardly room to get around and filling the place with smoke. He remonstrated. She went to the door and pointed at the sky. Clouds were gathering. Rain, if it came, would have spoiled the half-smoked meat had the rack been outside.

She started in on the second load of meat and he fell to beside her, cutting wide, flat strips and spreading them on the rack to smoke. She worked swiftly, without hesitation and with no waste motion. She'd turned out all of a sudden to be quite a help. She'd been working for him since she'd started the day by catching and cooking his breakfast.

"Look here," he said. "No use our acting more simple-minded than we have to." He indicated himself, "Adam," he said.

"Adam," she repeated.

He pointed at her.

"Ayunita," she said.

"How about just Nita?"

She nodded and went on with her work.

"Now that we got us a start," he said, "might as well keep at it." He held up his knife and named it.

"Knife," she repeated.

They worked on, while from time to time he named other articles. She was interested but kept busy, glancing up only when he indicated some new object. Her voice was low and clear and on the whole she seemed to take readily to the English words, except for some difficulty with "kettle" and with several of the r sounds, as in "shirt."

The smoke thickened in the cave until he tried closing the door. After that it curled slowly upward to escape through some hidden crevice in the irregularly vaulted ceiling toward which it was carried by the summer outgoing current of air from the main cavern. The rain came in late afternoon and developed into a continuing downpour.

Adam set the hump and ribs of the fatter cow to broiling beside the cooking fire. By the time their work at the drying rack at last was finished these portions, browned and sizzling, were ready. They sat at the fire and began to eat. Nita held back, waiting for him to exercise a man's privilege to eat first. He was annoyed by this example of Cherokee manners.

"Sit down," he ordered impatiently.

He cut a smoking slice and shoved it at her before taking any himself. She gorged like an Indian, tearing at the rich meat with her sharp, white teeth, gulping, then reaching for more. They ate steadily, silently, until they could swallow no more.

Adam went to the water bucket and washed the grease from his hands and mouth. When he had finished she did likewise. He got his pipe and returned to the fire. She also came back and sat down. Since Bert had left they'd been busy every minute. Compared to their former silent animosity the exchange of a few spoken words had been a kind of relief. Even eating together, both of them tired and hungry and able to feel they'd earned their supper, had been oddly companionable.

"Pipe," he said, holding it up.

"Pipe," she repeated, with something less than her earlier interest in his announcement of English words.

She sat looking into the coals with a composed, almost contented, expression on her face. Seldom, even during the language exercises, had she looked directly at him. She did not now. Her hands folded in her lap, continuing to stare into the fire, she seemed to be waiting.

He got up uneasily and went to the door. It was dark and raining harder than ever. Without having given the matter much thought he had anticipated sleeping outside. But it was nonsense to go out in this rain. He'd put the pack horses in the horse pen so he couldn't sleep in the shed. Anyway, it was foolish to let her run him out of his own cave.

He crossed to his bed, gathered up an armful of cedar boughs, carried them over and dropped them against the wall on the opposite side of the drying rack. Over them he spread one of the blankets. She was still staring into the fire. He walked to the door and drew the heavy oaken bar into place to lock it for the night and then came back to the fire. She didn't move or look up.

"Me—I'm going to turn in," he announced, unnecessarily, it seemed, as soon as he had said it.

She still did not move or look up. She sat there, as quiet and still and yet as pliable as a doll. She was leaving every move to him. Where before she had opposed him in everything now she was opposing him in nothing. She wouldn't even go to bed without his telling her to go.

"Stay up if you want to," he said, resentfully.

He went over and sat down on his blanket, loosened his

belt, arranged rifle, powder horn, shot pouch and tomahawk within immediate reach, took priming horn, flint and steel and whetstone out of his hunting shirt pocket so that he would not roll on them in the night and then stretched out with a long and elaborate yawn. She continued to stare into the fire with that odd air of waiting that was becoming each moment more disturbing.

The air was pleasantly heavy with the oily, rich smell of the smoking meat, the sweetness of the burned fat that had dripped from the roast, the tang of charring wood. Rain beat against the door but within there was the complete stillness, the utter shut in feeling, of the great cavern. They were surrounded and enclosed by a mountain. Two people could not be more alone.

"Go to bed," he commanded.

She turned then to look at him, gravely, questioningly, ready to obey his wish, whatever it was, once she was certain it was clear to her. There was no mistaking her attitude now. Something had turned entirely around in that strange, contrary mind of hers. All day she had worked for him like an Indian wife. Now that night had come she was still prepared for her duty.

"Bed," he commanded again.

"Bed," she repeated, as in the earlier language lesson. Then her eyes lighted up. "Bed," she said again, for the first time bringing out a word as if it were her own instead of an imitation of one of his. Suddenly, in a clear, childish voice, she added: "Go to bed—you sleepy head."

Adam raised on one elbow and stared at her. "You remembered that," he accused her. "I didn't say it—you remembered it. And it was English."

Already the light had gone out of her face. She shook her head vaguely. She looked almost frightened. But Adam was excited and more than ever disturbed. He'd known she was white. Now he knew that she had dim memories of a childhood in some English family. No matter how she acted she was not a savage.

He got up. "No time now to worry you about what else you might remember," he said. He didn't want to learn more about her now. Anything that served to make him more aware of her as a person and, more than that, a person of his own kind, could only add to his disquiet. He took her by wrist and led her to her couch.

"There's your place," he said.

She looked up at him comprehendingly. She didn't seem insulted or disappointed or relieved but merely acquiescent.

Adam went back to his own pallet. He found himself

breathing hard. He could hear the faint rustle as she composed herself. This was never going to work, he decided. Not for a whole month. He'd have to take her to Logan's after all.

He got up and went to the door. The rain had stopped. Light from a late moon was cold and wan on tumbled masses of slowly drifting clouds. Everything was moving slowly for him. No matter how hard he pushed, the trip to Logan's would cost him three more days. It would take some time and a bit of talking just to account for her to Ann and Ben. He'd not relish that part much. And there was no telling how she'd act. Not that she'd made him so much trouble since they'd got to the cave. Except for that flare-up against Bert, for which she could hardly be blamed. Still, she could switch again any minute.

Suddenly he remembered Bert's story about the new station being built by Sam Glover's uncle on Green River. That was only half as far as Logan's. Also, it was not on the main Wilderness Road, with movers swarming through and scattering all over Kentucky. It was off by itself and news would take a while to spread from there. Sam himself might be there and Sam and he had always gotten along well. Glover's was the place to leave her while he finished his work here. This decision seemed so completely practical that he was able to go back and go sensibly to sleep.

The first thing in the morning he got the watch out of the niche in the rock where he had kept it laid away, along with the three silver dollars that remained to him. By the time he had fed and watered the horses Nita had the cooking fire going and the leftover buffalo ribs warming at it. She moved about so quietly and kept so carefully out of his way that, except for the work she did, her being here was not actually so very different a good deal of the time from his being alone in the cave. She never even looked at him except when he spoke to her.

After they'd eaten he picked up his rifle and indicated that she was to go with him. She followed him out, taking the skinning knife as she passed through the doorway. She thought they were going hunting.

He set off to the west at a good, steady gait. She followed a pace behind in the proper place for an Indian woman. In country as rough as this they'd make better time on foot than with horses. Occasionally he indicated and named things along the way—beech, hawk, rock, rabbit, sumac, cloud. Each time she repeated the word and after she had said it over she didn't forget it. When they paused for a brief rest she proved able to name promptly everything for which he had given her a name the night before—rifle, knife, moccasin, eye, nose, hand.

They started on.

"Snake," she cried suddenly. "Snake."

From under a rock around which Adam had just stepped there glided sluggishly the black and white coils of a big pine snake. The serpent was of no interest to him but what she had just said was.

"Snake—that's what you called it," he declared. "And that's another word you remembered by yourself. What else do you remember?"

"Snake," she whispered, shaking her head helplessly and again looking a little afraid as if again her remembering were an accident she could not understand.

"And you were scared, too," he said. "Just as you'd have been when you were little. If you'd have stopped to think you'd have seen it was only a common pine snake. But you were scared. You weren't thinking—you were remembering."

She only went on shaking her head, her whole attitude confused and troubled and marked by no understanding of what he was saying and apparently as little of what she herself had just said.

"Well, come along," he said impatiently.

In another hour they came upon a raw, new trail, a white man's trail marked by the prints of shod horses, coming from the direction of the main Kentucky settlements and extending to the southwest. It was too well traveled to be a trail only to the single station at Glover's. It probably led also to the new settlement beyond on the Cumberland that Bert had said they called Nashboro. Adam lengthened his stride. Every new path or word of new settlement reminded him of how much he had still to do and how far he was falling behind in getting it done.

Shortly after noon they came out on the treeless crest of a ridge. Below them the Green River sparkled in the sunlight and in a meadow beside the river stood a cluster of three cabins within a half-finished stockade. Nita's eyes narrowed the instant she saw these habitations. She stopped, almost in midstride, like a deer that has caught the first whiff of a threatening scent.

"Come on," commanded Adam. "That's where we're going."

She stood still. Her face had taken on the Indian look.

"Do as you like," said Adam. "But down there's where I'm going."

He strode off down the trail. Presently he could hear the

soft pad of her moccasins just behind him. He kept on, without looking around, as if it were of no moment to him whether she tagged along or stayed behind. The path wound into the forest that clothed the lower slopes of the ridge. She was still at his heels. When he reached the open at the edge of the meadow he paused and called out. It was never a good idea to get too close to a station until you were sure the people in it were equally sure you were a friend.

The shouting back and forth developed that old man Glover, the head of the station, had gone to Logan's to trade in some deerskins but that Sam Glover was somewhere around. He was spearing sturgeon in the river, somebody said. Then Sam was scrambling up the bank.

"Take it easy, Sam—and keep your powder dry," yelled Adam, referring to the time on Corn Island when, drunk in the night, Sam had relieved himself in his own powder horn.

Sam recognized the voice at once. "Well, if it ain't the old mouse killer himself. What yuh hung on, Adam? Come on outta the bushes where we kin git us a look at yuh."

Adam started out across the open. Nita followed behind, now so close that he could feel her breath on his shoulder. Yelling children and barking dogs boiled out around the end of the uncompleted palisade. The uproar increased as, goaded by the imprecations of their elders, the children fell to stoning the dogs in a useless attempt to quiet them. Sam, still favoring the leg he'd broken when he'd fallen off a roof that first night at Vincennes, pushed ahead with outstretched hand.

"Come in and make yerself t' home. We ain't got much but greens and drippin's but what we got yer welcome to."

"This," said Adam, drawing Nita up beside him, "is a captive I just got away from the Cherokee. She's been with them so long she's forgotten what English she ever knew."

The women of the station swarmed forward, exclaiming over Nita with mingled curiosity and sympathy, Madeleine, Sam's French wife he'd courted the winter he'd served Clark as town major at Prairie du Rocher, tried to take her hand. Nita drew back and edged closer to Adam. She wasn't liking this any better than Adam would have liked walking into a Cherokee town.

"No use standin' here knee deep in brats and dogs," said Sam. "Come on in."

He led the way toward the nearest cabin. Everybody held back until Adam and Nita had followed Sam in and then they all tried to get through the doorway at once. A year-old toddler was knocked down and set up a furious outcry.

Madeleine swooped down, caught him up and began soothing him. Nita's eyes lighted up. She spoke to Madeleine. The French woman quickly replied.

"You're talking French," cried Adam.

Madeleine nodded, bewildered by his sudden excitement. Adam grabbed each woman by the arm and shoved them from the crowd in the center of the room to a bench along the wall. When he had them seated he knelt, facing them. Everyone in the room had fallen silent. The child in Madeleine's arms, blinking back the tears, stared, puzzled, into Adam's face.

"Look," said Adam to Madeleine. "So far I haven't been able to find out a thing about her. I don't know Cherokee and she doesn't know English. Is she French?"

Madeleine asked Nita and both women shook their heads.

"Then how come she knows French?"

Madeleine questioned Nita again. Nita answered readily, apparently impressed by Madeleine's friendliness and, more than that, by Adam's sudden interest.

"She *adopté* by *vieille* Cherokee," explained Madeleine. "Theese Cherokee *femme* she long time before live wiz un trader *français*. From her theese one learn to spik *français*."

"How long's she been with the Cherokee?"

"From time she was so," interpreted Madeleine, holding out her hand to indicate the height of a three- or four-year-old child.

"How'd they get her?"

This brought on a much longer discussion between Madeleine and Nita, during which Madeleine several times clucked with sympathetic dismay. Nita was no longer answering readily. The subject had become a painful one, no doubt. But she did not seem as much grieved as strangely angered and ashamed.

"Theese ees what she say," reported Madeleine. "Long time ago—very many *années*—zer ees white familee zat come down ze Tennessee *Rivière*. At place where ze water go round ze rock very fast—ze place ze Carolina people name The Suck—ze *bateau* she sink. Everybody die. Only theese one—so big—she wash up on ze bank."

"What was the name of this family?"

Madeleine questioned Nita, who kept shaking her head, almost defiantly.

"She not know."

"The Cherokee would have tried to find out—so they could ask for a ransom. Didn't they?"

"Maybe so—maybe no. They nevair tell theese one nozzing."

130

"Where was the family from?"

There was another long discussion between Madeleine and Nita but it came to little.

"Ze *vieille* nevair say. *Mais* one time—long time ago—when ze Cherokee *enfants tourment* theese one—they call her 'Carolina.'"

That the girl's family was from Carolina was almost certain. As early as the middle sixties a number of parties of Carolina settlers had set out to make their way through the Cherokee country to take up plantations at Natchez which the King's Proclamation of 1763 had inadvertently left open to legal settlement.

"She must know something more than that about who she is," insisted Adam.

"She know only her Cherokee name," reported Madeleine after more questioning. "Zat ees Ayunita. In Cherokee zat ees 'Little Otter.' The Cherokee name her so when she—so very small—come safe out of ze water."

Adam stood up. One of the women thrust into his hands a bowl of wild lettuce sprinkled with ham fat. He moved over to Sam and drew him to one side. The bowl of greens seemed to be in his way. He put it down.

"I brought her here," he told Sam, "because I'm camped alone in the woods and can't take care of her. Sounds like she might have kin in Carolina. I want to leave her with your women until I can figure some way to send her there."

Sam's joviality vanished. "Be another mouth to feed."

Sam was one who was a match for Bert at driving a bargain. Adam took out the watch and placed it in Sam's hand. He'd taken the trouble to wind it. Sam listened to the tick and then, happily, the watch started striking the hour. The room was so quiet that everyone could hear it. The delicate chiming was followed by a general murmur of appreciation. To cover up how much he wanted the watch Sam shrugged his shoulders and laid it upon a shelf.

"Well," said Sam, "a watch ain't just what we got the most need fer around here. But we'll keep her fer yuh—fer a spell, that is."

Adam, turning to tell Madeleine to break the news to Nita, saw that in an eager whisper she was already doing so. Nita sprang up.

"*Non,*" she said sharply. "*Non.*"

"Tell her that she has to wait here," said Adam. "Until I've had time to find out about her folks in Carolina."

"*Non,*" said Nita, without waiting for Madeleine to tell her anything.

Sam's aunt, a huge woman, big enough to make three of Nita, waddled up to her and put an arm around her.

"We'll look arter yuh jus' like yuh was one of our own, dearie," she said, hugging Nita against her and holding her there in spite of her instant struggle to break free.

Nita snatched the knife from her belt. The big woman jumped back. Adam walked over and took the knife out of Nita's hand. The big woman grabbed her again.

"Tell her," said Adam to Madeleine, "she's got to start behaving like a white woman and the sooner she starts to the better. And lock her up until she does—if you have to."

His voice shook. He was just as angry as Nita. He turned and pushed his way out of the door. Sam followed hastily.

"Non," Nita cried once more in the house behind them.

"We'll take right good care of her," said Sam, peering into Adam's scowling face, worrying lest he repent of the bargain.

"See that you do," growled Adam.

He started across the meadow, walking very fast. By the time he was in the woods he found himself running. He slowed down to an ordinary walk. There was no reason he should feel he was running away.

When he came out on the open crest of the ridge he did not look back until it occurred to him that this was only another sign of foolishness. He came to a stop and turned deliberately to look down at the station.

He was startled, then, to see that Sam's cabin was on fire. There were men on the roof with pails of water. Adam started to run back along the trail but almost immediately pulled up. There were no gunshots, no sign of an Indian attack. Also the men on the roof were already getting the flames put out. It had been just an accident. There'd been a cooking fire on the hearth when he was in the cabin. Probably a burning end had rolled out against the wall or the stick and clay chimney had caught fire as they so often did.

He'd turned to go on when there came the low, broken call of a quail: "White—bob white." It was Bert's call but not Bert's voice. He strode from the trail over to the edge of the woods.

Nita was standing just beyond a blackberry thicket. She was breathing hard from running but her face was remarkably serene. She glanced down toward the station, then over the hills in the direction of the cave and then at him. She appeared still to be leaving everything up to him but she wasn't giving him much of a choice.

"They'd hardly take you in again," said Adam. "Not after setting their place on fire. You might as well come on."

He set off toward the east. She fell in step behind him. After a while he swung around and confronted her.

"I suppose you know," he said, "you cost me a good watch."

"Watch?" she repeated.

"Yes—watch," he said.

She shook her head, puzzled. He went through the motions of taking it out and holding it up to his ear, as Sam had done. She smiled, relieved to discover his trouble was one so easily cured, reached into the bosom of her dress, brought out the watch and handed it to him.

TEN

ADAM scraped the accumulation of saltpeter crystals from the bottom of the kettle, scooped them into the leather sack, jerked the thong tight and tied it. This was the last sack. His cargo was complete. His work here was done.

Already he'd thrown the remaining wood on the fires. The flames were leaping high, driving the shadows farther and farther back into the great cavern. Flashing reflections, cascading past with the stream, became an avenue of light rushing away from him, multiplying the flames again and again before finally disappearing in the distant darkness in one last shower of sparks. The great white icicles of lime, hanging from the cathedral-vaulted ceiling above and thrusting up from the rock-ribbed floor below, glistened as if encrusted with jewels. Beyond the most distant gleam hung the black velvet curtain of the underground's utter darkness. The bleak, cold cavern, where formerly he had known only unceasing labor, and frustration more exacting than any labor, had suddenly become a magic new world—a world out of which any favor of fortune might well spring.

He sat down to watch, deliberately wasting a moment for the first time during the month, in recognition of the fact that the month was ended and ended in success. As deliberately, he summoned up the image of Cynthia, as so often before he had seen it here in his dreams. What he had done had been for her—meant now that he could have her. Tomorrow he was leaving for Trace Creek to claim the place which was to be their home, and there would be no end to the journey until he had rejoined her in Virginia and claimed her as well. The image of her took shape before him against the magnificent, wild background of flames and jewels. It was an image that had become so fixed in his imagination that he could call it up almost as often as he tried. She was standing, waiting, leaning nearer, in that last instant before, with his own final step toward her, his arms would close around her.

He could see her so clearly that he was getting to his knees and his arms were actually reaching out when the chimes of the watch striking noon sounded their shrill little tinkle. He looked around, startled and irritated. Nita, moving noiselessly as always, had entered, come up behind him and was holding the watch near his ear to remind him it was time to eat. She was smiling, pleased that she had learned to tell time by the watch so well that she could even foresee the exact second the hour would strike.

During the month the watch had taken an important place in their life in the cave. It divided their day into equal periods. He slept afternoons and she slept nights so that always there was one of them awake to keep the cavern fires going. Bedtime had not again posed an awkward problem.

"I'm coming," he said, ungraciously.

He followed her out. The aroma that rose from the brass kettle over the cooking fire in the cave lightened his ill-humor.

"My God, what you got in there?" he asked.

Nita had been able often to vary their regular diet of dried buffalo. She'd collected berries and wild vegetables, caught trout, snared waterfowl, quail, partridge, and once a turkey. But this was something new. Then he saw the discarded shells.

"Turtle," he exclaimed.

"Terrapin," she said, nodding.

That hadn't been his name for it. But he no longer called attention to it when another word chanced to come back to her out of her distant childhood. It put her off when notice was taken. Sometimes, when she wanted to say something and didn't stop to try to think, a whole phrase would come back to her at once—and these times were getting more common every day. When she herself noticed what she'd done she was always upset. She'd stop talking and attempt to go back to communicating by signs. But he'd refused to have anything more to do with signs and, whatever the occasion, had insisted on stopping right then until she'd either recalled or learned the word she wanted and then had used it. She'd had no objection to English as such. In fact, she was constantly eager to learn words from him. It was the sudden and always unexpected flashes of memory that troubled

134

her. At any rate, between the uncomfortable remembering and what she'd learned from him, she was getting so that talking to her was almost like talking to anybody. She understood practically everything he said. And this last week she'd taken to speaking right out herself in a way that astonished him.

Before ladling out the main dish she gave him slices of smoked turkey that had been dipped in goose fat and then in honey. The serving of the stew released a new, sharp fragrance made up not only of the richness of the terrapin but the tang of leeks and wild celery and some other wild herb that was strange to him. On the floor beside him waited a basket of wild strawberries. She'd done well enough before but she'd outdone herself today as if she, too, had felt this last day had called for some sort of recognition.

He leaned against the wickerwork back rest, one of the many comforts her Indian domestic skills had added to their daily existence in the cave, and regarded her approvingly.

"Have some yourself," he said.

By the time he'd eaten all the terrapin he wanted there wasn't room for many strawberries. He lit his pipe, settled against the back rest and stretched out his legs.

"Well," he said. "Tomorrow we go."

She nodded soberly. Her smile had faded before he spoke. Maybe one of the reasons she always seemed to understand most of what he said was that she generally seemed to know what he was going to say before he said it.

"Is it far?" she asked. "To Kentucky?"

"Not very."

Her face clouded.

"How long—you stay there?"

He ran over the probabilities in his mind. He'd leave her at Logan's, go to Harrodsburg to sell his saltpeter, then cut across to Trace Creek to settle with the Wyeth brothers. If the sale hadn't made him quite the whole amount he needed he'd make Bert go his note for the difference, using his pack horses as security. Bert could be sure of being repaid because there was always more saltpeter to be had. In any event the whole business shouldn't take long. Then he'd be starting out for Ingles' Ferry and Cynthia. On the way he'd pick up Nita at Logan's and take her to Carolina. That might cost him considerable extra time, at a moment he'd least want to spare it, too, but that's what he'd have to do, just the same. If he left her stranded in Kentucky she'd likely as not run back to the Indians. And if she stayed in Kentucky among strangers it would be just as bad. Either way, people

135

would never get over talking about how he'd taken advantage of her and then left her to shift for herself. Getting her permanently settled somewhere she belonged was his job —he had to face that—and one he had to finish.

"Maybe two, three weeks," he said.

"Where you go then?"

"I'm taking you to Carolina—to look for your kin."

"Carolina is very far," she said, brightening. In the Cherokee country they knew about Carolina where the Cherokee themselves once had lived. "It is over the mountains." The prospect of so long a journey still before them seemed to leave her with no further concern.

She rose briskly and picked up the nearly finished new deerskin hunting shirt she had been making for him. She held it up to show him, very pleased with it herself, as she had a right to be. He was pleased with it, too, because it was simple and plain and strong and without any Indian-style attempts at ornamentation. He was able to appreciate, because he had once had to hack and punch out a shirt for himself, the beautiful precision of the sewing. She gestured for him to get up and held it against him to see how near she had hit his size.

"Wait—I'll try it on," he said.

He pulled off his old shirt and put on the new one. She walked around him, tugging at a seam here, pinching a wrinkle there. She was not going to be satisfied unless it fitted him perfectly.

Her head was bowed just enough so that he could glance down into her face without her noticing that he was looking at her. He'd been so busy and had had so much on his mind that he'd not stopped to think much about how she looked since she'd stopped making him trouble. During the month at the cave when she'd been out in the sun so much less, some of her tan had faded. Her skin was still golden, though. She kept herself so clean that it looked almost transparent. There couldn't be smoother, fresher-looking skin than that on her cheeks and neck and even her arms. That was her best feature. Her face was too thin, however, her cheekbones and chin too marked and her mouth too wide. The way she parted her hair and pulled it flat back into those two braids made her forehead seem too high and added to that odd air of childlike gravity that went so poorly with her actual temper and willfulness and resolution. Her eyes, of course, were another good feature. The long lashes gave a violet shade to their blue and they seemed larger and brighter now that her eyebrows had started to grow out. Balancing the good features against those not so good it still wasn't a face at which he'd have been likely to take a long second look, even during those roving years before his return to Cynthia. She looked too much like what she was—too independent, too different, too much just herself—to suggest the kind of promise that made a woman look inviting to a man. He'd told Bert the truth. Her presence had been almost like having a boy around. And a month of her company had made no difference.

She backed away, her head cocked, took one more glance at the way the shirt hung on him, then gestured for him to take it off.

"You are more big than I think," she observed.

She sat down and began ripping out a seam. He knocked out his pipe. Ordinarily at this hour she'd have gone back to the cavern to tend the fires and he'd have been going to bed. He rubbed a hand reflectively over his chin. They'd be leaving too early for him to shave in the morning. He might as well get that done now. One of the several comforts of Nita's housekeeping was the basket of water, kept hot by heated stones, always beside the fire. There was soft soap, too, she had made of grease and ashes.

After the pleasant coolness in the cave it was hot and sultry outside the door. He shaved slowly and carefully, enjoying the sense that this afternoon, for once, there was no need to hurry. When he had finished shaving and was bending to splash cold water on his face his hair hung down in his way. It had gotten much too long. He got out his knife again and began cutting it off, a handful at a time. Without a mirror it was an awkward process.

Nita came out and stood watching and laughing at his efforts. She seldom laughed and he liked the sound of it. After a moment she took the knife out of his hand, pulled him down to his knees, and herself began to cut his hair. So personal a service made him uneasy but he submitted rather than admit his uneasiness. She worked swiftly, pushing his head unceremoniously this way and that, like any barber.

He shivered, tickled by the hair dropping down over his bare shoulders and chest. She laughed again and brushed him off. She could not have been behaving more impersonally. Yet the feel of her soft finger tips lingered. She resumed her barbering. Her encircling arms were at times so near they touched his face. Her skin was damp from the heat and the faint scent of it was pleasant. Just in time he checked an impulse to sniff approvingly. That was another of her good features. Everything about her was young and fresh and sweet.

137

She moved around in front of him and her upraised arms revealed the curling little tufts of new dark hair in her armpits. He was startled by this glimpse. According to Indian ideas about personal appearance she could never before have let hair grow anywhere except on her head. She must have given up this Indian practice the day, weeks ago, he had reproved her when he had come upon her plucking her eyebrows with clamshell tweezers. She had appeared to have given up so many of her former Indian ways but the discovery of this change in her took possession of his imagination as no other had. He remembered her smooth, unrelieved nakedness that day on the raft. That alien and heathen hairlessness no longer existed. Her slender figure was now beginning to be marked according to the shadowed mystery of a woman of his own race. He could picture this as vividly as if the modest covering of her deerskin dress did not exist.

Desire, sudden and demanding, seized him. There seemed so little reason he should deny it. He couldn't understand why he hadn't come to before. There'd been no sense in his being so choosy. She was not only young and sweet, she was willing. She was eager to do anything to please him. Any day this whole month she'd been ready. He'd probably been disappointing her, as Bert had said, but he didn't have to any longer. He didn't even have to make any awkward approaches. She was so near that they were already on the verge of an embrace. All he had to do was to take hold of her. There'd be no talk, no argument, no struggle —just a sudden release for both of them.

"So," she said, stepping back to survey her work.

She moved closer again and ruffled his hair briskly to dislodge the loose ends and then once more brushed off his shoulders and chest and back. He got slowly to his feet.

"Come," she said, handing him his knife and taking him by the arm to turn him toward the doorway. "It is time for you to sleep."

He shook free. "Maybe," he said. "But not in there."

He strode off toward his pool below the horse pen. That had been about as narrow an escape as he'd ever had and he'd had some close ones. After having kept his mind on what he was doing for the whole month he'd been right on the edge of making a fool of himself the very last day. It was the way she'd ruffled his hair that had straightened him out. She'd been as familiar as if they'd lived together for years.

The air was getting heavier and hotter by the minute. There was a coppery haze in the west and beyond that a bulging cloud line. Chances were there'd be a thunderstorm before night. He took a swim, pulled on his pants, crawled into the shade on a bank of ferns and, still relieved, went promptly to sleep.

He was awakened by Nita's despairing call. "Adam, Adam." She was running along the stream bank, looking for him, and she was frantic with fear. "Adam!" she screamed.

He got to his knees. He could see no sign of danger. The horses were restless but they weren't looking in any definite direction. She hadn't brought his rifle as she had when she had heard Bert's approach. She saw him then and rushed to him. She seized hold of him and when he was slow to rise she beat on him with her fists.

"Run," she kept saying. "Run."

He rose to his feet and then he could see it over the bush under which he had been lying. It was, indeed, not a threat against which his rifle would have been any help. A huge black cloud was boiling up in the west, filling the sky. Though here around them the air was still calm, to the west the whole forest was whipping and bending toward the cloud. Sudden terrific claps of thunder rolled over the hills. Then from the midst of the cloud a long gray funnel dropped toward the earth, its lower tip writhing and swaying like a monstrous snake searching for what it might devour. The tip touched the crest of the wooded ridge half a mile away and instantly whole trees were jerked up by the roots and went flying upward into the monster's interior with a roar that swallowed up the thunder. A sudden gust of wind boomed across the meadow, driving Nita against him. Having touched the ridge the tip of the funnel gave one long bound, settled again, then bore down the slope toward them, tearing a great furrow through the forest as a plow would cut through the softest soil.

"Come," Nita was begging. "Come now."

He ran with her to the door of the cave. It was too late to try to save the horses. In the cave, a step beyond, he and Nita would be safe no matter how near the tornado came. They turned in the doorway, clinging to each other, to watch, fascinated, as it continued its onward rush. Its roar was now earth shaking, as it marched with its strange, bouncing motion directly upon them. Trees and boulders were spiraling upward across its nearer face. The horses, belatedly terrified, were throwing themselves against the walls of their pen but their screams were smothered in the all-enveloping din. The split maple by the shed gave way in the rising gale now rushing toward the storm.

The writhing gray funnel came on until its terrible lower

tip reached the stream bank just below Adam's pool. To the upward current of its fearful digestive process was added a geyser of water and mud. But after a moment's hesitation, as if with the whim of a wild beast it had decided the horses not worth its attention, the monster swerved suddenly northward, now beginning to take great hops, the funnel dangling at times in the air above the waving forest, at times touching the earth to leave new islands of disintegration. In its wake torrents of rain fell.

"Even missed our horses," Adam exulted.

Only then did he realize that he had drawn Nita against him protectively. He was still stroking her hair soothingly. She was trembling, unable to get over her fright. Her arms were wrapped around him, her eyes were closed and she was rubbing her cheek against his bare chest as if trying to reassure herself that they had come through safely. Then, though she was still trembling, she was beginning to smile and to whisper something which must be Cherokee or French, for he couldn't catch the words. The whispering was mixed up with odd little sounds that were somewhere between a sob and a laugh. He stopped stroking her hair and started to let go of her. Her arms tightened and she slowly turned her face until instead of her cheek it was her lips that were pressed against his chest. He could feel the warm, moist tip of her tongue.

"No," he said, pushing her away.

She looked up at him, wide eyed, not in anger but with a patient attempt to understand.

"Why?"

"Because it's wrong."

She considered this point of view. "Wrong for me? Wrong for you?"

"Wrong for both of us."

He stalked into the cave. She followed, beginning for once to look remorseful.

"I forget," she volunteered.

"You forget what?"

She sought helplessly for some way to tell him what she'd forgotten but she was stumped. Before he could remonstrate she'd lapsed into making signs. In swift succession she made the ones for warrior, for fasting and prayer, for woman, and for complete negation. She thought he'd taken a warrior's vow. Nothing was more common among Indian men than religiously to stay away from women while planning war or engaging in serious hunting or trying to track down the meaning of a dream or for whatever reason.

He pretended he hadn't caught what she meant in order to give himself an extra minute to think. He'd been able to understand how being alone in a cave with a man had changed her so quickly from being ready to kill him to being ready to go to bed with him. All her savage young life she'd never been used to keeping a check on her most passing feelings. But he'd not been able to understand at all why she'd not furiously resented his refusal of her readiness. Now even this was accounted for. In her Indian way she had taken it for granted that a vow was the natural and only possible explanation.

"Vow," he said. "Warrior's vow."

"Vow?" she repeated.

He nodded.

"How long?" she asked.

"For quite a while yet."

She sighed and picked up the shirt she'd been working on.

"I'd better go look at the horses," he said, making for the door.

The horses had already settled down and were picking at the remains of their morning feeding. He cut more cane and threw it in to them. Now that it was over he realized how close he'd come to losing the entire pack train. He'd have to pay Bert for the horses before he did anything about his own affairs. What chilled him most was to reflect that the threat had been so great on this very last day. It was as if he had been given a warning. There could be Indians aplenty out by now. And it was on the way to Logan's he'd lost Oriole. You couldn't stir pack horses out of a walk and four of them left a trail wide enough for a blind Indian to spot from a mile away. All day tomorrow he'd be plowing along through the woods, inviting trouble every slow step he took.

The rain was slackening. It would be clear by night and there would be a pretty fair moon a little later. If he got started by moonrise he could be past the worst stretch of country before daylight.

He began carrying out the sacks of saltpeter and stacking them near the door. The sacks were too heavy for Nita but she began getting together the camp equipment and busying herself with cooking their last meal in the cave. She was accepting the earlier move with calm. She had apparently prepared herself for going anywhere he did, even though it might be among crowds of strange white people.

Each time he came into the cave with another sack on his

back he saw her bent over the cooking fire or rolling blankets or packing a basket of buffalo jerky. She was doing her part while he was going right on trying to fool her. It wasn't fair to her to let her think all she had to do was wait awhile. This hiding behind that vow story was no good. He was fooling himself, too. The longer he put off making her understand just where they both stood the harder she was going to take it.

He put off saying anything until he had finished carrying out the cargo, and until he had surveyed the weather which was clearing up as he had expected, and until they had eaten. Even then he still found it hard to begin.

"When I get to Kentucky," he said, "I'm going to buy me a farm."

"What is a farm?"

"It's a place where you grow corn and beans and keep horses and pigs—like the fields around a Cherokee town— only this won't belong to everybody in town—it will belong to me."

She was intensely interested, as she always was in anything he said about himself. "Then you will stay—all the time—in one town?"

"No. In a house I'll build on the farm."

She looked around at the cave. "The house—it will be better than this?"

"Much better."

"Who will hoe your corn?"

"I'll hoe it myself—at first."

She was more dubious about this than about the house. "You will work very hard."

"That's right."

"Why?"

This was a simple question but he had to stop to think to give it a real answer. "So that I can have what I want."

"What do you want?"

This seemed as good an opening as any. "What I want most—is a woman in Virginia."

She wasn't thunderstruck. She was puzzled.

"Where is Virginia?"

"About as far as Carolina—only more to the north."

She pondered this with a faint smile. "You are here. This woman is there. You do not want her very much."

"I've wanted her since I was a boy," he insisted, indignantly.

Nita was more than ever puzzled. "You take her then— and you still want her again now?"

142

"No, I didn't take her then. I came to Kentucky. I was away all the time."

"And you never forget her?"

"Never," said Adam, hoping he was at last making some progress.

"And all this time nobody else want her?"

"Of course they did. Any man would. But she's a widow now." He was beginning to sweat and to fumble with his pipe worse than Bert ever had.

"Widow?"

"A widow's a woman whose husband has died."

"Widow," repeated Nita. "She cut off her hair and make scars on her face?"

"No. White widows don't do that. Anyway, she's been a widow a long time."

Nita considered these several pronouncements. "This widow you never forget—she is old now."

"She's as young as I am."

"She have many children?"

"No."

Nita rose, strolled thoughtfully about the cave and then came back to confront him. "This widow—what does she look like?"

He got to his feet and faced her. He had to go through with this now that he'd got it started. "She's got brown hair —and brown eyes—she's taller than you"—he held up his hand indicating a point a full head over Nita's—"and— and"—his hand moved down in a vague gesture describing feminine curves—"more of this than you—and—" His hands dropped helplessly. "She's beautiful," he declared desperately.

Nita glanced down at her own slight figure and with her hands imitated his gesture, though somewhat enlarging upon it, to indicate considerably more of breast and hip than she possessed. "So—she is more tall than me—and more big than me—and more—like this—than me." She nodded complacently. "She is already old. Soon she will be fat." Her interest in the topic waned. She bent to pick up the new hunting shirt. "Your shirt—it is finish."

"I tell you," said Adam angrily, "when I get to Virginia I'm going to marry her."

"Marry?"

"She will be my wife. She will come to live with me."

Nita considered this statement. For a moment there was a dangerous sparkle in her eyes but for a moment only.

"But first we go to Kentucky?"

"Yes."

"And then we go to Carolina?"

"Yes."

Her calm was fully restored. "It is very far to Kentucky —and to Carolina." She held up the shirt for him to put on.

ELEVEN

ADAM was finding that telling his story was even more trying than he had foreseen. Ann was listening closely but not once had she nodded understandingly or stopped him to ask a question. She was just letting him go on talking. Logan wasn't being any help either. He was listening with a wicked twinkle in his eye and several times even chuckling and slapping his knee. Nita was being the least help of all. Since sighting the station she'd spoken no single word, had acted so scared you'd think any minute she might jump out of her skin. She was sitting, as he talked, on the floor at his knee, her fingers constantly edging out to touch his moccasins or his leggings, her eyes wide and frightened except when she looked up at him. The way she was carrying on, a young fawn he'd dragged in from the woods could not have seemed more shy or out of place.

They'd got to Logan's an hour after dark. Long before there'd been a glow in the sky that had made him wonder if the place was on fire. It had turned out to be only the campfires, strung along the Wilderness Road for a mile outside the gate, of movers too numerous to crowd into the station. One war whoop would likely have sent the lot of them running for the rest of the night, yet forty or fifty families, their children, slaves and livestock, were scattered around in the full light of big blazing fires as if there weren't a man among them who had ever heard about Indians. In the general confusion and visiting back and forth between fires no notice had been taken of his passing with Nita. There hadn't been so much as a curious stare and she hadn't had the faintest excuse to start shivering and hanging onto him as she had.

She'd had even less excuse when they got to the Logan house. Ann and Logan had been in bed and they'd gotten right up and taken them in with as warm a welcome as Adam had expected. But, after one look at Nita and then at him and then back at Nita again, Ann's smile had faded. And Nita had gone right on acting as if he were her sole hope in the world, her one friend in the midst of enemies, her father and mother rolled into one. She'd refused to eat or to talk or to do anything except to hang as close to him as she could get.

"Well, that's about all," he finished. "Then we came here."

Ann looked down at Nita with a cluck of sympathy. "Tch, tch. The poor child."

"She's not such a child as she looks," said Adam. "I mean—"

Logan snorted and coughed hastily when Ann looked at him. Ann's gaze came back to Adam.

"Yes? You mean?"

"I mean she's as much a child as when I first ran into her." None of this was going the way he'd planned. "I suppose you think she'd have been better off if I'd turned her back to the Indians."

"I'm not so sure I don't."

"That's only because you don't know as much as Ben or I do about Indians. I told you what I did do. I took her to the nearest white settlement—only she wouldn't stay there."

"And so you took her back to your cave for a month. And now that the month's over you want us to take her off your hands?"

"Only until I can get to Harrodsburg and Trace Creek and back."

"She's counting on your coming back?"

"I *am* coming back. I've already told you I'm going to take her to her folks in Carolina."

"That's all she's counting on?"

"Yes."

Ann looked at Nita crouched by Adam's knee. "I declare she has an odd way of showing it."

Adam drew his knee away from Nita's plucking fingers. "Don't be fooled by the way she's been acting since she's been here. And she understands every word we're saying."

"That's good," said Ann, "because we're not talking about anything that ought to be kept from her."

"Nobody's been keeping anything from her. She knows that soon's I leave her in Carolina I'm going on to Virginia to get married."

"And she thinks that's just fine?"

"Doesn't make any difference what she thinks. Nothing's happened to give her a right to think anything." In spite of his great need to placate Ann, Adam's temper was get-

145

ting away from him. "I can't drag her with me all over Kentucky. I have to leave her somewhere—and if it's not here it'll have to be somewhere else."

"You've no call to feel put upon," Ann said. She looked at Nita again. "Well—I suppose we have to keep her for you. Nothing much else we can do. But I do wish I had some idea how she really feels about it."

"You can't miss how she really feels about something whenever she's a mind to let you know," said Adam. "She's probably just saving herself for the hell she'll try to raise when I start out in the morning. Remember what I told you about what she did at Glover's."

Ann rose. "She won't have to start any fires here. She'll be able to come and go as she pleases. We're certainly not going to keep her locked up." She bent over Nita. "Speak up for yourself. Do you want to stay?"

Nita's only answer was to look up at Adam. The expression in her upturned face, the faint quiver of her lips, the silent pleading in the big eyes, proclaimed more clearly than any words that she didn't want to stay, she'd sooner die than stay, but if he really wanted her to stay, then she'd stay. Adam nearly choked. This new pose of adoring, helpless submission was worse than anything she'd done to him on the island or on the raft. He shoved her away and stood up.

"If it's up to me it's settled. She stays."

A flicker of hope rose in him as he watched Ann. She was too smart to be taken in by this last performance of Nita's. But the eyes of the two women had suddenly met in a strange, intent look. Ann bent and squeezed Nita's shoulder reassuringly. "He'll be back," she said. "If we have to send and fetch him."

Straightening, the look she gave Adam was strangely speculative, as if, in spite of having known him well for years, she was just beginning to know him.

"Well," said Ann, suddenly commonplace, "time for bed. I'll find some blankets." She went into the other room.

"Don't take Ann too hard," said Logan. "She'll likely be pleasant as pie in the morning. She always gets riled when she thinks somebody is gettin' the worst of it."

"Who's been getting it any worse than me?" demanded Adam.

"I don't see how you could have done no different than what you did." Logan was ready with some mild masculine support now that Ann was out of the room. "Or than what you're aimin' to do. Only one thing bothers me. If you don't even know the name of her folks—how you figure to find

146

any of her kin in Carolina when you do get her down there?"

"Couldn't have been so many families leaving for Natchez that long ago. Somebody'll remember."

Ann came back, carrying two blankets and dragging a straw tick. "We haven't got all the room we'd like," she said. She dropped the tick and one of the blankets beside Nita. "You can make do on the floor with these until we get time tomorrow to fix you something better." She handed the other blanket to Adam. "And you can crawl up in the loft with Davy."

Adam took the blanket and started hastily for the ladder.

"No," said Nita, jumping up.

She overtook him at the foot of the ladder. There couldn't be any question she was overdoing it now. Ann would never put up with this nonsense.

"I can always tie her up," said Adam.

But Ann's calm was broken by nothing more encouraging than a tight-lipped smile. "I never thought I'd stand for anything like this in my house," she said. "But after a month in a cave I don't suppose there can be much harm in your spending one more night in the same kitchen."

She went out. Logan started to follow, a little reluctantly. He turned in the doorway.

"Ain't had a chance to tell you. Seen Clark in Harrodsburg the week before last."

The name was like an echo from another world. "How is he?"

"Madder'n ever and busier'n ever. He hung onto the Illinois country through the winter all right. Scared off the English and Indians and the Spaniards at St. Louis, too. The Spaniards claim to be helpin' us but they'd have their hands on it soon enough if nobody was lookin'. Then he come to Kentucky and tried to raise an army to go for Detroit this year. But he couldn't get but three men and a boy to join up. Most everybody thinks the war's the same as over and they're all beaverin' around stakin' out land claims. Clark he sweat and swore and argued and then he couldn't wait no longer. He run back west again to build Fort Jefferson on the Mississippi."

"On the Mississippi?"

"That's right. Just below the mouth of the Ohio. Good place, too. Keeps the English from makin' too free with either river and keeps the Spaniards rememberin' that this side is our side. When he got back even the three men and the boy had wandered off—figurin' they'd bettter grab what they could before the new movers got all the land that was

147

left. Clark he locked up the land office so people couldn't file land claims and said he'd keep it locked until he got back from Detroit so that them that stayed behind couldn't take advantage of them that went with him. Good many said he had no right to do it but he said Kentucky land would be no good to nobody unless we got the English out of Detroit. No way to tell how closin' the land office might of worked because just then word came that Sinclair with fifteen hundred Sioux was on his way down the Mississippi to take St. Louis and Kaskaskia and maybe break all the way down to New Orleans. Clark he had to drop everything and make off west again to face up to Sinclair."

These were more than echoes from another world. Until last spring that had been Adam's world. Campaigning with Clark had kept a man feeling that he was right in the middle of whatever was happening. He found himself half wishing that he was in that westbound canoe with Clark and with nothing more on his mind than going along wherever Clark had to go. "Good thing Kentucky has a Clark," he said.

"That's a fact," said Logan. "Could be me and Bowman made a mistake not joinin' up with him at Vincennes last spring. Anyway, what I was comin' to—Clark he give me a message for you. He'd heard about your new station on the Licking. He said don't worry about comin' back to him. He said there wasn't no place you could be as much use to him and to Kentucky as makin' sure a station that close to the Great War Trail was hung on to."

"Ben," called Ann.

"Comin'," he replied. He withdrew and closed the door.

Adam turned to look disgustedly down at Nita. The personal word from Clark had been an immense comfort to him. Many times during the winter he had reflected uneasily upon the one feature of his plans with which he could not be quite satisfied. Obviously what he was doing meant any thought of return to service with Clark was postponed indefinitely. It was something to be told now by no less authority than Clark himself that what he wanted to do and was bound to do was still some help. But just at the moment he wasn't helping anybody hold anything. He was shut up in a kitchen with the most annoying female in creation.

Nita was no longer pretending. Her most stony Indian look had settled over her.

"Might as well go to bed," he said. "You've made all the trouble you can for one day."

She got up, stepped over the mattress, wrapped her blanket around her and sat on the floor against the wall. He kicked the straw-filled tick nearer to her.

"It's for you," he said. "Use it."

She shook her head.

"Suit yourself," he said. "You always do."

He blew out the candle and rolled up in his blanket against the opposite wall. The mattress lay on the floor between them.

There'd been no sleep for them the night before but he was too angry to sleep and he judged by her breathing that the same was true of her. Still, it could have been even worse, he decided. Bad as had been the reception of his story by Ann he had not had to tell it before a more severe tribunal. He shuddered to think of the Wyeth brothers and their wives listening to it while they watched Nita's traitorous antics. One thing was sure. Neither Ann nor Nita needed to worry about his getting back here as fast as he could. And getting Nita to Carolina as fast as he could. And seeing the last of her as fast as he could.

The door to the Logan bedroom creaked. "Adam," came Logan's hoarse whisper.

"Yes?"

"Can't figure why it didn't come to me before. Old Tom Gunter—he's got him a tomahawk claim right out here on the headwaters of Quail Creek."

"Who's he?"

"About as no 'count as they come—even to Kentucky this spring. But for years he used to trade with the Cherokee—before they run him out when the war started. He could have been around when that boat upset or leastwise heard about it. He just might know something about her family."

Adam sat up. "Where'd you say he was?"

"I'll take you out to see him first thing in the morning."

Logan closed the door. Adam dropped back on his blanket but felt less than ever like sleep. It didn't seem possible that something even faintly hopeful should have turned up. However little the old trader might know about Nita's family, if he knew anything at all it would simplify the Carolina search. And any saving of time was a godsend. He sat up again and looked across the dark kitchen toward Nita's shadowy figure. She must have heard Logan's story. She should be excited, too.

"Ever see this trader—Tom Gunter?"

"No."

"Ever hear of him?"

"No."

"But Logan says he was in the Cherokee country for years."

149

"There were very many traders with the Cherokee—and many Cherokee towns. My town was Hiwassee. This trader never come there."

"What makes you so sure?"

"When a white trader come everybody know. This man never come."

"Just the same—I'm going out to talk to him in the morning."

She did not reply. He was irritated by her lack of interest.

"You act like you're afraid of what he might know about you."

"I am not afraid."

"Then what does ail you?"

Her calm broke. The voice coming to him out of the darkness was suddenly cold and harsh. "Already I know who I am. Already I am me. I am not nobody. Always I have been somebody. With the Cherokee I belong to a clan. I am of the Aniwaya—the Wolf People. The woman who adopt me is the woman chief of the Aniwaya. In the Woman's Council nobody stand in front of her. I am proud —and I can stay proud. Why do I want to ask a trader who I am? Why do I want to learn that with white people I am nobody?"

"You can be prouder of belonging to the poorest white family," said Adam angrily, "than to the fanciest Cherokee clan."

"Maybe I have no white family," said Nita. "But if I have—they are lower than poor. They are no good. They are not like a clan. They do not care who belongs to them. At first—with the Cherokee—I am a captive and I am very small. But nobody ever come from Carolina to look for me."

"You don't know that. You don't know for sure how any of it happened."

"I do not want to know."

"Now wait. You keep remembering English, don't you— in spite of yourself? Every day you come out with new words. Every day you speak it more easily. You never talked English with anybody in the Cherokee country, did you?"

"No."

"Then you're remembering the way your own family spoke it while you were still with them. And you know how that was, don't you? Like educated people. You've never remembered a word that sounded like your folks were trash. Why don't you try to remember more about them?"

She didn't reply for a while. She seemed to be giving this some thought. Her hard breathing slackened. "Sometimes I try," she whispered. "But it is no good. When I try it is like it is dark all around me."

"Try harder."

"Always it is only the dark that comes back—like—like water in which I sink."

"This old Cherokee woman that adopted you—she must have known something about you. Didn't she ever tell you anything?"

"When I ask her she beat me. Always she is good to me. Only when I ask her about the white me—then she beat me." Nita's voice became firm again. "She is right. I am Ayunita. That is enough."

"The hell it is," said Adam. "Tomorrow I'm taking you with me to see this trader. He just might know more than you think. And if he doesn't we'll still keep at it. We'll keep digging until we find people you belong to. Now settle down and get some sleep."

The silence continued until Adam decided she must have dropped off. Then it was broken by her soft whisper.

"Adam."

"Yes?"

"You want me to have a white family?"

"What do you think I've been talking about?"

"Then you will still take me to Carolina?"

"How many times do I have to tell you? Now go to sleep."

Before it was full light Ann had a kettle of squash and salt pork bubbling over the fire. They ate hastily, mounted and were halfway over the ridge toward Quail Creek before the sun was up

"I'm going with you," Ann had suddenly announced at breakfast

It was well she had, as it turned out. When they reached his miserable little log and brush cabin they found the old trader still abed with his fat, one-eyed Choctaw wife. But he came scrambling out, scratching and grinning and pulling at his forelock, to greet them with a genial enough welcome.

"Well, fry my lights, if'n it ain't Colonel Logan hisself," he declared. "And his bonny lady along with him. Push right in and set yerselves down." He turned to bellow into the cabin behind him. "Betsy, larrup together a pot of this here deer meat fer these here folks to eat."

There was a quarter of fly-dotted venison hanging beside the door. It had started to spoil in the late spring heat.

"We don't aim to stay," said Logan. "We only come past

to ask you about something that happened down in the Cherokee country a good many years ago." He indicated Nita. "Every see her before?"

Gunter gazed at Nita with unaffected interest while he pawed thoughtfully with one grimy, taloned old hand at his tousled hair and beard. "Nope, Colonel, I don't reckon I ever did," he said, regretfully.

"And you're sure you never saw him?" Adam asked Nita.

She shook her head. The squaw, accompanied by as many flies as were clinging to the venison, waddled into the doorway to peer with slack-jawed curiosity.

"Or her?"

Nita shook her head again. "Choctaw," she said disdainfully.

Neither Ann nor Nita had dismounted. After one sharp glance at the squalid hut and the even more squalid pair that inhabited it Ann was carefully smoothing her horse's mane to save herself having to look again. But Nita continued to stare contemptuously at the old trader. Yet she was pale under her tan. Adam shifted a step closer to her. Her moccasined toe in the stirrup pressed hard against him. He could feel her leg trembling.

"Ever been to Hiwassee?" he asked Gunter.

"Rid through it mebbe oncet or twicet but never spent no time there."

"Where was your store?" asked Logan.

" 'Nother Cherokee town they called Coyate."

"That's right on the Tennessee, ain't it?"

"Smack dab on the bank, Colonel."

"Then you must have seen movers' boats on their way to Natchez."

Gunter overflowed with eagerness to talk. He continued to answer readily—even enthusiastically. "Every year, Colonel, every year. Not so many at first. But arter word got back about the good land at Natchez there wuz more."

"Then maybe you remember about one that got wrecked with everybody drowned but one little girl," said Adam.

Gunter stopped scratching and grinning and gave this suggestion solemn consideration. He seemed to be searching his memory, anxious to be helpful. "Nope. Never heard nuthin' about thet," he decided, blinking reflectively.

"Must have started a good bit of talk at the time. With you living right on the river seems a wonder you wouldn't have heard something about it."

The old trader shook his head, saddened that he must disappoint them. "Seems like I might—fer a fact. Injuns they do a

152

lavish o' talkin'—but they fergit quick, too. Besides—The Suck's more'n a hundred mile down river from where I wuz. The story must o' petered out before it got up to me."

"If you heard nothing about it—how'd you know it happened at The Suck?"

Gunter chuckled complacently. "Sounds like yuh purty nigh catched me there, don't it? Only reason I named The Suck wuz thet wuz the chanciest place on the river—where anybody's boat wuz most apt to run into trouble. Oncet—when I wuz down thet way lookin' fer a no-good injun thet owed me—I seed three boats in a row tip over there."

"But you never heard a word about the one we're talking about?"

"Nope. I never did." There was a faint edge of defiance in his tone.

Ann leaned over and laid her hand on Nita's arm. "I'm sorry," she said, consolingly.

Nita seemed anxious to get away. She looked down at Adam.

"You have more—to ask him?"

"No," said Adam.

Again refusing the old trader's invitation to share the venison, they started homeward. They rode on in silence. The fiasco had been a sad letdown after the excited interest with which they had set out in the morning. Adam was beginning to foresee the similar frustrations that might await his inquiries in Carolina.

"Too bad we wasted your time, Adam," said Logan after a while. "Bein' as he was down there the very year it happened you'd of thought the old fool might have heard something about it. 'Course the Cherokee are spread out over a big stretch of country and it was a good many years ago."

Ann suddenly pulled in her horse.

"He was lying," she declared.

"What makes you think that?" demanded Logan. "What would he want to lie to us for?"

"He was lying," repeated Ann.

She turned her horse around. Gunter heard them coming and came out to greet them again.

"Tickled to see you changed you' minds," he said. "The kettle she's a-boilin' good by now."

Ann rode right up to him.

"We didn't come back to eat with you," she said. "We came back to find out why you lied to us."

"Now, Mis' Logan," remonstrated Gunter. "You got no call to say nuthin' like thet."

153

"The only reason he'd have for lying to us," said Ann to Logan and Adam, "is that he knows something he's afraid to tell us."

"What a man ain't able to recollect," argued Gunter stubbornly, "nuthin' kin make him recollect."

"I'm not so sure about that," said Ann. She moved her horse another step toward him, forcing him back against the wall of his cabin, and leaned down from the saddle. "You're living among white people now. Unless you start telling us the truth right this minute I'll tell you how I'm going to help you remember. The very next time an Indian so much as shoots a cow or steals a horse anywhere around this settlement I'm going to start reminding every woman down there that you lived among the Indians for years and that you've still got one living here with you. You can guess how long it'll take people to come up here and burn you out."

"Ben Logan," implored the trader. "Yer colonel and magistrate in these parts. Yuh got no right to stand fer nuthin' like thet."

"Takes more than a colonel or a magistrate," said Logan dryly, "to stop women talkin'."

Gunter put one hand to his head and the other to the small of his back as if he were assailed by pain in both places at once. "I'm too old to take to the woods again," he whined. "Some days my rheumatiz is so bad I can't git me around a-tall." He studied the faces of his inquisitors and sighed deeply when he saw no sign of sympathy. " 'Tain't no use yer bearin' down on me so hard. Thet wuz a good many years ago. Like I tol' yuh right off—I surely crave to help yuh but a man my age can't allus recollect every little smidgen o' talk he might o' heered thet fur back." Still he saw no hint that his visitors might be relenting. "Come on in and set yerselves down—like I said. I got me a crock o' corn likker. Might be arter we've passed thet around a time or two could be somethin' 'ud come back to me." Nobody moved. His glance shifted helplessly to the ground at his feet, to the edge of the woods, to the sky over the surrounding hills, as if he hoped against hope aid might yet come to him from some quarter, however unlikely, and, finally, came back to the muzzle of Ann's horse. He again sighed deeply and his shoulders drooped more dejectedly than ever. "What year'd yuh say this wuz?"

"How many years were you with the Cherokee?" Adam asked Nita.

"Fourteen."

"That makes it the spring or summer of '66."

"H'mm," mused Gunter, beginning once more to put on a

154

show of trying to remember. "The year arter word o' the King's Proclamation begun to git around. The Cherokee they'd turned peaceable fer a spell and people from Carolina wuz startin' to go through their country to take up land at Natchez." Suddenly he clapped his hand to his brow. "Now, it comes back to me. I did hear somethin' or other about a boat wreck down river thet year. Almost the first one thet come through—it wuz. Everybody wuz lost but one little gal." He beamed ingratiatingly at Nita. "Well, well, fry my lights and liver, too, wuz yuh thet little gal?"

"We already know what she can tell us," said Adam coldly. "We want to hear what you know about that family."

"I don't know nuthin'. I never laid eyes on 'em."

"He's still lying," said Ann. She swung her horse around. "We might as well go."

Gunter jumped forward and grasped her bridle. "Give me time to think. Could be it's beginnin' to come back to me a little. It just could of been the same folks I seen comin' past my store at Coyate. The man thet owned the boat wuz singin' foolishlike, so thet I reckoned he wuz drunk. He had a toy brass cannon in the bow and he fired it off when he come around the bend. His wife wuz right purty. This gal here puts me some in mind of her. Thet's the one reason it's comin' back to me a-tall. They had a young'un along—mebbe three, four years old. And seven or eight niggers. And so much livestock and stuff the boat wuz ridin' terrible low in the water."

"Was that why the man stopped to see you?" asked Adam. "To sell you some of his overweight cargo?"

Gunter stepped into the trap. "Nope. He didn't want to sell me nuthin'. He—"

"Yes. Go on," said Ann. "Why did he stop to see you?"

"He didn't. I only seen the boat goin' past."

Logan's voice was as cold as the tap of a knife blade against a rifle barrel. "Tom Gunter, you're the worst liar I ever had to listen to. Damn me, if I see why we should wait for women talk to get around when we can start runnin' you out of this country right now."

The trader shrank back against the wall. Many far bolder men than he had quailed before the look that was coming over Logan's face.

"I'll tell yuh just how it wuz, Colonel," he said, his last shred of resistance collapsing. "He stopt to give me a letter to take to his brother back in Carolina the next time I went over the mountains."

"So he gave you a letter," said Adam. "Then you know his name."

The trader nodded. He seemed dazed. "Sheldon," he said.

"Sheldon," breathed Nita. "Sheldon." But her face did not brighten. "He is making this up," she added. "So nobody will hit him."

"Be quiet," said Adam. "What was his first name? And the girl's?"

"I got no idee," said Gunter, helplessly. "Only full name I'm sure of wuz the Sheldon the letter was to—the brother in Carolina. Thet was John Sheldon." Finally he was telling as much of the truth as he knew. "He had a place down on Deep River—big place—big family—four five boys and as many gals. I stopt there thet summer on my way out to Charleston to buy goods. This John Sheldon he wuz sick and in no shape to travel to the Cherokee country hisself to buy back the little gal so he asked me to see what I could do."

"How much did he give you?"

"A hundred pounds." The trader's spirit was completely broken. "When I got back I went down to Hiwassee. The young'un had been adopted by an old woman they called Agigaue because she wuz the head woman of the town. She wuz the widow of a French trader named Alex Menard and he'd left her well fixed. She'd made up her mind to keep the gal. She wouldn't sell her fer no amount of money."

"So you kept the hundred pounds."

"Thet's right."

"And what did you tell John Sheldon?"

"I sent back word the little gal wuz dead."

Adam looked up at Nita. "Now you know one thing about your people," he told her. "They didn't forget you. And you know another thing. You belong to a big family. We'll find Carolina full of Sheldons. You can take your pick."

"Sheldon," she said again, as if trying out the sound of it. "Ayunita Sheldon."

"What's wrong with that?"

"I am still me," she decided.

On the way back Ann rode ahead with Logan. But Nita remained grave and silent. She rode on, staring straight before her, not once even glancing at Adam.

"Are you wondering about how you'll get along with your Carolina relatives?" he asked.

"No. They are still far away."

"Not so far away as they were yesterday."

She didn't reply.

"Then what are you thinking about so hard?"

"I do not know yet what I think."

They rode on in silence. Ordinarily, he felt mingled alarm and annoyance when he could tell there was something on

156

her mind and yet could make no slightest guess about what it might be. But today was different. A great weight had been lifted off his own mind. Thanks to the luck of stumbling on miserable old Tom Gunter he could once more be sure of what he was doing and where he was going. He wouldn't have to wander around Carolina asking simple questions. He could know exactly where he was headed—Harrodsburg, Trace Creek, Logan's Station, Deep River—and then Ingles' Ferry. He could almost count the days.

And that wasn't all. Before this he'd had to foresee the chance that her kin in Carolina might turn out to be so worthless that he'd have felt uneasy about leaving her with them. Now he was rid of that worry, too. People who could pay hundred-pound ransoms were very substantial people. He could leave her among that kind of relatives and go on about his business, free of any further concern for her.

The trail winding down the lower slopes of the ridge began to offer occasional glimpses of the open flat below. A man was riding out from the station toward the foot of the trail. From time to time he pulled up and surveyed the wooded slope above. When Adam and Nita came out of the trees onto the flat he saw that Logan and Ann had pulled up their horses and were talking to him. Then he saw that the man was Bert.

Bert's unexpected reappearance so far from the side of his bride put an end to Adam's recent satisfaction. Something had happened, something unforeseen and undoubtedly disturbing.

"Figgered I'd best come back to help you with the pack-train," Bert announced, as Adam and Nita came up. "So's you could make better time."

"What's gone wrong now?"

Bert laughed in huge delight. "Fine thanks I git for comin' all this way to help you. Right away you start talkin' about what's gone wrong. Nothin's gone wrong, my boy." He laughed again. "Nothin'," he repeated. "Trace Creek's in better shape right now than most new settlements that's been goin' two, three years."

"Then what brought you here?"

"I'll tell you. Day before I left, Joel and Blake and Paul they got in with their families and so much stuff it took forty pack horses to carry it all."

"You told me a month ago they were bringing out their families this year."

"But I didn't tell you all this was bringin'. 'Cause I didn't know. Nobody did. So I come to tell you now"—he shot a meaning glance at Nita—"so's you could slide this one under

157

a basket—quick. Your gal—she come along with them." He added for emphasis: "She's at Trace Creek now—a-waitin' for you."

"The widow from Virginia," said Nita in a clear but expressionless voice.

Bert nearly fell off his horse. "You told me yourself she didn't know a word of English," he accused Adam. "How was I to know she could tell what I was talkin' about?"

Adam didn't try to explain to Bert. All he was able to think about was that Cynthia hadn't waited for him to come to get her. She'd set out to join him. She was already in Kentucky. He had only a few miles to travel and he could be with her.

"You don't have to worry about what she hears." Ann was grimly explaining her views on Nita to Bert. "Nothing's being kept from her and nothing's going to be."

"Yes, ma'am," agreed Bert politely. He turned to Adam, happy to get back to his news. "She brung along her forge, and them big niggers, and their wives—and all her own stuff. And when the new company had the land drawing she drawed for her piece along with the rest of them." He leaned over and stroked his horse's neck as if what he had left to report was of little importance. "And after that—long's you wasn't there to draw for yourself—she drawed for you, too."

Ann put her hand on Adam's arm, studying his face with the first flash of her old warmth and sympathy she'd shown since he'd walked into her kitchen with Nita.

"This the same one you wanted the letter for?"

He nodded.

"You've really set your mind on her?"

He nodded again.

"I'll tell you how set he is," said Bert. "He's so set that he ain't paid no real attention to no other woman since he first seen this one nine years ago."

"Well—that's that," said Ann. "Nobody's to blame—and anyway nothing can be done about it." She turned to Nita. "We'll keep you with us—and, when we can, we'll see that you get to your people in Carolina."

Nita shook her head. "I will wait for Adam. He will take me."

"Whatever makes you think that?"

"Because that is what he has said—many times."

The horses, restive at being held in one place, were stamping and kicking at flies.

"She's right," said Adam, himself as surprised as the others by the sudden edge in his voice. "Seeing she gets there is my job—nobody else's."

All at once Ann was more worked up than she'd been about hiring Indians the night Hamilton had come to dinner. "I can believe this other woman is the one for you—that you should go to her and stay with her. That I can believe. Your plans, what you want and what she wants, even the land you're taking up—all that goes together and probably belongs together. I'm ready to believe nothing else would ever be right for you or her or even for Nita. But there's one thing that couldn't be more wrong. That's for you to ride off leaving this girl sitting here counting on your coming back to take her to Carolina. Tell her the truth now, Adam Frane—tell her now she'll never see you again. About all you can do for her now is to stop fooling her—but at least you've got to do that."

"She's got nothing to forget," said Adam. "And nobody's fooling her. All there's to it—is this: I was the one that took her away from the Indians—and I'm the one that's got to see that she gets where she belongs. I owe her that and that's all I owe her."

"You owe her a deal more than that," said Ann. "She's the same as in a trap—and you've got to let her out. That's what you really owe her."

"Call it a trap if you like," said Adam. "But it was none of my setting."

Ann's indignation reached a new pitch. "It is a trap and, whoever set it, you're the one that's leaving her in it. You know in your heart that once you get back to this woman you're so stuck on you're never going to turn right around and walk away from her again. You'll take hold of each other and neither of you will want to let go—and neither of you should."

Adam's sudden rage was not directed toward Ann. It was the truth in what she was saying that had hit him. Taking Nita to Carolina was certainly no way to spend the better part of a summer which otherwise could be spent with Cynthia. Yet, if he didn't he'd be taking back the word he had once given. He would be crawling, and no mistake. Ann saw his anger and was the more aroused.

"Let me tell you this," she declared. "If you go—leaving this girl here waiting and wondering and hoping—and you're not back within two weeks—so help me—Ben and I will bring her to Trace Creek looking for you."

Bert straightened up with a jerk. "Hey, wait a minute." He spoke with a note of authority Adam had never heard in his voice before. "I don't aim to mind your business, Adam —nor yourn neither, ma'am. If you feel like keepin' a gal in your cave—that's your lookout—and if you feel like takin' her under your wing—that's yourn, ma'am. But when there's talk about movin' the ruckus up to Trace Creek—that's different—that's talk I want in on. I got me a family up there —and there's a slather of other families—all workin' at gettin' a new settlement started." He was addressing himself entirely to the two Logans now. "This other gal of Adam's that's just come out from Virginia—she's got a blacksmith shop—her niggers are good ironworkers and one of them is a first-rate gunsmith. There ain't nothin' a new settlement needs like that kind of an outfit. If somethin' happens to make her pull up stakes and head back to Virginia two hundred people that had nothin' to do with it—one way or t'other—will be losin' somethin' they can't afford to lose. This or that might be right or wrong with the way Adam handles his women— but you know as well as I do—better, most likely, because you've been through it—that it's all wrong to go out of your way to make trouble for a new settlement. Now, I've had my say."

"And now I'll have mine," said Adam. "I'm getting mighty sick of all this talk about my two women. I've only got one. But the talk about what I've done to Nita will go on—and get worse. And if I leave her here it'll keep on getting worse. You three are my oldest friends—and look how you carry on. A man can hardly guess how much the story will grow when it really spreads. The only way to stop such talk is to make people understand there's nothing to it. And I'm beginning to see there's only one way to do that. The woman I intend to marry and her whole family besides are at Trace Creek. To make it entirely clear where I stand—and what I think of all this talk about what I have to keep covered up —I'm not going to leave Nita waiting here or anywhere else. I'm going to take her up there with me right now. We'll face the music before anybody goes to Carolina. Whatever anybody has to say—we can drag it into the open and have it out. I can't see any other way to get it through everybody's head that there's been nothing between Nita and me that we have to hide or side-step—or be ashamed of."

"Man, you've gone clean crazy," shouted Bert.

"You'd actually push this child into a hornet's nest like that," cried Ann. "I won't let you. I tell you I won't let you."

Logan spoke up for the first time. "You've all been doin' a sight of palaverin'. But nobody's stopt to ask the gal what she thinks." He looked at Nita. "How do you feel about goin' up there with Adam? Want to chance it?'

There were spots of color in her cheeks and sparks in her eyes. "Yes," she said promptly.

160

"You can't know what you're saying," protested Ann.

But Nita seemed to know quite well. "Before we go to Carolina," she explained, "I would like to see this widow from Virginia."

TWELVE

TOWARD night Adam dropped behind to make certain their trail was not being followed. No war parties of any consequence had been reported anywhere in Kentucky since the snow had gone off. But you could always count on a scattering of young braves hanging around in the woods, alone or in twos or threes, anxious to earn distinction by stealing a horse or snatching a scalp. They hid and waited, sometimes for weeks—sometimes until they all but starved—for the chance to jump some unwary hunter or mover. And this unsettled country between Dick's River and the Kentucky, bordering on the main settlements and skirted on either side by the forks of the Wilderness Road, was just the place to look out for that sort of devilment.

He stretched out on a high rock and waited. The squirrels and woodpeckers and parakeets presently forgot their excitement over the passing of the train and went back to their ordinary aimless and conversational pursuits. The blue jays ceased their scolding and no single one started in again anywhere within earshot along the back trail. Adam moved higher up the slope to a point from which he could see an open meadow they had crossed nearly an hour before. Five deer and two elk were grazing placidly in the meadow. At least, the pack train was not being followed yet.

While Bert unloaded, tied the horses in a sapling grove and cut enough young cane to keep them quiet during the night, Adam circled the camp site, fixing every natural detail in his memory so that he could move about readily in the coming darkness, in the event there was need for it. The afterglow was fading behind Burdett's Knob in the west as the three settled down hungrily around the food basket from which Nita was taking out what they had to eat. Adam, his nerves edged by the approaching end to his journey, had vetoed a fire, but they did not do too badly, since they had their pick of Nita's buffalo jerky, smoked partridge and goose liver pemmican, together with wheat bread, ham and a dozen hard-boiled eggs Ann had given them.

No one spoke while they ate. The animosity between Bert and Nita prevented either from making idle remarks, while Adam had too much to think about to feel like saying anything he didn't have to. The darkness deepened and flowed out of the forest to engulf their fireless camp. In the silence the munching of the horses was at first the only sound. Then there arose various twitterings and rustlings in surrounding thickets as the lesser life of the wilderness began its nightly search for food. The oriental singsong of a frog chorus began to squeal and thump in a near-by marsh. In the distance a wolf howled.

Adam recalled the wolves the night he'd left Nita tied up under the willow. He'd had to go back and get her then. He'd had to hang onto her ever since. The wolf howl was like a reminder that he had never been able, even up to now, to find a place in which it was right to leave her behind. She was sitting there, unmoving, listening, as was he, to the night sounds. Her face was but a faint blur but it was turned toward him. He got the impression that she was waiting for him to say something to her. It could be that for all her willfulness she sometimes felt the darkness closing in around her, sometimes felt the need for reassurance. She moved. He could see the pale glimmer of her arm reaching toward him as if she felt the sudden impulse to touch him. But she was only reaching for her blanket.

She picked it up and retired under a cedar a dozen feet away. Bert yawned, stretched, then moved to a sleeping place beyond the horses so that in case of any disturbance he and Adam would be on either side of them. After a time Adam followed and squatted beside him. Bert was already peacefully asleep. Adam shook him awake.

"I've been thinking," he announced.

"You don't say," said Bert. "What you got to think about?"

"Coming in on Cynthia all of a sudden this way could give her quite a start," continued Adam.

"Whatever could of put that into your head? You got no call to fret about nothin' like that. Like as not she'll figger your showin' up out of the woods with a wild girl on a string is just one of them things that goes on all the time out here in Kentucky."

"Nita's not so wild as she was at first."

"She still looks it." Bert sat up. "And that's somethin' I didn't think about when I should of. We'd ought to of made Mrs. Logan give her some white woman's clothes. Then

162

she might look a little less like somethin' you knocked out of a tree."

"Ann wanted to. I wouldn't let her."

"You wouldn't? Why not?"

"My story's that I saved her from the Indians where she'd been a captive for years. The story's true. But it never hurts when you've got something to tell to have everything look the way you're telling."

Bert gave this a moment's thought and grunted dubiously. "You can paint her face and stick feathers in her hair but I don't know whether that's goin' to help you much or not. Was that what you woke me up to tell me you'd been thinkin'?"

"No. I've been thinking that it's a mistake to let this come at Cynthia as a surprise. It's only fair to her to give her a chance to get herself set. So you get started soon's it's light and ride on ahead to Trace Creek. You can get in before dark tomorrow. Tell her that I'm coming with Nita and tell her why I am."

"How much else you want me to tell her?"

"Tell her everything you know about it. You can leave out some of the things you've been trying to guess. Tomorrow night I'll camp where we found Paul and Eli camped that day and I'll come on in to the station the next morning. That'll give Cynthia overnight, at least, to think it over."

Bert shook his head so hard the bones in his neck creaked. "It's your foot that's in the bucket—not mine," he said. "But you been makin' a sight of mistakes—and now you're makin' another one. The trouble with you is that you've never paid no attention to the way a woman tracks except when you was watchin' for a chance to catch up to her in bed. The way a woman works the rest of the time is like this: You're always doin' somethin' to make her mad with you and the longer you give her to think about it the madder she gits. When you're within reach she can start right in takin' it out on you. That wears her down and after a while she uses up everythin' she wants to say and do to you and she's played out. But when you're out of reach she just gits hotter and hotter the longer she thinks about what she'd like to be tellin' you and can't because you ain't there to listen to it."

"Cynthia's got more sense than that."

"Beats me how come I ever used to hang to the idea that you knew so much about women."

But Bert obediently set out an hour before dawn. Adam, following at the pack train's slower gait, swung wide around Boonesborough to avoid the curiosity Nita's appearance might arouse among the settlers there, and, in late afternoon, reached Paul's old camping place on the head-waters of Trace Creek. A steady drizzle of rain had commenced. The brush and sapling hut had fallen in. He set to work propping it up, rethatching it and adding a lean-to. The oiled elkskin sacks would shed water for a time but might not save the saltpeter from dampness if the rain lasted through the night. He tied the horses in a clump of cottonwoods where they could gnaw the bark, piled the sacks in the hut and then crept away through the darkness to the crest of the slope. In the valley below he could just make out, through the slanting veil of rain, the faint glimmer of light within the stockade.

He sat on the ground, wrapping his arms around his drip-ping, leather-clad knees. There seemed literal need to hang onto himself. Cynthia was down there, so near that if he rose and started walking he could be with her in a few minutes.

He tried to guess what she might be doing in that glimmer of light behind those log walls. Bert must long since have told her. She might be talking it over with her brothers, while the family considered the stand it was right for all of them to take as a family. She might, on the other hand, have told none of them yet. She might be alone—walking up and down—making up her own mind. Or she might be sitting still while she did her thinking. She could be sitting by the fire. He liked this thought. He could see the gleam of the firelight across the curve of her cheek and on her hair and in her eyes. Possibly, though, she was already in bed. This thought was even better. The surge of feeling that came along with it was strangely comforting. She must un-derstand how he felt about her. It was a feeling so strong that she must know how strong it was. Women knew things like that.

There was a rustle behind him. He snatched at the deer bladder, waterproof cover over the lock of his rifle. But it was only Nita. She squatted beside him and stared at the dim glow in the valley.

"Get back in out of the rain," he said harshly.

"She is down there?"

"Yes."

"Bert maybe is telling her now about me?"

"What makes you think that?"

"Last night when you talked to him—I came close. I like to hear what you say." Her low laugh was throaty with malice and satisfaction. "Maybe tomorrow I feel very bad. But tonight she feel bad."

"Get on back like I told you."

"The rain and the woods and the night—they are good. We sit here and think that we still are up here. That is good, too."

He grabbed her by the wrist and towed her back to camp. It was too dark in the hut to see anything at all. He felt among his sacks of saltpeter to make sure there was no threat of leaks. The remaining space was so small they had to stretch their blankets almost side by side. For a second Nita's head and shoulders were faintly outlined against the comparative grayness outside as she leaned into the doorway just beyond his feet to wring water from her unbraided hair. Then she drew back again into the complete blackness beside him. He could hear a faint, slithering whisper.

"What are you doing?" he demanded.

"My dress—it is wet. I am taking it off."

"No," he protested.

"It is all right," she replied calmly. "You cannot see."

It was true he could not see but it was almost the same as seeing to have her so near and, by what he could not help hearing, to know every move she made. She dried herself on the blanket, spread it on the ground, lay down upon it and squirmed about in search of a comfortable position.

Again there came her low, malicious laugh. "She is down there alone. She think about us up here together. She think we are like we are—so close as this." She reached out and touched his face. "She never believe that nothing happen. That is almost so good as—"

"Will you shut up and go to sleep?"

She was quiet for a while. "No," she murmured. "It is not so good. But it is better than nothing."

"I suppose tomorrow you will make all the trouble you can."

"I cannot tell yet how I will feel tomorrow."

"You try to make everything worse than it is and I'll wring your neck."

"My neck it is here," she whispered. "Why do you not wring it now?"

Adam turned over away from her and drew his blanket around his shoulders. His wet leather shirt and hip-length leggings were cold and clammy. There was no reason he should spend an uncomfortable night, he decided angrily. Grunting and swearing under his breath, he sat up, peeled off everything down to his breechclout and rolled into his blanket again.

There wasn't much use in trying to get to sleep, with all he had to think about, but, at least, he didn't have to shiver all night. He wished it were morning now. He couldn't any longer even find comfort in thinking about Cynthia, as he had back there on the crest of the slope, with Nita lying so near the sound of her breathing was almost in his ear. He remembered how near he'd come to taking her that day she'd cut his hair. What a good thing it had been that he'd backed away in time. His thinking became more confused. Next, he was awakened by Nita clutching one of his feet.

She was crouched in the doorway, looking out and listening. It was still drizzling but the clouds had lifted and thinned and had been turned lighter by the moon behind them. There was light enough for her slender figure to stand out distinctly against the dark belt of woodland beyond. Her black hair was flowing over her shoulders, making her body look very white. She shook his foot again.

"Somebody come," she whispered.

He sat up, reaching for his rifle. He'd gotten so annoyed while they were going to bed that he hadn't taken the cover off the lock or recharged the piece. He stripped off the cover. The powder in the pan still smelled dry. Somebody was coming, all right. But it certainly wasn't an Indian sneaking up on the camp or the horses. Whoever it was was clumping though the blackberry patch like a buffalo coming through a dry canebrake.

"It is Bert," said Nita.

She wheeled out of the doorway and dropped back into the darkness beside him. From Bert came the familiar quail call, a little wheezy this time on account of his being winded. A moment later he loomed in the low doorway, stumbled over Adam's outstretched feet and sprawled forward, putting out one hand to save himself.

"Gawdamighty," he cried, jerking his hand back as if he'd put it into a fire. "Put my hand right on her bare bottom." He lurched sidewise to get Adam between him and the scene of his mishap and spoke into the darkness beyond Adam. "I didn't mean nothin'. I can't see a thing. Don't come at me out of the dark with no knife."

"Nobody's coming at you with anything," said Adam. "What the hell ails you? What you doing here?"

"I wouldn't put nothin' past her," said Bert, hanging onto Adam. His clutch made him suddenly aware that Adam also was bare. He sank back to a sitting position and slapped Adam jovially on the back. "Well, well, gittin' in your last licks, eh? Don't know as I blame you."

"We got wet," said Adam. "We're trying to dry off."

"Bad to sleep in wet clothes, all right," agreed Bert. "Could bring on a spell of lung fever."

"You can go to hell," said Adam. "Now—speak your piece."

"Just as well I come up to speak it, too," said Bert. "You better git yourselves all dried off come daylight. Because Cynthia's comin' up here to look you over first thing in the mornin'."

"Why's she doing that?"

"All I know's she's comin'. She didn't say nothin' about why. Could be she's runnin' to meet you 'cause she can't wait no longer to see you. Could be it's Nita she wants to take a look at. Could be she wants to size things up a little before you and Nita plow in among her brothers and the rest of the folks at the station. Could be she's comin' to tell you you might's well turn right around and head back for your cave. Your guess is as good as mine. Anyway, I figgered you'd better know about it so's you wouldn't be dryin' yourself off at the wrong time."

"She knows you came up to tell me?"

"Nobody knows. I even told Alice I was takin' Pete Lamb's shift guardin' the horse herd."

"How'd Cynthia take it when you told her about Nita?"

"You got me there. I couldn't tell what she was thinkin' no more'n you can never tell what Nita here is thinkin'. She listened until I got through and then she asked some questions."

"About what?"

"Mostly about what Nita looks like." Bert started to back out. "Sure is a wet night, for a fact. Beats me—the kind of times you pick to drag me away from home. Be a relief when I don't have to travel so far to keep you straightened out. Be a bigger one if you'd git yourself settled one way or t'other whilst I still got me a wife to run back to." He stuck one hand out to test the drizzle. "Night like this I could stand some dryin' out myself. Wait a minute." He squatted in the doorway. "There's another thing maybe I better tell you. There's a young doctor named Naylor that come out when all the Wyeths come out. He's bought him a piece in the land company. I didn't pay no attention that first day they got in—before I come down to Logan's to see you. All I noticed was he acted like he was mighty good friends with the whole family. There was talk like they all growed up together back in Albemarle. But Alice she's been noticin' more than that whilst I was away. She says this here sawbones is after Cynthia mornin', noon and night and that Cynthia she ain't what you might call slappin' him down real hard. Now don't start tryin' to get your elbow in your mouth. Chances are that once you're back you'll find you got

167

no need to worry about him. Reason I'm tellin' you is because his pushin' around might even turn out to be some help to you. Every time she squawks about Nita you can come right back at her with a squawk about the doc. Well, here I go."

Bert backed out of the doorway, muttered profanely as he stepped into a mud puddle and again as he hit the en-tanglements of the blackberry patch. Adam dropped back on his blanket.

"Maybe this man," said Nita, "maybe he will take her."

"Go to sleep."

"He follow her out here. She did not tell him to go back."

"I want to sleep—whether you do or not."

"I say only this. Maybe everything it will still come out all right. Now you can sleep."

There wasn't much likelihood of his sleeping. This young doctor wasn't somebody who'd just happened along by acci-dent. He was an old friend of the family. He was part of the land company, too. Very likely he was the one Joel had al-ready had in mind that first day he'd talked about shares and had mentioned taking in a doctor. Anyway, he'd come out with the Wyeths. That could have had something to do with changing Cynthia's feeling about Kentucky enough so that she had come out at the same time. Nita could have put her finger right on it. He'd hardly have come out with her unless he'd been given some reason to think he had some chance.

The drizzle had stopped and it had turned much warmer. The air in the hut was stifling. The blanket and the pile of wet buckskins beside it steamed. Adam wanted to get out-side and walk around. But he didn't want Nita to see that he was that much disturbed. There were no stars out yet so he couldn't tell how much longer the night was to last. Probably a good many hours. Again he didn't realize he'd been asleep until he was awakened, this time by the sun breaking over the crest of the eastern mountains and striking across his eyes.

Nita was no longer beside him. He scrambled into the doorway and looked out. The first thing he saw was her deerskin dress spread out to dry on a bush up the stream a little way. Then he saw Nita herself bathing in a pool beyond. Her wet hair and arms and shoulders glistened like the ripples on the sunlit water.

"Get your clothes on," he yelled.

"It is all right," she called back. "Nobody come yet."

He stood up, looked toward the blackberry patch and jerked his own clothes on. They were still wet, which was perhaps just as well, since the only way he could have kept dry during the night was to have spent it in the hut with Nita. He took his blanket to the stream, sopped it in the water and rubbed some mud on it before spreading it over a rock as if to dry. Having gone this far he got angry, bundled up the blanket and threw it back into the hut. He started to build a fire, remembered his three-day beard and instead went down to the stream to shave.

When Nita came back she was dressed in her still damp deerskin, her hair neatly braided, everything about her glowing with her usual morning cleanliness. There was another kind of glow in her eyes but her outward manner was placid and cheerful. She got out the food basket and then, while waiting for him, began rolling the blankets and packing for the day's move. She looked toward him when she found his blanket soaking wet but he didn't say anything and she didn't either.

When he came back to the hut she was slicing pemmican on a rock by the cold fire pit. He considered building a fire and decided there was no use. The slightest decision seemed a task. He hadn't eaten since yesterday morning. He must be hungry, whether he had sense enough to know it or not. He crammed a handful of the pemmican into his mouth and began dragging out the sacks of saltpeter and loading the horses. He finished this and then staked them out on a strip of grass along the stream. Still Cynthia had not appeared.

"Maybe she not come," suggested Nita. "If she really think to come maybe she never tell Bert."

"This time you stay here," said Adam.

He started for the blackberry patch. From the other side he could see whether or not she was on her way up from the station. The second he reached the crest of the slope overlooking the valley he dropped flat.

Cynthia, bareheaded, wearing a tight-fitting green dress and riding the gray stallion, was almost up to the top. But he couldn't rush to meet her or even give himself the pleasure of a long second look at her, for riding beside her was a man—a black-browed, black-eyed, lean, long-legged young man wearing a plum-colored coat, doeskin breeches, silver-buckled shoes and a three-cornered hat trimmed with a touch of lace—who could only be the doctor. The two had pulled their horses into a slow walk, were riding very close together, talking earnestly. He was begging her to do some-

169

thing or not to do something and she, if not quite agreeing, was listening sympathetically. You couldn't miss seeing how he felt about her.

Adam started to rise to face them and dropped flat again. At first sight of them he'd taken cover instinctively, as any woodsman would do upon catching sight of something unexpected. Now it was too late to show himself, no matter how naturally he tried to greet Cynthia, without looking as if he'd been hiding here spying on them. He squirmed backward into the blackberry patch. Bent double, he swerved through the tangle of vines and ran for the camp.

"She's coming," he warned Nita.

Nita had been watching his face as he came up to her. She smiled. The worse things went for him today the better she'd like it. He went down among the horses and began fussing with their tie ropes. He could hear their horses in the blackberry patch. Now that they were near they were coming faster. Nita knelt down by the food basket as if she, too, were busy.

"Adam," called Cynthia. "Adam."

They pulled up their horses in the little open space between the two cedars on the opposite side of the hut from the doorway. Adam ran toward them. There had seemed to be a ring of genuine welcome in her call.

"Cynthia," he yelled, echoing her greeting. "Cynthia."

He hoped he was sounding surprised. He hoped he did not sound as if his throat were as tight as it felt. She looked just the same. She was looking right at him as he came up. She didn't look mad. She looked glad to see him.

"But you've lost weight," she declared accusingly. The stallion wheeled restlessly and she paused to pull him back around. "Adam," she said, "this is Gilbert Naylor. He insisted on coming along"—she laughed—"to protect me from Indians."

Gilbert lifted his hat. He'd been eying Adam with sharp curiosity but now his grin was immediate and cheerful. If he'd been anybody else Adam might have taken a liking to him on sight.

"Glad finally to lay eyes on you, Adam Frane," said Gilbert. "The reports on you have been so good that I made sure I'd be disappointed—and, I might add, I'm disappointed that I'm not."

He wasn't backward, anyway. Before the first chip had hit the ground, he was staking himself out a piece of whatever land was going to be cleared here. Adam couldn't stop looking at Cynthia long enough to give him more than a curt nod. She had quieted the stallion and he was stepping forward to lift her down when he saw she was looking past him. Nita was joining them. She had on her Indian look and it was like a stone mask.

"This is Nita Sheldon," said Adam, "the captive girl Bert told you about."

Cynthia looked at Nita with perfect composure. "Why Bert said she was little and scrawny. But she's quite nice looking."

Nita came closer, her expressionless stare fixed on Cynthia. Adam held his breath, afraid to reprove Nita too soon lest this only make her harder to handle. She walked slowly all the way around the stallion, studying Cynthia's person from every angle. A spot of color appeared in Cynthia's cheeks but she exchanged an amused glance with Gilbert. Nita completed her survey.

"She does not look so old," she decided. "But—like I said, Adam—before very long she will be fat."

"Good heavens," said Cynthia. "She speaks English. Bert didn't tell me that. She's not very polite but she sounds almost like a white girl."

"She is a white girl," said Adam, glaring at Nita. "Though she's so ignorant and mean you'd seldom guess it."

Nita remained impassive. "I am young," she announced. "I can wait. You will not always stay with her."

"As I live and breathe, Cynthia—you have a rival," cried Gilbert. Nita had turned away toward the fire pit as if for her the incident was closed, but she turned back to look at him. He swept off his hat and bowed low in the saddle to her. "Heaven prosper your suit, fair maid of the woods—all my hopes and prayers go with it."

Nita continued to stare at him and with a growing interest. "If you want her—why do you not take her?"

"A consummation most devoutly to be wished," he replied, "though one still teetering, I fear, most precariously on the knees of the gods."

"Gilbert was at Princeton College with my brother, Deck," Cynthia explained. "As you can notice—he loves to parade his learning."

"So brief a biography scarcely does the subject justice, my dear," remonstrated Gilbert. He addressed Adam. "I later pursued my thirst for knowledge at the Pennsylvania College of Medicine. And still later was separated from the Continental Army as a consequence of a most unprofessional prejudice against bleeding men already wounded. So finally you see before you a physician employed chiefly in an earnest endeavor to heal himself."

Nita had resumed her examination of Cynthia. She ad-

171

dressed Gilbert again. "She is strong. She will be able to work hard. And she is a widow—she will also know how to work well at night."

"Shut up, Nita," threatened Adam, "before I take a stick to you." He glanced swiftly at the two on horseback. He didn't know whether to like it or not when he saw they still looked amused. "The worst of it is—she's not so simple as she makes out. She knows what she's saying. She just likes to make trouble."

"Bert says you made up your mind to bring her here," said Cynthia, "so we could judge for ourselves how much trouble she'd made you."

"She was fourteen years with the Cherokee," said Adam. "In a good many ways she's the same as an Indian. You can see that."

"Yes—I can see that." He still couldn't be sure how much of the glint in Cynthia's eyes was just amusement. "That brings up the practical reason I came out here this morning." She reached into a saddlebag behind her and drew a bundle that seemed to include a blue sunbonnet and a brown homespun dress. "Most of our people down there have never seen wild Indians. That makes them very touchy on the subject. Some of them even stand off from old Eli Skaggs because of the story he once had a Chickasaw wife. I think we might make a more comfortable entrance with her if your wild girl looked a little less wild. See if you can get her to change into these."

Adam took the bundle she was handing him, swung around and thrust it at Nita. She looked at it suspiciously.

"Take it," said Adam.

She took the bundle, handling it as if she thought there might be a snake wrapped up in it, let the dress unroll and looked at it. It was plain homespun but there was an edging of white linen around the throat and cuffs. She started to push it back at Adam, then paused to give a more reflective second look, first at the dress, then at the sunbonnet.

"A new dress," murmured Gilbert, "hath charms to soothe the most savage feminine breast."

"Put it on," said Adam. "Do as I say for once."

"Yes, Adam," said Nita.

She withdrew around the corner and went into the hut. Adam turned back and looked up at Cynthia. She was watching him expectantly. He reached up and swung her to the ground. When she was standing, facing him, he did not let go of her arms and he could feel that she, too, was not letting go of his. Their eyes met. Hers did not waver. He could see

172

suddenly that she was trying just as hard as he was to figure everything out.

"We've come a long way, Adam," she said.

"Far enough?"

"If you're going to kiss him," said Gilbert, "let me know in time to turn my back. I don't want to see it."

She was going to kiss him. And it was a good one—as good as that first under the oak. For a moment she clung to him as fiercely as he was clinging to her. His arms tightened about her. She pulled her mouth away from his.

"Still skyrockets," she murmured, "if nothing else."

"Everything else," he insisted.

"Better not drag it out," said Gilbert. "You have a less resigned observer."

Over Cynthia's shoulder Adam saw Nita at the corner of the hut. She had changed into the homespun dress and upon coming out to show herself in it had been confronted by the spectacle of the embrace. The sunbonnet she had been carrying by the strings slipped from her fingers. She bent swiftly and snatched up the knife with which she had been slicing pemmican. Adam let go of Cynthia and strode toward her.

"Drop that," he demanded.

Nita stepped to one side so that she could see Cynthia past him. Her eyes had narrowed and her teeth were showing. But when Adam reached for the knife she dropped it and looked up at him, smiled cheerfully and was immediately calm again. She glanced down at the homespun dress as if there were nothing else on her mind. While it was a clean, almost new, dress, it was so long it touched her moccasins and enough too large for her to hang on her a little like a flour sack.

"This dress," she said. "I do not like it."

"Just the same you're going to wear it."

"No," she said, with complete finality.

Cynthia walked over to them. Like Nita she seemed now concerned only with the dress.

"Don't be silly," she said. "It suits you quite well."

She picked up the sunbonnet, slipped it over Nita's head and tied the strings under her chin. Nita didn't move. Cynthia stepped back to survey the effect.

"There—you look very nice. Doesn't she, Adam?"

Nita took off the sunbonnet, tore it in two, dropped the pieces on the ground and stalked into the hut.

"Come back out here," commanded Adam.

When she did not reappear he went in after her. She was

pulling the homespun dress off over her head. He grabbed up the deerskin. She got one arm disentangled and snatched at it. He jerked it away from her, took it out with him and tossed it high in the nearer cedar. Cynthia and Gilbert was watching, more fascinated every minute. In the silence there came from within the hut the ominous sound of tearing cloth. The shreds of the homespun dress came flying out the door.

"Something tells me, my friend," said Gilbert, "that you're about to be up a tree."

Cynthia began to laugh. All the time Adam was climbing the tree her laughter was ringing in his ears. Sliding down, he threw the deerskin through the door into the hut.

"I'm so glad you brought her, Adam," said Cynthia, wiping her eyes. "I'm just beginning to guess what you've been through."

Before he could reply she began to laugh again. Adam wheeled to see what Nita was up to now. He was relieved to see she'd slipped on the deerskin dress again. At least she hadn't come out naked. But while he'd been up the tree she'd taken time to paint her face with horrible elaboration, evidently having used pemmican grease, a charred stick and the yolk from one of the boiled eggs. He grabbed her, dragged her to the stream, washed her face with sand and water and dragged her back again.

Cynthia had stopped laughing. She was watching thoughtfully. Adam released Nita and waited grimly for what she might try next.

"He has to treat her like a child," Cynthia said to Gilbert. "You can see that."

"True," said Gilbert. "Though a child of rather interesting dimensions."

Nita suddenly sprang away in the direction of the horses and put the whole strength of her lungs into an earsplitting series of war whoops. The peacefully grazing horses, startled into a frenzy, broke their tie ropes and bolted. Before Adam could catch and control Nita the whole pack train had stampeded. Only Cynthia's quick thinking saved Adam's saltpeter from being scattered over miles of wilderness. Leaping into the saddle she called to Gilbert to help her and galloped in pursuit. They managed to head off the pack horses, to soothe them and to herd them back to camp.

Adam was tying Nita hand and foot. Cynthia rode up and sat in the saddle, looking down at the conclusion of the grim and efficient process.

"Well, it's some relief," she said.

"What is?"

"To see that's the only way you can handle her."

"How else could anybody?"

"I don't know. Maybe I'm a weak character. But I've an idea that after month in a cave with you I might be rather docile."

"I doubt it," said Gilbert, "if he were making off for another cave."

Adam stood up, walked over and pulled Cynthia out of the saddle none too gently. He held her by the shoulders and forced her to look at him.

"Have you another halter for me?" she asked.

"Let's have this out here and now," he said. "There's been nothing between me and her—in that cave or anywhere else."

"I actually believe you," she replied. "Not that it would have made a fatal difference—to me."

"What would make—that much difference to you?"

"Nothing—that's happened so far."

"You mean it's all going to depend on what happens down there at the station?"

"No, Adam. On what happens between you and me."

"If you're working up to another kiss," said Gilbert, "may I suggest postponing it to a more opportune moment. The prostrate young lady and I do not constitute a truly sympathetic audience."

Adam released Cynthia and stepped around the stallion.

"Get down off that horse," he said.

"I'm not fond of being told what to do in quite that tone," said Gilbert. "But under the circumstances I'm only too happy to oblige."

He sprang to the ground and moved toward Adam. He was just as ready for this kind of trouble as he was ready to talk out of turn.

"Some other time, maybe," said Adam impatiently. "All I want now is your horse"—he indicated Nita—"so I can tie her in the saddle. That'll save dragging her by the heels all the way to the station."

Gilbert grinned cheerfully. "I yield," he said, "to the prospect of your triumphal entrance."

"But, Adam," said Cynthia, "that won't do at all."

"What won't?"

"Taking her down there all tied up."

"How else are we going to get her there?"

"But people will never understand."

"Wait a minute," said Adam. "Maybe we haven't settled so much, after all. What makes you so afraid of what people down there understand? What have they got to do with it?"

"Since my chief function today seems to be that of a neutral observer," interposed Gilbert, "maybe I can help clear that up."

"And I'd also like to know," said Adam, "just where you come in on all this."

"Then I'll tell you," said Gilbert. "I heartily wish it were in a manner that could cause you more concern. I'm here instead of one of Cynthia's brothers to keep the introduction of your captive into the station from seeming a purely Wyeth enterprise. There are twenty-six families down there besides the Wyeth households. You know how people crowded together in a station make everybody else's business their own. What we're trying to do is to make your arrival with the girl seem something perfectly normal and usual."

"Leaving the Wyeths free," said Adam, "to decide among themselves how they're going to take it."

"And why not?" asked Cynthia. "What other reason did you have for bringing her here?"

Nita had been watching and listening with the utmost intent interest. She now sat up and stretched out her bound hands to Adam. "No more today," she said, "will I do what you do not want me to do."

Adam promptly began to untie her.

"How do you know the performance won't start right in again?" asked Gilbert, astonished.

"Mean as she is," said Adam, "you can trust her to do what she says she will do."

"Then—when we get in sight of the station," suggested Cynthia, "will she ride along with me? Can you get her to do that?"

Adam looked at Nita. "Will you want me to?" she asked.

"Yes."

"Then I will."

"Beware the Greeks," murmured Gilbert.

"What's that?" demanded Adam.

"I was merely reflecting somewhat idly upon the various quarters from which you have been receiving gifts."

Adam walked down to string together his pack horses. Nita tied the food basket on the back of Gilbert's saddle, mounted and wheeled the horse around beside the stallion. The procession set out, the two women riding slowly ahead, Adam and Gilbert walking together beside the lead horse of the train.

When they reached the crest of the slope Adam stopped. Many people, apparently everybody in the settlement, were assembled on the strip of flat grassland before the open gate. There was the faint squeal of a fiddle. The carcass of a buffalo was hanging over a barbecue pit. A horse race was in progress. Other men were engaged in a turkey shoot. And others were cheering on a wrestling match.

"Last night Jane Archer, the miller's wife, had a boy," explained Gilbert. "Everybody decided to knock off work for the day to celebrate the first child born in the settlement."

"Brings 'em all together to watch us come in," said Adam.

"That's so. But it also gives them something else to think about."

Adam took his first careful look at the way the station was laid out. He could see much to approve. Some hundreds of acres of bottom along the lower stream had been put into corn and the corn was doing well. A pasture for horses and stock had been fenced. The stockade was high and strong with good blockhouses at each corner, while the houses inside were bigger and more substantial than was common with new settlements. The station occupied the flat in the center of the horseshoe bend between the two falls. There was an outlying building, with an overhanging, loopholed upper story, at the lower falls and a mill wheel rumbling beside it. An addition of equal size was in the course of construction. At the upper falls another structure was going up.

"Tom Archer's building his gristmill right alongside Menifee's sawmill at the lower falls," explained Gilbert. "There's power enough from the one big wheel to run both. Cynthia's building her shop at the upper falls because in time she'll want water power, too, so that she can add a tilt hammer to her forge. As you can see, the mills are within gunshot of the stockade. They'll have garrisons at night and serve as outlying blockhouses, adding to the strength of the station."

Adam nodded. The Wyeths planned well and carried out what they planned.

"As you probably know," Gilbert continued, "the Wyeths kept the land on the east side of the stream and turned the west side over to the company and to the small farmers they've brought in to add to the population for the sake of defense." He shot a glance at Adam. "We're standing on Cynthia's tract. It stretches from beyond her millsite all around this head of the valley."

"Where's mine?"

"Over there along the west slope—the next but one beyond Cynthia's boundary."

"Who's got the one in between?"

"I have. You see, my draw came just before the one Cynthia made for you."

"How about trading?"

"You seem to be laboring under one misapprehension, at least. I'm by nature incurably hopeful—to the last. Actually, the occasion could arise, you know, when I might be eager to keep mine and to buy yours."

"If that occasion does arise," said Adam, "you won't have to buy my piece. I'll give it to you as a wedding present."

"And if it goes the other way you'll expect me to do the same?"

"You can suit yourself."

Gilbert laughed. "It's a pleasure to know you, Adam. You're a bold fellow. And you give me new hope. Cynthia's never liked being dominated." He gave this statement a second thought. "At least, she's never thought she did."

THIRTEEN

PEOPLE were keeping right on with whatever they were doing, without paying any attention to the approaching party.

"Gate wide open and nobody looking," grumbled Adam. "How do they know who's coming?"

"The Wyeths do," said Gilbert. "And if you know Joel you can guess the station's never really off guard. They post sentries every night—at the gate and around the horse pasture—and every morning at daybreak Eli Skaggs takes three or four men and goes out to scour the edges of the woods. As soon as he can get around to it—maybe today—Joel's going to organize a militia company. Practically every man here has seen service in the Continental Army or the Virginia militia."

Cynthia and Nita rode on ahead, splashed through the ford and turned toward the gate. Several women on the nearer fringes of the crowd glanced around. It was only after a second look that they seemed to realize that Cynthia's companion was a stranger. Had Nita been wearing the homespun and bonnet Cynthia might have slipped her into the stockade without any fuss at all. But Nita's Indian-like deerskin and moccasins and braids were enough to make people suddenly curious. More and more of them were looking around. Then, as if timed to cover the two women's entrance, a drum began to beat, drawing everybody's attention the other way. Cynthia and Nita rode through the gate without attracting further notice.

One thing, at least, was already clear enough. The Wyeths, as usual, had closed ranks and adopted a plan. Cynthia and

Gilbert's coming to meet him, the homespun and bonnet, the drum—possibly even the barbecue—were parts of the plan. They'd told nobody Nita was coming or that she was a recently rescued captive. They hadn't wanted anybody outside that close family circle to take a hand—not at first, at any rate. With Nita once safely in the stockade and in one of their houses they'd be free to deal with the situation any way they chose.

The pack train was crossing the ford. Three men were coming out to meet him. The rest of the crowd kept on toward the plank table under the big elm between the mill and the stockade where the drum was beating. He saw the three were Paul, Blake and Bert. Paul got to him first, seized his hand, punched him affectionately in the ribs.

"Adam—good to see you," he roared. "Bert says you had a hard winter—but I knew you'd never let a little cold weather get you down." He waved proudly toward the stockade, the mill and the cornfields. "Been a big change since you were here last, eh? Ever see a finer location?"

Blake was not as loud but his welcome was just as warm. "Big day for us," he said. "Brought the station its first child and the company its last partner."

"Big day for me, too," said Adam. "Been a couple of times I wasn't so sure I'd ever get here."

"I'll take the horses," said Bert.

He gave Adam a broad wink that was apparently intended to be reassuring. Paul was pulling Adam toward the table under the elm where the men of the station were collecting.

"We're having our first muster," said Paul. "Joel wants to see you before it gets started."

Joel came around the end of the table with outstretched hand. "Glad to see you, Adam," he said. "And specially glad you got in today. We're organizing a militia company and electing a captain for it and we can use your help."

Adam glanced toward the gate through which Cynthia and Nita had disappeared. "First I better take a look to see how Nita's getting along. I mean the white girl I took from the Cherokee. Cynthia must have told you about her. You could never guess the trouble she can get into."

Joel didn't seem to feel the problem one of great moment. "I can guess at little—from what Cynthia did tell me of what she had heard from Bert. But the women can look after her. It's mainly their affair, anyway." He kept hold of Adam's arm and led him around the table to the side facing the assembling crowd. "Take a look at them," he murmured. "You'll see what I meant about maybe being able to use a little help."

Adam looked, trying to take the interest it was no more

179

than sensible for him to take. These men were likely to be his neighbors for some time to come. They'd be closer than neighbors, for that matter, as people were bound to become when they were crowded together within the walls of a station. Summoned from their various diversions by the drum, some had come running but others had only sauntered and there was a good deal of nudging and shoving and horseplay. Several were already drunk enough to be noisy. Adam was familiar with the difficulty of handling frontiersmen whenever any considerable number of them were gathered together. Each had to show himself to be as independent as the next. He could sense the restlessness in this gathering. Many were not happy at being called by a drum. Others were taking on either the humorous or the argumentative look normal to every frontier town meeting. Not that any of these were real frontiersmen yet. They were just farmers in butternut and linsey-woolsey. They came from a part of Virginia where not since their fathers were young had people had to hunt for their keep and fight off Indians to stay alive. But they were fast taking to the ornery behavior that went with the West. No matter how willing a man might have been to keep his place, back where he came from, the minute he got over the mountains he carried a chip on each shoulder. The drum stopped.

"Big circle," called someone. "Down in front," yelled others. "We can't see the major," added a voice.

The last complaint brought several laughs. The men in front began sitting on the ground. Behind them the nudging and shoving continued. Joel seemed to take no notice of any of this foolishness.

"Before we start," said Joel, putting his hand on Adam's shoulder, "this is Adam Frane. You've all heard enough about him to be as glad he's joining us as those of us that know him are. He came to Kentucky before the first settlement was founded. He knows the country as few do—white or red. He was with Clark at Kaskaskia and Vincennes. He's a man able to meet any Indian on his own ground. As an example of that—there's what's just happened to him. The Cherokee stole a horse from him. He followed the thieves right into the middle of the Cherokee country, and when he saw they were keeping the horse where he couldn't get near it he took something away from them they valued much more. He stole a young white woman they'd held captive for years and brought her back with him. She's in the stockade now."

Adam stirred restlessly. The Wyeth plan was marching on. A number of women on the outskirts of the meeting turned and hurried toward the gate, immediately more interested in

180

getting a look at the surprising new arrival than in the further proceedings of the muster. And leaving Nita to her own devices among strangers was about as safe as leaving your powder horn beside a fire.

"A captive white girl," exclaimed a young man standing in the back row. "Ask him does he know where he could steal me one."

Joel joined in the laugh, pressed Adam to a seat on the bench and himself sat informally on a corner of the plank table.

"Now, to our meeting," he said, his manner as easy as if this were no more than a conversation among friends. "Since we've been here it's been our way—whenever we've had to make up our minds about something—to talk it over first and give everybody his say. Somebody has to start the talking and maybe you're used to my doing that."

"We sure are," said someone.

"But we like it," said another, good-naturedly.

"What we're here to talk about today," Joel went on, "is the right way to defend ourselves. We've been working hard, building and planting. Everybody's been doing his share and more than his share. But having enough to eat and a roof over our heads won't do us much good if we let the Indians come and take both away from us." The crowd was sobering. "Now the right way to defend ourselves is not something that can be left to each man's separate judgment. I think we're all agreed that we must organize ourselves into a military company to which every man and every boy over fifteen will belong."

There was a general murmur of assent.

"The next thing I feel we must keep in mind is this," Joel continued. "When we have differences of opinion on other matters we can discuss these differences until we reach an agreement—and talk as long as we need to, in order to reach one. But that can't hold when it comes to defending ourselves. Once we're attacked it'll be too late to stop to talk. Therefore it seems to me that the most satisfactory first step in organizing ourselves into a military company is to make up our minds who's the man best fitted to command it. Does anyone have a different view?"

Adam could see the notion of one-man rule was none too welcome. But each man present was waiting for the other to raise the first open objection.

"I'm sure we're all agreed on that," Joel continued after the briefest pause. "However, the selection of a military commander is the most important decision we can make. We'd do well not to rush it. Whatever talking we have to do—let's do it now and get it over with. I suggest we recess for two hours and come back with our minds made up on the man to whom we can all give our full support."

Everybody was surprised by this postponement. They'd evidently expected Joel to push his program right through. The meeting broke up into groups which drifted away, the men arguing vigorously among themselves. Blake, Paul and Gilbert moved away, too, leaving Adam alone with Joel.

"We could have put our man over by bringing it to a head without any more fuss," said Joel. "We have the votes. But we didn't want to seem to force it. We want everybody willing to go along."

"Who's your man?"

"Gilbert Naylor. At first we thought of putting in Blake or Paul. Both have been Continental officers with plenty of command experience. But there's some feeling the Wyeths are taking too much on themselves. That we own two thirds of the place and have paid for most of the rest only makes it worse. Gilbert's got another advantage. He's a doctor, not a soldier. A good many of the men here have served in the army and have had their fill of regular officers. On the other hand, the post is too important to let it go to just anybody that can get the votes. That's what brought us around to Gilbert. He's smart. And we can trust him."

"Who's against him?"

"Nobody, actually. Everybody likes him. But there's a good many against giving any one man so much authority. There's some talk of a committee of public safety, instead. Halponstall, the storekeeper—the fellow over there with the long nose that's going around whispering his misgivings into everybody's ear—is the one pushing the committee idea. Then there's that heavy-set man in the black coat just now scuttling through the gate into the stockade. He's Uriel Barr, the minister. He feels the church should be guidance enough to do us. Since we haven't given him all the rope he wanted he's set against anything he thinks we're for."

The pushing and elbowing Joel was concerned about came up in every new settlement. If anybody ever was able to handle this sort of thing these Wyeths were. And Adam would be glad to see Gilbert get the captaincy. A man could hardly take on more grief than that which went with the military command of a new settlement.

"I'll vote for your doctor," Adam said, getting up.

Joel laughed. "Now that you're here we're expecting a lot more than your vote. People will listen to you. You're a stranger and haven't yet taken sides. They all know you were with Clark, that you know Kentucky, that you know

Indians and that you know what it takes to defend a station. They'll take stock in your judgment. The sticking point is not Gilbert. It's bringing themselves to give one man the authority he has to have. You can make them see that if there's ever a place that needs one-man command it's a new settlement."

Adam nodded. But his eyes were still on the gate. All the Wyeth women, and very likely half the women of the station, could be swarming around Nita by now.

Joel's eyes twinkled. "If you're worried about building up a rival—don't give it another thought. Cynthia has known Gilbert a long time. His getting command of half a company of farmers isn't going to startle her."

"I've got more than Gilbert to worry about," said Adam.

But the chance to pin Joel down evaporated. A woman was coming out through the gate. She kept on through the crowd and headed straight for Adam. She was a handsome, rosy-cheeked, redheaded woman, nearly as tall and big as Paul, glowing with the same exuberance, and, in fact, looking a great deal like him. She seized Adam by the arm.

"I'm Phoebe—Paul's wife," she announced. She leaned past him to Joel. "I promised Julia I'd fetch him. She can't wait to have a look at him."

Joel had been about to object but his face softened at the mention of Julia.

"How is she today?" he asked. "She was asleep when I left this morning."

"She's fine," said Phoebe. "She ate a good breakfast."

Julia's breakfast seemed to carry the day with Joel. "But don't keep him long. He's got work to do. Tell Julia I'll drop in soon's I can."

Phoebe steered Adam toward the gate. "Julia's Joel's wife, I suppose you know," she explained. "They've been married for twenty years and for the first time there's hope she's going to have a baby. She's staying in bed to make sure she doesn't lose it. She'd spend her whole time hanging by her heels if she thought that would help." Four boys, ranging from six to ten, were scampering before them, staring over their shoulders at Adam. "My four oldest. You've been with George Clark and that makes you a great hero to them—to all of us, for that matter. Even Joel's impressed." She gave Adam a quick, intent look and nodded judicially. "And now that I've seen you I'm beginning to understand what set Cynthia to wondering. In her own way she's usually got as much of a mind of her own as any of the Wyeth men."

"I've noticed signs of that," said Adam.

"You're not exactly backward yourself," said Phoebe.

"Bringing your wild girl straight here." She chuckled. "Nothing could have set Cynthia to wondering harder." She chuckled again. "It's worse than some of Paul's tricks I can remember."

Adam blinked. After having braced himself to withstand the certain diapproval of the Wyeth women, to be met instead by their amusement was like stepping into a hole when your attention was fixed on the trail ahead.

Inside the gate, the first three in the row of plank houses were twice the size of those beyond. "Ours, Joel's and Blake's," explained Phoebe. "Cynthia's living with Blake and Amy. That's where she took your little stranger." Five more children, ranging from two to six, were playing about the steps of the nearest house. "My next five. We've got ten." Adam took another look at her. She couldn't be much more than twenty-five and the bloom on her glowing face was that of a girl of sixteen. She laughed. "Scandal for fair, isn't it? But they've just seemed to keep coming—one every year." From within the house there came a violent wail. "The youngest. He's heard me—and he's hungry. Come in a minute."

The big kitchen smelled pleasantly of the newly sawed pine planks. The fireplace was of brick instead of stone and the pots and kettles ranged about it were shining brass and copper instead of dull iron. The long table running down the center was of old mahogany and so large and heavy no pack animal smaller than an elephant could have brought it over the Wilderness Road.

A smiling Negro woman lifted the baby from the cradle. "Sit down," Phoebe said to Adam. She herself sat on a low stool in the corner so that when she opened her dress and took the baby only her head and shoulders were visible over the cradle. The infantile yells ceased with a sudden indignant gurgle. Adam couldn't go on grinning and nodding to encourage Phoebe to keep on talking, so he looked at the mahogany and the bricks.

"Paul knocked the table down and put it together again after we got here," Phoebe explained. "It took three mules to pack it over the mountains but Paul likes to see us all sitting around it. And he found clay for the bricks on that slope beyond the salt spring. He fired enough to see how they'd do. They came out fine. Once the Indians clear out enough so that we can build real homes, all of us can have brick houses if we want."

For sure, Adam reflected, no movers had ever come to Kentucky with a capacity to strike down instant and vigorous roots equal to that of these Wyeths.

"Faster, Georgie," said Phoebe, glancing down. "If we keep Adam more than another ten minutes Uncle Joel is going to start beating that drum of his." She looked up again to smile at Adam. "You're Adam to everybody else in the family, Mr. Frane, so you might as well be Adam here, too."

"Good," said Adam. He didn't mind being patted on the head by such a fine, big woman. "I've certainly never run into people I wanted more to get along with."

"I'd hardly say that falling on the neck of an outsider was a Wyeth family tradition," said Phoebe. "But they did take to you on sight. That's one reason Julia and I had to get a look at you. Hurry up, Georgie. There isn't time to be polite, Adam—or even civil—so I'll come right out with it. Julia's and my main reason was—that we could tell the Wyeth men had already decided what they thought about your bringing the captive girl here. This seemed to us something that might turn out to be a little too complicated to leave entirely to the men. So we made up our minds—Julia and Amy and I—that we better try to keep track of it, too."

To Adam it was like the moment you had caught a glimpse of the shadow of a stag and could know as you slowly lifted your rifle that his next step would bring him into view. He could know, at last, just what he faced. All he had to do was ask. He did.

"Just what ideas do the Wyeth men have?"

"The same as they always do. They're waiting to see how Cynthia takes it. They want her to have anything she wants—and the way she wants it."

"And the Wyeth women have different ideas?"

"Not this time. If what Cynthia wants is a man—we want her to have him. The Wyeth brothers' wives would like very much to see Cynthia settled with a man of her own."

There it was. After all his worrying it was as simple as that. The Wyeth men were willing to wait and see and the Wyeth women were wishing him well. What it all simmered down to was that everything depended on Cynthia. That was wonderful. That was the way it should be.

"What makes you so sure I'm a better bet than this young doctor?"

"We're not sure. Cynthia never says much and for all we know she hasn't made up her mind. That's another reason Julia and I wanted to see you right off—to see if we agreed with Amy's guess that she had. But even before seeing you the chances still seemed all in your favor. Gilbert's been after her all his life. First he lost her to Henry Rowan. Since she's been a widow he's been trying hard again and still has never quite made it. While from the talk at Draper's Meadows you got off to a flying start the very first time you met her—that night at the Ingles dance." Phoebe seemed to read his mind. "Oh, her brothers like you. Make no mistake about that. But they'd turn on you in a minute if they thought you meant the slightest harm to Cynthia."

"Well," said Adam, "I don't. And maybe the sooner I tell her so the better. You say she's at Blake's house—next door?"

"First we've got to see Julia," said Phoebe, replacing the baby in the cradle.

The other kitchen was much the same except that the fireplace was of stone and the table, pine. Julia lay on a couch by a window. She was still beautiful in spite of the streaks of gray in her dark hair and the lines of suffering upon her pale invalid's face. She looked stern, severe, even cold, until you noticed the glow of happiness in her deepset eyes. She turned her head on the pillow with the slow, careful movement of one husbanding every ounce of her energy.

"I am happy to meet you, Mr. Frane. It was good of you to come directly to see me."

She exchanged a glance with Phoebe.

"But I am not surprised," Julia continued. "Joel is so much taken with you and he is seldom mistaken in his judgments. Please sit down—both of you—here where I can see you."

"Have you had a glimpse of the captive girl yet?" asked Phoebe.

"Cynthia had her in for a minute," said Julia, smiling. "She's such a shy, big-eyed little thing. But she took a most sympathetic interest when she learned why I was in bed. She earnestly advised me to eat plenty of bear meat—so that I would have a small baby—as the bears do."

"All her life she's lived among Indians," said Adam quickly. "In most ways she's still the same as one."

"Well, she's not among Indians any more," said Phoebe. "Joel wants Adam back out there right away. So I'll tell you straight off what I think—or rather what I don't think. I don't think her being here has to be such a problem unless we make it that. She's here. There's no help for that. But we can make the best of it. There's only one way to do that—and that's to make a place for her in a perfectly normal, ordinary way—just as if she were any other unfortunate young woman who had just escaped from the Indians. So how about this? With all my children I could use some extra help. I'll hire her to work in my house. That'll

186

give her a home with us. That's certainly better than letting her go on staying with Cynthia at Amy's. She looks quick and smart. She can learn. I've an idea it won't take long to teach her decent manners. Presently everything else will follow along. She's pretty enough. With as many snorting young bachelors as we have around it won't be much longer before she'll be married and settled in a place of her own. You brought her here, Adam, and I suppose that makes you responsible for her—as much as anybody is—but what's wrong with letting it work out that way?"

"She's got relatives in Carolina," said Adam.

"Relatives she's never seen," replied Phoebe. "That have long since forgotten her. Why should she have to go back to them?"

"You don't know her," said Adam. "She's a terror. Didn't Bert tell you about her setting Glover's on fire? She'd be no help to you. She'd give you nothing but trouble."

Again the women exchanged glances.

"Why did you bring her here, Mr. Frane?" asked Julia.

"Taking her from the Indians was an accident. But once it had happened I saw no reason to try to hide what had happened."

"It wasn't because you saw how she felt and was sorry for her?"

"Sorry for her? She's a little hellcat. Nobody could be around her very long and still be sorry for her."

"Would you object to her marrying one of our young men?" persisted Julia quietly.

"Why should I object?" demanded Adam, getting up. His temper was beginning to slip. So much interest and support on the part of Cynthia's sisters-in-law was an advantage he hadn't counted on, but he wasn't a bug crawling up the wall, its progress to be observed and speculated upon by the entire Wyeth family. "I'm not worrying about marrying off Nita. I've my own marrying to think about. You keep telling me everything's up to Cynthia. That's what I want it to be." He turned in the doorway and grinned back at them apologetically. "You've been mighty good to me—both of you. A whole lot better than I deserve. Could be I'll come running back wanting you to take me on your laps."

Outside, he turned toward Blake's house next door and came to a disgusted halt. A dozen women were clustered about the steps. The cackle was like a hen yard. But Amy caught sight of him from the doorway and came running to him.

"Oh, Adam," she whispered, "I'm so glad you've come back." Her voice dropped to a lower whisper. "I can't believe your little wild girl is going to make any real difference. Cynthia's been trying to be very patient and amused—though down inside she's boiling. But it's never been her way to let anything get between her and what she wants—and I know—I just know it, Adam—that she wants you. Oh, I do hope nothing goes wrong."

She gave his arm a squeeze and went flying back into the house. Adam didn't like her idea that something might still go wrong. Anyway, now was the time to push right in and find Cynthia, no matter how full of strange women the house might turn out to be. The ones around the steps were staring at him and whispering. The door was ajar. Adam was too anxious to get away from the women to wait to knock. He pushed it open and walked in.

He found himself in another big kitchen. Nita was sitting on a stool by the fireplace. Standing over her was the only other person in the room—the preacher. Seen at close range he was perhaps fifty, short, deep chested, thick shouldered, with small, sharp eyes and a square-jawed, pugnacious, florid face that did not go at all with his ministerial black coat and oratorical voice.

"Confession, repentance and prayer," he was declaiming to Nita as if from a pulpit, "these are the steps by which the most confirmed sinner may return to grace."

Amy came hurrying in from another room. "The Reverend Uriel Barr—Mr. Adam Frane," she said.

The minister gave Adam a quick, searching look and then strode forward to clasp Adam's hand in both of his. "A very great privilege has been granted you, Mr. Frane." His voice reverberated through the kitchen and his handclasp was like a blacksmith's. "In wresting this poor creature from the foul clutches of the infidel you have not only saved her temporal life but opened the way to saving her immortal soul as well."

"Who is this man?" Nita asked Adam.

"He is a white medicine man," said Adam. "The head one of this town."

"Do I have to listen to him?"

"Yes. He wants to help you think like white people think. And you have to learn that as fast as you can."

Nita folded her hands composedly in her lap. "I will listen. I want to learn how white people think. But I cannot yet tell what *I* will think."

Adam eyed her impatiently. Apparently she'd been trying to behave since she'd given him her promise up on the hill. Still, it wasn't too safe to leave her alone here with this preacher. If the man kept at her, as he showed every sign

188

of doing, she'd probably wind up going for him with the fire shovel. But he had to find Cynthia. That had to come first.

"Well," he said to Nita, "whatever you think—stop and think some more." He turned to Amy. "Where's Cynthia?"

"She went out somewhere with Blake. They wanted to talk."

Talking with Blake. Talking with Gilbert. Talking with anybody but him. Adam started for the door.

"Adam," called Nita.

"Yes?"

"You will come back?"

He swung around.

"You've got only two things to worry about," he snapped. "One's to stay out of trouble and the other's to do as you're told."

She seemed almost pleased by his anger.

"Yes, Adam," she said meekly.

He was still angry when he reached the gateway. In the meadow beyond, the turkey shooting and the horse racing had been resumed. A good many men were more interested in the whisky barrel and the barbecue pit. Others were just standing and arguing. Seemingly countless children were scampering in and out among the groups of their elders. Some of the more impatient women had managed to persuade some of the younger men to help them get the dancing started. Upward of two hundred people, counting the blacks, were milling around, all foolishly intent upon their own foolish concerns. Then he saw Cynthia. She was at some distance, sitting on a stone by the corner of the horse pasture. Sprawled on the ground around her were Joel, Paul and Blake. All were talking earnestly.

He started for them. These Wyeths seemed to think that everybody could go on being calm and polite and friendly while their women took time to sit around talking about ways to help him up if he didn't fall down too hard, and their men took time to sit around studying him and talking about how near he might come to measuring up to what they thought was good enough for Cynthia, and Cynthia herself took time to sit back and wonder just what she did think about him after all. He didn't have to stand in a corner waiting to be told when he could turn around to see what they had for him. But after a dozen strides he pulled up. He'd better wait until he could see her alone. He'd already waited so long he could afford to wait another hour or two.

Men standing near him were beginning to eye him and

189

several to sidle toward him. Then a couple of the boldest came over to shake hands and to introduce themselves. Others followed and then more. He remembered that he was supposed to be advising them and to be working for Gilbert Naylor. The Wyeths had given him a job to do for them, while they were making up their minds what they were going to do for him. But whether he felt like it or not he couldn't side-step giving his opinion. Everybody that came up asked him what he thought about the captaincy idea. They set a high value on his judgment. They thought he knew. Well, he did know—as much as a man was ever able to know about anything that was as seldom twice the same as the way Indians could come at a settlement. And since this was going to be his settlement he had to tell them what he really thought, whether or not it helped the Wyeths. The advice he gave had to be repeated again and again as new groups came up. The burden of it each time was:

"Certainly you need a captain. Somebody has to keep a roster and keep track of whose turn it is to stand guard and to sit up to watch the stock and to go out to look for Indian sign. It's a mean job and any man's a fool to want it, but it's a one-man job and a poor man can do it better than a good committee. But you don't have to fret too much about who you give it to. When the Indians do come you'll have to look to old Eli Skaggs, anyway. He'll be able to figure out how many of them there are—whether so few that you can run out and chase them off—or so many you'd better lie low back of your palisade. He'll know what to do and how to do it. Bert's another one that will know."

Nearly always as he turned away, some man's hoarse whisper followed him. "Why ain't he himself the man fer the job?" And always someone else had an answer. "He's so close to them Wyeths be just like havin' one of them."

No one ventured to ask him directly if he wanted the post. He hadn't turned back to protest the whispers lest this merely stir up talk that might otherwise die out. For he certainly didn't want it and wouldn't take it. He'd never wanted to be an officer with Clark. Between battles the responsibility of command was a never-ending annoyance. When shooting started it was worse than an annoyance. Much less did he want that kind of responsibility here.

But he couldn't help taking notice of these men. The average was way above most new settlements, which generally were burdened with a fair proportion of real no-goods. He might have known that in selecting settlers to bring out with them the Wyeths wouldn't have included any outright nincompoops. Most of them were willing to listen to advice

190

from anybody they thought knew better than they did. They wanted to do what was best. And they were trying to guess what they weren't at all able to guess, and that was what it might be like—most any day—to find bullets thudding into the stockade, and the bodies of three or four of their friends down by the edge of the cornfield, stuck full of arrows, and Indians howling in every clump of brush around—and the women and children up on the roofs with buckets of water. Even the Wyeths, who thought of almost everything, likely hadn't yet thought too clearly about that day.

The group then questioning Adam became involved in persuading a drunk that the loss of the lower half of his ear, chewed off in the course of a wrestling bout, was not a provocation which required going after the biter with an ax. When next Adam looked toward the corner of the pasture fence Cynthia and her brothers were not in sight. But the barbecued buffalo had at last been pronounced done and the blacks presiding over the operation had begun to cut off smoking hunks. Adam was intercepted on his way to the gate by Bert with a slab of hot meat.

"Come over here by the crik and eat with us," he said. "You ain't seen Alice yet."

Alice was sitting on a low, flat stone. She didn't look around or start to get up until they were beside her. When she did she seemed to keep right on rising. She was a good head taller than Bert. She was also thin as a rail and had mouse-colored hair and big hands and feet. At first glance she was about as homely a woman as you'd often run across. But there was something about her that made you take a second look. She had more bosom than most skinny girls, her lips were full and soft and red and her eyes were green as a cat's. She was alive, too. When she looked at Bert you could tell what she was thinking as certainly as when Amy looked at Blake.

However she appeared to other people, Bert was as pleased with her as if he were drawing back a curtain to show off the Queen of Sheba.

"This," he said, "is Alice."

Then his face fell as he noticed the way Alice was looking Adam up and down.

"So you're Adam Frane," she said.

Adam was dumfounded. If there'd been anyone in the settlement, after Bert, upon whose support he had relied, it had been Bert's wife. He wondered uneasily if she knew something he didn't know yet. There'd been all those women swarming around Nita. And the preacher, too. On the other hand, Alice might only be badgering Bert. A bride didn't always take to her man's old friends.

"No, I'm not," he said, for Bert's sake, to let the moment pass into frontier-style teasing.

"You're not what?"

"I'm not Simon Girty. Wasn't that what you said?"

Bert tried to save the situation. He gave Alice an elaborate nudge. "You'd best git on the good side of him. Ain't nobody alive can tell you more about me."

She gave his arm an immediate playful slap and as she looked at him there was a light in her green eyes indicating that ordinarily such little exchanges worked up quickly and well for Bert. But when she looked back at Adam her glance was as cold as before.

"Bert counts you his best friend," she said.

"That's what I count him, too," said Adam. "We've both counted on it for a good long while."

"Then what beats me," she said, Bert's familiar phrase sounding very odd in her thin, high voice, "if you're such a friend of his—is why was it—when he was startin' to git along here so well—you had to bring that white squaw here to make trouble fer him—and fer all of us?"

Bert grabbed her arm and shook it warningly. "Here comes Blake. Look, sugar—Adam's goin' to stay at the mill with us. You can pick your bone with him tonight. Save it for then."

"Always we have to worry about what the Wyeths might think. I suppose now you'll want me to start worryin' about what Adam might think. You can do as you like, Bert Cogar, but—"

Bert shook her so fiercely that she stopped. She jerked away from him but she didn't say any more.

Blake joined them. "Hope you've eaten, Adam." He grinned at Bert and Alice. "Sorry to take him away from you." He took Adam's arm and turned him toward the gateway. "We've had a mysterious summons from the church."

"What's up?" It had been a mistake not to get back to Nita sooner.

"All I know is," said Blake, "that the spiritual shepherd of our little flock sits glowering in Julia's kitchen. He demands the presence of the entire Wyeth family. He demands yours, too."

Amy met them at the door and contrived to whisper to Adam. "She won't wear any of my clothes—though I'm just her size. But every other way she's been behaving like a little angel. Practically every woman in the station has been in

192

to see her—they're all so curious—and she was pleasant to all of them. I took her over to see Jane Archer's baby. She was very interested. The minister came twice to talk to her. She even stood for that. She's asleep now—she's worn out, poor child."

The Reverend Barr sat at the head of the table and, as Blake had said, he was glowering. All the Wyeths were present, Paul and Phoebe side by side at the table and Joel sitting on the floor beside Julia's couch. But Adam saw only Cynthia. She was on a stool back in a corner, leaning forward on the low seat, her fingers laced about her knees, her dress pulled smooth and tight over the roundness of thigh and hip and shoulder, her body drawn into a series of gracefully submissive curves. She seemed thoughtful but quite calm. She smiled faintly when their eyes met and gave a little shake of her head as if warning him to keep calm, too. He followed Blake and Amy to places at the table.

"I hope you'll make this as brief as possible," said Joel. "Julia mustn't be tired more than necessary."

Barr got to his feet, clasped his hands behind him and strode up and down as if to gather his powers. "This is a matter of the utmost urgency," he pronounced. "Otherwise I would not have insisted that every one of you be here."

"Well, stop galloping in circles and take the fence," said Paul.

"This Kentucky is a godless land," said Barr, ignoring Paul. "To my knowledge I am the only ordained minister in the entire province. Throughout this benighted wilderness, in this settlement only is there any disposition to acknowledge the demands of Christian conduct. It is my duty to make certain that these demands are not challenged—that this lone candle in the dark forest is not extinguished."

"If you're bringing up the chapel question again," said Joel, "we can only say what we've said so often before. As soon as the other two mills are finished we'll see that lumber is sawed for your church."

"A place of worship is indeed the most essential feature of a Christian community," said Barr. "But that is not the protest I am here to make. We can hold services in God's open air—or in a stable—or anywhere that godly people gather themselves together. What I am here to protest is the sudden flowering of heathenism in our very midst."

"Good gracious," said Phoebe. "He must be talking about the poor little wild girl."

"I am, indeed. My heart bleeds for her. I pray unceasingly

193

that light may come to her. But the terrible truth is that in giving her refuge we are sheltering a sorceress—a practicer of witchcraft."

The Wyeth women, including Cynthia, gasped. The Wyeth men were smiling in equal disbelief but the nature of the charge had not been the same surprise to them. Adam saw what was happening. They'd sent for him to undertake Nita's defense because there was for them a double advantage in this. If he successfully quieted Barr, well and good. He'd have saved them the trouble of doing it. Meanwhile, they realized what slippery ground this put him on and could watch how he handled himself on it. They had him in a tighter spot than when they'd first started looking him over the morning he'd reached Blake's house or during the land survey when they'd taken so long to make up their minds. He couldn't just jump up and give the preacher the clout he was tempted to give him. His real opponent here was the Wyeth family.

"Witchcraft—your grandmother," he replied. "I don't know what she's told you—or anybody else has told you. But let me help you get everything straight. She may be a little ignorant because she's lived among Indians most of her life. But she's no more of a witch than you are."

Barr shook his head sadly. "None is so blind as he who would be blind. The truth is—the Devil in his unremitting endeavor to promote evil sometimes finds strange instruments—and she is such an instrument."

"Come—come," said Joel. "This is hardly Salem. What actual evidence have you—that you, at any rate, can regard as evidence?"

"I have indisputable evidence, I regret to state. I myself have questioned the girl at length. There is, moreover, the testimony of Jane Archer. It is unmistakable and it is damning. When the girl was permitted to see the new infant she noticed that the cradle was lined with deerskin and immediately asked if it was a female child. When told that it was a boy she at once became strangely excited. She said it must be taken from the cradle at once. She reproached the mother with ruining the boy. She said a girl baby should be laid on fawnskin so that when she grew up she would be shy and pretty and graceful, but that a boy baby must always be cradled on pantherskin to make him supple and strong and capable of making prodigious leaps upon his enemies. She did not stop there. She further reproached good Sister Archer with remaining in her bed in the midst of her family. She said this had contaminated all of them. She said that childbirth was unclean and that Sister Archer should have withdrawn to a hut in the woods—to remain there for weeks and until she had purified herself by various pagan rituals. In failing to do so, she insisted, a mother brought misfortune upon her other children and upon her husband and upon all who were near and dear to her. When I saw Sister Archer she was in tears and suffering a severe sinking spell. Make no mistake, my brothers and sisters. What I have described to you is sorcery—it is witchcraft—and its practice among us is a work of the Devil."

"All foolishness," said Adam. "Everything you've been saying. I told you she'd been raised among Indians. Your fawnskins and pantherskins are only some of the most ordinary things all Indians believe. She knows no better. But that doesn't make it witchcraft."

Barr paid no attention to Adam. His attention remained fixed on Joel. "Seems to me it's an opportunity for you," suggested Joel. "It's your bounden duty to convert her."

"I have already begun struggling toward that end. But she is very obdurate. However, I shall persevere until I have saved her poor troubled soul."

"That seems to settle it," said Paul. "Why, then, all the shouting?"

"I am only now coming to that." Barr strode forward and pointed his finger at Adam. "There stands the man I am here to accuse."

"He doesn't stand," said Blake. "He sits."

"Don't point," said Adam. "I don't like it."

"There stands the man," resumed Barr, not at all confused by the interruptions, "who introduced this taint of heathenism among us. And how have we received him? We have taken him to our bosoms. We have rushed out to cover him with honor. So much so that this family—I am given to understand"—he looked about the room in sudden malicious triumph—"the leading, the most respected, God forgive us, of our whole community—that this family is planning to make him a member."

"And there," said Blake, "hops the cat out of the bag."

"You see, Adam," said Joel, "he's getting at us more than he's trying to get at you. I think I told you he wants a greater hand in running the place. Now he thinks he sees a chance to make us knuckle under for once."

"Well, he's got a poor chance with me." Adam stared at Barr until the minister looked at him. "Whatever you're driving at—come right out with it."

"That is what I came here to do." Barr addressed the Wyeths again. "There is but one stand we can take if we are honest men and women with that regard for the sanctity of family life which dwells at the heart of the Christian attitude.

195

We must give this man his choice. For weeks he has lived in a cave and in the woods with this young heathen female. Now he has brought her here with him. We must insist that he take her as his lawfully wedded wife, so that hereafter we may hold him responsible for her conduct, or we must cast them both from our midst." He gazed about him solemnly. "You shake your heads, you smile. You do not agree with me. But before you give me your final answer—reflect, I beg of you—reflect and take counsel."

"I've already reflected," said Adam. "My answer is that you're crazier than a loon. So get on with whatever you're threatening to do about it. What comes next?"

Barr continued to ignore Adam.

"I feared that you would harden your hearts. Once more I have held open for you the gate to the fold. If you will not enter I must still do my duty. I shall make the matter the first order of business when the meeting reassembles this afternoon."

"They'll howl you down," said Joel.

"Some may try to. But there will be others who will give heed. The seed of righteousness, once planted, will take root. It will grow"—his face glittered with sweat and his voice boomed—"it will flourish—it will spread until, like the tree of life, it shelters this community of ours from every heathen wind that may beat upon it."

"It's a fact," said Paul with a rueful chuckle, "he can raise a hell of a stink."

Adam got up. The Wyeths had been holding back to see how he'd try to deal with this. The time had come to show them. He started around the table. Barr did not flinch. Instead he gathered himself as if quite prepared to offer resistance if violence was in prospect.

"Don't get your feathers up, mister," said Adam softly. "I'm not going to lay a hand on you. But you better listen—even if you're not used to listening. You call this a godless country. Maybe it is. But it is not a lawless country. Because every man is his own law. One more word out of you—in this house—or outside—or anywhere—about me—or about anyone that has anything to do with me—and I'll kill you. I'd no more stop to think before shooting you than I would a Mingo jumping at me or a rattlesnake trying to bite me."

Barr looked around appealingly at the others in the room.

"Certainly sounds to me," said Blake cheerfully, "as if he means exactly what he says."

Adam stepped aside and Barr started for the door. By the time he had reached it he had recovered at least a shred of his dignity.

"I can forgive you," he said, raising his hand in benediction, "for I am certain you know not what you do. It could be that the unbridled fury of your defense indicates your innocence. I will pray for further guidance."

He went out and Adam went back and sat down.

"Would you have shot him?" asked Paul with genuine interest.

"I may still have to," said Adam. "He looks to me like the kind that hates to quit."

Adam saw the Wyeths hadn't been shocked. They were regarding him with approval. Cynthia's eyes were particularly bright. He himself was already vaguely ashamed of his display of violence, but apparently they were able to take a threat to kill a minister of the gospel as something quite for granted as long as the threat was made in their interest.

"I think we're all beginning to see," said Joel, "that Adam is going to be quite a help."

The incident seemed closed.

"Now that we can talk reasonably again," said Phoebe, "what does everybody think about moving Nita over to our house?"

It was a general question but all looked at Cynthia.

"Don't look at me," said Cynthia. "Let Adam decide. He knows her better than we do. What do you think, Adam?"

Everybody was looking at him now. They still had him in that corner.

"We might try to find out what Nita thinks," he said. "She'd ought to have some say about it."

"Quite true," said Joel dryly.

He called Julia's black girl and sent her for Nita. Phoebe and Amy started talking about Phoebe's oldest boy's refusal to eat corn bread. Joel and Julia were talking in low whispers. Cynthia leaned her head back against the wall and closed her eyes. Paul was whistling under his breath. Blake began telling Adam about a bear cub that had torn Eli Skaggs's pants off. Yet the waiting was as awkward as if they were sitting in an uncomfortable silence. The door opened and Nita stood in it.

"My God," whispered Amy to Adam. "My best dress."

Nita walked slowly into the room. She was no longer clad in the sleeveless deerskin and her braids were wound around her head, making her look taller. Amy's peach-colored silk fitted her to perfection and she carried herself well in it, so that she seemed suddenly as much the lady as any woman present. Joel got to his feet, as did Paul and Blake.

"Who told you you could wear that dress?" demanded Adam.

197

"Nobody," said Nita. "I wear it so that everybody can tell I do not belong in it."

"You certainly don't," said Adam. "Go back and take it off."

Nita seemed not to hear him. She addressed the Wyeths.

"I do not belong in this dress. I do not belong here. I do not like it here."

"But this is where you are," said Adam. "And it doesn't make any difference whether you like it or not."

Nita continued to speak to the Wyeths.

"I did not come here because I wanted to come. My home it is with the Cherokee. I never leave them because that was what I wanted to do. Adam he take me away. He tie my hands. He tie my feet. He carry me on the raft. He carry me on his back. He keep me with him when I want only to get away from him."

"I've wished a thousand times since I'd let you get away," said Adam.

She turned to him. "But you bring me here. I do not want to stay. I want only to go back to the Cherokee. That is where I belong."

"The hell you do," said Adam, getting up. "You belong with your real people in Carolina. And that's where I'm going to take you."

There was a momentary gleam in Nita's eyes. Cynthia's cool voice cut the silence.

"Sounds to me as if Adam had decided something, after all."

Adam turned from Nita to face Cynthia. He was caught, and had been fool enough to do the catching himself.

"I haven't decided anything," he said. "I haven't had a chance to. But where else would you say she belonged?"

In this crisis, as usual, the Wyeths seemed to move according to plan, as if each, at all times, knew what the other thought. Neither Blake nor Paul had even glanced toward Joel. Yet they immediately drifted toward the door.

"Well, we don't have to settle everything right this minute," said Joel. He looked out the window. "It's getting late. Time to get the meeting started again."

He linked his arm companionably with one of Adam's. The three, moving out the door, carried Adam with them. Blake and Paul walked on ahead. Joel still had his arm through Adam's. He might almost have been a prisoner.

"Cynthia's a little touchy about that girl," said Joel. He was talking as man to man about the mysterious, though on the whole pleasing, weaknesses to which the best of women were heir. "You can hardly blame her. But it'll blow over—if you give it time. Phoebe will take the girl off her hands and when Cynthia's had a chance to think she'll realize there's no reason to make too much of it. My sister's got a temper—as you may have noticed—but she can be very reasonable, too. I think the best move you can make is to start out first thing in the morning and take your saltpeter to Harrodsburg. I heard yesterday from Casper Gonday—the storekeeper there. They're short of gunpowder everywhere in Kentucky. You take it to him and you can get most any price you ask. And by the time you get back Cynthia'll probably feel like running to meet you. Oh, Jesse." A slightly stooped man in a red waistcoat, old enough to have a snow-white beard but still vigorous and bright eyed, was waiting in the gateway. "Excuse me, Adam,—Jesse Baker, my overseer. Well, Jesse, how's it look?"

"Good, Major," said Jesse. "Good." He thrust a friendly thumb at Adam. "After he got through talkin' to 'em they was all hell bent for the one-man scheme."

"Fine," said Joel. He took Adam's arm again and walked on with him. "Well, that's another thing off our minds, thanks to you."

Everything managed to suit the Wyeths. Everything going the way they wanted. Getting him off to Harrodsburg out of the way for a while. Making Gilbert captain. Giving Cynthia time to back and fill. Adam pulled away from Joel and crossed to Bert who was strolling with a group moving toward the elm. He drew Bert aside.

"Tell as many as you can catch before the meeting," he instructed Bert, "that I've had a falling out with the Wyeths over Nita. Tell the storekeeper first."

Bert's eyes grew wide. "You don't say. But Joel was just walkin' with you. I seen it myself."

"Don't argue," said Adam. "Do as I say."

He watched while Bert caught up to Halponstall. He whispered to him. The storekeeper grabbed the man next to him. Other heads bent into the circle. The circle broke up, each member becoming the center of another circle. The report spread through the crowd moving slowly toward the elm like the ripples set up by a school of fish cruising near the surface of a placid stream.

Adam stayed in the back row. The drum stopped beating. The crowd's buzz of excited whispering kept on. Adam knew what was coming. He knew these men as the Wyeths could never hope to know them, because he was so much nearer to being one of them. But it came sooner than he had expected. The storekeeper, stuttering in his haste and excitement and sense of importance, spoke up before Joel or anybody could get in a word.

"Mr. Chairman, I move that it is the sense of this meeting—that we here and now form ourselves into a military company—and that we elect one man captain—and give him full authority and—as a necessary part of this motion—I nominate the best man for the place—Adam Frane."

There was a yell from the crowd, partly of approval and partly of surprise from those the last-minute word hadn't gotten around to yet. Adam was watching Joel. Joel didn't change expression. His eyes swiftly searched the crowd until they met Adam's and then they still remained veiled, merely thoughtful. Adam met the glance with his own calm stare, likewise giving no sign of what he felt. A sense of again being fully alive took possession of him, as if he'd just come up out of deep water to take a first long breath.

Jesse Baker turned around from his position up front and faced the crowd. He'd undoubtedly had had fixed in his mind his assigned part in keeping the election from getting out of hand. He was more than a little confused by the complete unexpectedness of what had happened, but he dutifully did what he could. He spoke out as soon as the meeting had settled down enough to give him a chance.

"I ain't got no manner of doubt this Adam Frane is a mighty good man. But folks never got in no trouble by stoppin' to think. We better stop long enough to puzzle out if we know what we're after. I like the way he looks and acts, too, but how can we know for sure what we're a-votin' for? To most everybody here he's a total stranger."

Blake was leaning lazily against the trunk of the elm. He spoke without straightening up.

"So much the better. He can give orders without hurting anybody's feelings."

The drawling remark brought a nervous laugh. Nobody could be quite sure whether he was making light of Adam's qualifications or Jesse Baker's argument. A number who had yielded on the spur of the moment to the impulse to oppose the Wyeths were relieved by this first hint that the Wyeths might not take an inflexible stand on the issue.

Bert stood up. He was solemn but there was no hesitation about his taking his position. "Adam ain't no stranger to me. And all I can say is—we couldn't do no better—'less we was to send for Clark himself."

This brought a bigger laugh, in which the undercurrent of relief was clearly evident. Bert was known to have been a firm partisan of the Wyeths. His switching so early was leading many to think that they'd have the fun of crossing the Wyeths without getting themselves too involved in the risks of an outright collision with them. Paul jumped up, putting an end to all doubt.

"And I move," he bellowed, "that nominations be closed."

"All in favor say aye," directed Joel.

Many of the ayes were little more than gasps of amazement. Several of the slower witted had been completely taken aback by the lack of any contest. To some of the shrewder it had begun to seem that this might have been the result the Wyeths wanted all the time. There were accusing glances at Bert and he was looking just as accusingly at Adam.

"The ayes have it," ruled Joel.

Adam knew there had been a contest, all right, that it had been between him and the Wyeths and that he had won it. He became aware of Gilbert at his elbow.

"As I think I remarked before," said Gilbert, smiling, "you are a bold fellow. My one immediate consolation is that I trust your duties will keep you most of the time in the depths of the woods."

"If they do," said Adam, matching Gilbert's grin, "I'll need a doctor with me."

He began to push through the crowd to meet Joel who had started toward him. Everybody fell back and then moved closer again to observe this meeting. Joel's gray eyes were frosty until they met Adam's and then they warmed with a kind of guarded approval.

"The democratic process," he said, offering his hand, "sometimes moves most mysteriously to fit the right man to the right place. So far, Captain Frane, we are at your service."

The "so far" enlightened Adam. They hadn't foreseen losing control of the election and they hadn't liked losing it, least of all to him. But they hadn't felt free to make a fight of it. They were still protecting Cynthia's possible future interests. They had still to be prepared, if need be, to close ranks around him, to make him one of them. Their devotion and their magnanimity at once impressed and confused Adam. He felt the need of making some concession himself.

"I'll still go to Harrodsburg in the morning," he said. "I want to get rid of that damn saltpeter."

FOURTEEN

THE summer twilight lasted late into the evening. Adam had spent the remainder of the afternoon drifting among the crowd, talking casually, fixing each man's face and name in his mind, finding out what weapons he owned and how familiar he seemed with them, learning how much and how well he hunted, noting in passing how he held his whisky—and deciding in each case whether, when it was the man's turn to serve his time on guard, he had better be kept at the gate, or could be trusted to take care of himself through a night in the open around the horse pasture or was one of the few up to ranging the woods with Eli Skaggs.

The dance had finally got going. Phoebe and Amy had come out to join in it for a while. Practically every woman of the station able to walk had. But Cynthia had not. And no Wyeth came near him with a message from her. Once he saw her in the gateway, talking to Gilbert.

"Put the doc on the first watch at the horse pasture tonight," Adam said to Bert, who was helping him draw up the guard roster.

If a meeting with Cynthia did happen to work out tonight he didn't want Gilbert around. At dark he ordered the dance stopped, insisted that everyone withdraw into the stockade, rounded up various bemused couples lingering in the farther shadows and stationed the first watch at the horse pasture.

"How good's the chance of the Indians jumping you on your way to Harrodsburg?" asked Gilbert cheerfully.

"Not so good as their jumping you here tonight," said Adam. "Keep your eyes open."

"I do," said Gilbert. "Though I can't say I like everything I see."

Adam placed the young Ealor brothers on the first watch in the stockade, Caleb at the gate and Jonas walking the circumference of the rifle platform. Having learned from Bert that both were courting Sally Halponstall it seemed a good idea always to assign them to the same watch, lest the one on duty leave his post to see what the other was up to. Then he took the guard roster to Blake's house for Blake, as his lieutenant, to keep for him while he was away.

Amy let him in. She and Blake were alone in the big kitchen. Amy saw Adam's quick look around.

"Nita's moved over to Phoebe's," she said. "She seemed quite willing to go. The children over there are utterly fascinated with her. And Cynthia was tired. She's gone to bed."

"Been a long day for you, too," said Blake. He reached for a bottle on a shelf. "How about a nightcap?" His smile was not quite as warm as usual but he still seemed friendly enough.

"Thanks," said Adam. "But I'd better turn in, myself. I want to get a good early start in the morning."

"Harrodsburg's quite a trip to go it alone with four pack horses keeping you slowed up. Aren't you taking any help?"

"I'll get along. Eli Skaggs and Prosper Doane and the Spenser boys are going out along Stone Creek to hunt buffalo tomorrow. That'll cover me 'til noon. After that there'll be stations every ten or fifteen miles and I can make a run for it from one to the next."

Amy walked with him to the door. "Nothing that's happened yet has made me change my mind about what I'm sure Cynthia really wants," she said, squeezing his arm. "Only—do hurry back."

"Before she wants something else?"

"Oh, no. I only mean—why take chances you don't have to? Anyway, with something that's so important."

Adam jerked his head toward the board wall at his shoulder beyond which Cynthia lay in her bed, possibly sleeping, possibly lying awake and thinking and listening to the murmur of their low voices.

"Sensible way would be for me to go in there, get her up and ask her straight out what's what."

"Oh, my God, no," said Amy, pushing him out the door.

Starting for the mill, he recalled irritably the lesser difficulty now before him. He still had Alice's strange animosity to face. Jim Menifee was sitting on the step outside the closed door of the mill.

"Set down," he invited hospitably. "They'll call us soon's supper's ready."

Behind the heavy oaken door Adam could hear Alice talking steadily. Her voice was too low for the words to be distinct but the tone was bitter. Adam settled down beside Jim.

"I allus pull out for a spell when they gits to squabblin'," said Jim. "Bert he holds up his end better when there ain't nobody watchin'."

"They fight much?" asked Adam.

"Not so much as most," said Jim. "But—when they do go at it—generally it's a purty good one." He turned his head toward the door. The low drone of Alice's complaint had ceased. "Bert's got her stopped already. Now listen." Oddly dragging footsteps receded from the kitchen and then from somewhere beyond there was a light squeak. "That's their bedroom door. Won't be long now before we eat."

Jim bent forward, spat out his cud of tobacco and with a forefinger began scraping the remnants from his teeth. "Don't never take that Bert too long to git around her. He makes out a sight better'n I ever was able to with her maw."

The two men waited. The silence inside continued. Through Adam's mind ran memories of Bert's one-time bashfulness with women. After a time Jim turned his head again. The inner door squeaked once more. Jim drew his feet under him. Bert threw open the door above them and peered out.

"What you doin' a-settin' out there in the dark?" he demanded. "Supper's been a-waitin' and me I'm hungry whether you are or not."

They went in and followed Bert to the table. Alice was bent over the kettle that swung on a crane in the fireplace. There wasn't much of a fire but her face was red. She began serving them. She didn't look directly at Adam or say anything to him but the plate she gave him was heaped with choice pieces of the stewed venison.

"Give him some more," directed Bert.

Alice gave Adam a quick look and blushed more than ever. "Adam knows he can have more," she said humbly, "whenever he wants it."

She gave Adam another quick look, this time accompanied by a conciliatory smile. Adam stared at Bert. Bert laughed complacently.

"Trouble with Alice was—she thought you'd been keepin' the wild girl back in the woods for me and then had brought her here so's I could git at her again. What give her that idea was my sneakin' off them three times in a row to see you and not tellin' her nothin' about Nita before you showed up here with her. Took me 'till just now to git it through her head Nita was all yours and nobody else's."

Jim tramped hard on Adam's moccasined toe but there was only the faintest twinkle in his eyes as he regarded Bert. "It's a fact," he told Adam, "nobody can tell Alice that Bert he can't have any woman he's a mind to—and that every last one o' them ain't allus after him."

"I can remember a good many that were," said Adam, gravely nodding his agreement with this point of view. "Every place we went. Only reason some of them aren't still following him around was that he always made them see it was no use."

Alice didn't laugh. She was listening with shining eyes and believing every word. She sat down at her place with a contented sigh, glanced at Bert, blushed, hastily picked up her spoon, dropped it again and leaned toward him. She spoke with sudden fierce passion.

"And for one o' them it ain't never goin' to be no use."

"Not any," Bert pronounced firmly.

From outside came the subdued, yet sharp, broken call of a quail. Adam started up. So did Bert and Jim. They were reaching for their rifles.

"It's only Nita," said Adam, trying to act as if he saw noth-

204

ing out of the ordinary in her being outside the stockade. "I'll be only a minute."

He glanced back from the doorway. Jim and Bert were exchanging knowing masculine grins.

"You don't have to hurry it," said Bert. "Alice she'll keep your stew warm."

His loud laugh petered out as he encountered Alice's stare.

"Who's she whistlin' fer—around this house in the night?" she demanded. "Answer me thet, Bert Cogar."

Adam closed the door behind him. His eyes were unused to the darkness.

"Nita," he whispered angrily. "Where the hell are you? What you doing out here? What's the matter with you?"

He felt his way around the sawmill and among the piles of boards and beams assembled for the construction of the gristmill. He could see better now. Still he couldn't find her. Then her low laugh caused him to look up. She was straight above him, perched on one of the crossbeams of the half-erected framework. Her slight figure was distinct against the stars. As she leaned over her braids fell forward and swung as she giggled. She looked like a little girl playing hide and seek and seemed as childishly delighted by his delay in finding her.

"Come down here," he commanded.

"You will only take me back," she said. "First I want to talk."

"You're damned right I'll take you back." He started climbing up after her.

She sprang to her feet, ran fearlessly along the beam, swung around the corner upright and ran on along the next beam. Pursuit was useless. She could keep ahead of him, circling continually around the framework beyond his reach. He dropped back and sat down. She returned to her perch above him. She'd stopped laughing.

"How'd you get out?"

"It was easy. White people sleep very hard."

Adam jumped up. "The very first night, eh? That lunkhead at the gate's going to wish he'd stayed awake."

"He is not asleep."

"Then how'd you get past him?"

"I did not go near him. I came over the wall at the back."

"What happened to the guard there?"

"All the time he walk—and look only where he walk."

Adam sat down again. "So—you just came out to talk. Well—talk."

"You go to Harrodsburg in the morning?"

"Yes."

"You take me with you?"

"No."

"Because she would not like it?"

"Because I would not like it."

"When you come back?"

"Maybe five days."

"Then we go to Carolina?"

Adam paused to consider his answer. She dropped from her perch and sat beside him. After peering up at his face she nodded her head thoughtfully as if they had come upon something which, while not good, was still no worse than she had expected.

"So soon as I look at her I know."

"What did you know?"

"That for long time she would not let you go to Carolina."

"Now, look here. There's no use your making a fuss—as if this were something new. I've made no secret of it. I've told you from the start I'm going to marry her. I am. Make up your mind to that."

"You are a fool." She snatched up a stick of wood and struck at him furiously. He warded off the blow, took the stick away from her and held her until she had quieted.

"Could be. But what makes you think so?"

"I will tell you. I have watch her. Many hours I have watch her. Her skin it is smooth like Amy's dress—she have the shape everybody turn around to see. But she have something more than that. With the Cherokee I have seen the women who are like her. Such a woman have something that is different—something other women never have. It make every man want her. Every boy, every warrior, every old man, they come to her. They come from other towns. They all want her."

"You mean I'm a fool for wanting a woman that any man would want?"

"Yes. For you it is better to have a woman that is only for you. You do not want a wife that is also wife to the town."

"I'd ought to just slap your mouth shut and be done with it. But you talk so much—to anybody—that I suppose I'd better straighten this out for you. After all, you don't know any better. Maybe among Indians a woman that stirs men up like that always takes them, too, as they come. But among white people it's different—at least, it's generally different—and it's certainly not that way with this one. She's not had other men—since her husband—and when I marry her she'll be wife to nobody but me."

"It is the same. There is no difference if she take men or

if she do not take men. You want her for something in her that all men want in her. It is not something that is for you alone." She became suddenly and strangely calm. "I do not like it when you are a fool. But one thing you still must do."

"What's that?"

"You have said many times you will take me to Carolina."

"I know that."

"Then you must do it."

"I intend to."

"When?"

"I can't say for sure, yet."

"I do not like it here. I will not stay here long."

"You'll have to stay 'til I'm ready."

"I will go to the Cherokee."

"No, you won't. I'll catch you and bring you back."

"Then when will you take me to Carolina?"

"Probably not before fall. Something I didn't count on at all has turned up. They've made me captain here. I can't run off during the summer. That's the season there's the most chance of Indian trouble. When the first snow comes I'll take you."

"That will be too late."

"Why? You're being well taken care of."

"Before that you will marry her."

"You might as well make up your mind to that—and that nothing's going to stop it. That's sure."

She stood up. "Only one thing is sure."

"Talk is no good." She started away.

"Hey, where you going?"

"What's that?"

She paused as if she had not before considered this. "Back over the wall," she said.

"Wait a minute. You'll get yourself shot."

She started to run. He overtook her, seized her by one wrist, forced her to a walk and to approach the station with caution. They crouched in the shadow of the stockade until Jonas Ealor, walking the circumference of the rifle platform above, had passed by. Adam held her up by the ankles until she could grasp the top of the palisade.

He watched only long enough to make certain she had dropped down on the other side, ran to the mill and called to Bert. Bert came out, closed the door quickly behind him and peered around suspiciously.

"What'd you do with her?"

"Put her back over the wall—the way she came. But I haven't much doubt she'll try making another break. I need you to help so we can watch both sides of the stockade."

"You mean—right now?" asked Bert.

"Yes—now."

"What'll I tell Alice?"

"Anything you want."

"She won't believe it—no matter what I tell her."

"Be a man," counseled Adam.

Bert reluctantly opened the door and called through it. "Adam wants me to go with him to take a look at the guard posts."

"Don't make no difference to me where you go," Alice replied. "Or if you ever come back."

Adam pulled the door shut and Bert off the step with one abrupt movement. "No time now to argue with her," he said. "Besides, it won't be five minutes before she'll be leaning against that door—listening and waiting for you."

"And suppose she ain't?" said Bert bravely. "Case a man don't now and then let 'em know who wears the pants they'll run right over him."

"Come on," said Adam, pulling him away from the door.

The two ran around the stockade to the side opposite the gate.

"You take the far corner," whispered Adam. "And keep down out of sight. I want to catch her right in the act."

"You ain't figgerin' on us squattin' out here all night?"

"No. Just a little while. If she comes out at all it'll be right away. She'll only wait until she thinks I've had time to get back to the mill."

Bert muttered but trudged off toward the farther side. Adam sat on the ground. Above him the sharpened tops of the palisade logs were clear against the night sky. From time to time he could see the head and shoulders of the guard pacing past along the rifle platform. But no matter how hard he stared during the intervals between these passings he caught no glimpse of Nita's furtive shadow. After an hour he gave up and moved around to pick up Bert.

"She's fooled me," he admitted. "I had an idea she'd try again tonight. Let's go to bed."

"Sometimes you slip and think yourself up somethin' smart," said Bert. "Though lately it ain't been often."

He didn't say any more until they were almost to the mill. "What makes you think she wants to run off?"

"Because she keeps saying she will."

"Anyway, there ain't but one way to handle that. Give her a pat on the bottom, a compass and a sack of grub—and a horse, too, if she wants it." He peered up at Adam's face. "What makes you want to hang onto her? Nobody knows you like I do. But you got me treed, too. What you coverin' up?

Why can't you just shut your eyes and let her go? Don't look to me like anything could work out better'n that."

"Not tonight—it wouldn't. You're forgetting that when she turned up missing tomorrow it could look like she'd gone with me to Harrodsburg."

Bert chuckled. "It surely wouldn't look like nothin' else, for a fact." His chuckles became an unfeeling laugh as the situation grew on him. "And you tell me to be a man. You don't dast keep her here and you don't dast let her git away. You wouldn't listen when I tried to tell you. I never knowed a man so set on workin' up trouble for himself as you was when you brung her here."

The kitchen was empty and lighted only by a burning rag floating in a tin of grease. Bert hardly waited to bar the outer door before making a run for the other. He pulled up a step away from it, grinning sheepishly.

"Jim he sleeps back in the mill," he said, gesturing toward the business section of the building beyond the kitchen. In his impatience to free himself of Adam's presence he kept repeating the gesture, as if he were shooing a fly. "Alice put a mattress in a storeroom in there for you. Take the slut lamp so's you can see. Wouldn't want you fallin' into the saw—stumblin' around out there in the dark." He laughed briefly at his own joke. He was trying hard to show a host's proper concern for his guest's welfare but where Adam slept was the last thing on his mind. A thought of much more import occurred to him. "I'll help you load up when you git ready to go—but if you aim to git goin' real early you'd best call me. Sometimes I'm a little slow gittin' started in the mornin'." He laughed as if he wanted this considered another joke, picked up the lamp and thrust it at Adam. Another much-less-happy idea came to him. "You scarce had time to finish your supper. If you're still hungry there's more deer meat there in the pot."

"I'm sleepier than I am hungry," said Adam.

Bert sighed with relief. With the first step Adam took in leaving the kitchen Bert wheeled to his bedroom door.

"Sugar, I'm back already," he called through it softly.

His hand fell on the latch. It resisted. He pushed at the door. It did not yield. He placed his shoulder against it. The door was undeniably barred. His contented smirk was replaced by an expression of frantic concern.

"Hey, sugar," he cried, beating on the door.

"Never do to stand for that," advised Adam. "Get an ax."

But when Adam returned to the kitchen with the first streak of daylight there was already a fire snapping on the hearth. Alice, bending over a second skillet of broiling bacon, was humming happily and Bert was in the middle of an enormous breakfast of bacon and fried corn meal.

"Take you on a load of this side meat and mush," advised Bert. "The way you'll be travelin' you'll need somethin' that'll stay with you."

Peace had again descended upon the Cogar household. The two men were halfway to the horse pasture before Bert made any comment.

"That Alice," he observed. "They don't come no better'n her. Sometimes she puts on like she's real mean. But the way she really is ain't that way a-tall. Sure is a purty mornin', ain't it?"

It was. The first curls of smoke from chimneys in the stockade were rising in the fresh, still air. The green meadows and even greener fields of young corn in the valley bottom glistened with dew. A few wisps of mist wreathed the edges of the woods. Eli Skaggs and his fellow buffalo hunters had completed their dawn circuit of the rim of the valley and were riding over the hills to the west on their way toward Stone Creek. Young Jasper Croak, who'd been on guard the second shift at the horse pasture, stood watching them.

"Looks like they didn't find no injun sign," he said, almost regretfully, to Adam and Bert as they came up. "Ain't bin none since we bin here."

"There'll be enough—soon enough," said Adam. "One thing for you to do while I'm away, Bert. Make sure Blake doesn't stand for any slacking off in the kind of watch that's kept. You know how quick Indians generally are to take a look at a new station. Their holding off this way is a bad sign —not a good one."

They caught the horses and started back with them to pick up the saltpeter at the mill. The stockade gate was open. Phoebe came running out. She had some kind of a green woolen dressing gown belted around her and her red hair, cascading down her back, gleamed in the first rays of the rising sun. Her face was flushed and her eyes bright.

"Nita's gone," she announced. She watched Adam curiously to see how he took the news.

"When'd she go?"

"I don't know. Nobody saw her, of course. But it must have been almost daylight. I was up with the baby just before that. She was still in bed then and she seemed sound asleep. She's not in the stockade now, though. The children have looked everywhere."

"You take the horses," Adam directed Bert.

Bert stared at him. "What you goin' to do?"

"Bring her back, naturally."

"Want me to help you trail her?" Bert's tone indicated his conviction that Adam hadn't the remaining wit to pick up the tracks of a Conestoga wagon.

"No. You get the horses loaded. I know right where she is."

Phoebe, too, was staring at him. But it was a waste of time to stop to try to explain now. He went around the sawmill, dropped into the bed of the stream and ran up that, screened by the fringe of brush on the bank from the view of anyone higher up the hill to the southwest.

He passed the upper falls, with hardly more than a glance at Cynthia's giant blacks at work on her mill, and kept on up the stream. When he reached the upper woods he circled higher and to the west until, when he came out to the edge of the woods again, he could look down the slope to the station as well as down upon the route he would have taken in setting out for Harrodsburg. It was the nearest fold of the hills from which both could be observed. He had been nearly certain that Nita would be found here. Had she been serious about leaving for the Cherokee country she would have left early in the night. But he let out a grunt of deep satisfaction when he saw her. It was almost worth the delay and so much entirely unnecessary annoyance to be able for once to take her at so great a disadvantage.

She was lying in the tall grass, watching the station and the trail heading west from it. She had chosen a spot from which she could slip back into the woods the moment she saw him coming up the slope to look for her, and from which, on the other hand, had he started out before hearing she had gone, she could reach the trail in time to run ahead to wait for him somewhere along the way or to follow the pack train as long as she pleased before showing herself.

He moved down toward her so noiselessly that he was standing over her before she realized he was there. She was chewing a blade of grass and smiling from time to time, certain she had gained the upper hand and enjoying the idea. When she saw him she spat out the grass disgustedly and sat up.

"You catched me," she acknowledged.

"Come on," said Adam.

She rose without any protest at all and followed him. He swung off down the slope. He could hear the soft pad of Nita's moccasins behind him. She'd never before seemed so nearly subdued. His outguessing her had certainly taken the wind out of her. Maybe it had been a lesson that would last a little while, at least. It hadn't cost him a great loss of time, either. And it had been worth something to prove to people at the station that he didn't have to take any nonsense from her.

Around the settlement below, the day's activities were getting under way. Several men with hoes over their shoulders were going down to the cornfields. Another group was setting out to cut wood and timber. Joel, Paul and Blake were riding off somewhere. Adam noted that every man who left the gate had his rifle with him. They'd listened to what he'd said yesterday. He was getting everything under control, even with Nita. Everything except with Cynthia. And that would come.

Again he was approaching Cynthia's mill. This time he looked with interest. Saul and his sons maintained the high quality of their workmanship no matter to what they turned their hands. The upper floor and the interior partitions were being fashioned of carefully matched tongue and groove, while the outer walls of exactly squared timbers fitted along lines as straight and even as if they'd been drawn by a ruler. Adam could see that the lower section of the building was to house forge and shop and living quarters for the help but that the upper story contained additional apartments.

He paused to stare. Evidently Cynthia was planning to live in that upper story. A sudden gust of excitement beat upon him. If so, then there before him, only half formed as yet but still with the clearly indicated shape of walls and floors and windows and doors, were the very rooms in which Cynthia and he would presently begin to live together. There were the stairs they'd climb, the floors across which they'd walk, the walls to shut out all but themselves. Viewing the actual boards and rafters made the meaning of their life together suddenly real, as it had never been before. Always before, his thinking of her had been compounded of dreamlike efforts to remember how beautiful she seemed to him and equally dreamlike fits of desire to capture that beauty for himself. Here, though, was something more substantial than dreams. Here was the precise place they were to live as man and wife, experiencing details of daily companionship as real as the chairs, table and bed they'd be using. He'd balked at that reality when her house had stood beside the Valley Road in Virginia. But here it was different. Here he would be a member of the company, a landowner, a commander and in every respect the recognized equal of any of her brothers. And anyway, this place was only a start. Before long he'd have bought out or squeezed out Gilbert, thus joining his own land with hers in one magnificent sweep around the whole head of the valley, and then he'd build a proper house for them to spend the rest of their lives in. The entire prospect seemed already as definite as the oak sill Saul was laying in the doorway at the head of the stairs. And it was a reality that might as well start taking shape right now. He'd dismiss all this foolishness about giving her time to simmer down while he went to Harrodsburg. Before he went anywhere or did anything he'd get hold of her and make sure everything was settled, up to and including the date of their wedding. He became aware of Nita's steady, speculative gaze fixed on his face.

He scowled and strode on, veering away from the mill as he passed. Then, forgetting Nita's curiosity, he stopped again to stare. Saul and his sons had paused in their labors to eat. They were being served not only by old Hebe but by two young black women of a stature very nearly as impressive as that of the men in the family. One had a skin the color of coffee and the other of the darkest chocolate, but otherwise they were as alike as twins. And they were more than just big. Their bodies and arms and legs were beautifully shaped and their faces bright and handsome. Full bosomed and broad hipped, they were so tall they still seemed gracefully slender. They smiled calmly and spoke in low voices, carrying themselves with conscious pride and dignity. In their simple white cotton shifts, with scarlet bandannas on their heads and gold rings in their ears, they might have passed for African goddesses.

"That's Bessie and Betsy," said Nita.

"Who?"

"Wives to Herc and Sam."

"Herc and Sam?" Then Adam nodded. Saul's sons had apparently been named Hercules and Samson. "How do you happen to know so much about them?"

"They sleep in the stockade. I see them last night. People talk to them. I hear."

"You hear a good deal."

"Yes. I listen." She looked thoughtfully at the young giantesses. "They are new wives. For long time she look for women for Herc and Sam. All the women she find are too small. She look more and more far away. Finally she find these two. They come this spring—in a ship from a place called Maaka."

"Jamaica?"

"Jamaica," assented Nita, accepting the correction. "Where is that?"

"It's an island out in the ocean."

Sudden anger seized her. "Always she look—no matter how far—for what she want."

"What's wrong with that?" Adam approved of the quest for Bessie and Betsy. This magnificent black family helped to

213

make the kind of an establishment in which Cynthia belonged.

"She think only what is the best for her," Nita persisted.

"Come on," Adam said impatiently.

But the cloud was still on her face. Instead of following him, she very deliberately sat down. "No," she announced.

"Get up."

She shook her head. She seemed at peace again, as she always did when she resisted him. He bent down, seized her by the arms and lifted her to her feet. She didn't struggle. She merely let her body go limp. He threw her over his shoulder and turned to start on. Only then did he see what she had seen behind him just before she had sat down. Cynthia was coming along the path from the stockade. It was too late to avoid the meeting or the manner of it. He strode on toward her.

She stepped out of the path to allow him to pass with his burden. She was wearing a crisply starched, blue-figured gingham dress and a blue poke bonnet that shaded her eyes. As he drew nearer he saw that she was pale. But she was smiling.

"Didn't take you long to catch her," she observed.

"She wasn't running away. She was only hiding up the hill. She had an idea she wanted to go to Harrodsburg with me."

"Apparently she still wants to," said Cynthia. "Can't be that you handle her just right, else you wouldn't find her so hard to manage."

A hiss of anger came from Nita. She reared up and began to struggle to escape from his grasp. Not even during their first flight from the Cherokee camp had she opposed him so violently. She struck at him, clawed at him, tried to bite him. Her every panting breath was accompanied by animal-like little cries of fury. Impeded by his rifle, he found it nearly impossible to control her. He thrust the rifle into Cynthia's hands. Then, grasping Nita by the base of her braids, he held her away from him while he took off his belt. With the belt he bound her arms to her sides. Swinging her under one arm, he took his rifle from Cynthia and grimly started on. Nita could kick as furiously as she pleased but that was about all she could do.

Fifty yards beyond Cynthia, Nita ceased the kicking. She became suspiciously quiet and the next moment she laughed contentedly.

"She see the trouble you take with me," she said. "She know you will never take so much with her."

"There'll never be need to," shouted Adam, enraged anew to learn the whole outburst had been put on. "She's a woman—a sensible and cultivated woman. She's not a half-

214

grown, half-witted brat—a miserable, Indian-loving, screech-ing little hoot owl like you." He plunked her down on her feet and jerked his belt off her. "There—I'm through. Go where you please. Go back to the Cherokee."

She looked up into his face with a slow, satisfied smile. "You get very mad with me," she said softly.

"Go on back to the Cherokee," he repeated. "Nobody'll stop you."

"No. I do not want to go back to the Cherokee."

"Where do you want to go?"

"With you to Harrodsburg."

Bert and Jim had the pack horses loaded in front of the mill. Alice was standing in the open doorway. All were watching with interest. Adam grabbed Nita by the wrist and dragged her over to them.

"That empty storeroom I slept in last night," he said to Bert. "You won't be needing that for the next few days." He pulled Nita another step forward. "Lock her in there and keep her locked there until I get back."

"Hold on a minute, Adam," said Jim, reasonably. "She's a white girl. We ain't hardly got a right to keep anybody that's white locked up."

"I have," said Adam. "She's spent all her life among In-dians. As military commander here I've certainly got the right to decide it isn't safe to let her run loose around the station. In case you were attacked there's no end to the mischief she could make."

"Once you put it that way," conceded Jim, "it makes sense—plenty of sense."

"We'll keep her for you," said Bert, drawing an uneasy long breath.

Alice spread her arms in the doorway. "No, you don't, Bert Cogar. You've told me this and told me that and you've fooled me so far. But you ain't goin' to fool me no more. You ain't bringin' your wench right into my house— not so long's I'm in it, you ain't."

Bert advanced slowly toward Alice. She bristled and braced herself in the doorway.

"I ain't never told you nothin' but what was so," he said. "Nobody's been foolin' you and nobody's been tryin' to— you've been doin' all the foolin' your own self."

"She ain't comin' in here," screamed Alice. "You kin git such notions as thet right out of your head."

Bert was white around the lips and little beads of sweat were popping out on his forehead. "No good your yellin'," he said. "And, whatever you think about what I been doin' before, I ain't foolin' now—so you better listen. Adam's my friend and he's in trouble. I'm goin' to help him just like he would me was it the other way around. I'm goin' to keep the gal for him while he's gone. If it ain't here then it'll have to be the camp up by the blackberry patch. I'm goin' to keep her one place or t'other. You can have it whichever way you want."

Alice, sobbing wildly, ran across the kitchen and through the squeaking door. Bert took out his handkerchief and mopped his face.

"You bin shootin' purty close right along but you sure took the turkey on that shot," said Jim, wagging his head in marveling approval of his son-in-law. "Wisht I'd had thet steady a hand back when I was in shoes like yourn—there'd bin many a year since I'd of had smoother goin'."

Adam pulled at Nita resentfully. "She's raised enough hell for me," he said to Bert. "No use letting her upset your cart, too. I'll find some place else to leave her."

"No," said Bert. "I said she's goin' to stay here and that's the way it's goin' to be."

He led the way to the storeroom. It occupied a corner position in the mill and had been fitted as a blockhouse. There was a ladder leading up to a rifle platform and loopholes near the ceiling which let in air and some light. Adam released Nita. She walked calmly forward into the room and looked around without resentment.

"I will like it better here than in the stockade," she said. "You will come back in five days?"

"Maybe six—or however long it takes me."

"However long—I will be here." She seemed as satisfied with her situation as if in getting herself locked up she had won some new advantage over him. He turned from the doorway to look back at her suspiciously.

"That's right. You're here and you're going to stay here. No use your trying to get out."

"Why should I try? You will know I am here. You will have to come back."

Adam went out and slammed the door. Bert brought hammer and nails. They attached cleats to the door and frame and fitted a bar in place. Walking on ahead, Bert crossed the kitchen without a glance toward his bedroom door and sat down on the step outside the open outer doorway. Adam stepped over him and paused.

"You and me's always stood together," said Bert gruffly. "There's plenty of use hangin' onto somethin' like that—'cause it's somethin' we know we got. And standin' together against a pair of women—that makes it more use yet. You git goin' and git back—without wastin' no more time."

Adam dropped his hand on Bert's shoulder for a second, untied the lead rope, picked up his rifle and set off with his pack train. The first thing he saw as he rounded the corner of the mill was a flash of the blue bonnet, bright in the sun, up by the other falls. Cynthia was sitting on a rock, chin in hand, staring into the water.

He tied his horses under a tree back of the upper millsite. Saul and his sons glanced down incuriously and went on with their hammering and sawing on the second floor. Adam started around toward the falls. But Cynthia had come to meet him and their meeting was in the midst of all the carpentering to-do, with Hebe hovering around and Bessie and Betsy watching, while, each strong as a man, they went on handing up boards to their husbands above.

"I'm glad you decided to stop," said Cynthia. "I wanted to show you what we're doing here." She kept on, chattering along politely and cheerfully, as if the thing that interested her most at the moment was showing off her new house or mill or whatever she called it. "The main workshop will be where we're standing—the forge over there and the gunsmith there and a workbench along that side. Saul's family will live back there behind the kitchen. Next summer he'll put in a water wheel so we can have a power hammer alongside the forge there. All the rest is upstairs."

She ran ahead of him up the flight of stairs. The floor above was already laid and the outer walls were going up rapidly.

"This will be the dining room," continued Cynthia. "There'll be a brick fireplace—like Paul's—and the bedroom will be there—and another room there—a sort of combination sitting room, sewing room, guest room and office." Her gestures included the whole living area with pleased satisfaction. "It's not very big but it'll do for the time being while everybody has to live within gunshot of the stockade."

"Saul," rose Hebe's shrill voice from below. "You and Herc and Sam come down here and eat. It's all ready."

Adam had seen them eating some sort of a meal only a little while ago. They couldn't eat every hour. Anyway, Saul and his sons laid down their tools and disappeared down the stairway. Suddenly he and Cynthia were alone—for the first time since they'd said good-by nearly a year ago. She was looking at him thoughtfully.

"Well?" she asked.

He had tried to hang onto himself as long as she was able to keep herself so safely calm. "I want to know where I stand," he said.

"Where do you stand, Adam?"

"Nowhere. I'm hanging in the air. And I don't like it."

"And you can't make up your mind where to come down? Is that it?"

"*I* can't make up *my* mind? *I* can't? After I've spent nine years with nothing else on it. After I all but deserted to travel clear to Virginia just to get a look at you. And then traveled all the way back to look for land for you and your family. After I've run through the woods to Pittsburgh—and paddled six hundred miles down the Ohio—and boiled saltpeter in a cave all winter—to fix up a place where you could live alongside your brothers if it turned out that was what you wanted. Don't talk to me about making up minds. Not when everybody from here to Ingles' Ferry is standing around with a finger to his lips, whispering—'S-s-s-h—don't move— don't make a sound—Cynthia's thinking!' "

"Can you wonder? That I should know what to think would be much more wonderful."

"If you're talking about Nita and me in the cave—let's settle that once and for all. I told you before—up there on the hill—and I'm telling you again. Nothing happened between me and Nita—there or anywhere—that needs to make any difference to you."

"Whatever happened—what difference? It's past now— along with the other women you may have had—and the husband I once had. After all—you and I are that grown up —I hope?"

He was baffled. "Then what is it you're trying to figure out?"

"You. You might remember you haven't done all the traveling. I've come a long way, too. I've given up every plan I ever had—moved out to this wilderness—made over my whole life. We finally met again yesterday morning—after all these months—and—well—we met yesterday morning."

"Are you trying then to say that after coming out here on my account you're not sure that's what I want?"

"Are you sure, Adam?"

"How often do I have to spell it out? Anyway, let's stop pawing the air and get that, at least, straight and clear right now. I'm completely sure of what I want. I want you to marry me. Will you?"

"Yes," she said. She was beginning to smile. "And don't look so surprised. Though I suppose you might well be—as might I, too. We're probably not at all suited to each other. We'll each try all the time to run over the other. I might much better take that blessed Gilbert. But that just doesn't seem to be the way it is."

"No," he said slowly. "That doesn't seem to be the way it

is." She'd said yes right off. Her answer had been as straight and clear as his question. But it was no moment of triumph for him. What everybody had been trying to tell him about the way it was with her had been the way it really was. She *had* been taking time to think. She'd gone over it in her mind until she'd decided he'd make the right Kentucky husband for her—one of which her brothers approved, one able to fit into her plans and the Wyeth family's plans. Having at length made up her mind she'd made him come to her. Worse than that, she was now going to beat him completely. She was standing before him, smiling, waiting, just as always in his dreams, for him to reach for her. And that was what he was doing. He couldn't help it. No matter how much time she spent thinking or how little she spent feeling, he had to reach for her, he had to have her.

He took hold of her roughly. She lifted her face to his. She was that honest, at least. This part of her he could have. Their embrace was as sudden and violent as the one under the oak or the other on the hill. Only this time there was nobody around to interrupt. Here there was no need to think of others or even of themselves. He drew her harder against him, prolonged the kiss savagely. He was ready to hurt her, if he had to, to make her feel something, at any rate, while he was feeling so much. She did not flinch. Then he realized that she was holding to him, too. She was no longer merely yielding. She, too, was reaching. And then, she, too, was becoming aware of the difference. Her eyes had been closed. Now they opened. They stared into his, at first only startled, then widening with surprise, with what amounted almost to dismay. His sudden triumphant reassurance was so great that he began to laugh. Her face flamed but she did not try to avoid the issue.

"Don't laugh," she murmured fiercely. "How was I to know? It never happened to me before."

He'd won, after all. She'd not thought this one up. She'd not planned his genuine surrender. He couldn't stop his exultant laughing. Not until she stopped it with her mouth upon his. Her response was now as urgent as his demand, her arms and lips as eager as his.

"When?" he asked, finally.

She laid her head on his shoulder. Her voice was peaceful. "Today—if you want. Only I don't suppose we'd like setting up housekeeping with Blake and Amy. And you do have to go to Harrodsburg, don't you? So—suppose we say—the day this house is finished."

"How long will that be?"

"Not more than a week, according to Saul. Hardly longer

than it will take you to get to Harrodsburg and back." She leaned away and looked up at him. She was smiling but her eyes were no longer peaceful. "There'll be a door there at the head of the stairs when the house is ready. The day it's hung you can open it and come in—if you mean to stay."

"If," he scoffed. "If. When I get back I'll help Saul and his boys finish the house—and I'll hang the door myself—from this side."

He began kissing her again. The pleasure to be had of her seemed a delight to which there could be no end. But there had to be one, at once, if he was to get started today at all. And he had to get on to Harrodsburg, and get back and get that door hung. He pushed her away.

"Such strength of character," she mocked him.

"Laugh while you can," he warned her.

His kissed her hard once more and ran down the stairs.

Saul and his giant brood straightened and regarded him, not so much inquisitively as hopefully. He grinned at them with affection and pride and new approval.

FIFTEEN

IT was so hot in the warehouse that sweat was pouring in streams off the blacks unloading the horses. Casper Gonday thrust his hand into one of the opened sacks and let the dry white crystals run through his fingers.

"H-m-m-m." He managed to make the one grunt express his doubt that the saltpeter was of sufficient quality to give it any value at all and at the same time his astonishment that it was as good as it was.

"Poke into as many as you want," said Adam.

He walked to the doorway where the air was a trifle less suffocating and looked out at Harrodsburg. The place had at least ten times as many people as when last he had been there. Many more lived in shacks and tents and brush huts outside the stockade than could find room inside. And just now every one of them was making all the noise he could contrive, filling the sultry air with a din of gunshots, yells, songs and pan thumping. For the news of Clark's latest victory had but just come down from Louisville. Another English lieutenant governor had been discomfited. Sinclair, commander at far-away Mackinac, and his fifteen hundred Sioux—a strange new name never until this year included in the long list of

Kentucky's Indian enemies—had been not only defeated but humiliated. According to the story—before Clark, traveling fast and almost alone, had even reached the banks of the Mississippi, the mere report of his approach had thrown the invading horde into confusion. Adam somewhat doubted everything had been quite as simple as that. But there seemed no question the siege of St. Louis had been lifted, the advance upon the Illinois broken off and all threat to Kentucky removed, or that the whole enemy force, pursued by a single company of Clark's men, was in headlong retreat back toward those distant northern forests from which it had emerged. People who'd been too busy even to listen to Clark's appeals for men when he'd been right here among them only a few days ago were now shouting themselves hoarse in his honor, howling with pride because he was a fellow Kentuckian, calling him their immortal commander and the savior of the West. You could be sure that when he came back they'd again be too busy to listen to him. Clark might go on working wonders with his handful of followers but with no better backing than he was getting from the people he was defending no victory would ever be final.

Adam walked back to Casper. The storekeeper brushed off his hands, sat down on a sack, took off his wig and with his sleeve mopped the sparse gray stubble on his shaven head. The handsome wig was his one extravagance. Casper was all of sixty and had a face like an elderly monkey's, but with the glossy black wig clapped on his head, always a trifle askew, he counted himself a dashing young blade, well able to win feminine favor. Though the one rich man in Kentucky he was too close-fisted to further his amorous aspirations by the investment of one penny beyond the price of the wig, continuing to cling to the hope that he would yet prove successful. At the moment there was a large louse crawling among the carefully combed strands of his treasure. Casper snorted with anger when he perceived the intruder, caught it and crushed it venomously against his thumbnail. He looked up at Adam, his scowl switching to a grin as promptly as if his face were working by strings.

"You been workin' real hard and I'd like to see you make somethin' from it," he said, flipping the tiny carcass into the nearest open sack. "I'll give you twicet what your stuff's worth. Only reason I can do that is 'cause I happen to know some folks that want it bad."

"You mean half what you'll get from them."

Casper looked grieved. "I mean a dollar a pound—and that's twicet what I ever heard of saltpeter ever fetchin' before."

"I'll take it," said Adam. "You're talking about silver, of course."

Casper jumped as if he'd been stuck with a knife. "Silver," he cried. "You must of been walkin' around with your eyes shut and your thumbs stuck in your ears—since you come out of that cave of yourn—else you'd know there ain't no silver in Kentucky—no, nor copper neither." He began waving his arms. "If you don't believe me go find out for yourself. Then come back and maybe we can talk business."

"You might be right," said Adam. "Everybody acts that way, for a fact—including some that have probably got a sockful tucked away under a floor board. But just the same I have to have silver. I didn't work all winter just to earn me a wad of mattress stuffing."

"There ain't none—whether you think you got to have it or not. Try to find some. Try Louisville. Try Boonesborough. They're harder up than we are here. Who do you think's got silver? Answer me that."

"The Spaniards," said Adam. "And this saltpeter's no trouble to pack around. Hardly half a canoeload. I can get silver for it at St. Louis—or for sure at New Orleans."

"Then them's the places for you to go," advised Casper. He got up and went into his office with a great show of disinterest.

Adam untied his horses and led them to the watering trough. While they drank he took off his shirt and plunged his head and shoulders into the cool water. He was taking his time, waiting for Casper to follow him out.

Everybody talked about Casper's stock of corn. The whole back of his warehouse was piled high with sacks of it. The moment the ice had gone out of the Ohio, Casper had shipped a dozen boatloads down river from Pittsburgh. People, close to starvation after the hard winter, had had for a time to pay anything he demanded. But the spring had been surprisingly warm and favorable and by now the new crop was flourishing. No one was buying a cupful more than he had to have. The price was falling daily. Casper must already be nervous about being stuck with a surplus. Adam had an idea, what with people swarming to Kentucky as they were, most of them arriving too late to get in a crop of their own, that by fall corn would be in short supply again. But whether that proved true or not, corn right now had a value for him as definite as silver. His agreement with the Wyeths was payable in terms of bushels of corn at the stipulated rate of twenty-five cents a bushel. Casper, overloaded with corn, might let some of his go at half that. If he could work Casper up to, say, twenty-five hundred bushels, in exchange for the saltpeter, then he had a safe deal. The sum he had to have would then be at least in sight. After the proceeds from the sale of the watch and the Hamilton coat and the Calloway pants were added, he'd need only a comparatively small loan from Bert to make up the full thousand dollars, or its equivalent—four thousand bushels of corn.

He sat on the edge of the trough to dry in the sun. When he saw that Casper was strolling out to join him he turned around and began putting on his shirt.

"I been thinkin'," said Casper. "Might be I could help you out some."

"I wouldn't fight you off—not very hard, that is."

"This is what I been thinkin'," continued Casper, elaborately offhand. "Long's you say you're a mind to go all the way to New Orleans—you might's well take a full cargo. Down river you can make it with a bargeload of corn just as easy as you could with half a canoeload of saltpeter. And here's the meat in the nut. At New Orleans they got plenty of gunpowder but they almost never got plenty of corn—and when they do they can ship it straight off to market in the West Indies."

Casper had taken bait, hook, sinker, line and pole. "I never thought it out that far," said Adam. "You could be right. Trouble is—it's saltpeter I've got—not corn."

"I have a little corn," said Casper. "Just to help you out I might trade you some."

"I surely have to feel obliged to you," said Adam. "Might be I better think it over." He paused, frowning, to think. "Of course, it could be I'd not have to go all the way to New Orleans. Suppose I could sell the saltpeter at St. Louis? Nobody there ever wants corn."

Casper was trying hard to show a purely friendly interest in the problem. "Be worth your while to go all the way to New Orleans—no matter what—was you to take enough corn."

"How much would you reckon is enough?"

Casper's lips moved in the processes of his thoughtful calculation. "Just to help you out—I might go three thousand bushels for your saltpeter."

He waited, smiling, for Adam's eager acceptance of an offer so patently generous. Adam did blink. Casper certainly wanted the saltpeter bad and he probably wanted even worse to work off some of his excess corn. Adam was calculating, too. A bill of sale for three thousand bushels would see him through without borrowing anything from Bert. The thought of Bert, however, reminded him of Bert's way in a trade. "Never take any but the last offer," Bert always said.

"That sounds to me like a fair-to-middling proposition," Adam conceded. "Might be pretty near all the saltpeter's worth. There's only one hitch. That much corn is still a short boatload. And I'd still have to hire two men to help me with the boat—just as if it was a full load. And that would cost a good share of what I might make."

All of Casper's pretended geniality vanished. "Take it or leave it," he said.

"I guess I'll have to leave it," said Adam.

Casper stamped back into his warehouse. Adam looked after him, angry with himself. The kind of bluff he'd been putting up could well have been apparent to far dimmer wits than Casper's. He'd talked big about St. Louis and New Orleans when actually he didn't have time to take his saltpeter as far as Louisville. He had to sell to Casper here today for whatever he could get and be on his way back to Trace Creek. A faint relief came with the thought of the watch, coat and pants. He had to sell them to Casper, too. He'd give Casper an hour. Then he'd come back, not to talk about the saltpeter but about this other stuff he had to sell, and once they got on the subject again he'd take what he could get for the lot.

He led the horse back to the front of the warehouse. Casper's blacks had disappeared. So had Casper. Adam slowly retied the open sacks, carried them out and reloaded the pack horses. He took his time but Casper remained out of sight. Adam cinched up the last pack and started around the corner of the warehouse with his train. There wasn't grass enough left to keep a goat in any pasture within half an hour of Harrodsburg but at least he might as well find some brush for his horses to feed on during the hour he had decided to wait before coming back to tackle Casper again.

Casper stuck his head out of his office window and addressed Adam's lead horse. "A man can get so stubborn he beats hisself."

"Happens like that all the time," agreed Adam, keeping on going.

"Never like to see a young man tryin' hard to get ahead and still makin' a fool of hisself."

"Neither do I," said Adam, pausing.

"I'll make it four thousand," said Casper. "And that's positively my last offer."

"Four thousand, eh?" said Adam, still clinging to his pose of thoughtful consideration, though the figure was ringing in

224

his ears like the clang of a bell. Not thirty-five hundred. Not thirty-seven hundred. But four thousand. The exact full amount. It was a return that freed him of the need of borrowing from Bert, saved him the blue coat to get married in, even left him the watch to trade for the kind of riding horse a landowner and captain ought to have. "Maybe I better take you up on that."

"Then you better get in here and sign a bill of sale—before I figure out how big a fool I'm makin' of my own self."

The blacks popped out of nowhere and began to unload the horses again. Adam went into Casper's office.

"I can't put that much corn in my hip pocket," he said. "Write me an order to furnish it on demand when I get ready to send for it."

Casper grunted and set his pen to scratching across a second piece of paper. Adam signed the bill of sale for the saltpeter, folded Casper's note and tucked it into the waterproof pouch where he kept his flint and steel. An order on Casper Gonday was as good as money—better than the money going around in Kentucky these days.

"For one winter's work—you done right well for yourself," said Casper, still disgruntled.

"Not bad," conceded Adam.

He went out to his horses tied at the rail. A man and a woman were looking them over with critical interest, feeling of their legs, flapping handkerchiefs in front of their eyes, peering into their mouths. The man was big and black bearded and black browed, with the aggressively domineering look of an overseer who'd long been in charge of a big place where the hands were kept under tight control. The woman was little, with straggling light hair, red nose and eyes and a perpetual snuffle.

"Middlin' horses—fer Kentucky," said the man. He had a deep, harsh voice that carried the sound of authority.

Adam nodded and began loosening the nearest tie rope. He had no time to gossip with strangers.

"My name's Peleg Snowden," said the man. "This is Mrs. Snowden. Heard these here horses might be fer sale."

"They're not," said Adam. Bert might be willing to sell, since he had little need for pack horses any more, but even if so he would certainly want to handle the selling himself.

"Buy 'em, Peleg," directed the woman. Her voice was weak and asthmatic.

Peleg turned hastily back to Adam. "We could make you a real good price fer 'em," he said.

"Price wouldn't make any difference," said Adam. "They're not my horses. They belong to a man over on Trace Creek."

The explanation had no apparent effect on Mrs. Snowden. "Buy 'em, Peleg," she repeated.

Peleg edged sidewise a little, as if a whip had just cracked beside his ear. "You see, it's this here way," he informed Adam earnestly. "Naomi she's sick of Kentucky. She wants to git out. And we got to have horses to git out."

Adam grasped the lead horse's mane, setting himself to swing up onto his back. In spite of his impatience he was entertained by the big man's awe of his diminutive spouse.

"Been here long?" he asked.

"Too long," said Naomi.

"We got here just this mornin'," said Peleg, anxious that Adam should fully comprehend the situation. "We come to Louisville by boat. We can't afford to throw away what stuff we got left. But the only horses we been able to find—they was hardly up to gittin' us from Louisville here."

"They was no good at all," said Naomi, "like everythin' else in this country."

"We need real horses," said Peleg. "Naomi she likes to travel fast."

"A body can't travel fast enough," said Naomi, "gittin' away from here."

Adam mounted and grinned down at her. "What don't you like about Kentucky?"

"Everythin'," she said. She wrinkled her nose. A faint breeze, stirring the stagnant, dusty air, brought with it the full flavor of Harrodsburg, where hundreds of people lived huddled together among the accumulated waste of camp and stock pen. "Beginnin' with the smell."

Adam laughed and jerked the lead rope to get his horses started. "Harrodsburg's had quite a smell, all right, since the last snow went off. But before you give up you'd ought to get around a little and see some of the country. Still plenty of fresh air in Kentucky."

"See some of the country," jeered Casper from the warehouse doorway. "From the story they give me when they come to me for horses this mornin'—there ain't never been movers that has seen more of this country. They come down the Tennessee with Donelson last winter. But that new Tennessee country everybody else speaks so well of—it wasn't good enough for them. So they come on down river to the Ohio—and then up to Louisville—and then over Lexington way—and then here. They seen the best there is out here and still it wasn't good enough for 'em." His indignation grew on him. "What's wrong with Kentucky?" he demanded of the Snowdens. "Tell me that."

Peleg shifted uneasily but his wife was ready with an ex-

226

plicit answer. "The folks—mostly. Dirty, lazy, shiftless, out-at-the-elbows trash—a-settin' around all the time whittlin' and gassin' about their thousand-acre tracts when nary a one of them's got gumption enough to farm one acre or to fight off the injuns when they come to take his cow. And so far as the country goes—it might be bigger than Carolina but it ain't no improvement no other way."

Adam stopped chuckling and pulled in his horses. "Carolina? That where you come from?"

"And that's where we're a-headin' back to," said Naomi.

"Anywhere near the Deep River country?" Even the longest shot was sometimes worth trying.

Naomi stared suspiciously. Peleg made haste to reply before she could take some further offense. "Nope. We come from quite a ways over the hills to the south—on the Haw River."

"Ever happen to run across anybody from Deep River?"

Peleg grinned. "Yessir—I reckon you might call it thet— yessir, I surely did—oncet. I married up with her." He bethought himself and shot a placating glance at his wife. "Naomi she sharecropped a cotton patch one summer over on Deep River—back when her first husband was still alive," he exclaimed with more circumspection.

"Peleg he done more'n what you might call run acrost me," added Naomi, giving her husband a sudden, complacent smile which obviously bewildered him. "He follered me around fer most a year."

Adam laughed sociably and began fishing for pipe and tobacco, as if willing, after all, to sit and talk awhile. "Back when you lived on Deep River—ever know a family named Sheldon?" he asked her.

"No," said Naomi. "Not if you mean the Sheldon family thet had a big place down by Pine Fork. They was too uppity fer the likes of us to know."

"I mean a John Sheldon."

"He died near twelve years ago. But last I heard, his boys was still runnin' the same place."

Adam swung to the ground. When so long a shot hit the mark it surely made you feel good. "Might be I could fix it so you could have these horses."

"Look out," advised Casper. "He'll have your eyeteeth."

"We aim to pay what they're worth," said Naomi. But she was still on guard. "What more do you want?"

"No more than this," said Adam. "There's a girl at the settlement I come from who's related to those Sheldons—a niece of John Sheldon's. She's been a captive to the Cherokee most of her life. I'll see you get a deal for the horses if you'll take her to Carolina with you and see that she's turned over safe and sound to the Sheldon family."

"That's something we'd be bound to do whether we got the horses or not," said Naomi. "A gal belongs with her own folks."

"She may not be too easy to handle. She's only been away from the Indians a month and sometimes she talks about going back to them."

"We say we'll take her to Carolina," pronounced Naomi, "that's where we'll take her."

"Where's your stuff?" said Adam. "I'll pack you over to Trace Creek with me and we'll get this worked out."

Naomi, as Peleg said, certainly liked to travel fast. They stopped to eat at dusk but when the moon rose they started on again and kept on until well after midnight. By the third hour of daylight the next morning they were over the rim of hills and could see the valley of Trace Creek spread out below them.

"Right pretty bottom," said Peleg.

"Looks like fever country to me," said Naomi.

Adam strode on ahead, leaving them to lead the pack horses. It was hard for him to let out a breath without letting a yell out with it—to relieve the way his heart seemed to fill his chest. All of his old confidence in his luck had returned. He'd worked hard for the saltpeter and he'd planned on selling it to good advantage. But encountering the Snowdens had been pure luck. A man might take satisfaction in overcoming difficulties but there was no satisfaction like the feeling that things had started to break his way of their own accord. Nothing could make a man feel as good as that.

He lengthened his stride, weaving in and out among a belt of vine-covered fallen trees laid low by some tornado of other years. Suddenly he came upon Gilbert, sitting on a log with a fowling piece across his knees. Gilbert wasn't making the slightest pretense at hunting. He was just sitting there watching the trail from the west. When Adam came into sight he rose with his usual cheerful smile.

"Lo, the bridegroom cometh," he called out. "I'd hoped to the last something might have happened to you. And I didn't want to leave until I was certain nothing had."

"Nothing has so far," said Adam. "When are you leaving?"

"Before the wedding, at any rate. There's little enough my tears could add to that occasion."

"The way I'd feel if it was the other way around," agreed Adam. He was too excited and impatient to attempt to cope tactfully with Gilbert's ideas of humor.

228

"I'll leave the deed to my land on the altar," said Gilbert. "Or whatever the Reverend Barr uses for an altar. And, by the way, he's become your loudest champion. First time in his life, I venture, he's ever expressed approval of anybody but God and himself. What did you do to him? Amazing—the way you—literally on first sight—took this entire community by storm. Caesar was a laggard. Now don't give me any argument about the land. You wouldn't have listened to any if—as you say—things had turned out the other way."

Adam didn't want to argue. He wanted only to go on. "Going back to Virginia?" he asked.

"No. They need doctors most anywhere in Kentucky. I'll hang my shingle in some deserving settlement not too far away—where I'll be within call. After all—something can still happen to you. Cynthia's been widowed once already, you may remember."

"And could be again—that's a fact," agreed Adam. "Well, if she is—better luck the next time." He started to edge past.

"You're wild to be on your way—and no wonder. I'll keep you no longer. I've been able to convince myself once more you're real flesh and blood and not just a remarkably bad dream. So hasten on to your journey's end. Cynthia's house looks about complete—in case you're interested—except for one door. Ah, that does interest you. For some reason I can't begin to fathom they've tied that door up on the roof. In spite of your great desire to be off, I can see that I'm not altogether boring you."

"Far from it," said Adam. "But something will happen to me right here and now if I wait to hear any more. I have to get a look at that door."

He plunged on down the slope. Coming out at the lower edge of the woods he was near enough to see the door dangling from the ridgepole, just where, coming from the west, he could not help seeing it with his first look even had he not been warned it would be there. He began to run and then to laugh as he had laughed when Cynthia, in his arms, had suddenly discovered how much more she was surrendering than she had intended. She was used to the idea now. She was flaunting her surrender.

As he drew nearer, the place seemed a beehive of activity. Many blacks besides Cynthia's were at work, carrying in furniture, cleaning up around the yard, laying the last shingles on the roof. The other Wyeths had sent help. To get the house ready in time had become a family enterprise. As he reached the nearer corner Cynthia was running around the farther one to meet him.

"But you got back so soon," she was calling.

He came to a stop, watching her, enjoying the sight of her running to him. "Too soon? Want me to go back?"

"No," she said. "You can come right in and help."

Breathlessly she threw herself into his embrace, and then leaned back to look into his eyes.

"No use your looking so smug," she taunted him softly. "How you must have hurried to get back so quickly."

He glanced at the door dangling from the ridgepole. "Thought I better get that hung where it belongs before the wind blew it away."

"Tomorrow," she said, "you can get a ladder and go up after it."

"Tomorrow?"

She nodded, her eyes not leaving his for a second. Slowly he bent nearer her mouth. She lifted her face. Her lips parted.

From somewhere just above came Blake's voice: "Hip—hip—"

"Hooray," came a chorus, followed by applause.

Adam looked up to see all the Wyeths, except Julia and Paul's children, leaning from the windows above.

"Most interesting view when you look down on it like this," said Blake. "Do it again."

"The way they carry on," said Cynthia, "you might think you were marrying the family. But you're not. You're marrying me."

"So far as I go," agreed Adam, "we need see them only at church on Sundays."

She took his arm and walked with him toward the door. The Wyeths came boiling out to overwhelm him with their affectionately jeering congratulations. The three men were shaking his hand and beating him on the back. Phoebe and Amy were kissing him.

"You've never had a chance," said Joel consolingly. "Not since that first dance with her at Ingles'."

"I'm mighty relieved to have some competition in the family," boomed Paul. "Of course, I've got a head start of ten—but the way you get around might be I'll have to keep moving to stay ahead."

"I'm so happy I could die," whispered Amy.

He hardly heard what they were saying. He saw their laughing faces through a delightful haze of sympathy and good cheer and good will, as through the dancing golden dust in a sunbeam.

The Snowdens pulled in the horses on the slope just above and waited, politely impassive. Joel's sharp eyes noted them at once.

"Find you a tenant farmer?" he asked.

"No," explained Adam. "They're on their way back to Carolina. I brought them here on the chance Bert might want to sell them his horses. The woman used to be a neighbor of the Sheldons'. She's going to take Nita back with her."

Cynthia squeezed his arm. "Really?" She seemed pleased but no more so than she might have been by some unexpected small gift he had brought her from Harrodsburg. "Thank goodness for that. So much the best way for her."

The other Wyeths were more openly impressed.

"Kentucky can hardly be full of Sheldon neighbors," said Paul. "Whoever told you about this one."

"Nobody. Just happened to run across her."

"Luck like yours, Adam, is more than luck," murmured Blake. "You have to call it destiny."

"Well, I better get along with them and get the horse trading under way," said Adam. He glanced up at the door and then down at Cynthia. "When I come back—do I have to bring my own ladder?"

"No," she said, smiling. "I'll have one waiting for you."

Adam pointed out the sawmill to the Snowdens and strode on ahead again. The intermittent scream of the saw in the mill covered the sound of his approach. He stood in the open doorway, for a moment unnoticed.

Alice was bent over her spinning wheel. Nita was beside her, watching with intent interest and then taking the yarn into her own fingers.

"Thet's right, dearie," said Alice. "Thet's jes right. You do ketch on quick."

Nita was wearing a green-dotted white calico dress that must have been one of Alice's cut down, though this had been done so neatly that it fitted her well. Around her neck hung a gold chain and locket, presumably also Alice's. Her hair, no longer in braids, was done up on her head, while across her brow its straightness had been altered by a curling iron into a wavy fringe that made her face almost pretty.

She saw Adam and started to her feet, one hand fluttering to her breast in an astonishingly feminine gesture. All of her stubborn childlike quality seemed lost. She looked instead like a sedate and demure young woman who had been suddenly startled by the entrance of a total stranger.

The thumping of the wheel stopped and Alice, also, looked around. There was no hint of welcome in her glance of recognition. She jumped up to take a stand, as if protectively, beside Nita. Adam walked on into the kitchen.

"Well, well, this is fine," he said, as heartily as he could. "So she's been behaving so well you could let her out?"

"There was never no call to lock her up," said Alice. She thrust one long arm around Nita's shoulders and gripped her tightly.

"Where's Bert?" Adam asked, backing away.

"He's a-sawin'. Can't you hear it?"

Adam started for the door.

"Adam?"

It didn't sound like Nita at all. Her voice was changed as much as her appearance. It was timid—almost trembling.

"Well?"

"You will marry her today?"

"Tomorrow."

He waited for what else she would have to say, bracing himself for the outburst. But she only closed her eyes and sighed gently. Alice glared at Adam.

"Yer Bert's friend," she said. "Ain't no other reason I'd ever stand fer yer steppin' in thet door."

Adam found Bert in the mill.

"Gawdamighty," said Bert. "Back already? You must of flew." He gave Adam a meaning dig with his elbow. "Had somethin' on your mind, eh?"

"How'd you like to sell your horses?" asked Adam.

Bert shook his head. "Ain't no money goin' around now worth one good horse's behind."

"You wouldn't want to talk to a man who had some real money left?"

Bert stopped his headshaking with a jerk. "Who? Where? How much?"

Adam took him around front and introduced him to the Snowdens. Then he backed off and sat down on the doorstep. Bert's elaborate bargaining would give him time to think about how best to deal with Nita and Alice. He got out his pipe and pouch but had only started frowningly to break up a twist of tobacco when to his astonishment he saw Bert and Peleg shaking hands and then moving toward him.

"What?" Adam exclaimed. "A deal that quick?"

"When the price is right," said Bert, "ain't never no use goin' on gabbin'."

"We might's well git us started, Peleg," said Naomi. "We kin make it 'most to Boonesborough afore dark." She turned to Adam. "Where's this here Sheldon gal?"

"These people are taking Nita to Carolina with them," he explained to Bert. He saw how quickly Bert's grin broke down. "What's wrong with that?"

"Ain't nothin' wrong with that," said Bert. He leaned over to take an uneasy look through the open doorway. "Not if you can work it out."

232

"It has to be worked out," said Adam. "Come on in and we'll get at it."

Nita was again standing beside Alice and Alice's arm was again protectively around her. Nita's eyes were downcast and she was trying to look shy and frightened. Alice could have been scowling no more antagonistically at the strangers coming in behind Adam if he had been bringing a parcel of Shawnee into her kitchen. She—or more likely, Nita—must have been listening.

"Nita," said Adam. "This is Mr. and Mrs. Snowden. They're from Carolina. Mrs. Snowden used to live near the Sheldons. That makes her almost the same as a neighbor to you."

"No, it don't," said Alice. "And who ast these here folks into my house?"

"I did," said Bert manfully.

Naomi seemed not in the slightest disturbed by Alice's animosity. She walked over to Nita and studied her judicially.

"She's got the Sheldon look, all right," she pronounced. She continued to regard Nita. "I never seen your paw and maw but I heard tell of the time way back when they took out fer Natchez. Nobody ever knowed but what you was dead, too. But that's all over now. We've come—Peleg and me—to take you back to Carolina—back to your own people."

Nita raised her eyes, not to look at Naomi but past her at Adam.

"I do not want to go to Carolina."

"And there ain't nobody goin' to make her," Alice burst out. "She kin stay right here in this house so long as she's a mind to. Tell 'em, Bert. This is our house. And this is a free country."

"This is a free country, sure enough," said Bert. "But there ain't no manner of doubt where at she belongs in it."

Nita shrank away from Naomi and clung to Alice.

"She belongs where she wants to," asserted Alice.

"Nita," commanded Adam.

"Yes, Adam."

"Come here."

She came over to him, timidly obedient. He led her out the door.

"And you, Alice," said Bert, equally commanding, "git these folks somethin' to eat. They got a ways to go before the day's out."

Adam stopped in the yard and faced Nita. She still looked odd in the print dress, with the locket at her throat and her hair done up, but her face had become as composed and expressionless and Indianlike as ever.

"Now," he said. "Let's talk sense."

"Talk—it is no use."

"Yes, it is—when you talk sense. Now try to listen for once. That woman in there is just the same as a neighbor to you—no matter what Alice says. She wants to take you to where your own family down there is waiting for you. Your home is there. Everybody ought to have a home. It's where they belong. Maybe you don't know that because you can't remember ever having one. Maybe you don't even know the word. But it's an important one. Say it."

"Home," said Nita.

"And that's where you're going. Home to your own people."

"Not with that woman," said Nita.

"Why not?"

"Many times you have said that you would take me to Carolina."

"So I have. But this is just as good a way to get you there. Finding these people to take you is just the same as taking you myself."

"No. It is not the same."

"Well, whether it is or not, there's where you have to go sooner or later. Why don't you want to take a chance as good as this and go now?"

She began deliberately to survey him, as if making an inventory of his every separate feature. "I will tell you. If I go to Carolina now—maybe I never see you again."

"Certainly you may never see me again. But what of it? You know I'm getting married, I'm marrying another woman tomorrow. Can't you get that through your head?"

"Yes. That is in my head all the time."

"Then what can be the use of wanting to hang around here?"

She was still looking thoughtfully into his face. "Maybe you will not stay with her—so long as you think."

He laughed shortly. She was as bad as Gilbert. "What's your real reason?"

"I will tell you that, too. She will not like it if I stay here."

"But you're going to go," he shouted. "You're going to go if I have to tie you up and pack you as far as the Hazel Patch myself."

She was delighted, as always, by his anger. "Every time you get very mad with me," she exulted.

Suddenly she began to laugh, as maliciously as ever she had laughed on the raft, and darted into the house. He bolted after her. Instead of running to Alice she kept on toward the storeroom in which she had been locked. He came to a stop, deciding it might be more sensible to wait until she, and

234

he, too, had cooled off a little, before renewing the battle.

Alice, glaring at him as he passed, rushed after Nita. He gestured impatiently for Bert to follow Alice and to do what he could to keep her, at least, in hand. Bert obeyed reluctantly. The Snowdens were sitting at the table, busily eating and paying no apparent attention to the goings on.

Adam went outside. Presently Bert came to the door. Never had even Bert looked so worried.

"You better come in here," he said.

Adam followed Bert through the kitchen. The Snowdens were still eating. Bert led the way to the storeroom. Nita was in Alice's arms, her face hidden against Alice's bosom.

"There—there—there," Alice was crooning.

"What's up now?" demanded Adam.

Alice glared fiercely and then quickly looked away, blushing a deep red. "Tell him, Bert," she directed.

Bert coughed a couple of times and finally spoke hollowly. "She says she's goin' to have a baby."

"Who is? Alice?"

"No. Nita. She says it's yourn."

"She only this minute told us," added Alice, her voice hushed tragically.

"Why—the miserable, Godforsaken, two-faced scurvy little liar," Adam whispered. "After all she's tried to do to me— now she's even come to trying this. She's no more going to have a baby than I am. She's had no more chance to get one than if she'd been kept locked up in her grandmother's hope chest. I've never so much as touched her. I've never touched her, I tell you."

He brushed Bert aside, tore Nita away from Alice and began to shake her.

"Look at me," he cried. "Look at me."

She raised her downcast eyes. For an instant he saw in them a flash of that same dreadful enjoyment of his complete frustration that he'd seen in them when she'd thrown her dress in the river. He shoved her away and turned frantically to Bert and Alice.

"You've not gone out of your minds, too," he stormed. "You must be able to see that she's lying—and that I'm not. You, Bert—you know me well enough to know I'd never deny a thing like that if I had ever done it. I've never been near her. She's as much a virgin as she was when I first saw her. You got to believe the truth. You do, don't you?"

"Sure I do," said Bert gloomily. "But who else do you guess is goin' to? Look at her. Little and sad and mopin' around in corners—and pretendin' to be sick—and everybody knowin' she's just come from weeks in the woods with you—

235

how many do you think is goin' to believe you instead of her? Not another soul in this settlement—that's how many. Beginnin' with that preacher. You scared him half white oncet but how he's going' to jump at a chance like this to git back at you! And after him there's every woman around the place. They're all goin' to take it like Alice here. Far as they go a man's always wrong—whether they're real sure he is or not." He jerked his thumb at Nita. "Take you another look at her. Droopin' like a flower somebody's stepped on. Maybe the way she's actin' turns your stomach but it won't turn nobody else's. No, sir. She's got you nailed to the post. That's what she has. And the fire lighted."

Adam swung around and grabbed Nita by the wrist. She looked up at him again, smiling this time, expecting physical violence from him and exulting in her expectation. He yanked her with him out the door.

"Stop him, Bert," screamed Alice. "Stop him. You've got to help her. He's goin' to kill her."

"Shut up," growled Bert. "She don't never need help no more than you ever do."

Nita made no effort to pull free or even to hold back. She ran beside Adam, laughing softly once or twice, as he crossed the kitchen with her, crossed the dooryard, circled the tethered horses and started along the path that led upstream past the stockade. It was only when she saw that they were headed toward Cynthia's mill that she pulled back.

"Wait, Adam."

"Well?"

"Where do we go?"

"You want to tell your story, don't you? Well, we're starting out to make the rounds and tell everybody who wants to listen. And we're starting with Cynthia. She's the one you want most to tell it to, isn't she? And her whole family's up there with her. You want them to hear it, too, don't you?"

Nita seemed less to be listening to what he was saying than endeavoring to grasp what he was thinking.

"What's the matter? Afraid to tell her?"

"No. I would like very much to watch her face while I tell her."

"Then come on."

"Wait, Adam."

"What for?"

She was still studying him, still trying to make up her mind about something.

"You think maybe they will laugh at me? That is what you want?"

"How do I know who they'll laugh at? Maybe at you.

236

Maybe at me. But it won't take long to find out. Come on."

"But you want them to laugh at me."

"What's all this talk about laughing? Nobody's ever felt like laughing—except you now and then."

"Wait, Adam. You have made me think."

"Then it'll be the first time."

"You make me think that you are sure now."

"Sure of what?"

"That you will never want to see me again."

"I should say I am. Never will be too soon."

She continued to confront his anger with the strange new calm that had come over her.

"You make me sure, too."

"Of what?"

"That you are sure you want me to go."

"For God's sake—what else have I ever tried to make you sure of?"

"So I will go."

She turned and walked quite fast back toward the sawmill. He gaped after her, unable to comprehend that all had at last been resolved, and, at the end, so suddenly and simply. He was dazed. So recently he had been filled with fury. Now he felt oddly empty.

Bert came running out, quivering with curiosity. "What the hell kind of a hex did you put on her to bring her around all of a sudden like that?"

"They'll never make Boonesborough by dark, walking and leading these pack horses," said Adam. "They'll need some extra ones to ride. And you and I better go with them that far. Once they hit the main Wilderness Road they can join up with some party of other movers, but they'll be alone until they get to Boonesborough."

Bert stared at him. But all he said was: "Anyway, somebody's got to go along to fetch the extra horses back." He went off to borrow the horses.

The Snowdens came out. They'd not seemed ruffled by any of the commotion. Having decided back in Harrodsburg to take Nita along Naomi had evidently taken it for granted, as with all her decisions, that that was the way it was going to be.

Through the open doorway Adam caught a glimpse of Nita. She was back in her Indian dress and her hair was once more in braids. She'd stopped pretending. She was herself again. Upon his last sight of her today she'd look just as she had the day he'd first seen her.

He walked over to the horses and removed his camping equipment from the packs. The elkskin roll containing the

237

blue coat and the doeskin breeches he left lashed in place among the Snowden effects.

"Something in that I want you to take with you," he told Peleg. "It's mainly a blue coat that once belonged to Lord Hamilton. If you look around for somebody that can afford it you can get a good price for it."

"Why you givin' it to Peleg?" demanded Naomi.

"Just might be that once you get to Carolina Nita may make you more trouble than you think—finding her people and getting her to them. I want to make it right with you so you'll feel able to go to whatever extra trouble there's need for."

"We've already said we'd get her to her folks," said Naomi. "And it'll be right side up and all in one piece." Her shrewd glance was fixed on his face. "But you kin give Peleg the coat if thet will make you feel any easier."

Bert came back with the extra horses. Alice began to weep noisily but she kept out of sight in the kitchen. Nita's face was like a mask when she came out. She mounted and waited impassively for the caravan to get under way.

Adam rode ahead up the long slope, through the blackberry patch and on past the camp. It didn't seem possible that less than a week had gone by since last he had been here. There was the spot where Cynthia had slipped down from her horse and into his arms. There, also, was the hut in which he had spent the night with Nita and the pool in which she had bathed that morning. He wondered what she might be thinking now, as, following with the train, she, too, rode past. He put down an impulse to signal to her to come up and ride with him. There was nothing he could say to her if she did. Everything between them had already been said.

He kept on, reversing the course he had taken with Bert and Nita when he'd packed in the saltpeter, and before that with Joel and Blake on their way to see Trace Creek for the first time. Presently he was crossing the meadow where he and Nita had been overtaken by the rain that afternoon of his second approach to Trace Creek. There was the rock beside which she had stopped the horses to tighten a pack rope. He kept his attention on the way ahead. Beyond the meadow was the stretch of beechwood and next the belt of cane and then the hills from the crest of which you could look down on Boonesborough. From there the Snowdens and Nita could go on unattended.

In the beechwood Bert galloped up beside him. He glanced over his shoulder toward the train behind.

"Wouldn't want me to keep ahead for a spell, would you?"

"Why should I?" asked Adam.

"Oh, nothin'. Just wondered."

Bert dropped back to wait for the others.

At the foot of the hills Naomi came up to ride with him for a moment.

"We'll wait at Boonesborough until we kin join up with a good strong party goin' east," she remarked, more as if thinking aloud than addressing him.

She pulled in again without waiting for his nod.

It was early evening when Adam rounded a shoulder of the hills to an open slope from which he could look down on Boonesborough below. From here there was a hunter's trail leading down to the riverbank across from the town. He could see several boys, guarded by two men with rifles, driving stock from outlying pastures to pens near the stockade for the night, and the new ferry being pulled across the river. The others came up. Everybody dismounted. Bert began to string together the five extra horses that were to be taken back.

Adam walked over to Nita. Her face was chalk white but with no more expression on it than if it had been made of chalk. She was shivering a little, though the evening was oppressively warm.

"Talk," she said, "is no use."

There was no answer to that or to anything else either could say. He took out the watch and thrust it at her. The suddenness of the movement broke her calm. She gave a little cry.

"Why?" she asked.

"Because I want you to have it. That's why. You'll find out there'll be things you'll need. Clothes, maybe. A dowry, maybe. No need your being a complete drag on your relatives. You wouldn't like that. Now don't get your back up. I wouldn't be giving it to you if I didn't want you to have it."

She stared at the watch. Her hand closed over it again and she looked up at him. Into her eyes, which had always been so unafraid, there came a look of terror, like the suddenly realized panic of a child awakening in the darkness of an unfamiliar room. She whirled, clutching the watch, and began to run, her braids swinging. The Snowdens had already started on with the pack horses but she passed them and ran on ahead of them down the trail. A few steps beyond there was a fringe of laurel at the head of a draw, and when she was lost to Adam's view it was behind this laurel. When first she had stepped into his sight it had been out of such a laurel thicket. It began to seem to him that all that had happened between them from that first moment to this one, in which she had as suddenly faded from his sight, was already as if it might never have happened.

SIXTEEN

No cooling came with the gathering darkness. The heat of the day seemed instead of have settled in a sweltering blanket upon the earth. Bert rode ahead, leading the three other horses. A sultry haze obscured the night sky and it soon became too dark for him to see, but he kept on, giving his mount its head, trusting, now that they were homeward bound, that the animal would keep to the way.

Adam rode at the end of the line with no concern other than to keep his horse's nose close to the tail of the next horse ahead. Everything at last was settled. He could stop thinking. He could let himself sag in the saddle, as he had to do, anyway, to avoid the low branches that kept coming at him out of the darkness, and let his mind go blank. He gave up making the slightest effort to take notice of their progress and became aware of how far they had traveled only when they came out into the open meadow by Nita's rock.

For a moment he could see her again, standing here on this same spot, tightening the pack rope. The rain drops glittering on her long lashes had made him wonder until he'd come closer. He should have known better. There'd never been so much as a suspicion of tears in her eyes, not even during that last moment before they had parted.

He rode up beside Bert. "No use your doing it all," he said. "I'll lead for a while."

"Better save yourself," counseled Bert. "A man needs to keep up his strength for the kind of day that's comin' at you."

Adam yanked the lead rope out of Bert's hand and rode on.

"Never aimed to rile you," Bert called after him.

"You didn't," said Adam.

It must be after midnight. If so, then Bert was right. This already was his wedding day. After a time the haze began to clear. He could see a little now and hope to make better time by guiding his horse around the fallen trees and other obstructions and by keeping him from dawdling. The camp was just ahead. In spite of his preoccupation with the horse he was getting sleepy again.

He'd been far from nodding the other two times he'd come up from the south along this same path. Beyond the blackberry patch was the crest of the slope from which he'd first looked down upon the valley of Trace Creek and, again, crouched in the rain and darkness, had stared toward the stockade while he'd tried to imagine how Cynthia looked at the moment and what she was doing. She was still down there tonight and this time he knew what she was doing. She was waiting for him.

At the edge of the blackberry patch his horse snorted, came to a sudden, stiff-legged stop and stood, trembling, his ears cocked forward his nostrils dilated. Adam could not smell what the horse had smelled. But he could hear the furtive rustle in the midst of the thicket ahead. Then a stick snapped. No animal other than a panther or a bear could have so terrified the horse. But the rustle was too gentle for a bear, the weight that had broken the stick too great for a panther. There was every chance that the unseen presence was that of an Indian's.

Adam was roused from his lethargy as by a reviving dash of icy water. There could be one Indian—or forty. However few or many, it was too late to withdraw. He gave the low, sharp whistle signal which in Clark's command called upon men engaged in thick woods, where they could see neither friend nor foe, to charge straight ahead. He heard the immediate thump of Bert's rifle butt against the rumps of the other horses.

All five horses plunged forward. He let out a series of wild yells in which Bert, after a second's astonishment, joined. The horses crashed through the tangle of vines. The commotion might have passed for the onrush of a score of whooping horsemen. Adam caught one acrid whiff of the grease Indians smeared on their bodies. But there were no answering war cries, no blaze of gunfire or twang of bowstrings. The horses swept on through the blackberry patch and over the brow of the hill. They were halfway down the slope before he and Bert were able to get the animals under control again.

"What got into you?" demanded Bert. "Come to all of a sudden like out of a bad dream?"

"There was at least one Indian back there in the berry patch that was no dream," said Adam.

"You don't say." Bert relaxed. "Come daylight I might take some of the boys and go catch him. We could show him in a cage to help celebrate your weddin'."

"You mean to help you work up a new wrinkle for your shivaree."

Bert laughed heartily. "You're recollectin' Sam Glover's weddin' night the time he married up with that French gal at Prairie du Rocher and we let the wildcat down his chimney."

"No. I'm thinking of how many of you Saul and his big boys will throw in the creek if you come bothering around too close tonight."

The jeering, down-to-earth talk gave another lift to Adam's spirits, already revived by the brush with the Indian. The men of the settlement would undoubtedly signalize the nuptial night of their new young captain with a charivari that included every frontier trimming. Right now he could feel what it was going to be like in that closed-in upper room, with Cynthia beside him in the darkness, listening to the outrageous outer din of gunshots, tub thumping, iron clanging and stones clattering on the roof, accompanied by the most indelicate songs and shouts of encouragement.

The first gray of dawn was in the eastern sky but the valley bottom was still night black. The stockade was shrouded in silence and there was no sign that the settlement's repose had been disturbed by the uproar on the hill.

"Looks like a couple of guards' heads could use some knocking on," growled Adam.

Then, as the horses splashed into the ford, a shot rang out from the parapet. The bullet whined close overhead.

"Hold your fire!" Adam yelled. "This is Adam Frane and Bert Cogar."

A low babble of many voices ran along the rifle platform. Far from the station being off guard, it sounded as if every man in the place must be up and about. Above this general chatter rose Paul's angry bellow: "Who fired that shot? You've been told a hundred times not to shoot 'til you see what you're shooting at. Come on in, Adam."

"Soon's we put the horses away."

"No. Bring 'em in here," shouted Paul.

The gate swung open. It was still too dark to see much, but Adam could tell everyone in the station was milling around and that all the stock had been driven in. He dismounted to find Blake beside him.

"Were you anywhere near that yelping up on the hill?" he asked.

"That was us doin' it," explained Bert. "We was scarin' an Indian before he could scare us."

"Then they must be getting here already," said Blake cheerfully.

"Who?" demanded Adam.

"Come talk to Joel," said Blake. "He's heard more than I have. I've been helping Paul get in the stock. Joel's in Paul's kitchen."

All around were huddling, whispering knots of women and

242

children. Above, visible against the graying sky, loomed the heads and shoulders of the men of the settlement lining the parapet.

The single candle in the kitchen seemed, by contrast to the outer darkness, to give out a glare of light. Gilbert and Jesse Baker were lifting Eli Skaggs from the floor while Phoebe shoved a mattress under him. Eli was limp and he was breathing heavily. Gilbert dragged the mattress into the adjoining room.

"Relief to see you back safe and so soon," said Joel to Adam. "Eli's not hurt. Only worn out, apparently. He ran nearly forty miles without stopping and that's quite an effort for a man of his age. His heart skipped a few beats just now but Gilbert says it's ticking along again. However, before he collapsed Eli got out the gist of his story. He'd decided to visit Riddle's Station to find out if that band of rangers that works out of there along the Ohio had seen anything. But he never got to Riddle's. He found the woods up that way swarming with Indians. By the number of boats and canoes on the Licking he thinks there's six or seven hundred of them."

"What kind?"

"All kinds. But mainly Shawnee."

"Any Tory rangers with them?"

"Yes. He saw what he took to be at least a company marching across a meadow."

Here again, as at Logan's, were echoes from another world —this time echoes that thundered and reverberated. The familiar images of forest warfare filled Adam's mind. "That's bad," he said. "Means the whole thing was planned in Detroit. Could be they've timed it so as to come at Kentucky just when they could count on Sinclair's Sioux keeping Clark and his army busy on the Mississippi."

"I'm no judge of Indian tactics," said Joel. "But if they really are operating according to a military plan they wouldn't be coming this way. They'd be striking at Louisville to cut Clark completely off from Kentucky."

"Anyway, one of them's come this way," said Blake. "Adam and Bert ran across him just now right up here on the hill."

"That doesn't mean too much," said Adam. "If they're across the Ohio with a force as big as Eli says this one is they'd be sure to scatter spies all over Kentucky to keep track of what we do."

Paul rushed in, as happily excited as if he were on his way up a tree into which his dogs had chased a bear. "Let 'em come. We've got plenty of corn and bacon, plenty of water, plenty of gunpowder and plenty of men. We can hold 'em off as long as they want to stay around and make 'em suffer every minute they do."

"We certainly should be able to hold out," said Adam. "If we can't it'll be the first Kentucky stockade that's ever had to surrender. But we've got more than that to do. We've got to find out more about how strong they are and which way they're moving. No good our sitting here holding our breath waiting for them to get here when they may be running off the other way toward Lexington or Louisville."

Joel was listening but his eyes had suddenly become sharp and watchful. "That's true. Still, isn't our first duty to make sure we do hold this place?"

"Everybody's first duty is to hold his own place," said Adam. "But that's only a start. According to what Eli saw this may be a good deal more than just an uncommonly big raid. They don't need seven hundred braves and a company of greencoats to steal horses and kill cows. It could be a try to take over Kentucky. That's what they've been talking about in Detroit for the last three years. Maybe now they think they can do it. Our people can't deal with that kind of an attack if every man stays in his own stockade. We have to know just where they are and just which way they're moving so all our people can come out together—from every settlement at once—and run them back across the river. The only way to find that out is for somebody to go out and look for them and see that the word is gotten around. That's what Bert and I have to do."

All three brothers were eying him now.

"The alarm must surely have spread to other settlements already," said Joel.

"We don't know that," said Adam. "Riddle's Station could have been cut off before they knew what was happening. Thanks to Eli Skaggs's run we may be the first to hear anything about it. But anyway, we have to find out for ourselves whether or not they are coming at us—and find it out in time for us to send aid or send for aid to other stations."

"How long would you be gone—presuming you were able to get back?" asked Paul.

"No use our going out unless we get back—and that should not be later than tomorrow night."

"I can see the advantage in sending out spies, all right," said Blake. "But you're our commander here. And Bert's our second most experienced man. Shouldn't you send someone else?"

"No. We haven't got anybody else who stands one chance in ten of getting anywhere near them—or, if he did get near enough to see anything, who'd know what to look for or be able to get back to tell what he'd seen."

"Come in where you can hear this, Cynthia," said Joel, looking past Adam. "It concerns you about as much as anybody."

Adam turned to see Cynthia in the open doorway. She must have left her bed without pausing longer than to throw on the blue silk wrapper she had wound around her—and somewhere in her haste she had lost a slipper, for one of her feet was bare. Her eyes were wide and dark in her pale face which was made to seem even whiter by the cloud of her loosened hair hanging about her shoulders. With every step she took forward into the light she seemed to him more beautiful.

Paul nudged him and whispered loudly: "Since the first alarm she's been up on the rifle platform—watching and listening. She knew you were due back."

Cynthia kept on slowly toward Adam until she was confronting him, her questioning gaze fixed on his face. As always, when she was near him his one impulse was to take hold of her. He reached out but she thrust his hands away.

"*Why* must you go?" she demanded. "Why?"

Adam was amazed by her vehemence, so unlike her usual self-control. Before he could reply her brothers hastily took upon themselves the burden of trying to make her understand.

"Somebody has to," said Joel. "And nobody else can do it."

"Eli's the only other man who could," said Paul. "But look at him. He'll be no good for maybe a week."

"It's Adam's place to go," said Blake. "Surely you must see that."

"I certainly don't," she declared. "His place is to command here. The more danger—the more true it is that his place is here."

"You were outside the door for a while before you came in," said Joel. "Didn't you hear anything of what he was saying?"

"I heard it all. Everything about how anxious he was to take the whole war on his shoulders. But I didn't hear what really makes him think he must be the one to go."

Blake turned to Adam to offer him some explanation. "I'm afraid Cynthia's singing a familiar tune. She's always been convinced her brothers welcomed every excuse to rush to arms. Apparently she finds even less sympathy for a bridegroom's martial spirit."

"No," said Phoebe sharply. "That's not what she means at all."

"Of course it isn't," said Cynthia. "And Adam knows it."

"I know Indian fighting," said Adam stubbornly. "I know

245

better than any of you how I can best do what has to be done. And since I am in command no one else can decide for me."

He looked down into her upturned face. Her eyes sought his. She was no longer bitter. She was making an appeal meant only for him. A fold of the wrapper had fallen away from her throat to reveal the first promising swell of her bosom, but when she raised her hand it was not to replace it but to brush back her hair. She might have been offering herself to his attention, beseeching him to take notice of her. He was taking notice. Tonight she could have been coming to him wrapped in this same blue silk, her smooth brown hair again streaming heedlessly over her shoulders, her eyes bright in the last gleam of the candle before he blew it out. She could have been lying in his arms as he listened in the darkness to the rude tumult of the charivari.

But tonight he would be miles away, creeping through another kind of darkness. He would be listening for a far ruder tumult—the sound of a single snapping twig that might mean the approach, not of hilarious friend, but mortal enemy. He should be frantic with resentment against this sudden turn in his prospects. He was. He didn't want to leave her. He'd never wanted more to stay beside her. Yet he was being seized by an odd kind of excitement, an urgent sense of the need to rush away into this other darkness. His mind was already leaping ahead to the dangers with which he would have to deal before this time tomorrow.

"I still have to go," he said.

She turned away from him abruptly, walked to a stool and sat on it with her back to him. Phoebe placed a comforting hand on her shoulder. Adam wasn't able to feel quite so tender toward her. His main impulse at the moment was a growing irritation that she should be trying, just as might any ordinary woman, to twist a time like this into an excuse for a display of feminine pique. Amy came running in and stared with frightened questioning from one face to another.

"Adam thinks he has to go spy on the Indians," explained Phoebe.

"No—oh, no," cried Amy in incredulous dismay. "You can't, Adam. You just can't—not today."

"Nobody's yet thought of any good way to persuade the Shawnee to wait until after the wedding," said Blake.

He drew Amy against him and began stroking her hair soothingly, shaking his head slightly to warn her against saying more. Then he was startled by something in her expression as she looked up at him. Though she had not even been in the room she already seemed to have leaped, like Phoebe, to some conclusion the men had missed. Blake looked quickly at Adam, his eyes narrowing speculatively. Joel and Paul, watching Blake, suddenly stiffened. These Wyeth brothers seemed so often to be able to share one another's thoughts without the need of words.

"If you have to go," advised Cynthia harshly, without turning around, "why don't you go?"

Adam was beginning to understand. They weren't objecting to his going but to his readiness to go, as though in some way he was failing her—that he was giving her something less than her due. His irritation deepened into anger. There was no use their expecting a war to start and stop to suit the whims of the Wyeth family.

"Joel, you'll take command while I'm away," he said. "Turn the stock out to pasture by day so's to save corn. Push patrols out three or four miles every morning and evening. When Eli comes to, put him to ranging farther if he's able to get around. Post a garrison of five extra men in each mill. Keep everybody set every minute as if you expected the main pack of Indians to be coming at you the next half hour. Get a man off to Boonesborough with Eli's story. They may send you some help. You don't need more men to hold the stockade but you could well use a few more who knew their way around in the woods."

"I accept your instructions as a command," said Joel, very formally. "I might also say I completely agree with them."

Adam picked up his rifle which he'd leaned against the wall when he'd come in. He turned to face the Wyeths once more. He waited a second. Cynthia did not turn around. No change of expression came over any Wyeth face, even Amy's. He went out.

It was light enough now to see the individual shapes of the horses and cattle and people crowding the open square between the two rows of houses. On the parapet the riflemen, having been able to see in the growing light no sign of the enemy, were lowering their rifles and beginning to talk in hushed, excited tones with their neighbors. Bert was not in sight. The moment he'd heard about Eli's story he'd probably known what had to be done. It had been only natural for him to hurry home to break the news to Alice. Adam set out for the mill.

The stockade gate was opened for him but before it had quite closed behind him he heard a whisper of silk and turned to find Cynthia darting through. She threw herself into his arms and clung to him convulsively.

"Oh, Adam—Adam," she cried. "How can I be such a fool? How can I work so hard to make you hate me—just now of all times? After all, the world isn't coming to an end,

247

is it? Of course you have to go." She leaned back to look up at him. Tears were streaming down her face and yet she was half laughing with what seemed almost her usual self-possession. "But you have to come back, too. More than that —you have to want to come back. You *have* to. And I have to believe it. We can have so much—you and I, Adam. We can't lose it—no matter how wildly I talk—or how impatient I get with your being so slow to see what I'm talking about. While you're away you musn't think of me as a woman who screams and scolds. I'm not really like that. All the time you must think of me as I am." She caught one of his hands, guided it beneath the folds of the wrapper and pressed it against her breasts. "You must think of me like this." Her low laughter was genuine now, and openly and confidently provocative. "Don't remember so continually, mind you, that you let some Indian catch you. Only remember when it is safe to remember and when you have time for the remembering to make you want to run all the way back."

The pressure of his finger tips against the soft warmth of her body had aroused in him a surge of sensation so strong it was all but painful. Then over her shoulder he became aware of the half-dozen grinning riflemen looking down from the parapet over the gate. He scowled up at them and they hastily looked away.

When he looked back at Cynthia he saw that she was angry again.

"Oh, I *am* a fool," she whispered.

She began pushing him away. His one hand was entangled in her wrapper and the other was holding his rifle. Before he could get hold of her she had torn completely away from him and was running back into the stockade. He stared at the gate closing behind her. He should be rushing to overtake her. She deserved the reassurance for which she seemed to feel so mysteriously deep a need and they both deserved the solace of a less frenzied farewell embrace. But it could be no great kindness to her to subject her to the tumult of yet another parting. To take her into his arms again for one more moment would be a wonderful privilege for him. But not for her. She had chosen to read something tragic into their separation. She might as well be spared further harping on it. He turned and trotted toward the hill, comforted to find himself sensible enough to think first of her.

Jim Menifee had come out of the mill and, rifle ready, was working his way along the creek bank, peering into the fringe of willows. Jim was old enough to remember Indians on the Virginia frontier and to know that the first light of day was the time to make sure they were not crawling close up, looking for a chance to jump at an unwatched door or gate.

The door of the mill was barred but Bert opened it before Adam had hardly started to scratch on it. Alice was stirring tallow and maple sugar into a bowl of corn meal and stuffing the mixture into Bert's game sack. This was the familiar warpath ration—one of the frontier tricks long since picked up from the Indians. A man could carry enough to feed him for days without his needing to hunt to keep going. So she already knew Bert was taking to the woods. She was biting her lips and her face looked a little lopsided as if it were being squeezed in a vise, but she was showing no real signs of throwing the fit Adam had expected. Bert walked back to her and resumed holding the sack. She lifted her head to stare coldly at Adam.

"Fer once," she said, "I'm right glad yer as mean as yuh are, Adam Frane. Yer enough meaner'n any Indian so's maybe you'll be able to git Bert back safe."

"Adam and me—we've been places before," said Bert with forced heartiness. "We'll git each other back safe. And likely before you've had time to make that venison pie we're countin' on your havin' ready and waitin' for us."

He leaned over and gave her a playful slap on the behind. She grasped his wrist and hung on to it so tightly that her knuckles whitened.

Backing off the doorstep Adam turned to face a cheerfully grinning Gilbert. The doctor was dressed in borrowed moccasins, leather shirt and coonskin cap.

"I'm going with you," he announced.

"Not a chance," said Adam.

"I can save you the trouble of listing all your objections," said Gilbert. "I know them all. They boil down to the supposition that I can be of no conceivable use to you and that as a matter of fact I'll be a drag on you since you and Bert will have to spend half your time playing nursemaid to me to keep me alive. But I have some answers, too. Though I don't know much about Indians, I've hunted all my life and I can get around in the woods without making any more noise at it than you will. If you do get into a fracas three guns are better than two. And I can run as far and as fast as either of you. When the time comes to get back with news there'll be more chance of one out of three getting through than one of two."

"Whatever gave you such a fool idea?"

"It's not such a fool idea from my point of view. Actually, it's the pinnacle of wisdom. Reflect, my friend. Perhaps you seldom do but I have all too often been required to. At any rate, surely you can see that I can scarcely sit at home holding Cynthia's hand while you heroically brave the manifold dangers of the wilderness. Were something to happen to you —and that is my fond and only remaining hope—even that hope would fade. Neither she nor I could ever successfully forget that I had crouched in safety behind her petticoats while you had gone forth to confront the savage enemy."

"What enemy could you confront with that popgun?" demanded Adam, pointing at Gilbert's fowling piece.

"This popgun," said Gilbert, "may not shoot as far or as unerringly as that long-barreled squirrel nemesis of yours. But it's double loaded with buck shot. At any really critical moment—such as our chancing to be set upon by Indians at close quarters—you'll be surprised by how many fall before one blast."

Bert came out, very red in the face and pretending to be preoccupied with hitching the straps of his powder horn and game sack over his shoulders.

"Well, might's well be on our way," said Adam.

Bert looked at Gilbert. "He goin' with us?"

"That's what he says."

"Folks always allow," remarked Bert, showing no surprise, "that three's a crowd. But just could be we'll git us in a fix where we could use a crowd."

Adam set off at an easy lope, the other two following in single file. He kept on down the valley of Trace Creek, past the salt lick, abandoned by the buffalo since the establishment of the station, though still frequented by many deer and an occasional elk. This morning there were a dozen does and their fawns shouldering each other away from the patches of salt-encrusted mud. Adam swung wide of the spring so as not to startle them off into telltale flight.

At the estuary where Trace Creek emptied into the south fork of the Licking he paused to survey the hills across the river and to consult Bert.

"According to Eli they came up the Licking in boats. Coming that way they could have been planning to head for the settlements around Lexington. Stands to reason after coming as far as Riddle's, where Eli saw them, they'd never cut all the way back to the east to come down the Great War Trail to get at our station or Boonesborough. I think we can be fairly sure that if they are coming south at us they'll be coming through the woods down this side."

"You never can be sure about Indians," pronounced Bert. "They don't think like humans. All the same you're right about keepin' to this side. If we don't run into them—soon or late we'll run across where they been—and if we see by their sign they've started to circle to the east we can still git us back to the station before they can git there."

Gilbert had naturally no comment to offer upon these brief deliberations of men acquainted with the mysteries of the wilderness, but he listened closely to every word, his eyes bright with interest.

Heading north, along the western slopes of the valley of the south fork, Adam kept to the crests of the ridges, where game trails made the going easier and the height gave him frequent glimpses of distant expanses of country across which he could look for traces of smoke or the behavior of game in the open meadows. He ran on with long, smooth strides, his body leaning slightly forward, his glance ranging constantly from the ground at his feet to the limits of the horizon, permitting nothing to escape his attention, from the faintest field mouse tracks in the dust to the flights of birds over the ridges beyond the river.

No warning signs appeared as he swung on mile after mile. As he ran, his eyes were constantly watchful but his thoughts kept drifting back to his parting with Cynthia. He might have handled that better. A woman often became overwrought when her man was suddenly snatched away from her. Its being her wedding day made it worse. He should probably be glad that she'd taken it so hard. But Phoebe and Amy had been just as foolish. Even the Wyeth men. Others, too. Alice had called him mean. That had been because of the way he'd handled Nita. But there hadn't been any other way to deal with her. Still, Alice might have had hold of something there. For more than a month Nita had been with him every day, almost every minute. He'd got to know her better than most men, probably, ever learned to know their wives, because he'd had to keep thinking all the time about everything she said or did. And yet when she'd disappeared behind that laurel he'd felt next to nothing at all. He'd only gotten sleepy as if something that had been keeping him awake had suddenly stopped keeping him awake, like a string might snap.

He came to a stop as suddenly as if he had brought up against a wire stretched across the game trail. There in the path at his feet the tracks of a stag which had been ambling along peacefully, after watering at the spring a mile back, showed that the animal had come to as sudden a stop. He had stood stiffly here for a second and then, wheeling, had plunged down the slope to the west. He could have seen no more than Adam could see now through the thick walls of shrubbery shielding the path. Some sudden sound or scent had come to him. There'd been something down the other slope toward the river which had set him into instant wild flight! It could be near or far, since the wind, though from that direction, was fitful.

Bert came alongside, took one look, grinned at Adam and glanced at the priming of his rifle. Signaling Gilbert to keep a few paces back, Adam turned from the game path down the eastern slope.

He kept on running. This was no time to be overcareful. They'd come out to find Indians and the sooner they found some the sooner they'd begin to learn some of the things they had to learn. New life seemed as suddenly to have flowed back into him. His senses had sharpened. He was aware of the faintest breath of air against his cheek. No sound was so indistinct that his ear did not pick it up. His eye instantly caught the slightest temble of the most distant leaf.

Bert had swung to the right where he could see behind trees Adam was approaching. Adam was likewise watching the cover in front of Bert. Each depended for his protection against a hiding and waiting enemy upon the keenness of the other's eyesight. Adam's sense of exhilaration mounted. Nothing called upon all that there was in a man like knowing there was extreme danger just ahead and that he still was keeping on going into it. And when you got right down to the truth there was no excitement you could share with anybody else equal to what you felt when you knew your life depended from minute to minute on the quickness of another man, as his did now on Bert's, while you were equally responsible for him. No experience with any woman could ever come up to that pitch of excitement.

╡ SEVENTEEN ╞

OUT of the corner of his eye, Adam caught a passing glimpse of Bert's face. Bert was as watchful and tense as a cat ready to pounce, but back of the outward watchfulness there was a complete serenity. Bert had left behind him a devoted wife and an agreeable home. He had no right to be looking as if he'd knocked off work in the middle of a hot day to make a run for the nearest trout stream. Then there came over Adam the realization that he was feeling a serenity of his own. He might be shot the next minute but this present minute he could breathe easily. He could be breathing no more easily had he shaken off a burden at the edge of the game trail. It was like being a soldier again. From now on it was as if each step he took were timed by the beating of a drum. He was free again as only the soldier can be free.

Just ahead a tremendous elm had fallen, carrying with it a number of lesser trees. The resulting tangle of prostrate trunks and outthrust branches, long since enlaced with vines and briers, was an ideal spot for an ambush. Adam and Bert pulled up and approached with the utmost wariness. First one and then the other watched, rifle ready, from the protection of a tree, while the other darted nearer. Gilbert, obediently hanging back, observed with the most intent interest this exhibition of approved forest tactics. But all their wariness was wasted. The giant brush pile proved to be untenanted. And beyond stretched a mile-wide grove of hardwood, with beautiful straight trunks rising from a flat forest floor on which there was no vestige of undergrowth. You could see nearly as far through these woods as across an open prairie. They were empty.

"Could be," said Bert, "that buck dreamed up his Indians like you could of that one of yourn last night."

Gilbert laughed. Adam swore. It still was necessary to be sure before they went on. It cost an hour's circling to locate the first moccasin print and then another hour to work out the carefully covered sign left by one Shawnee and one Mingo who had reached the west bank of the river by canoe, climbed to the top of the ridge, returned to the canoe and pushed off again. The mission of the Indians had obviously been to examine the network of game trails west of the river for traces of the possible movement of any white man through this area. Two lost hours was a price to pay for learning no more than this, but it was at least an indication that the main force of the enemy was still located somewhere to the north. Also that it must be moving westward, if moving at all; for if it were marching in this direction they'd have sent many more spies out this way and be keeping them out.

Adam swung on northward, the silent drum seeming again to be timing his strides. But it only drove; it did not guide. The marsh which bordered the estuary where the next tributary emptied into the south fork was impassable. Discovering this only after spending some time trying to find a way through, they were forced to retreat and make a wide circuit on higher ground. Returning to the direct cross-country course they had decided to hold, they came upon a seeming-

253

ly endless expanse of burned-over land where the new undergrowth was so thick as almost to deny them passage and altogether to deny them a view in any direction.

"Might's well be travelin' with a blanket over our heads," grumbled Bert. "Was the whole of Burgoyne's army camped ten rods ahead we'd walk right into his tent."

"Eli knew his way around patches of bad country like this," said Adam. "You've been at the station over three months. Didn't you ever talk to him about the general lay of the land up this way?"

"Eli he's never no hand to talk," said Bert. "And since I been here I never had no time to see for myself. I was too busy runnin' back and forth lookin' after you."

They struggled on through the matted brush. Adam tried veering nearer the river to find easier going, but instead found a belt of cane in the river bottom that was worse. With the gradual widening of the river valley the line of low ridges had fallen away to the west. To swing that far to the left, in search of more open country, would take them too far from their route.

The afternoon became blistering hot. The brush, reaching just above their heads, shut out every breath of air. They plowed doggedly on, Adam and then Bert taking a turn at breaking a way by throwing his weight forward, all crawling ignominiously when this became necessary. Hours passed, their lack of progress making them seem longer.

"Give me a crack at leading for a while," volunteered Gilbert. "You two have been taking all the beating."

The others grunted and stood aside, mopping their faces. Gilbert began breaking the way. Almost at once he brought up hard against a low outcropping of limestone which was yet high enough to enable a man standing on it to see out over the brush.

"All we been lackin'," said Bert, "was a guide that knowed his way."

The three scrambled up onto the stone. The whole valley to the north was immediately exposed to their view. To Adam the drumbeat seemed to accelerate to a sudden ominous roll. Ten or a dozen miles to the north, in the general neighborhood of Riddle's Station, clouds of buzzards and eagles were hovering and circling in the clear evening air.

"Somethin' up there dead," said Bert. "A lot of somethin'."

Gilbert was watching the grim faces of his companions, seeking a clue to their conclusion. "The Indians could have suffered heavy losses," he suggested, "trying to take the station."

"You want to make a wish," advised Bert, "then wish for

somethin' likely—such as eight hundred of them dyin' off in one night from smallpox."

"But if they'd taken the station they'd have burned it, and then wouldn't there be smoke?"

"Takes buzzards longer'n a fire to finish up," said Bert.

"Indians carry off their dead," said Adam.

Fixing the direction and distance across the intervening valley, he led the way back into the underbrush and on down the slope. At the foot they came to the end of the brush but to the beginning of the cane, which now extended all the way across the flat river bottom. The new green growth was very nearly as thick as the brush, while the old dry stalks, killed by last winter's unprecedented cold, were as hard as iron rods and rattled like iron when jostled.

"Might be we should fire us a shot now and then," said Bert. "So every Shawnee within eighteen mile will know for wure we're comin'."

"Be no use," said Adam, fighting his way between two stalks as big and as rigid as gateposts. "The rate we're going it'll be morning before we get near enough for them to hear a shot."

Though it was now dark, he could tell his direction by noting the stars, visible through the swaying tops of the twenty-foot cane above, but he could also tell they were making far too little progress. Coming upon a buffalo path that led toward the river, he followed it. On the other side the going might prove better. It could hardly prove worse.

At the riverbank they crouched and listened. Curls of mist were rising from the dark water. No faintest sound broke the stillness. Even the ordinary wildlife seemed to have withdrawn from the unnaturally silent wilderness. Tying together some bits of driftwood to form a raft upon which to ferry their weapons, powder horns and food sack, they swam to the other bank.

They found that cane could be worse, after all. The valley bottom on this side was flatter and wider and the growth thicker. But there was no use recrossing the river. Riddle's Station was on this side. They began pushing on northward, making the best time and the least noise that they could manage. Sooner or later they were bound to come out into the cleared country around the station.

By midnight, Adam judged, they had made perhaps half the distance between the rock from which they had observed the circling buzzards and the scene of whatever the disaster which had attracted the scavengers. The next time he glanced up he realized that the difficulties under which they had so far been laboring were being multiplied many times over.

The mist was thickening to form a blanket of fog over the tops of the cane, which shut out the stars. Stumbling on through the maze of giant cane they were no longer able to make more than a guess at the direction to which they were trying to hold.

To keep to the riverbank was no help. Since the river meandered to follow its course would add miles to the distance they must cover. Already they could barely hope to arrive by dawn. Occasional game trails wound through the labyrinth, but any one of these was as likely to lead in one direction as another.

Adam plunged on savagely, becoming, after a time, more and more obsessed with the conviction that he was headed south instead of north.

"No good lookin' at the worst side," was Bert's comfort. "Chances are we ain't goin' south—but just in circles. That's what folks generally do when they git themselves lost."

"We have to keep going," insisted Adam. "Even if we haven't a chance in a hundred of coming out where we want. We can't just squat and wait for daylight."

"Right," said Bert. "Besides we got to keep actin' like we're headed somewheres—whether we know which way or not. Gilbert he come along to watch how a couple of old hands like us git around in the woods. We let him see we're bushed he's liable to lose confidence in us."

Gilbert cleared his throat. "A compass be any use to you?"

"Only next to sprouting wings," said Adam. He grabbed at Gilbert. "You mean you've got one?"

"Yes," admitted Gilbert. "Didn't seem sporting to mention it. I brought it because I thought it might come in handy—in case I got separated from you."

"First the rock—now a compass," marveled Bert. "When we start for home I don't want to get separated—I want you to take me by the hand."

They knelt around Gilbert's compass. Adam struck a spark from his flint and blew on the ignited tow until he could see the quivering needle. They went on a hundred yards and repeated the operation. They were traveling no faster but at least they could know they were moving in the right direction.

Another hour passed. There was no change in the thickness of the cane or the character of the river bottom. Each clump he shouldered past, each slow step he took, forcing his leg forward through the rubbery new growth stooling out from the base of each stalk, seemed to Adam to leave them where they were. They might have been on a treadmill, pushing endlessly against the same piece of ground. Before long dawn would break. Time was running out on them. Suddenly Bert hissed. All paused. The fog had settled right down to the ground. Bert was so near their sleeves brushed but Adam could not see him.

"I don't hear anything," whispered Adam.

"Me neither," replied Bert. "But I had me a kind of an idea I smelled somethin'."

He took several slow steps forward, sniffing at the warm, moist air, then paused again.

"Give us your light."

Adam crouched beside Bert and blew on the smoldering tow. The object on the ground which was the occasion for Bert's intense interest became visible.

"A cow pat," murmured Bert with deep satisfaction. "Never expected to see one I'd feel like kissin'."

Delighted by the humble proof that they were at least within grazing range of the station, they pushed on, taking more care now to move silently. The cane began to open up. They were reaching an area where it had been more heavily browsed by feeding stock. Bert paused, sniffing again. Adam, too, was aware of this new taint hanging in the heavy, wet air. At first this smell was elusive but also from the first it was horrible. They went on. The smell, still faint, yet was fearfully offensive. It was the odor of flesh, now dead but so recently living that death was made to seem still present. Suddenly there was a rustle in the cane immediately ahead, followed by a swishing. The beating of invisible wings drove the air against Adam's face. Disturbed by their approach a buzzard had risen from his feeding. Bert crept forward and groped about along the ground.

"A pig," he whispered, relieved.

They went on. The cane, grazed off by the station's livestock, had fallen away to a mere stubble, but Adam still could see nothing through the encompassing fog. He felt his foot sink into plowed earth. They were at the edge of a cornfield. The three men crouched and listened for minutes. No sound informed them of what might lie ahead. Bert nudged Adam. He looked up. The fog overhead was becoming tinged with gray. Day was about to break.

They crept on into the cornfield. When daylight came they might have desperate and immediate need of its cover and they had a greater need to find a spot from which they could see what lay beyond the corn. The fog was slowly becoming gray enough to look like fog. Adam could make out the blurred outline of the other men and of the nearer cornstalks.

The corn had been wildly trampled as if stock had been driven headlong back and forth through it. A whiff of charred timbers mingled with the heavier odor of death. The gray fog seemed a nightmarish curtain concealing horrors unbearable were they to be revealed. There was another rustle immediately ahead. Shadow-winged shapes rose into the air, flapping awkwardly, setting the fog to swirling. The sharp smell of soured milk mingled with the heavier odor of decaying flesh. They came upon the carcass of a cow, bristling with vengeful arrows as evidence of the special Indian hatred for cattle. Horses they were always glad to steal but a cow they abhorred, since they had come to regard it as a sure sign that wherever the white man brought cattle he had come to stay.

It was growing rapidly lighter, though the fog still shrouded everything more than a few feet away. There were many more cattle carcasses scattered through the corn and buzzards were rising by the dozen. Adam recognized the risk that the continuing flight might give notice of their approach, though it was normal, after a night's gorging, for buzzards still able to fly to flap off at dawn to roost in the nearest tree.

He crept around the carcass of a horse that must have been struck down by some unintended wild shot and then came to an instant stop. He had reached the station edge of the cornfield. The three men lay prone behind the last row of corn and listened. The oppressive silence continued.

A faint breeze stirred the fog. The wind freshened. The fog thinned as suddenly as a curtain might be drawn aside. Thirty feet away there was a woodpile. Across it was sprawled the body of an old woman. Scalping had left her but a fringe of wispy gray hair. Her clothing had been torn from her, exposing the pitiful meagerness of her aged frame. Beside the woodpile lay the bodies of three very young children —two little girls and a boy. They had been killed by being swung by the heels to crush their heads upon the chopping block.

"Every now and then," whispered Bert, "somethin' comes along that gits you real sick of Indians."

Gilbert was observing the bodies with a professional eye. "Those unhappy children appear to have been dead all of two days," he pronounced. "Possibly a few hours less—considering the heat. But the old woman—they broke her arms and legs and left her there on the woodpile. She only expired about an hour ago."

Adam stood up behind a cornstalk. The fog was withdrawing toward the river. The whole area around the station was coming into view. The buildings and the stockade were heaps of ashes. Riddle's had been a big and prosperous settlement. The number of dead cattle strewn about ran into the hun-

258

dreds. More fearfully revealing was the array, almost as numerous, of naked, mangled and mutilated corpses of men, women and children. All had suffered more grievous wounds than had been required merely to end their lives. Their contorted and dismembered limbs seemed to have stiffened in attitudes of continuing supplication, as if death itself had brought no release from their agony. Nothing moved among these windrows of the dead, except the buzzards and eagles still on the ground, slowly shifting their bloated weights from one leg to the other. The savages seemingly had gone on. Even they could have been oppressed by this desolation they had themselves contrived.

"They must of got in on them by some trick—most likely in the night," muttered Bert. "This was a good stockade with a big blockhouse at every corner and they had near two hundred men. They could of stood off all the Indians betwixt here and Detroit for the rest of the summer."

"Whatever the trick—it took all the fight out of them," said Adam. "They surrendered. Notice how many were hit by hatchets and clubs and how many there are in that long heap over there. They had to be prisoners that had been lined up first."

"There just might be somebody left alive out there," said Gilbert. "I'm going to have to take a look."

"No," said Adam sharply. "Stay out of the open. The settlements in Kentucky that haven't been taken yet—they're the ones we have to think about now. And we still don't know for sure which way these devils went when they left off here."

The fog was lifting and dissipating in the warmth of the rising sun. Adam made a quick survey of the clearing, as the whole of it was now for the first time disclosed, noting in particular the patches of cover to which they might take if the need suddenly arose or, on the other hand, in which some party of Indian stragglers might still be hidden. The chief features of the area were the mile-long cornfield and the belt of willow and sycamore along the immediate river-bank. The cornfield stretched in a half-moon around the ashes of the station with the points of the crescent extending toward the river but leaving an intervening strip of open pasture. Just beyond the woodpile there was a narrow, brush-choked gully that cut diagonally across the clearing past the south horn of the crescent, leading all the way to the river. He took this route, the others creeping behind him.

When at last he could see through the willows and out over the river he paused with a mutter of satisfaction. Many barges and canoes were beached along the west bank and a curl of smoke rose in the woods beyond, probably from the campfire of a party left to guard the boats. The Indians had started, at least, moving west toward an area where the settlements were thickest and among which a force of settlers could be most rapidly rallied were the alarm spread in time.

Before trying to cross the river to follow until he had made sure that this was what they were doing, it was necessary to get some idea of the disposition of the Indian boat guard. Handing his rifle to Bert, he climbed a willow sapling, swung his weight sidewise until the sapling bent to drop him into the lower branches of a sycamore, then pulled himself up into the greater tree until he could see well out over the flat river valley on the other side. But the first Indians he caught sight of were on this side, though they seemed to present no immediate threat. Thirty or more were sprawled out on a sandspit a scant hundreds yards up river. Some were on their stomachs, some on their backs, one or two half in the water —many in such odd, tumbled positions that for a second Adam surmised hopefully that all were dead. Looking more closely, he realized they were only drunks, sleeping it off.

Nearly every one was festooned with scraps of white clothing, women's aprons and petticoats seeming to have attracted the most favor. Even from his distance Adam could see the blood, now dried black, with which all were splotched and smeared. They had gorged on the station's beef and swilled the station's whisky. The excitement of firing its walls had led to the greater excitement of butchering its cattle and then to the ultimate excitement of murdering its inhabitants. Exhausted by their own excesses the Indians had not been able to march on to new attacks until a day, and maybe two, had been lost, and even then these sots on the sandspit had had to be left behind when the main force had gone on.

Adam wondered who was in command of it. The expedition semed too ambitious an undertaking to have been trusted to Tory partisan leaders like Alexander McKee and Matthew Elliott. The nominal command had probably been given to some English regular officer. Whoever he was his Indians were giving him almost the trouble he deserved. However he'd felt about the massacre of the prisoners, if he had any sort of military judgment at all he must have been driven frantic by the heedless killing of the stock. Three hundred head of cattle, if kept alive and driven along on the hoof, would have fed his invading army for a couple of weeks. To try to manage pigheaded white frontiersmen was task enough for any commander, but it was nothing like the task of maintaining any kind of control over a pack of Indians.

Keeping the trunk of the sycamore between him and the sleepers, Adam turned to survey the other bank. His grip

260

tightened suddenly on the branch to which he was holding. An incredible sound had come rolling across the river—the unmistakable boom of a cannon. It came from the direction of Martin's Station, five miles to the west, and it was followed by the firing of a second.

Before the dull explosions had ceased to echo through the silent wilderness Adam knew everything he had set out to learn. He knew where the enemy was, what they had done, what they were doing and what they could do. He knew that for the first time in Kentucky's violent history Indian invaders had managed to bring with them cannon from Detroit. The strange surrender of Riddle's Station was no longer a mystery. The station had had no choice but to surrender, for no simple stockade of wood could withstand artillery fire. The cannon were now before Martin's Station. It, too, must surrender. And with the same result. Each succeeding station in Kentucky must fall if each waited to be attacked. The one hope was for an alarm to be spread in time for every man to come out from behind his stockade, band together with his neighbors and do battle in the open.

Adam took a second look at the sandspit. Another Indian, this one very much awake, had appeared. He was running about, vigorously kicking signs of life into his sleeping companions. He kept pointing down river toward the sycamore. Adam dropped to the ground. There was no use wasting words on the cannon shots. Bert understood their meaning as well as he did.

"There're some thirty Indians still on this side," he said. "They'll be taking after us in another minute. If we get separated—remember this: You, Bert, and you, Gilbert, get back to Trace Creek. Tell Joel to send the women and children to Boonesborough. And to get ready to move his men wherever they're needed when word comes of wherever that is. Tell him whatever happens not to let himself get cooped up in his stockade. I'm going to cut around Martin's Station and get the word to Lexington and Harrodsburg."

Bert and Gilbert nodded. Adam led the way back. They were half the distance up the gully when it suddenly became all too apparent that more than the one Indian had been awake. A group of six loomed against the morning sky on the bank just above. Adam whipped up his rifle and, according to the long-established understanding with Bert in the event of such a choice of targets, shot the one on the left. Bert's shot took the one on the right.

But four remained. Staring down at the two white men desperately reloading, they fully comprehended their advantage. Deliberately they lifted their weapons. One had a rifle,

261

two had trade muskets and the fourth a stubby elkhorn bow. Adam saw that he was destined to receive the attention of the rifle and the more ancient of the two muskets.

Gilbert was a few paces back and had so far been obscured from the view of the Indians by a clump of alder. The sudden roar of his double-charged fowling piece took Adam almost as much by surprise as it did the Indians. Two of them dropped in their tracks. The other two doubled up and pitched forward into the gully. With the butt of his rifle Adam finished the one that had rolled almost to his feet. But before Bert could get his knife into the fourth, that one had raised on one elbow and with one last vengeful effort was throwing his tomahawk.

Adam sprang to the top of the gully bank and looked toward the river. The formerly sleeping Indians had not yet emerged from the belt of willow. He completed reloading and slid down into the gully bottom. Bert had reloaded but Gilbert was sitting down while he somewhat slowly recharged his piece.

"Come on," urged Adam. "We've still got time—but none to waste."

"Gilbert's hit," said Bert.

Gilbert got to his feet, keeping all of his weight on one leg. The other was drenched with blood from a deep gash cut by the whirling blade of the tomahawk.

"How bad?" demanded Adam.

"Kneecap's broken," said Gilbert, as calmly as if he were diagnosing a patient's injury. "I can put a little weight on it as long as I keep it straight but I can't bend it." He sat down again with the leg sticking out and the fowling piece across his lap. "So you and Bert better get along. What you have to do is too important to lose any time fooling with me."

"We didn't bring you along to tell us what to do," said Adam. "You'll do as I say and exactly what I say. And don't argue. Crawl as fast as you can up the gully and through the cornfield. Bert and I will hold them off for a while from the bank here. When we think you've had time to reach the edge of the cane we'll run and catch up. Then will be time enough to worry about how we go on from there."

"Yes, my captain," said Gilbert with a conciliatory grin. He got to his feet again and handed Bert his fowling piece. "This will just be in my way."

Grasping at the brush along the sides he hobbled off up the gully. Adam and Bert gained the top of the bank in time to see three Indians making a break from the edge of the river-bank woods to the southern corner of the cornfield. It was just a nice distance for a moving target. The foremost two dropped as the rifles cracked and the third ducked back into the willows.

There was a considerable stir now of signal whistles and animal calls all along the edge of the willows. But the recently awakened Indians remained for the moment none too belliger- ent. They seemed more concerned with advising one another what to do than with embarking on an advance across the open. Adam tried a shot into one twitching bush and had the satisfaction of drawing a a yell of pain. Bert won a greater reward. After his shout into the same sycamore Adam had climbed, an Indian fell headlong, hitting the ground with a fine thud.

"Pack of 'em starting to work up the bottom of the gully," observed Adam.

This advance was protected from any direct rifleshot by a curve in the lower gully.

"Just what I been waitin' for," said Bert.

He picked up Gilbert's fowling piece and aimed it high. After a moment's frowning study and several thoughtful changes in the angle of firing he pulled the trigger. The charge of buckshot carried just far enough to scatter before plung- ing down into the lower gully. Yells of outraged astonish- ment burst from the Indians and the waving brush tops in- dicated the haste with which they were retreating.

"That's sure a fine little gun," said Bert, patting the piece fondly.

"We can push along now," said Adam. "Gilbert's had time to get quite a ways and if we wait too long they'll try next to work around behind the cornfield."

They crawled up the gully to its head. Adam glanced back. The Indians had not yet come out of the willows. He was gathering himself for the short dash past the woodpile when Bert grabbed his foot.

"Will you take a look at that."

Gilbert was hobbling out of the northern point of the cornfield and crossing the open beyond the ruins of the station. He'd not only taken an opposite route to the one he'd been told to take but he was deliberately heading straight for the Indians in the willows. And he knew what he was doing. He was holding up his hands to show he was offering him- self as their captive. Adam jumped to his feet.

"You crazy fool," he yelled. "Get back. You don't have to do that. Get back."

"Get back yourself," yelled Gilbert in reply. He'd never sounded more cheerful. "And don't argue. You can see it's too late now for you to do anything except what you ought to be doing. See that you get on with it."

A dozen Indians were running out gleefully to surround Gilbert. It was too far for the longest rifleshot to take effect.

"Don't argue, he says," stormed Adam. "He certainly took care we had no chance to argue. He started scheming this the minute he was hit."

"He can be my pappy and my grandpappy," pronounced Bert. "He's as double-charged as his gun. Twice in a row he's saved our skins."

"He was thinking about saving more skins than just ours," said Adam. "Well, let's get going. And fast, too. He's paid our way."

At the farther edge of the cornfield he pulled up.

"I'm circling to the north here. I'll have a better chance to get around the Indians at Martin's that way. Tell Joel I'll get some word to him about what's going on soon's I get to Harrodsburg."

"See that you get to Harrodsburg," said Bert. "And don't worry about things. I'll look after Cynthia same's I will Alice."

Adam started away. Cynthia seemed as far removed from him as if she were still in Virginia, as she had seemed before he'd left Vincennes. Everything else in his past life seemed that far away. All he could think about was what had happened at Riddle's and what was happening to Gilbert now and what would happen at Martin's before this day was out. There could be nothing else for him to think about except what he might be able to do to keep such things from going on happening all over Kentucky. The pounding drum was right inside him now.

He swam the river and kept on into the wooded hills north of Martin's Station. Occasionally faint bursts of yelling drifted up to him from the distant clearing. But there'd been no cannon firing since those first two shots. That must have been all that had been needed to bring about a surrender. Probably by now people there were beginning to suffer what had been suffered at Riddle's.

Beyond Martin's he dropped down to the Great Buffalo Trace which stretched across northern Kentucky from Blue Lick on the main Licking River to Lee's Town on the Kentucky River. Countless years of buffalo migrations had trampled the soil down to the underlying limestone, and in places the tremendous natural road was a hundred yards wide. From the shelter of the forest's edge he studied the broad avenue for a moment, then plunged out into the open and settled down to steady hard running. Ordinarily, in traveling through the wilderness he would not have dreamed of expos-

264

ing himself in a manner so foolhardy. He knew there was far more chance of his encountering Indians now that he was west of their main force, since they must have sent out parties to watch every trail leading in this direction in order to prevent word of their advance from preceding them. Still he kept to the trace, where he could get on so much faster, taking to the woods only occasionally, when approaching a stream crossing or a hilltop, where watchers were most likely to have taken up position, or when crossing expanses of grassland, where he could be seen from a distance. An hour passed, a second and then a third. Game seemed nervous but not unusually disturbed. This was a big country, he kept telling himself. No matter how many Indians were trying to watch it, one man on foot might go a long way through it without running into any of them.

He decided, however, against cutting south to Bryant's. That was the most exposed station, after Martin's, and Indians were surely infesting its approaches. Even were he able to get through to the station he might be unable to get out again. His news was too important to the rest of Kentucky to run that risk. He kept to the trace until he judged he was north of Lexington and then turned down a deer trail.

The country was more open now and it was more and more difficult to keep within reach of the patches of woods. Finally a mile-wide belt of grassland stretched across his way south. He had to chance it. He paused to take a dozen deep breaths and then started. Lifting his knees high so as to be less impeded by the thick, clinging grass he ran as hard as he could. He was a third of the way across when the first Indian horseman appeared over a low rise to his left.

It was already too late to hope to hide in the tall grass, for the Indian had seen him at once and was blowing a piercing blast on his war whistle. Eight more mounted Shawnee galloped over the rise, pulled up momentarily alongisde the first and whooped with satisfaction at sight of the white man stranded helplessly in the open. Jerking their dancing mounts into a new gallop, they swept down toward him, leaning forward along their horses' necks and continuing to yell in their eagerness to add to his consternation.

Adam whirled and plunged back toward the woods he had left, bounding and zigzagging like a fleeing jack rabbit to distract their aim. They began to shoot but their marksmanship was further disturbed by the jolting of their horses and he was not hit. They veered to the right when they saw where he was heading and raced to cut him off from the woods. Calling upon some deep-seated store of reserve energy, he put on a final burst of speed and won the race to the shelter of the trees by a margin so narrow he could hear the swish of one thrown tomahawk whirling past his head.

Once in the woods he could move faster and with more freedom on foot than they could on their horses. They wheeled back into the open and separated to encircle the grove. Since he had foreseen this, instead of trying to hide he dashed straight on across an adjoining meadow, knowing they had not had an opportunity to reload, and on into the next patch of woods. Before they had quite surrounded this one he had made his way along a brushy draw into a third and more extensive wood where he had more room to maneuver.

But the Indians seemed to have guessed his intention of making for Lexington. All except two fanned out across the open country to the south to make sure that whatever he did he made no progress in that direction. The two dismounted and set about tracking him through such cover as he found in his desperate twisting and turning. The deadly hare and hounds game went on. He was forced continually to swing farther westward.

It was past noon before he finally could feel any confidence in having shaken them off and could at last turn southward again. He was now nearly as far west as north of Lexington and had lost three precious hours. Moreover, once freed of the grim excitement of escaping the horsemen he began to realize how rapidly he was tiring. Guessing he still had fifteen miles to go he consciously doled out his remaining strength, setting a pace to which he felt he could keep until he got there.

An hour passed without new alarms. He noted more signs of human use of deer trails, an increase in the number of blazed trees marking land claims and even one grove of maple that had been tapped the past spring to make sugar. He was approaching the outskirts of the more settled area around Lexington. Then his luck, which had taken so bad a turn when he'd been sighted by the Shawnee horsemen, took almost as pronounced a turn the other way. He encountered another horseman, this one a white man.

He came riding up out of a marsh with a string of muskrat traps jangling at his knee. He was old, with a tangled, tobacco-stained white beard so long it mingled with his horse's mane; he was more caked with grease and dirt than was common even on this frontier, and one side of his face continually twitched with some kind of a nervous disorder. But never had Adam been so pleased by the sight of another man. The rat trapper pulled in his big, bony, wall-eyed horse and watched Adam's approach with the mildest interest.

"How far to Lexington?" gasped Adam.

"Mebbe eight mile."

Adam put a hand out to steady himself against the horse's shoulder. Coming to a stop had seemed to take a greater effort than to keep on running. He could barely hold himself upright.

"Give me your horse," he said.

The old man shook his head patiently. "No, sir. Don't callate I kin do thet."

Adam grabbed him by the belt and pulled him from the saddle with a great clatter of muskrat traps. The old trapper offered no resistance nor did he seem to feel concern over being handled so cavalierly. He released himself with a certain dignity and reached for the trailing ends of the reins.

"I have to have him," said Adam. "My name's Adam Frane. I'm from that new settlement over on Trace Creek."

"Mine's Simon Hite," murmured the old man politely.

"Listen to what I'm saying," demanded Adam. "I have to get to Harrodsburg as fast as I can—to tell them the Indians are back in Kentucky. You can save me a couple of hours if I can trust you to take the word to Lexington. Now get this straight so you can tell it just as I'm telling you. A pack of Indians and Tory rangers—a big one—maybe seven or eight hundred—is across the south fork of the Licking. They've already taken Riddle's and Martin's. They were able to take both stations right off *because they have cannon.*"

An unexpected spark of perception kindled in the faded old eyes. "Grasshopper guns?"

"No. Real fieldpieces. Big enough to knock down any stockade. Make sure the people at Lexington understand that. And make sure they send the word around to Stroud's and Todd's and McClelland's—and Bryant's, too, if they can, though it may be too late for that. I have to count on you to get the story to Lexington because I have to keep on to Harrodsburg to get them started rounding up some help for you people up here."

Simon sighed and handed Adam the reins. " 'Pears from all you say thet there ain't no question but what I got to let you have him. You'd never make it afoot—yuh look real tuckered out."

Adam pulled himself up into the saddle. Simon still seemed none too excited by his share in their common mission. He stepped back, pawed his beard and looked sadly at his horse. "His name's Zeke—though ain't much use callin' him one name or t'other. He's mostly too mean to pay no attention no matter what you call him. He's a good animal jus' the same. When yuh git to Harrodsburg—if'n yuh do—yuh kin leave

267

him with Eph Millikin. Eph's married up with my youngest granddaughter."

"Lexington," Adam reminded him. "Remember? That's where you're going. And *get going*." He pulled Zeke around and got him started off.

Simon called after him helpfully. "If'n Zeke he comes on to balk or lay down under yuh—jus' bite his left ear. Be sure it's the left ear. Yuh could chaw off the t'other without his payin' yuh no heed."

"Lexington," Adam yelled back at him.

Zeke set off at a lumbering gallop. His feet seemed to strike the ground at unexpected intervals and his action was peculiarly uneven, as if he were always either about to stop or to bolt. Unless pulled aside by main strength he also seemed as disposed to run head on into the next tree as to veer past it. Rocked and jolted, forced constantly to jerk and tug at the reins, Adam found the going more demanding than if he had been still on foot. He clung grimly to the saddle and counted the miles.

For the first hour Zeke exhibited no sign of the tendency to balk of which there had been warning. Then at the margin of a narrow stream, after having gathered himself for the leap across, he froze into sudden stiffened immobility. Adam pitched off over his withers into the water. Climbing laboriously back on, Adam remembered the admonition to bite his left ear. He did so. It worked perfectly. Zeke plunged ahead. He also threw up his head violently, striking Adam in the face and setting his nose to bleeding so that he had to return to the stream to stop the flow with cold water.

Mounting again, he worked Zeke into his awkward gallop and kept on. Thereafter, when the ear-biting was indicated, as it was, on the average of every quarter hour, he took care to avoid the tossing head. Worse than the periodic balking was Zeke's gait in descending hills. It was marked by irregularly spaced jumps, after which he alighted stiff-legged each time to produce a maximum jar. Worse than that was the cunning with which he would swerve unexpectedly to pass under any branch low enough to catch his rider. Adam began to wish for another brush with Indians in which Zeke might conceivably become the victim of a wild shot. There was one advantage in his rage, however. He'd never have found the strength to keep going, without even an occasional pause, had he not so bitterly begrudged the horse the benefit of a rest.

Coming out, at length, on the main Lexington-Harrodsburg trail, he turned down it, his destination now only a few hours away. He also began to meet an occasional traveler. He welcomed each chance to tell his story. Each added person to whom he told it made it that much more certain that the news would spread widely and swiftly. He had had at first none too much confidence in Simon's dependability and this confidence grew less every hour he rode Zeke. A man who possessed and valued such a horse could hardly have sense enough to travel the eight miles to Lexington and still remember what he'd been told to say when he got there. No one Adam met on the trail had previously had the faintest inkling of the Indian invasion. While the general ignorance of the threat to Kentucky made the general danger more obvious, it brought Adam a kind of comfort, too. It was some relief to realize that his own effort and Gilbert's sacrifice had not been wasted.

By nightfall he had begun to wonder, dully, if he was going to make it. He kept falling asleep and catching himself as he was about to roll from the saddle. Zeke, perverse as ever, seemed on the other hand to be growing stronger and pounded on harder than before. Each jarring impact of the horse's hoofs seemed to be against Adam's temples. His mind seemed as tired as his body. He began to wonder what he was doing and why he was doing it. Suppose, if he did get there, they didn't believe him. Suppose he couldn't remember what he had to tell them. He wasn't so sure, even now. In any event, it began to seem that whatever he had to say would be said too late. It must already have been days since he swam the river below Riddle's. It could be weeks. Or some other summer. Or some other Indian inroad that had long since been dealt with. He was becoming more confused. His eyes closed. He sagged forward, clutching at Zeke's mane.

This time he did not catch himself in time. Striking the ground awakened him. He'd tied the end of the reins to his wrist so that the horse could not go on without him. He hadn't the strength to climb back on. There was a bank near by. Zeke proved profoundly suspicious of it. With much difficulty he edged Zeke near enough, crawled up onto the bank and lurched into the saddle. It was only then that he realized he was in sight of Harrodsburg.

He stared in stupefaction. He must still be asleep and dreaming what he seemed to see. Several of the huts and sheds outside the stockade were in flames. Men with torches were running about setting fire to the others. They must expect an attack and be bent on denying the Indians the use of the outbuildings as cover for an assault. That made no sense. They couldn't know here that the Indians were coming. He hadn't told them yet.

The gate was opened to him and immediately his confusion

was a thousand times compounded. When he fell off his horse it was straight into the arms of two Indians. Reflections from the flames outside gleamed unmistakably on their shaven heads, their bristling topknots and the old war paint peeling from their faces. Worse followed—and his tired mind refused to grasp any of it. The two who were gripping him and pounding him on the back and calling him by name were not Indians. They were not only white men but old friends he'd not seen since Vincennes. This made the least sense of all. They couldn't be here. He had the wit left to know that. They belonged with Clark. They didn't belong here. This was Harrodsburg. He knew that, too. He'd worked hard enough to get here.

"You're not Indians," he said accusingly. "You're Jim Beggs and Cory Poynter."

"Thet Adam Frane—he's jus' as smart as he used to be before he turned farmer," said Jim to Cory. He grinned at Adam. "And yer jus' as right as yuh be quick. We only look like Indians—leastwise Cory does—'cause in the kind of country we bin through thet was healthier."

"We'uns jus' got in from Fort Jeff," explained Cory. "Old Vigo's cousin in Detroit he got word to Clark about what was a-comin' at you Kentucky folks—so Clark and Jim and me we tuk off to look after yuh."

"Clark's here?" stammered Adam.

"Right there in the gatehouse," came a dozen pleased voices from the crowd of men that had gathered around.

Adam slipped from the grasp of Jim and Cory and slowly sat down on the ground. So Clark was here. Clark had come because he already knew about the Indians. Clark would take care of everything now. That was a big relief. There couldn't be a bigger one. But an equally great depression settled over him. There'd been no real need for what Gilbert had done. His own desperate effort to get here had been unnecessary, too. Foolish, even. Still, now he could sleep.

"Was that Adam Frane I heard out there?" Clark stood in the lighted doorway of the gatehouse. "Bring him in."

Jim and Cory picked Adam up. Inside, eight or ten of the leading men of Harrodsburg were lined up along the walls. Their eyes were fixed on Clark as if they were troubled children and he was their father. Clark looked odd with his red hair shaved to a scalp lock. He'd taken the trouble to wash off most of the paint, however, and someone had loaned him a homespun shirt to cover his naked torso. His first keen glance at Adam, sagging between his two supporters, took in the significance of his condition.

"You've been traveling hard. Got some news?"

"Only what you already know," mumbled Adam.

"I know that an English captain named Bird left Detroit with a hundred or more Tory rangers. He's got Alexander McKee and the three Girtys with him. He's counting on picking up seven or eight hundred Shawnee and Mingo and coming at Kentucky. And that's all. What do you know? Is he across the Ohio already?"

Adam pulled away from Jim and Cory and straightened up. He had something to tell, after all—enough to make the difference between day and night. And he had for a listener the one man in the world who'd know best how much it meant and what to do about it. He spoke slowly and carefully, aware that he might not have the strength to speak his piece more than once.

"They've been across the Ohio nearly a week. They came up the Licking in boats. They've taken Riddle's. That was three days ago. This morning they took Martin's. By the way they're moving I'd say they're going for Bryant's next. Stations have to surrender on demand because they've got two pieces of field artillery. When you decide what you're going to do will you send word to Major Wyeth at Trace Creek? And I agreed to turn the horse I rode over to a man here named Eph Millikin."

He was starting to fall forward. Clark caught him by the shoulders and was letting him down on a cot in the corner. Then he was asleep.

EIGHTEEN

ADAM was headed north again—over the same ground he had covered so painfully when struggling south with his news. But everything was different now. He'd had a night's rest and been loaned a proper horse. He wasn't alone. Jim and Cory were with him. Next to Bert, they were men about as good as you'd want to have in the woods with you. Also with him were a dozen young Harrodsburg militiamen, to be used according to his needs—to carry messages, stand guard, handle the horses or to fight if he got into one. And—making the most difference of all—Clark was behind him. All Kentucky was arousing. Men were leaving their stockades by the hundred to join him.

"Find me Bird," Clark had said. "Keep me posted on just where he is and what he's doing. I want to be able to move

271

fast soon's Logan gets here with the regiments from his place and Boonesborough. I want to hit Bird and hit him so hard it'll cure his Indians of ever coming across the Ohio again."

Adam rode on, feeling more at peace with himself than he'd been able to feel for a long time. Not much more than a year ago he'd been so set on leaving Clark, at Vincennes, that he'd been ready to stoop to any trick to make the break. Since then he hadn't seemed to worry too much about that leaving, but all the time it must have been gnawing at him inside—to account for his feeling so good about being with Clark again now. He'd already made up a little for the time he'd taken off. Clark had made a great fuss over the news he'd brought and the effort he'd made to bring it. And now here he was in command of the vanguard, in effect, of Clark's army. With all Kentucky for the first time rallying around Clark, a greater blow might be struck than any since the taking of Kaskaskia and Vincennes.

The drumbeat seemed now a regular, reassuring tap. Everything he had to do from now on was ordered. Even the time for his eventual return to Trace Creek. That might not come for quite a while but he could even feel good about the delay. When he did get back there'd be none of the things he'd set out to do that was still undone. After Clark and Bird had come together there'd either be no Kentucky to worry about or Trace Creek would be as safe as Ingles' Ferry. Even Nita had had to fit into this new ordered pattern for everything. She must be halfway home to Carolina by now. Of course, that couldn't be. It had been only three days ago that he'd watched her running down the hill toward Boonesborough. He could still see her braids swinging, her hand tightly clutching the watch. He'd better keep his mind on what he could see down this hill ahead of him now. Most any time he could be getting into country where there could be Indians watching every trail or chasing settlers trying to get away.

But the main trail north from Harrodsburg remained deserted. Nobody in the northeastern tier of settlements seemed yet to have started running. The people of Lexington and the neighboring stations were just as pigheaded as people were everywhere else in Kentucky. They'd probably decided, as he'd been almost certain they would, to stick to their stockades, cannon or no cannon. As it was turning out, with Clark coming swiftly with help, it might be they'd decided wisely, and that all except Bryant's, perhaps, could still manage to hold out until Clark arrived. And their hanging on would serve a purpose. It would slow up Bird's advance.

Adam kept on, without pausing to look for minor Indian sign. He wasn't interested in the forward fringe of enterprising horse thieves that generally preceded an Indian invasion or in the network of spies thrown out ahead of the main body, nor could he dally at every stream crossing or narrow defile to worry about possible ambushes. His one object was to locate Bird's army and he had to assume, no matter how brusque the eventual contact, that some of his men would get away to take the word to Clark.

The hot summer morning wore on. From time to time Adam pulled down to a trot. There was need for haste, but a greater need to save the horses for the demands the day might yet make on them. The peaceful calm of the country remained unbroken even after they had crossed the Kentucky River. Buffalo and deer were grazing within sight of the trail. War and the movements of armies could not have seemed more distant or more unlikely.

The first actual evidence that anything out of the ordinary was afoot anywhere in Kentucky came when they were within a mile of Lexington. Five white men burst from a thicket to intercept them with yells of jubilation. They said they were one of the parties sent out from Lexington to beat the surrounding cover for Indians, and they were delighted to sight instead a squadron of friendly horsemen from the south.

"Things stayed so quiet last night," reported their leader, "that folks they begun to think old man Hite he was crazy with all his talk about cannon and injuns by the hundred. Since we come out at daylight, howsomever, we've picked up tracks where upwards of fifty injuns was a-crawlin' around durin' the night. But we ain't run acrost hair nor hide o' one o' them this mornin'. They've all tuk off agin."

"How about Bryant's?"

"We ain't heard from Bryant's since before noon yesterday. But we ain't heard no cannon neither—and it's only five miles."

"Clark's back in Kentucky," said Adam, gathering his horse. "He's raising men and on his way. Get your Lexington militia ready to join him. And get that word to Todd's and Stroud's and McClelland's. We're going to keep on until we find where they are. When we do we'll let you know."

Adam swept his little command on through the Lexington clearing, past the station and on along the trail to Bryant's. Another party from Lexington was working cautiously through the woods up the slope from the eastern edge of the clearing. They were startled by the sudden appearance of riders from the rear and stared openmouthed as Adam's men passed, rushing on with so little apparent concern for consequences.

The failure to use cannon at Bryant's had mystified Adam.

273

If the station had surrendered without the firing of a shot then by now Lexington should have been beleaguered. Instead, the Indian picket line, already posted around the station to prevent the people there from sending for help, had itself been withdrawn. The paradox opened up possibilities that caused Adam to urge his sweating horse on even faster. If Bird, after taking Martin's, had suddenly swung west along the Great Buffalo Trace, to strike toward McClelland's and Lee's Town instead of toward Bryant's and Lexington, there was more need than ever to get some prompt and definite word to send to Clark.

The trail broadened enough for Jim and Cory to ride beside him. He glanced at their faces. This pounding on headlong through woods they might discover any moment to be swarming with Indians was unheard of in wilderness warfare. But they only grinned as if this were something they'd been accustomed to all their lives.

The trail narrowed again. Adam's attention was fixed on each patch of cover they approached. For the last hundred yards there'd been no question about how many Indians had recently been in these woods—as recently as a few hours ago. The leaf mold was torn up in all directions by footprints and hoofprints. Each moment he expected a volley or an outburst of war whoops. Even if Bird had turned west he'd had left a screen of bush fighters to protect his flanks. But, just as when Adam had been going the other way, there wasn't time for caution or even common sense.

The trail curved around a big elm and suddenly they were out in the clearing surrounding Bryant's station. The snug little stockade was still intact—closed up tight—and bristling with riflemen. A number of dead cattle scattered about indicated the place had been so nearly taken by surprise there'd been no time to drive in all the stock before closing the gate. A husky cheer went up from the defenders at sight of the white horsemen. Adam pulled up beside the stockade. The faces of the men peering down were pale and worn. Bill Bryant leaned out to answer Adam's questions.

"How do we know where they went? We don't know for sure they've gone. All night there was hundreds of 'em howlin' around in the woods like they thought mebbe they could scare us to death. They only stopped long enough once fer Simon Girty to beller out his advice to us thet we'd surrender if we knowed what was good fer us." He pointed to the edge of the clearing where there stood a post with a blackened, still-smoking figure hanging to it. "They even burned poor young Abel Goff thet they tuk at Martin's and done it where we could see it and listen to him holler. But come daylight they stopt their whoopin' and fer the last two hours we ain't seen nor heard nuthin'. There ain't too many of you. You'd best git into the stockade here with us. Most likely they've only pulled off a little way and are waitin' fer us to come out."

"They'd have had you out fast enough," said Adam, "if they'd a mind to. They had cannon."

Jim and Cory were examing the edges of the clearing. Cory let out a yell. Adam joined him. He'd found the tracks. The cannon had been dragged down the trail from Martin's and wheeled into position. Then, sometime before daylight, they'd been dragged off again in the direction from which they had come.

The deep ruts stretched off through the woods. You could see them as far ahead as you could see the white patches on the trees along a newly blazed trail, but this didn't tell you much more than if you couldn't see them at all. Bird's sending pickets to Lexington for a night could have been part of an elaborate feint to confuse the people of Kentucky with regard to his actual intentions. But dragging the cannon to Bryant's and then immediately dragging them off again had cost too much time and labor to be a trick. There must have been some sudden change in his whole plan. At the rate at which the cannon could be moved there'd be no question of coming up within the next hour or two with whoever was with them. But there was no use telling Clark Bird's position had been established within ten or fifteen miles unless Clark could also be told at the same time which way Bird was moving. Adam divided his men into two detachments, leaving Cory with the second to follow a hundred yards behind. He had to take care that his whole party wasn't wiped out at once, with no one remaining to take back any sort of word.

The nearer he got to Martin's the more expectant he became. He signaled his first detachment into a widely spaced single file, so that the rearmost, though in sight, could wheel back successfully no matter what happened to those in front. He stayed in the lead himself, for he trusted no man's eyes, even Jim Beggs's, as he did his own. Watching, studying the country ahead, he kept on, now trotting, then galloping when the woods opened up, constantly pushing on, expecting each moment to find the silence breaking into stunning uproar.

But nothing happened. The ruts left by the cannon led on and on, into the deserted, blackened clearing at Martin's, then on beyond along the trail to the south fork and Riddle's.

"Wait here with the horses for fifteen minutes," he instructed Cory. "You might look around a little for any sign that might mean anything. Jim and I will go ahead on foot.

275

We're bound to run into them between here and the river."

Martin's had not been a large station. The heap of ashes that marked its site was pitifully small. Skirting the edge of the clearing, Adam saw there had been too few cattle for carcasses to be left for the buzzards. Only the strewn bones remained after the Indians had satisfied their own appetites. Neither were there human bodies. The people here either had been spared or taken somewhere else before they were killed.

He reached the trail and started on between the cannon ruts. These were no longer clear and sharp but were trampled by prints of hundreds of moccasined feet. The whole enemy army seemed to have reassembled for this strange march to the rear. Some of the prints were not an hour old. Gesturing for Jim to drop back fifty yards, Adam ran on.

The trail entered the bottom land cane. Still, nothing had happened and now there was less chance of an ambuscade, for the cover in which the assailants might wait, though thick, was but an arm's length away from the path. His mind was not as much occupied with his danger as with the deepening mystery of the sudden Indian withdrawl when their initial success had been so great and all Kentucky must have seemed to lie open before them. Already it was clear that they had not counter-marched west along the Great Buffalo Trace. At least he could know for certain that he was coming up with their main force. The sign they had left was as deeply marked as by the passing of a thirty-team wagon train. And he must be practically upon them. The south fork was just ahead. In another minute he would know something.

Then he was through the willows and at the river's edge and knew but little more than before. He dropped to the ground, Jim beside him, and swore softly while he studied the two shores of the river. The cannon ruts ran to the water. The boats were gone. There was no sign of disembarkation on the other side. The whole Indian army had taken again to the river. He considered this fact and what it might mean. The south fork was too shallow for the heavier barges with the cannon to make it farther upstream, supposing they had any idea of striking southward toward Trace Creek or Boonesborough. But afloat again and dashing down river with the current, Bird could land where he pleased. He had his choice of landing anywhere along two hundred miles of the wooded shores of the Licking and the Ohio. The beating of the silent drum seemed now to be mocking Adam. After all his reckless driving he had no clearer word to send back to Clark than that Bird could be expected to renew his attack at almost any place at almost any time.

The horseman arrived. Adam stood up and spoke to Cory

and Jim. "From the first it didn't seem to make sense—their coming at stations like Riddle's and Martin's way back here in the woods—wasting their numbers and their cannon and their surprise. They had so much more to gain by going for Louisville first off. It could be they've finally figured that out. And now that they're back in their boats they can make it around to Louisville in a hurry—while everybody in Kentucky is rushing off this way looking for them."

The answer did not come from either Cory or Jim but it came in an astoundingly familiar voice. "Would you like to know exactly where your Indians went?"

Adam whirled to see Gilbert sitting sidewise on Jim's horse, his wounded leg thrust out stiffly.

"Great God," cried Adam. "You're alive!"

"Never more so," said Gilbert. "Five miles riding sidesaddle with this leg catching in the brush has been enough to convince me of that."

He was naked except for the piece of an old blanket wrapped around his middle; most of him was smeared with black paint, while his head was plastered with clay. In every other way, too, he'd been treated by the Indians as they treated a prisoner they were getting ready to kill. Several of his fingernails had been torn off, his fingers had been chewed and his whole body was covered with gashes and bruises. But his chief trouble was still the leg. It was swollen to twice its normal size. Unless he kept on being as lucky as he was to be alive at all he'd likely lose it. And it must be causing him great pain. Drops of sweat were popping out through the black paint and trickling down him.

"Found him buried in leaves at the edge of the clearin' back there at Martin's," said Cory. "Never have noticed he was there if my horse hadn't stepped on him."

"Square on my good leg, too," complained Gilbert.

"Where do you think the Indians went?" demanded Adam.

"Back to wherever they came from—their own native and, I am sure, miserable towns."

"Do you know that—or only guess it?"

"Know is a hard word. Perhaps it will save time if I tell you what I saw and heard; then you can judge for yourself where they have gone."

"Do that," said Adam. "And tell it all. Don't leave out anything—whether you think it's important or not."

"My friend, everything that's been happening to me has struck me as having the most exceptional importance. But it will take a while to tell. If you'd have me lifted out of this confounded saddle that comes at me in so many of the places the Indians laid on the hardest. . . ."

277

Gilbert was lowered to the ground. He stretched out his leg with a sigh of relief. "To start with the last you yourself saw and heard. The Indians who ran out to welcome me were ecstatic to have me in their possession—particularly after they discovered what had happened to six of their compatriots in the gully. They seemed to have no interest in chasing after you and Bert. All their interest centered on me. They took me to the other side of the river where they were joined by an equally ecstatic group of their fellows. They stripped off my clothes—with very little regard for my bad leg, I may say —and at once began daubing a mess of black paint on me and rubbing wet clay in my hair. The black, I recalled with the deepest misgiving, was an extremely bad sign, but the clay baffled me."

"That was to save your scalp from the fire," put in Adam.

"Ah. In people who are in most ways so prodigal that seems oddly frugal. But you must be right. For others were assembling firewood about the base of a tree. All this was proceeding with the most unseemly haste. Their countenances were as bright and eager as those of ardent fisherman about to cast their lines for the first time in the spring. At this most opportune of moments, one of their white officers rode up. I learned somewhat later he was Alexander McKee—the King's agent for the western Indians. No doubt he is a consummate Tory scoundrel but I shall remember him in my will. For he began immediately to berate the Indians and a fearful argument ensued. All this was in the Shawnee tongue so that in spite of my natural interest I could make neither head nor tail of it, but I afterward learned the substance of the dispute. It seems that the English commander of the expedition —a Captain Bird—had been much exercised over the murder of the prisoners at Riddle's whose safety he had personally guaranteed before the surrender. He had refused to permit further use of his cannon unless the chiefs swore to observe the terms of all future capitulations. My Indians declared I was a special case but McKee, to my great satisfaction, argued so persistently that eventually I was dragged, along with the dispute, into the presence of Captain Bird. He had set up his headquarters in the clearing at Martin's, which had in the meantime fallen. He was already engaged in furious arguments of his own with the Indians, in his efforts to save this new crop of prisoners, and my prospects became entangled with theirs. The terrified captives were huddled on the ground around him. Yelling braves occasionally seized some unfortunate on the outskirts of the group and carried him away. They desisted only when Bird drew his sword. I naturally kept as close to him as I could. The Indian side of every
278

argument had to be interpreted to him so that I could now gather the gist of all that was said. The debate over the fate of the captives, with which I was so engrossed, was repeatedly interrupted by other instances of disagreement between the captain and his red legions. It appeared that Indians may never be commanded—they must be persuaded—even with regard to the most trifling decisions. Bird must have been shouting at them for days for he had all but lost his voice. His face was as flushed and his eyes as bloodshot as if he had contracted a fever. Though as a man he deplored the murder of captives, as a soldier he had been even more disturbed by the witless destruction of the cattle at Riddle's. This had left his army hungry and threatened with the early necessity of scattering to hunt in order to subsist. As another example of the difficulties which constantly beset his exercise of command, the Indians refused to help drag the cannon to Bryant's. This they asserted was a type of labor meant only for draft animals or squaws. The Tory rangers, themselves by now infuriated, were obliged to do it alone. Kindred disputes continued endlessly throughout the afternoon and into the night, accompanied by periodic returns to the subject of the captives. Because of my injury I was not closely watched and after darkness fell I was able to creep away into the edge of the forest where I found a small hollow and covered myself with leaves. I fully expected to be discovered and retrieved with the coming of daylight, but after nursing my anxieties for a time I fell asleep and slept until the horse of my good friend here was considerate enough to step on me."

"Bird was having no more trouble than you always have with Indians," said Adam. "What gave you the idea that he suddenly decided overnight to break off his whole campaign?"

"I have yet to tell you about the father and grandfather of all the arguments that took place. Along toward evening two Kentuckians reached Martin's. They had ridden hard and long. It seems we harbor a number of wretches in our settlements who make a practice of running to the English with information. These two reported that Clark had arrived in Kentucky with his army."

"And they was right," interjected Jim Beggs. "Me and Cory know—we was the army."

"The news had an amazing effect on the Indians. Where before they had been perpetually excited and insufferably boastful, the mere mention of the name Clark had made changed men of them. They became calm and sober and infinitely judicious. With the grave sensibility of so many chancellors of the exchequer they began to point out the military bankruptcy of their situation. They were without food, without sufficient ammunition and without the necessary numbers to dream of confronting Clark. Bird raved until his face turned from red to blue but they only stared at him in grieved silence, as at a friend who is going out of his mind. As I crawled away the last I heard was Bird calling them cowards and old women, while they, becoming angry, too, were calling him a fool and a madman. It was hearing that and then noting this morning that they had obviously taken themselves off that gave me the idea that they are getting out of Kentucky as fast as they can."

"It begins to give me the same idea," admitted Adam.

Jim and Cory had been whispering during the latter portion of Gilbert's story.

"Looks like the war's over, for a fact," said Jim. He glanced warily at Adam. "Long's it is and long's the doctor here is from your place you'll likely be wantin' to take him back there. Cory and me we'll just poke down river a ways and see how fast Bird he keeps goin'."

"You bet you'll poke down the river," said Adam. "And I'll be along with you to see that you do. The war's not over. It's hardly started. You know Clark. After what they've done here he's not going to let them stroll home singing. He's going to keep after them until he's hit them twice that hard. There's just as much need now as there was before for us to be able to tell Clark where he can find Bird, no matter how far he has to chase him to catch him."

Gilbert was regarding him with a thoughtfulness which he covered with a quick smile. "Paddle on, my two-legged friend. Unhappily I'll have to limp back while you rush off to keep on being a hero. What do you want me to tell Joel about your militia command and what do you want me to tell Cynthia?"

"Tell Joel to send my militia command to join Clark and tell Cynthia you're the one that's the hero." Adam stopped. "Tell her when I can start back I'll run every step of the way," he added, and then turned abruptly to the mounted men. "Get down off your horses and pay attention. I want you to remember everything you've seen today and everything you've heard—especially what Dr. Naylor told us—and what I'm telling you now—so that no matter what questions you're asked you can answer them." He counted off the six whose horses looked the most tired. "Take the three extra horses, fix a horse litter and see that the doctor gets to Trace Creek. Take it easy and go around by way of Stroud's. I'm sending six of you because I want him to have a safe trip. He's earned one. So keep your eyes open just as if you knew the woods were still full of Indians." He counted off the next three. "Take the Great Buffalo Trace to Lee's Town and keep on to Louisville. Tell Colonel Slaughter there that Bird's back in boats and on the Ohio and could change his mind and still come to Louisville." He faced the last three. "Ride as hard as your horses will stand for and tell Clark all you know. Tell him Jim and Cory and I think there's not much doubt Bird's on his way back across the Ohio and that we'll let him know for certain within a day or two." He turned to Jim and Cory. "And while they're riding their heads off all we have to do is build a canoe and float down the river."

"That's right," agreed Cory, grinning. "Course we kin fish a little when we git sick o' just a-floatin'—that is, if we're a mind to."

NINETEEN

ONCE you climbed up there and got yourself wedged in position you had a fine view through the knothole. Looking across the tongue of the main cornfield which stretched down to the Little Miami River you could see every house in Chillicothe, the southernmost town in the Shawnee country and the one Clark was due to hit first. The good accomplished by Logan and Bowman when they'd burned the place a year ago certainly hadn't lasted. The English must have helped in the rebuilding for nearly every cabin was of solid logs and the big one at the lower end of the street had a loopholed overhang like a Kentucky blockhouse. When Clark attacked he'd do well to drive in from the upper end, using the other houses for cover while advancing on the one that was fortified. In the meantime you could keep him informed of everything that went on here, count the warriors who were present at any given time and notice when Alexander McKee or one of the Girtys dropped in to talk to the chiefs. Each time you could pretty well guess the kind of news and advice they'd brought by the way everybody acted. Chillicothe had celebrated for days the capture of Riddle's and Martin's. But the town had finally begun to settle down a little. They hadn't burned a prisoner for the last two weeks. The captives still alive were probably now fairly sure of adoption. All such things as these you could see, but the trouble was that once you'd got here to take a look you had to stay here for the day and a day was a long time to spend in one position and that one this uncomfortable. However, having made it before dawn from the river to the base of the fire-blackened old sycamore stub, and crawled up its hollow interior to the knothole, you couldn't leave until it was dark again.

Adam squirmed until he'd shifted his weight from his right knee to his left. He'd spent every third day of the last month at this miserable knothole. He liked much better the other two days of each three which he'd spent ranging around Piqua, the larger Shawnee town to the north on Mad River. He hadn't been able to see anything like as much of what was going on at Piqua, but on the other hand he hadn't had to put in fifteen hours at a time as discontented with his situation as a treed coon. Still, having once located a lookout so serviceable, he'd had to keep on taking advantage of it.

Today hadn't been as long as most, at that. It had been enlivened—too much enlivened for a while—by a number of Shawnee activities right around the base of the stub. In the morning an old squaw had picked blackberries from the tangle of vines that covered the hole between the roots through which he passed to get into and out of the hollow sycamore. She'd pulled the vines aside in her search for the last berry but finally had gone away without noticing anything. A couple of hours later a little fat dog had appeared and had become much more inquisitive. After judiciously wetting two or three selected briers among those the old squaw had handled, he'd sniffed deeper among the vines, had stuck his nose into the hole and had begun to bark. And he'd kept on barking in an ever-increasing frenzy of excitement. A main Indian trail ran along the riverbank not thirty yards away and people were almost constantly passing. Adam had been certain that at any moment someone would become curious enough to investigate. But no one had and eventually some women working in the cornfield, annoyed by the protracted clamor, had come out to throw sticks at the dog until he'd withdrawn, whining his disgusted disapproval of this lack of appreciation of his diligence. Then, toward dusk, there'd been a final interruption which, while less threatening, had been no less irritating, because he'd been beginning to look forward thankfully to the moment he could safely get down. A young brave had persuaded one of the women leaving off work in the cornfield to return to town by this roundabout route. They'd selected the glade immediately below for the climax of their loitering. To Adam's huge disgust, watching impatiently from his position in which he was becoming so cramped he could scarcely hold to it, she'd unnecessarily prolonged the business by proving excessively coy and requiring her suitor to plead and cajole for a time that seemed as long as the little dog had barked. Even now, after her wooer had achieved success and was stalking off toward town, she was still sitting there, listening and peering toward the corn into which he had disappeared, evidently imagining he might return with renewed demands. As Adam could see and she could not, he was keeping on, however. Now, at last, she was getting up, sighing with resignation, and taking herself off as well.

Adam dropped to the ground within the hollow sycamore. For minutes he kneaded his stiffened legs until he was able to use them again. Through the hole between the roots he saw that it had become full dark. He rubbed soot from the charred walls of the sycamore over any white patches remaining on his skin. To gain his position in this lookout he'd had to come naked and blackened and armed only with a knife. Carefully parting the blackberry vines he crept out on the exposed root of the sycamore, paused to listen until he had made sure there was no unusual note among the night sounds in the town, stepped from the root to a rock imbedded in the riverbank, from that to a log, to another stone, jumped the trail to a piece of driftwood and let himself silently into the water without having left behind the faintest sign of his passing.

Now came the good part that almost made up for the hours of misery at the knothole. Swimming lazily down river, enjoying the peace and quiet of the summer night while the cool water washed off the soot and soothed his cramped muscles, was infinitely pleasant and never lasted long enough.

A mile downstream he brought up at the jumbled pile of driftwood that had lodged against a rock ledge in mid-river. Silt had collected and nettles and reeds taken root until the obstruction had become a tiny island. He crawled through the tangle of matted brush and uprooted trees into the nest in the interior where he kept his clothes, weapons and food sack. This also was the rendezvous where periodically he met Jim or Cory as they journeyed back and forth across the Ohio to take what information he had gathered to Clark. They had also brought him news each time. It had been a comfort during his lonely vigils to know how formidable was the Kentucky army Clark was assembling at the mouth of the Licking. Adam had been able almost from day to day to follow the movements of that assembling. Clark was coming up the Ohio from Louisville with a company of his own regulars. Harrod with the Harrodsburg levies was coming down the Kentucky and up the Ohio. Logan was marching across country from the south. The Trace Creek company was with him. Boone, Floyd, Todd, Slaughter, McAfee—practically every Kentucky leader was taking part.

Adam had expected to find Cory waiting for him tonight and was disappointed that he was not. He dressed, ate his cold supper of buffalo jerky and river water thickened with corn meal and sugar and, then, as Cory still had not come, went to sleep. Long before dawn he was awakened, to his great satisfaction, by Cory's arrival.

"Clark's crossed the Ohio," said Cory. "He figgers to hit Chillicothe day after tomorrow—first thing in the mornin'—then to go for Piqua."

"Go back and tell him that so far as I can make out they know both at Piqua and Chillicothe that he's come as far as the Licking," said Adam. "But they don't seem to have any idea how strong he is. They're worried but they haven't worked out yet what he's up to. Tell him that since Bird pulled out with his Tory rangers and the northern Indians two weeks ago there's been no sign of his coming back. He must have kept on to Detroit. So Clark will have only the Shawnee and Mingo that live here to deal with—together with McKee and the Girtys. I'll run up and take another look at Piqua to see if everything there is still staying put. Either you or Jim meet me here about this time tomorrow night. There might be something even as late as that that Clark ought to know about."

Cory nodded and cleared his throat. Something else was on his mind. "I seen Bert Cogar," he said. "They've made him lieutenant of his station's militia company. He give me a long rigmarole to tell you—made me say it over 'til I got it just right." Cory stopped to clear his throat again.

"Well, what did he want you to tell me?"

"He said to tell you that since what folks down yer way has bin hearin' about what you bin up to—some o' them has got the idea you belong right up alongside Clark and Washington and Lafayette—mebbe a couple of jumps ahead—and thet you better not let no injun keep you from gittin' back 'cause there's a door down there that's mebbe not shut so tight as you might think. Thet mean anything to you?"

"A little. When you see Bert tell him much obliged."

Adam saw the pale ripple as Cory let himself into the water to swim to the south bank. Then the water was black again. He was alone. The words Cory had spoken had been Bert's, and the tone Bert's idea of humor, but the message was as clearly from Cynthia as if it had been brought by one of her brothers. The message had come at him with so little warning that he'd been startled, almost unpleasantly so, as when a silence is broken by a sudden sharp noise that had been totally unexpected.

Now that he had time to think about it he was still startled. Evidently she'd regarded their parting at the gate as some sort of a definite break between them in order now to be sending him word that he should come back because she might let him in again after all. He'd taken it for granted that he was going back, that she'd be there waiting for him and that one way or another everything would work out as it always did when two people were so strongly drawn toward each other. Instead she was saying that if he behaved she would give him another chance. He didn't much like this idea.

Still, no good could come from his shutting his eyes to facts. He had to have her, on his terms, or her terms, or no terms. She probably knew that. He might much better be spending his time thinking about what he knew he did want instead of what he guessed he might not want. He began to single out and dwell upon the things about her that pleased him most. There were so many. Deliberately he let his imagination carry him the long way back to her, up the stairs and through the opening door.

Twice, working his way northward toward Piqua during the hours before dawn, he became so absorbed in the detail of these anticipations that he lost his way. But from daylight on there were things to watch that held his full attention.

There was little question that the Shawnee at Piqua were greatly disturbed about something but it also seemed that they were having trouble making up their minds what to do about it. From noon on they held council at the burning place in front of the blockhouse, which was much larger and stronger than the one at Chillicothe. The council was interrupted for a while in the late afternoon by a war dance and the burning of a prisoner and then they resumed their deliberations, with every last man present seeming to want to have his say. Like most Indian councils this one seemed slow to come to a conclusion.

After dark Adam crawled closer to make sure the council was still continuing and then he returned to the island in the Little Miami. Here he found Jim Beggs waiting for him.

"Clark's a little behind where he counted on bein'," said Jim. "But he still figgers on attackin' right soon after day-light."

"Tell him Piqua's stirred up but that they haven't started to send any help this way yet," said Adam. "He'll only have the seventy or eighty warriors that belong to Chillicothe to handle. I'm going to take me a couple of hours sleep. I need it."

Once he'd stretched out he was too sleepy even to make use of the opportunity to think, undisturbed, a little longer about Cynthia. But toward morning he awoke and began speculating on Clark's army pressing forward through the darkness. Keeping in hand a thousand men in the woods at night was a job even for a Clark. He became too restless to lie still and decided to go back to his stub. He might see something by the first streaks of light that would be a help to the attack if Clark were informed of it even at the last minute.

He didn't bother swimming upstream. There was no longer need to worry about leaving tracks. He trotted straight up the riverbank trail, crawled into the sycamore and looked out. At once his restlessness was rewarded. Chillicothe was humming like an overturned beehive.

The inhabitants must have become aware of Clark's approach. But they'd learned of it too late to send to Piqua for help. It was getting light enough to see women running out of the houses with bundles, putting them down, picking them up again, forgetting where they'd put them, chasing their dogs, snatching at their children. Even the warriors were running about as wildly and aimlessly as people do who've just discovered their house is on fire. Then Adam realized that their houses were on fire. The Shawnee had decided not only to make a run for it but to burn their town before Clark could take possession. They were catching their dogs in order to lock them in the burning houses. Anticipating immediate pursuit, they were taking care to forestall the possibility that their dogs, if permitted to accompany them, might by their excited barking betray the route of their flight. Every house was burning now and the imprisoned dogs were howling mournfully.

Then Adam saw the two brass cannon being trundled out of the burning blockhouse. He'd not guessed their presence there during all his watching. Bird must have left them there with some idea of their being used again against Kentucky. The Shawnee rolled the guns onto a barge, poled the barge to mid-river and dumped them overboard into deep water. Several bags of cannon balls followed. Adam chuckled. Once he'd told Clark where they were he'd have them snaked out on dry land again within an hour.

Then a group of five warriors came dashing through the cornfield, carrying sacks of cannon powder. This, too, they were hiding for later use. They began digging a hole near the base of the sycamore in the same little glade where the Indian lovers had cavorted.

A sudden bleat of signal whistles burst from the woods beyond the town. The Shawnee pickets came flying in, accompanied by a flurry of rifleshots. Clark's forward line of skirmishers broke into view. The few Indians still in town dove for their canoes and paddled across the river. A double line of white riflemen was now sweeping through the corn and closing in on the upper end of the burning town.

Adam glanced down at the Indian diggers at the foot of his sycamore. They had the hole just about refilled. Two of them became overwrought by the nearness of the white advance and bolted. The other three, however, stuck it out until they had smoothed over the place and carefully removed all traces of their digging.

They had lingered too long. Another of Clark's columns came into view, trotting up from the south along the riverbank trail. Seeing they were being surrounded and momentarily in danger of being sighted, the three Shawnee lunged into the cover of the blackberry vines around the stub. By the time they had got themselves settled, the feet and legs of two of them were stretched through the hole right into the base of the hollow sycamore below Adam. He was a prisoner in his own lookout, even though all of Clark's army was half a musket shot away.

His rifle and tomahawk were leaning against the inside wall of the sycamore within six inches of one pair of outspread Shawnee legs. Any moment the Indian might move enough to knock down the rifle or, one of them, squirming back into the deeper concealment of the hollow tree, rise to his feet and discover him. Adam thought of dropping down on them on the chance that the suddenness of his appearance might give him some advantage over their numbers but he concluded this was a foolish risk. To get at them he'd have to crawl out through the hole and while he was doing that they would have only to knock him in the head.

The advance swept on into the burning town. Two of the Harrodsburg companies made rafts to ferry their weapons and swam the river to see that the Chillicothe fugitives kept on running. After the briefest pause to eat, Logan's division reassembled. Adam could even recognize Bert and the three Wyeth brothers. Then Logan marched off up this side of the river. Adam guessed Clark was sending Logan to circle around behind Piqua so as to come at the town from both sides at once. The remaining two divisions of the army Clark set to cutting down the corn. It was still in the milk and too young for good eating but now it would never ripen to satisfy Shawnee hunger.

All this activity continued and yet no one of the hundreds of men in sight came near Adam's Indians. Looking down he could see the two pairs of legs as immobile as if they were

287

an outgrowth of the sycamore. Again and again he was on the verge of dropping down on them. But if he did he would be risking more than his neck. He had to tell Clark about those cannon and he had to take care that he lived to tell him about them. The guns might make a great difference when Clark ran up against that big blockhouse at Piqua.

A drum recalled the men from the corn cutting. Clark was preparing to cross the river and go on. He'd apparently decided he'd given Logan the start he required to get into position beyond Piqua. Desperately Adam thrust the blade of his knife through the knothole, hoping it might glisten in the sun and excite somebody's curiosity. But no one saw it. The army crossed. The smoldering town and the devastated cornfields lay deserted. The last white company disappeared in the woods.

Still the two pairs of legs remained as motionless as before. An hour passed. Adam waited. At last the legs began very slowly to move, as their owners inched away. They withdrew entirely from sight. Adam dropped, snatched up his rifle and thrust his head and shoulders out of the hole. The three Indians were not four feet away, crouched half erect, peering cautiously from the shelter of the vines to make absolutely sure their retreat was now safe.

The sudden appearance of a white man, emerging from an empty tree, and hardly an arm's length behind them, was too much after the long strain under which they had already suffered. They sprang, moaning, from the thicket and plunged into the river. The spectacle of their agonized flight was so soothing to Adam that he did not even take a shot at one of the bobbing heads.

After an hour's hard running he caught up with Clark at the head of the column. Clark wasted no time talking about how pleased he was about the cannon.

"Take Dolan's company," he said, "and go back and get them."

When Adam had watched the Shawnee dumping the pieces he had taken care to line up the spot with another sycamore across the river. Therefore he had little trouble locating the guns on the bottom. But it took time to twist sufficiently long ropes of grapevine and more time diving to attach the lines. After that, even with the whole company hauling with a will, there was more trouble getting the cannon ashore. The river bed was dotted with large boulders against which the axles kept catching. It was dark before the guns were on the bank.

Everybody cheered the final appearance of the dripping brass fieldpieces. They'd come a long way since their use had first been planned in Detroit. They'd been dragged and floated across hundreds of miles of wilderness. They'd made possible at Riddle's and Martin's the striking of a terrible blow at Kentucky. Now men were swearing and shouting in their glee over the prospect that they were about to become the hammer head of Kentucky's striking back.

Adam sent axmen ahead to widen the trail. The rest of the company laid hold of the lines and gave the first mighty jerk. The guns rolled forward. Lurching and skidding, they were hauled up the first long slope. On the downhill side they overran their human gun teams or swerved from the path to wedge themselves between trees. The straining struggle went on, up and down the next hill and the next. In the darkness obstructions were overlooked. The wheels caught on roots or sank to the hubs where there were no roots.

A storm was threatening. It broke just as the laboring procession was in the midst of a swamp between the third and the fourth hill. The poles cut to form a corduroy causeway sank into the softening ooze under the weight of men and guns. By main force the men, themselves up to the waist in mud, dragged the half-submerged guns on through the storm. Clark sent back another company to help pull and later himself appeared at Adam's elbow.

"I hadn't counted on having cannon to play with," he said. "But it might turn out we'll need 'em. This storm may delay Logan. If when we get there he's not yet in position on the other side of town it could well be we'll need 'em bad."

"We'll get 'em there," said Adam.

Throughout the night he could hear the intermittent rifle fire to the north. By Clark's command men were occasionally firing and reloading, lest the rain so dampen their charges that an Indian night attack might catch them with useless rifles. The rain ceased but the ground had long since been soaked and remained so soft that at every step the guns sank so deep the barrels dragged in the mud. Morning came and the cannon were still not within sight of the rearmost company of the advancing army. Then, in the place of the former scattered firing there came a sudden outburst of solid volleys which developed into a continuing din.

The battle had commenced. More men were sent back to pull at the guns. At Piqua the Indian defenders had not fled. Instead they were coming out of the town and were themselves attacking. Logan had had much farther to march and, delayed by the storm, was still miles away. The Indians outnumbered this half of Clark's army and were pressing their advantage.

Clark had a big raft waiting at the bank of Mad River. The

guns were pushed aboard. The river was shallow and swift. Near the other bank the raft stranded on hidden rocks and began to come apart. So many men waded out that they half carried the raft ashore. A wooded slope stretched up toward the firing.

Coming out finally on the crest Adam could see the battle-field. A belt of woodland wreathed with the powder smoke of hundreds of Shawnee rifles barred the way to the town beyond. Frontal attack on the woodland was made impossible by flanking fire from the big blockhouse. And the more numerous Indian line overlapped the white so that they were beginning to work around Clark's other flank. Either the woods in front or the blockhouse had to be stormed at once or the whole position given up.

The sweating, grunting men on the grapevine ropes pulled the guns to the top of the rise. A platoon of Clark's regulars ran up to take them over. The guns were wheeled around and loaded. Clark himself aimed the first shot. It tore a whole log from a corner of the blockhouse. The Indian garrison came running out as if the place were on fire.

Adam sat on the ground and watched contentedly while successive cannon balls splintered trees in the woods and plunged into other houses in the town. Indians, four and five at a time, were beginning to dart from the belt of woods back into the cover of the cornfield behind. Then by tens and twenties. The line of white riflemen in the foreground rose and swept toward the town. Adam picked up his rifle to join the advance. Jim Beggs came running up.

"Clark wants to see you."

Adam found Clark on horseback, forming one of the Lexington companies for a charge to clear the Indians from a patch of woods on the left flank. Bullets were whispering through the air. Being mounted, he was the most prominent target in sight but he was standing in his stirrups the better to see. He swung his horse around, leaned down and gripped Adam's shoulder.

"Your guns turned the trick—and just in time, too. We'll keep 'em on the run now. A good many may get away before Logan gets up to cut 'em off. But we'll burn their town and tear up their corn. They'll have to hunt to eat from now 'til next year's crop and that'll keep them too busy to make mischief in Kentucky for that long, anyway. And that's news I want spread around Kentucky as fast as we can spread it. Too many people—specially those who've just come—are starting to move back east. Nothing will stop that quicker than a batch of good news. That's why I'm sending one man to each settlement—today—right now—to get the story spread around quick. You'll find the rest of the runners assembling at a canoe down where you landed the raft with the guns. Get going because you're the one I'm picking to take the word to your station." All the time he'd been talking he'd been watching the course of the battle which was developing into a headlong Indian retreat. Now his eyes met Adam's for a second. He grinned. "From what I hear you won't feel any more like objecting to this order than you did the one last spring when I ordered you back to Virginia."

Before Adam could reply he had wheeled his horse and was galloping off toward the town. Adam stood for a moment looking after him. Maybe he'd already done enough. The trouble with Clark was he always left you wanting to do more. Then he turned and trotted toward the river.

Coming up the trail was the mule train carrying supplies for Clark's army. Adam swung off the trail to pass. The man with the lead mule glanced up. Adam came to a sudden stop.

"Peleg Snowden," he exclaimed. "I thought you were on your way to Carolina."

"That's where I aimed to be," said Peleg. "Only Naomi she changed her mind. When she heered about Kentucky bein' full of Indians she said thet was no time for folks to be runnin' off from Kentucky—leastwise folks like us. I jined up with the Boonesborough militia."

"Then Naomi and the girl—they're still at Boonesborough?"

"Naomi is. But the gal—she tuk off."

"She what?"

"She tuk off. 'Pears when she heered we was stayin' in Kentucky fer a spell longer she didn't like it."

"Where'd she go?"

"Not even Naomi was up to figgerin' thet out. Worst part of it was when she went she tuk along thet pack roll with her —the one with the Hamilton coat in it. How's the fight up ahead comin' out?"

"We've won it." said Adam shortly.

He strode on toward the river.

‖ TWENTY ‖

ADAM sighted the station just at dusk. He'd slowed up the last hour to avoid getting in by daylight. It angered him to be obliged to creep up on his own stockade. Here he was coming back from a campaign in which he'd done pretty well and coming to a place he himself commanded and still he had to snoop around like an Indian looking for a chance to shoot a stray calf. He swung over to the creek bottom willows and came out in the deep shadow by the corner of the sawmill.

"Where's Bert?" came Alice's sharp demand before he'd reached the door.

He saw her rising in the darkness from a bench set against the outer wall of the mill. He got the impression she might have been sitting there, listening, watching the trail from the north, ever since Bert had gone.

"Still with the army," explained Adam, quickly. "He was well when last I saw him. And his company didn't get in the fight at Piqua so he's surely still well. They'll all be back before long."

"How long?"

"Soon's they finish burning and tearing up the Shawnee country. Likely within a week."

"Another week, eh? Thet Bert. Whoever comes back last—thet'll be Bert." Her voice was harsh with longing.

"I wouldn't doubt he's twice as anxious to come back as you are to have him."

"Mebbe." She dropped wearily back on the bench. "All the same I git just as mad at him when he's away as though he was enjoyin' it."

Adam leaned his rifle against the wall and sat down on the doorstep. There was no use trying to fool around when dealing with Alice.

"Happen to know where Nita is?"

"No."

He speculated briefly on the chance Alice might be lying to him. He decided against it. That wasn't her way. And there was no ill feeling in her voice. She might have been speaking of something that had happened so long ago it no longer counted.

"You knew she'd run away from the Snowdens, didn't you?" he persisted.

"Yes."

"She must have come back here. Maybe she's hanging around out in the woods a ways waiting until she sees I've showed up. The camp by the blackberry patch maybe."

Alice slowly but emphatically shook her head. "Nope. She ain't in no woods around here. This is one place we know she ain't." She paused to shake her head again. "When Logan was here he had to lay over a day waitin' fer Clark to send him word whether he should go north by way of the Old Shawnee Trail or by the Dry Ridge. He put his whole outfit to lookin' fer her. Ann Logan she wasn't satisfied 'til near five hundred men they'd combed ever inch o' cover fer miles around."

Adam's mouth dropped open.

"Ann Logan—she was here?"

"She come back with me and Naomi," explained Alice impatiently.

"Maybe you better start at the beginning."

"Mebbe I better had. Yuh might's well know about it. Yuh was the one thet set it off. When Nita she first run off Naomi she rid up here to tell me. I knowed how much store Nita set by Mis' Logan so Naomi and me went down to Logan's to see if thet was where she had went. But she wa'n't there. Then Ann she come back here with us and stayed until —like I said—she was satisfied Nita wa'n't nowhere around here neither."

"You and Naomi—and then Ann, too," marveled Adam. Not in all Kentucky could you get together a search party more likely to find whatever they'd decided to look for. "And not one of you has any idea where she might have gone?"

"All we had to go on was somethin' she said once to Naomi. She said somethin' about 'goin' home.'"

"Home," said Adam. "That's it. I told her the word 'home' meant with her own people in Carolina. That's where she's gone. She's that stubborn—once she'd finally started there she was bound to keep on going whether the Snowdens did or not."

"That's what Ann and Naomi finally made up their minds to. But me—I think she want back to the Cherokee. Thet's what yuh druv her to."

"You're wrong," argued Adam. "She wouldn't have called going there going home. When she said home she meant Carolina. I pounded the word into her."

"Leastwise she's gone somewhere where she won't fret yuh no more," said Alice. She leaned her head against the log wall. "Yuh'll find your woman up to her mill. Yuh kin bed down with her there tonight. The preacher's run off so yuh won't have to worry none about waitin' fer him to marry yuh."

"You've no call to talk about her like that."

"What's wrong with how I'm talkin' about her? That's the way Bert and me done it. Yuh bin around long enough to know there ain't no other way to do it out in this country. What counts is that yuh come out next mornin' and tell folks yuh meant it. How else has wimmen ever got theyselves husbands in settlements where there ain't no church to take a man to? She ain't no better'n any of the rest of us—except mebbe the way she looks." Alice got to her feet. "Yuh might's

293

well get along and git at it. I'll tell folks over at the stockade what yuh said about Clark's layin' fire to the Shawnee country."

It would hardly do to run up the path toward the upper falls. Not while he was within earshot of Alice. Even after that his walk was deliberate. The dark outline of Cynthia's house loomed before him. The iron shutters were tightly closed over the windows. That was sensible. Saul and his great sons made a redoubtable garrison, and probably the last prowling Indian had been scared back across the Ohio for the rest of the summer, but still there was never any use taking chances. The lock of a rifle clicked as the hammer was drawn back.

"I'm Adam Frane," he called out.

Saul stepped around a big rock into the path, his crown of white hair pale in the starlight.

"Bless God," said Saul. "Come right into a house that will be overjoyed to receive you."

Saul hurried up the path before him. Hebe unbarred the door. The red glow from the forge spread a pattern of warm light and shadow across the room. Saul's sons and their statuesque wives were at supper. They rose, smiling and bowing, when they saw Adam. The door at the head of the stairs opened.

"Adam?" There was a catch in Cynthia's voice. "Is that you, Adam?"

"Yes."

"What"—her voice caught again—"what makes you so slow?"

He sprang up the stairs. She retreated from the doorway, watching him as he came in. He set his rifle against the wall and closed the door behind him. She ran to him then. She didn't give him a chance to kiss her. She only clung to him, pressing her face against his chest and sinking her fingers into his shoulders as if trying to convince herself that she did have hold of him.

"I'm here, all right," he assured her, grinning. "Turn loose of me for a second and I'll help you to believe it."

She released him but backed away. She seemed desperately glad to see him. Yet there was the same sense of strain as when they had parted. They might still be standing there at the gate.

"I'm beginning to believe it," she was saying. "But you're so thin. You must be starved. See—I was about to have supper. You're just in time."

She circled around him to open the door. "Hebe," she called. "Will you set another place?"

When she came back she left the door open. Maybe it was

only natural for her to seem so nervous. When last he'd been with her so much had gone wrong. He was very conscious of the door she'd left open, and was listening for Hebe's step on the stairs.

"Do sit down," Cynthia urged. "You must be worn out as well as starved." She was getting hold of herself. "And you don't have to talk—not yet. Just settle back—and give us both time to start realizing you're here."

Moving across the room he passed the other door—the one that led to the bedroom. It, too, stood open. He'd hardly looked but with the one glance he'd seen her bed with the covers turned down and the white linen sheet showing. He hadn't slept between sheets since the last time he'd been in New Orleans. Draped over the foot of the bed had been the blue silk wrapper. "Yuh might's well git along and git at it," Alice's words rang in his ears.

He sat in the chair across the table from the place already set for Cynthia. It was a beautifully molded maple chair that fitted in just the right places. Sitting down felt good. He hadn't sat in a chair for quite a while either. The table and sideboard were of the same polished maple. Saul must be as accomplished a cabinetmaker as he was a gunsmith. Cynthia was pouring two glasses of whisky from a decanter on the sideboard. She gave him one and clicked hers against it.

"Present company," she murmured.

"To present company," he repeated, and added quickly: "And future, too."

She gave him a half-smile for that. He tossed off the near tumblerful. He hadn't had a drink for weeks. The pleasing warmth shot through him. He looked around at the room so brightly lighted by a dozen candles. The radiance gleamed on the brass pot in the fireplace, on the copper bowl on the mantel, and on the array of glassware on the sideboard. She was wearing a yellow dress. The brilliant candlelight gave the yellow the cast of daisies in the sun, made her smoothly coiled hair seem more red than brown, made her eyes seem to glow when she looked at him.

"It does seem bright in here, doesn't it," she said. "When I'm alone I seem to like it better that way."

She moved around the room, blowing out half the candles. When she lifted her cupped hand at each candle the pose drew the yellow dress against the curve of her breasts. He became doubly conscious of the two open doors. They couldn't both mean anything. They canceled each other out.

Hebe came in with a tray. The thick slices of juicy ham, the platter of sweet potatoes browned with sugar and cheese and the crisp corn biscuits with accompanying butter and honey

295

looked and smelled like a dream of heaven. Hebe stepped back.

"Never mind coming for the dishes," said Cynthia. "That'll be all for tonight."

"Yes, ma'am. Good night, ma'am. Good night, sir."

Hebe closed the door carefully before descending the stairs. Cynthia met his glance with a calm smile.

"Eat," she commanded.

The ham and everything else tasted as much like a dream as it had looked and smelled. He was hungry but the food hardly seemed real. Nothing seemed real.

"How's Gilbert?" he asked. "Should have asked that right off. He's quite a man."

"He's doing very well," said Cynthia. "And he must be quite a doctor, too. At any rate, he saved his leg—though he'll probably always limp a little. And do you realize I haven't even asked about my own brothers?"

"They were well the one time I saw them. They still are, without doubt. There was no fight at the first town and Logan's division didn't get into the one at the second."

"Joel had a chance to send me one letter. He said you were spending your time crawling right into Shawnee towns getting news to send back to Clark."

He told her of the sycamore stub and the old berrypicker and the little fat dog and the Indian lovers. She told him of the solemn efficiency with which the Trace Creek women in the absence of their men had organized their own company of militia, elected officers, drilled twice a day. They'd finished eating. She moved the dishes to the sideboard.

"Smoke if you want to," she said.

He got out his pipe and started fumbling at his pouch before he remembered he'd long since used up the last of his tobacco.

"I have some," she said, bringing him a jar. "Lonely as I am, you see that I keep prepared for gentleman callers."

She sat down in her former place across the table from him and they went on talking as if they were no more than old friends who had much news to exchange. He was getting more uncomfortable than he'd ever been perched in that sycamore stub. She wasn't helping him much. She was just talking and smiling and waiting. She was probably thinking of the manner of their last parting and holding that against him. She was sitting back and making him come to her. She wanted him to crawl a little.

No. There was more to it than that. He put his pipe away so he'd stop fiddling with it. He knew the real shadow that was upon their meeting. It was darkening fast. He had to face it. He didn't want to face it because that would make him angry. And he didn't want to get angry because she was in the right. He'd been here two hours and hadn't so much as tried to kiss her. He was just sitting here, fidgeting and squirming, with the table still between them, while they talked about what a good thing it was that this year's corn crop was coming along so well. They'd even stopped talking now.

"Nita," he said abruptly. "I hear she's run away from those people that were taking her home."

Cynthia grew suddenly pale. There was a pinched look around her mouth and eyes.

"I couldn't believe it," she said. "I kept thinking it might be that—but I just couldn't believe it."

"Believe what?"

"Don't try to dodge."

"One thing's not so easy to dodge. I told her a dozen times that I'd see to it she got to Carolina."

"You're still dodging. You did everything sensible that you could about that. Is it your fault she ran off while you were away fighting Indians?"

"No. My fault is even mentioning it at all."

"Don't dare—don't dare for one instant—to talk as if I'm being unreasonable. We haven't seen each other for weeks. I couldn't know I'd ever see you again. And now that you're here—what happens? You sit for hours moping over that girl you don't care two sticks about—compared to the way you feel about me. Or do you?"

"I can wonder, can't I—or is that wrong, too—whether she got to Carolina—or back to the Cherokee—or whether she's dead in a gully somewhere?"

They had risen to their feet and were leaning toward each other across the table—not as lovers lean nearer but as antagonists.

"Well?" she asked, and waited.

"What else do you want me to say? That I don't give a damn what happened to her?"

"No." She was carefully keeping her voice steady. Then at once it broke. "Oh, Adam—what's happening to us? What's the matter with us? Nothing could be so wrong as what we're saying and doing." She regained some of her control. "Even aside from us—and how we feel—there are other people to remember. There's Bert. He's your best friend—and a more devoted one no man ever had. There are my brothers. They've literally accepted you as one of them. And all the people here. They've made you their leader. This past month they've become so proud of you it's hardly decent. They all but worship you. How can you give up all this to go trailing off heaven knows where looking for that crazy girl?"

"Who said anything about my going to look for her? But supposing I did—are you trying to tell me I could never come back?"

"I'm telling you you can't come back to me. A long time ago I told you you could come in that door whenever you were ready to come in to stay. I meant it then and I mean it now."

Her words came at him like blows. She was telling him what he could do and what he couldn't do. She was presenting the terms upon which he could have her and all that went with her. Worst of all, her terms were sensible and inescapably reasonable and no more than she had every right to set. He had given her every excuse to be standing there like a judge, measuring him, passing rulings, announcing verdicts.

Her eyes blazed. Her whole body was trembling. The intensity of her emotion had kindled all the fire in her. Never had she seemed to him so beautiful. She was beating him again. Only by possessing her could he ever win over her. In no other way could he assert himself against her.

He bumped blindly against the table getting around it. Her eyes widened, at first incredulously, then delightedly, as she realized what he was doing. With a gasp of relief she threw herself into his arms.

"How we work at trying to make fools of ourselves." As she whispered he could feel the movement of her lips against his neck. "We've always been that way. And the worst of it always seems to pop out in us come a wedding day." A purr of soft laughter interrupted briefly the low murmur of her voice. "And there's no reason for it. None at all. The fact probably is—whatever you ever want to do, Adam—I'll always want you to do. Anyway—we can talk over whatever it is you want to do about her—in the morning."

She laughed again, contentedly. She was certain enough about the morning. Over her head he saw the turned-down bed. This, she was saying, was their wedding night. Their marriage bed was but a step away. The significance of her words crept over him. When he awakened in that bed in the morning it would be too late to talk about what he might or might not do. Not any more would he ever be free even to consider whether he should stay or go.

TWENTY-ONE

ADAM came to a stop in the ankle-deep dust into which the first raindrops of the summer storm were beginning to hiss. Winding through the vast hazel thicket that spread over the hillsides for miles around, the trail was more like a tunnel than a path. To either side the thick growth was hollowed out where horses and cattle had nipped at it in passing but overhead it met almost to shut out the sky. The narrow track was torn up as if by the passage of armies but the early morning silence was that of the farthest wasteland. People who traveled the Wilderness Road waited for company until a good big party had assembled. Between such irruptions of activity the road remained as empty as it now was. He could see the most recent footprints were all of a week old.

He stood still, breathing deeply, for he had been running. He had to stop more than his running. He had to stop giving himself up to the waves of disgust and anger that kept sweeping over him. The sudden feeling that he couldn't stay with Cynthia had been so clear and strong that there had been no denying it. It still persisted and he hadn't once felt the impulse to turn back. He might as well give up trying to understand himself. A man who could spend nine years trying to get to a woman only to run right away from her again was beyond understanding. What was the farthest beyond understanding was that the desire for her that had been with him so long was still with him. And yet he wasn't going back or ever would.

But there was no good his spending the next nine years feeling the need to drive his fist into the nearest tree. Sooner or later he had to start settling down and it might as well be now. Before he took another step he had to stop and do a little thinking, for a change, about where he was going and how he was going to get there. He'd managed to commit himself to looking for Nita. At least, he could get on with that.

Standing here at the Hazel Patch, where the westbound trail forked to Boonesborough one way and Logan's the other, he could close his eyes and see the main Wilderness Road stretching eastward all the way to the Holston and Carolina beyond. He'd been over it often enough to know every step of the way. He could foresee also the end of his journey. For once he had found the Sheldon family there was but one

299

of two things he could learn. He could learn that Nita had long since arrived safely. That would mean his concern for her had been foolish and make the whole journey meaningless. Or he could learn that she had not arrived. That would mean even more decidedly that the journey had been a waste of time. He would know then that he should first have gone to see whether or not she had arrived safely among the Cherokee and that this far more difficult task still lay before him. A wrong guess now would cost him weeks and maybe months and possibly leave him with a trail too cold ever to pick up. This morning he had to guess right.

Some six weeks ago Nita had stood where he was standing now. She'd come south from Boonesborough and here she had had, as he was trying to do, to make up her mind whether to take the Wilderness Road east to Carolina or to strike south over the mountains and across the Cumberland to the Cherokee country. He tried to put himself in her place. When talking to Alice he had argued that home meant Carolina to Nita but that had been mostly because that had been what he had wanted to believe. Actually, from the first she'd taken little interest in the existence of her Carolina relatives. The only home she'd ever known had been with the Cherokee. There was as much chance that had been what she'd meant as that she had meant Carolina.

He grunted with sudden satisfaction. A way had occurred to him to find out within a day which course she had taken. Had she decided to go back to the Cherokee she'd not have swung east to take the Great War Trail. She'd have known there'd have been too much chance along that route of running into some party of northern Indians who'd have been far more likely to treat her as a stray white woman than as a Cherokee girl on her way home. No. If she had started south she'd have swung wide to the west toward the big bend of the Cumberland. And that would have brought her within an hour's travel of the cave. She couldn't possibly have gone on past without stopping there to take a look around. There was that much of the average woman in her. So all he had to do was to go himself now and take his own look at the cave. If he saw she had been there he'd know she'd gone on to the Cherokee. If she had not then he could set out for Carolina with at least some feeling that he knew what he was about as he went along.

As soon as he'd broken through the last of the hazel thickets he started running again. After an hour the rain stopped. By early afternoon he was in the creek bottom he'd searched the time he'd crossed the ridge to look for sign of Bert—the time he'd lost Oriole to Patched-Heel and Toe-Out.

The thought of his beautiful mare stirred new resentment in him. Right at the start Nita had cost him the chance to recover Oriole. Since then she'd cost him everything else that belonged to him. Now she was winding up by costing him all his time and effort for as many months as he could see ahead. It wasn't that he had so much else to do with his time and effort, but he couldn't be sure—no matter how much of it he spent—that he'd be able to discover just what had happened to her. Everything he tried to do could be a waste. He nursed his anger. Looking back it was easy to see how responsible she had been for every wrong turn his affairs had taken. It was some consolation to realize that when he had got to the cave he could know at least which way she had gone. That brought closer the time when he might be able to make her listen in detail to his views on what she'd done to him. She'd probably only laugh. She'd always been the more content the madder he got at her. Even whaling her with a stick had made no difference to her.

The sun was setting as he dropped down the slope past his wood lot. Briers and vines had already covered most of the traces of his cutting. He stepped into the stream and waded on. The new green growth in the cane was halfway up the old stalks. The hard winter hadn't killed the cane here as it had in some parts of Kentucky. Off to the right he could hear the coughing and grunting of a herd of buffalo feeding. Farther away a lone bull was bellowing. He was a month late with his rutting or maybe was just hard to satisfy. It was still light enough to see the trout darting away through the water ahead of him. The last time he'd walked down this stream he'd been carrying Nita on his back. It had been right after that she'd stopped openly fighting him. He'd left the door unbarred that night, but she hadn't run away. What a saving it would have been if she had.

The light was fading fast now. He stepped up onto the flat rock. The grass in the little meadow was four feet high in the three or four patches where the elk hadn't grazed it off. They'd even bedded down here nights and practically made a yard of it. That is, up to a month or so ago. They hadn't fed here much since. The grass was beginning to grow again. The bars of the horse pen and the whole of the shed were covered by a sprawling wild cucumber vine. Unless you knew about the door to the cave under the oak you'd have to look close to see that it was there. Moss had sprouted all over it and the edges of the frame were masked by a new growth of ferns. The ferns around the door might be a help in making sure whether she'd been here or not. You'd have a time looking for month-old footprints in that elk-trampled meadow. In another five minutes it would be too dark to look for any kind of sign. He pulled a handful of sugared corn out of his game sack, tossed it into his mouth and strode across the meadow to the door.

Even in the fading light he could see at once that the ferns around the edge of the frame had been frayed. Somebody had had the door open. They'd taken care not to touch the delicate coating of moss over the face of the door and to avoid stepping in the soft earth in front of the threshold but moving the door at all had disturbed the fringe of ferns. He pushed the door open. The usual summer's outrush of air brushed his face. Among the familiar smells of the cave was that of charred wood in the fire pit. There had been a fire there since his last time here. Whoever had opened the door had remained long enough to cook at least one meal. The darkness of the cave was like a bandage across his eyes. Instinctively he stepped sidewise out of the twilit doorway.

He touched his finger tips to the side wall of the cave and paused, staring into the darkness and listening. He could not see at all and could hear only the splash of the stream in the cavern. But he caught another new smell. Cedar boughs had been added to one of the beds sometime within the last month. Whoever had come to the cave had stayed long enough not only to cook a meal but to spend a night. A hundred to one it had been Nita. She had decided then, after all, to go back to the Cherokee.

Suddenly, seeming to come out of mid-air, as when Nita had held it suspended near his ear that last day in the cavern, the silvery little tinkle of the watch began to strike the hour.

"Nita," he cried. "Nita."

There was no reply. The watch had ceased its striking.

"Nita," he repeated.

Still she did not reply. He held his breath on the chance he might tell where she was by the sound of her breathing but could hear nothing.

"Nita," he cried again, beginning to get angry.

He reached out for her in the direction from which the striking of the watch had seemed to come but only jammed his hand against the wall of the cave. Still she did not speak. He set his rifle against the wall and reached again. Failing to find her, he became more exasperated and began lunging about the cave with outstretched hands clutching for her. From time to time he came to a sudden stop to listen in the hope of hearing some movement that might betray her location. He was filled with fury that she should try to make a fool of him by mockingly announcing her presence with the watch and then hiding from him. Still his waving arms encountered only empty air or the bare, cold walls of the cave. He became more heedless in his anger, stepped into the fire pit and fell headlong. He lay there for a moment, breathing hard and waiting for her laugh. But no laugh came.

It occurred to him then that she might have retreated into the passageway leading to the great inner grotto. He scrambled to his feet and felt his way along one wall until he was facing the cold, damp air of the main cavern. He stopped. She couldn't be hiding in that dark and dripping void. Not unless she were really afraid. And she had known it was he who had pushed open the door. That had been proved by her holding the watch to his ear. She'd set out to amuse herself at his expense. She'd only be making a fool of herself, instead, if she hid from him in this place. Anyway, if she was lurking somewhere back there he'd need a torch to look for her. He'd be damned if he'd take all that trouble. He turned back to the cave. The outer starlit sky framed in the open doorway was bright in contrast to the darkness within. More likely than anything else, he decided, she'd taken advantage of the door he'd left open. When he'd first reached for her his back had been to it and she'd slipped around him and outside.

He walked to the doorway. It was dark enough so that she could be sitting fifty feet away in the middle of the meadow and he'd not be able to see her unless she moved. Or she could be perched in the oak tree right over his head. She was crouched somewhere out there, listening to the foolish commotion he'd been making in the cave while trying so hard to find her.

"Nita," he said, holding his voice to a calm but firm conversational tone. "Come in here."

She didn't respond. She might be farther away. He tried the broken quail call. That should mean something to her. But it didn't. There was no answer.

He gave way again to his anger. He certainly wasn't going to give her the satisfaction of running around in the night, looking for her. He backed out of the doorway so she couldn't see him if she was watching and ate another couple of handfuls of corn. He could detect no movement in the meadow or around the horse pen. Disgusted, he felt his way to his bed and stretched out on it. She could come in when she got ready to come. He didn't have to give her the idea that it made any difference to him when she did or whether she did at all or not. There could be two sides to the joke.

He squirmed into a comfortable position. The fresh cedar boughs had been carefully laid to make a good bed. She could hardly have expected him to show up to use it. She must have been sleeping here herself. In fact, he could catch the faint scent of sweet grass that always clung to her clothes and hair. Suddenly curious, he got up and felt along the opposite wall. The floor was swept bare where her bed had been. She had moved to his place while she stayed here. He began to wonder how she happened still to be here more than a month later than she could have any reason for being here. She must first have started to go to Carolina and then changed her mind. He returned to his bed. His occupying it improved the part of the joke that was on her. When she did come in she'd have to work out for herself where she slept.

The daylight in the open doorway awakened him just as it had that first morning when he'd thought she'd run away. Then he'd awakened to an immediate sense of well-being because he'd been sure she had gone. Now he was well pleased for the opposite reason. He was relieved to know that she was here. It had saved him further looking for her. Just as she had that other morning she had probably been bathing in her pool and was now on her way up from the stream with a string of trout. She'd come in without a word, kindle a fire and start cooking his breakfast. He could pretend to be still asleep if he chose. Anyway, he'd not have to say anything either. That is, not at first. It would be almost as if they had never been away from the cave. All this seemed so certain to him that he sprang to the doorway to watch her approach.

A doe and her fawn were grazing in the meadow. The doe threw up her head at sight of him and trotted nervously away. There was no sign of Nita and the doe was proof that she was not anywhere near.

"Nita," yelled Adam.

He ran down to the stream and kept on yelling until he was hoarse. Finally he got himself in hand. He went back to the cave door and settled down to a painstaking examination of the approaches in order to pick up her trail in leaving so that he could follow it. She had taken care in coming in and out to leave the least sign possible that might attract the attention of some passing hunter to her occupation of the cave. After an hour's inch-by-inch scrutiny of the ground he was able to distinguish no more than half a dozen faint imprints of her moccasins. But each one had been made *before* yesterday morning's brief rain. She could not have slipped out the door last night. Even had she swung from the threshold into the oak, which was unlikely, she could not have dropped from the oak into the meadow without leaving the most obvious tracks, for there had been a heavy dew. There was no way around the conviction that she had not left the cave after he had entered it. Therefore she could only have retreated into the cavern. But there could be no reason for her remaining there this long. She couldn't know about the other exit on the far side of the mountain. Even if she did there could have been the least reason of all for her making for that. It would have taken her hours to crawl through it. And she hadn't had a chance to light the torch she'd have needed. More likely than anything else was that she had heedlessly run back into the cavern, had missed her way in the darkness and had become lost somewhere in its endless passages and chambers.

He ran into the cave, twisted a torch of cedar boughs, lit it and rushed on into the cavern. The light from the burning brand revealed to his first glance everything she'd been doing except where she was now. In the nearer dry corner where his sacks of saltpeter had once been piled was the pack roll containing the Hamilton coat and the doeskin breeches. Beside it was ranged a row of baskets. One was filled with dried blueberries, another with salted trout, another with smoked partridges, and two more with wild potatoes. She had been at the cave a long time. She must have come straight here from Boonesborough. She could have had no idea of going on anywhere else. She must have intended to stay here indefinitely. She had been thriftily laying up food for the winter. But the light also revealed something else far more important to him at the moment. Since his last firing a new thin sifting of saltpeter had been deposited across the floor of the cavern beyond Nita's cache. She couldn't have crossed that floor without leaving the tracks she would have left in newfallen snow. There were no tracks. She was not in the cavern.

Adam tossed the torch aside and ran back into the cave. He'd stopped worrying lest she might still be tricking him. A swiftly deepening concern had replaced last night's anger. He had to keep all his wits tracking and put his whole mind on figuring out what could have happened. Starting to run around again yelling like a wild man wouldn't help. If he was ever to make use of what sense God had given him he'd better buckle down and make use of it now.

Last night she'd been beside him, hardly an arm's length away, when she'd held up the striking watch. Since then she hadn't left the cave by the door or gone back into the cavern. She wasn't here now. All three statements obviously couldn't be true. The most logical one to doubt was that he had actually heard the striking of the watch. But that was no help. He knew he had heard it. It had startled him. It had been the last thing in the world that he had expected to hear. He couldn't possibly have imagined it. He could still hear the eerie, tinkling little sound coming out of the darkness almost beside his ear.

He moved over to the exact spot he had been standing last night. Just above the level of his eyes was the niche in the rock wall where he'd been accustomed to keep the watch. Suddenly his breath caught. He reached into the cleft. His fingers closed upon the cold, smooth case. He snatched out the watch and stared at it.

It was not running. He shook it. It gave several ticks. He fumbled in the case, found the key and gave it a couple of turns. The watch began ticking regularly. Last night it had been running. The striking he had heard must have been its last effort before it had run down.

The truth burst upon him. Sometime the day before yesterday she had wound the watch as usual and put it back in the hiding place where she kept it. Then early yesterday morning, before the rain, as he had realized from studying her moccasin prints, she had left the cave. She had not been setting out to go anywhere. She had intended to come back. Otherwise she'd have taken the watch with her. She'd never have parted with it. She'd merely been going out to pick more berries, or gather wild potatoes or attend to her bird snares. But sometime between then and his arrival something had happened to her to keep her from coming back.

He picked up his rifle and walked stiffly to the doorway. His dread was like a haze that hung between him and what he could see of the familiar meadow and stream and cane. For the moment, though, he did not need to see. He had to see with his mind. He had to use his imagination. He had to guess where she might be. She could not have planned to go any great distance. He would not have to look far. But he would have to look hard. Within a circle of the first mile from the cave were mountainsides, cliffs, other caves, cane-choked bottoms, thick woods, cataracts, deep pools, ponds, quicksands—and clear across the circle the twisting belt of uprooted and entangled trees left by the tornado. There was room out there for most any kind of accident. The most moderate mishap could be a disaster to anyone alone in the woods. A foot caught under a sliding rock would keep you pinned there until you died. The thought of Jeb Sproat kept prodding at him. Jeb had been an experienced old woodsman but he'd strolled out of this same cave of a morning and had never come back. One little misstep had been too much for him.

Adam began to run. There wasn't time to look carefully for sign. Whatever had happened to her must have happened nearly twenty-four hours ago. He could already be too late even when he did find her. He ran in ever-widening circles, swinging each time higher up the mountainside above the cave and plunging down again to break deeper into the cane. Every dozen strides he gave the broken quail call or cried out her name. No reply ever came. He kept on long into the night and only returned at last in the desperately nourished hope that she might have come back. But the cave was dark and lifeless.

The next day he selected a section of the region around the cave and examined it foot by foot, quartering back and forth like a good hunting dog thoroughly working a patch of cover. She had taken care during her month here never twice to use the same route in her goings and comings so that there were not the slightest trails to indicate the habitual range of her activities. Even between the cave and her bathing pool she had left not so much as the beginning of a path. Still, from time to time he found places she had been— where she had picked blueberries, dug roots, collected rushes for baskets, set snares for birds. But he came upon no sign of anything unusual, no faintest clue to her disappearance.

The third day he worked another section and the fourth another. He no longer had much hope. But he had to know. He speculated miserably upon what might have happened. He had so carefully covered the ground within what could have been the natural limit of her ranging around the cave that he was becoming almost certain she had not suffered any ordinary wilderness accident such as a fall or a snake bite. There was the other chance that she had been carried off. Cherokee, of course, would not harm her. But Choctaw and Chickasaw sometimes wandered this far and could have come upon her. And there was a type of white man worse than any Indian. Yet he had no basis for even this fear. Any such encounter would have left unmistakable traces and there had been none. No foot other than one of his or hers had been set down anywhere within miles of the cave. He was fast becoming helpless as well as hopeless.

The evening of the fifth day it began to rain. The rain became a pelting downpour that continued through the night. So heavy and prolonged a fall was flattening the leaves on the ground, muddying every scattered twig, beating down every blade of grass. Even were he to go on looking there would be nothing to look for tomorrow. The slate would have been wiped clean. All sign would have been rendered meaningless. The realization that his long struggle was ended left him without defense against his exhaustion. He had eaten only berries or roots that he had snatched in passing. He had slept hardly at all. He sat down in the canebrake where the rain had overtaken him. The burden of his dejection was so great he seemed scarcely able to breathe. He was too dispirited even to cut away enough cane to give him room to stretch out. He sat there, his head hanging between his knees, most of the night.

Finally, moved by no more than the instinct of the sick animal to crawl to his lair, he started for the cave. Due to the rain and the darkness and his own inattention he was a long time even finding the stream before at last he came upon it near his wood lot. He turned down it, staggering with weariness, falling repeatedly among the rocks that studded the creek bed. Striking his head against one, he was stunned and nearly drowned, face down in the water, before he could haul himself out onto the bank. Morning came. The rain stopped and the clouds began to clear. He struggled to his feet and stumbled on.

The sun came out but the glare hurt his eyes and he kept them half closed. He passed the flat rock without seeing it, floundered into Nita's pool and on into his own before he realized where he was. He crawled out then and dropped down under the bush where he had slept the morning of the tornado's approach.

But exhausted as he was he could not sleep this morning. The conviction that Nita was dead obsessed him. He would never see her again. Grievous as the thought was when he faced it awake, it became worse when his thinking it began to trail off into his dreaming it. He was afraid to sleep. His sense of desolation then became unendurable. The realization kept hammering at him. He would never see her again. That could not be possible when he could still see her so clearly. He saw her most often as she had run down the hill toward Boonesborough. Then all he would have had to do would have been to kick his heels into the flnaks of his horse and gallop after her. Instead he had let her go. And before that he had schemed continually to drive her away. Increasingly vivid memories of her swept over him. He saw her laughing in triumph on the raft, limping rebelliously beside the Cumberland, gravely handing him his watch at Glover's, leaning down toward him from the rafters at the saw mill. Always he had been scolding her, reproving her, pushing her away, holding her at arm's length. He'd fooled himself into thinking he didn't want her at all because he hadn't wanted her the way he had Cynthia. But he did want her. He'd wanted her all along. He wanted most of all just to be able to tell her he never wanted her out of his sight again.

The sun was hot on his eyelids. He started to throw one

arm up over his face and then let it drop back. There seemed not the strength in it to make even so slight an effort. He squirmed sidewise into the shadow of the bush. He was sore all over and barely able to move. He must have given himself a terrible beating falling so often among those rocks in the creek. There wasn't any wonder he was so weak, either. He hadn't eaten anything that counted since those last few mouthfuls of corn the night he'd got there. There was still some of that corn left in his game sack in the cave. He'd better crawl up there and eat some of it. If he did happen to go to sleep, by the time he awakened he'd probably not be able to. But it wasn't worth the effort. Nothing was worth the effort.

She'd always been so quick to run to him. No matter how often he'd pushed her away. Right here she'd done it twice. There'd been that morning she'd heard Bert's horses coming. She'd run to bring him his rifle. And then there'd been the other morning when he'd been sleeping under this same bush and she'd started frantically looking for him to save him from the tornado. He could still hear her calling: "Adam. Adam."

The sun was across his eyes again. He must have slept after all. For hours, because the sun was way past noon. Like a log, too. He was so stiff he couldn't move. But the same dream was going on. He could still hear her calling. "Adam—Adam." With a great effort he sat up. The dream was more confused than any he had ever had. Not even a dream should be so mixed up. For there in the middle of the meadow was Oriole. She was nibbling at the grass and then lifting her head to look toward him with her ears cocked forward. Never when he had been awake had she looked more real. He could see the trade blanket strapped to her back in place of his saddle and the Cherokee bridle with the rawhide bit. Even in a dream you had to try to account for things. Patched-Heel or Toe-Out would never have brought her back. He'd have guessed that it had been Nita—that she'd gone down to the Cherokee country to get the mare—if he didn't know better. But he didn't really know better. If, when she'd left the cave that morning of the day he'd got there, she'd walked in the stream all the way to its headwaters before coming out on the bank, she'd have got too far beyond the country around the cave for him to have found her tracks, with all his looking. It would have been like her, at that, to go for the mare. The doeskin pants, the Hamilton coat, the watch—and even Oriole. She had been a great girl to hang onto things.

"Adam—Adam." Nita's voice sounded real, too.

And now Nita herself seemed to be kneeling beside him, her hands clutching his shoulders. She was just as upset as she'd been about the tornado.

"Who was it?" she was demanding. "Who try to kill you?"

"Nobody," he said. This was the damnedest dream. He could even hear the sound of his own voice. "Unless I did it myself."

She let go of him, darted to the stream, wet the lower part of her dress and ran back to him. Drawing his head into the hollow of her shoulder she mopped his face. The dripping doeskin was soft and cool and pleasant. He saw that there was quite a lot of dried blood mixed with the mud she was wiping off. He had certainly given himself a fine banging around.

"Looking for you," he finished.

She didn't seem to be listening. She was feeling of his arms and legs and running her hands about under his shirt, trying to find out just how badly he might have been hurt. She seemed angry with him as if everything about this was his fault. But she was also beginning to look relieved. His hands closed upon her bare arms, gripping them, sinking his fingers into them. He should be pinching himself. That was what you were supposed to do to make sure you were not dreaming. Much better, though, to feel of her. He didn't care where *he* was. What he had to make sure of was that *she* was here. She must be. Her skin was as smooth and fresh as he remembered so well when her arms had been wound around him while they'd watched the tornado. And in the pleasant smell of her there were mingled the same faint hints of sunlight, open air, spring water, pine, wood smoke, sweet grass. She didn't look quite she same. She was paler and thinner. But she was just as young and strong and alive as ever. He could still feel the firm thrust of her shoulder and the vigorous pressure of her hands as she had examined him to discover how much he was hurt. She was kneeling beside him now. Her eyes, desperately searching his face, were filled with wonder and concern and almost as much anxiety as when she first had run to him.

"Adam," she whispered, as if she still were calling to him from a distance.

She'd ought to know he was here. She was usually so quick and she hadn't been dreaming. He was the one that had to be sure and then more sure. He pulled her down into his lap, with her shoulders across his thighs and her head cradled in the crook of his arm, and held her tightly against him. He didn't have the strength even to hang onto her as he wanted to but it was something to realize that he did have hold of her and that he didn't have to let her go. She was clutching at the fringe of his buckskin shirt and staring up at him. There was still something that she, too, was struggling to realize. Suddenly she started to look more worried than ever and to try to sit up.

"No," he said.

"But you hurt."

"What makes you think that?"

"You cry."

She could only be imagining that. Though his face *was* wet. He couldn't remember ever crying in his life. And he certainly never had felt less like it. There wasn't anything that needed talking about but maybe he'd better talk than make more of a fool of himself.

"How'd you get her away from them?" he asked, nodding toward the mare.

Even before she'd heard his question she'd been reassured by something. She'd relaxed and leaned back against him.

"That was easy. The Cherokee were glad to see me. They think I have come back to them. When it is night I just ride away with her."

"It's never easy to get a horse away from Indians."

"She belong to you. I want you to have what belong to you."

"That's right," he pronounced. This was no time to lecture her but there was an idea that could not be overemphasized. "And something for you never to forget. But whatever made you think I'd come here."

"You come very much sooner," she admitted, "than I think."

As she had said before at Boonesborough and at the saw-mill, talk was no use. He drew her closer to him. She wrapped her arms around his to help him hold her but she stopped looking up at him and instead pressed her face out of his sight against his shoulder. That was all right. She always seemed to know what he was thinking before he did. Or at least as soon. But what he was still thinking most was how good it was just to sit here in the sun and to keep on hanging onto her and to keep on reminding himself that he didn't ever have to let her go.

Oriole wandered over to them and nuzzled at the two of them inquisitively. She was certainly the prettiest mare in the world. She belonged to Nita now as much as she did to him. Everything he owned did. Or would ever own. That was all right, too.

ABOUT THE AUTHOR

DALE VAN EVERY was born in Levering, Michigan, and graduated from Stanford University. He is recognized as a leading authority on the opening of the great western wilderness immediately after the Revolution. Mr. Van Every has been widely acclaimed for his unsurpassed histories and novels of the west.

In addition, he has written for motion pictures and was a correspondent for United Press International.

He presently resides in Santa Barbara, California.

GREAT INDIAN WARRIORS
WILL HENRY

Will Henry is among the most honored of American historical novelists. His powerful books about the Great Indian Warriors of the west are alive with the grand spirit and bravery of the Indian people. The vivid characters and striking imagery of his Indian storytelling create memories of war dance and council fire which burn on in the reader's mind long after the last page.

☐ **FROM WHERE THE SUN NOW STANDS**
   (#14182-1 • $1.95)

☐ **THE LAST WARPATH**
   (#20398-3 • $2.50)

☐ **CHIRICAHUA**
   (#20718-0 • $2.50)

☐ **CUSTER'S LAST STAND**
   (#22684-3 • $2.50)

Buy these books at your local bookstore or use this handy coupon for ordering:

HISTORICAL ROMANCES

Read some of Bantam's Best in Historical Romances!

☐	12168	Bayou—S. O'Brien	$2.50
☐	20609	Black Ivory—S. O'Brien	$2.95
☐	14150	Lorelie—L. Lowrey	$2.75
☐	13132	Southern Blood—J. Channing	$2.50
☑	20404	Providence—E. Green	$2.95

CLAIRE LORRIMER

☐	13992	Chantal	$2.95
☐	20765	Mavreen	$3.25
☐	20542	Tamarisk	$3.50

REGENCY ROMANCES

☐	13691	Victory Summer—D. Lindsey	$2.50
☐	20100	Trafalgar Rose—C. Holmes	$1.95
☑	14812	Viscious Viscount—M. Gibson	$1.95
☑	13191	Rake's Reward—M. Gibson	$1.95